WIND WALKER

Wind Walker

P.E. CRAVEN

Little River Raven

To all the readers who spent their lives searching for a world where they belonged.
This one's for you.

Meropoli

Felysia

Veritasville

Maracabia

Sperfisia

Nysa

The World of Panchia

Prologue

Aryael seethed.

A rage boiled inside her that she couldn't master. Her ravaged throat spasmed as she screamed, her fingertips tearing as she ripped the bookshelves from the walls. She ignored the pain, the splinters lodged beneath her nails as wood crashed, books and trinkets smashing onto the ground. A delicate glass bowl followed, breaking into glittering icy pieces that skated across the floor. Her arms trembled as she hurled the side table next, screaming again as it crashed against the solid stone wall.

Her room was in shambles.

The bed lay broken and burnt, nearly every piece of furniture smashed; and still her fury would not abate.

In the corner of the room, on the only chair left unscathed, sat a wooden box, its lid flipped open. Burgundy velvet lined the box as if it contained a treasured gift, perhaps from a loved one.

But the truth that lay within was no gift.

It was a taunt. Undeniable evidence that Aryael was helpless in the face of the greatest challenge she would ever encounter.

Inside was the last of her bloodline to grace the earth.

Scarred and ragged, Suda's finger seemed to sparkle with crusted gore. It had arrived three days prior with no word, threat, nor promise. Meant as a message to crush all hope and chance of negotiation.

The Dark Born wanted nothing for the return of her brother, the last of her family. And now there was no further word that Suda even lived. Just silence, no answers.

Aryael sank to her knees, her head bowing to the once plush carpet, now singed and snagged. She roared into the floor. Screamed, and screamed. Hammering her fists until they were bruised.

Tears roiled through her as she succumbed, finally, to the panic that had been churning within her for days. Her traitorous heart hammered against her ribs, jolting her lungs. Visions of the torture Suda would be facing now wouldn't stop running through her mind. Both she and Suda had been horribly abused during their time of the occupation, but never by the Dark Born themselves. No one came back from that, except as one of their possessed.

Oh, Goddess. Was it possible she would have to kill her own brother? The only mercy available to those who had succumbed to the blood sorcery the twins were known for was death. But could she offer Suda that? Would she be able to burn the rot from him so he could rest in eternity?

A new kind of panic rushed through her, causing her body to shake. Her breath came in hot, short pants and she felt the acidic sting of bile at the back of her throat. How could she live through this? Her nails snagged in the carpet as she gripped at the fabric, trying to cling to anything that could bring her back from the hell she was falling into.

Strong arms wrapped around her but she pushed against them. She wasn't ready. She wanted to wallow, wanted to let herself sink into the dark cavern of despair. A sound like a wounded animal escaped her chest as she tried to pry herself from Symon's grasp.

"Shh," he pressed his lips against her head, "it's okay. I've got you."

His voice was calm, but she could feel the pain he tried to hide thrumming inside him. Suda's capture and evident torture was worrying to him. She allowed herself to fall into him for a moment. But this was *her* brother. *Her* blood. The only connection she had left to her childhood. How could she ever look her parents in the face when she finally rested in eternity, knowing she had failed to protect her last link to the past?

"No—" Aryael pushed again, not wanting the pain to ease. She fought Symon off to return to her dark, dank cavern of shame, regret... Vengeance. She knew what waited at the bottom. Something that would awaken and bring the Dark Born to their knees. "No! Let me go!" She pushed him away and he took a step back.

"Stop," Symon commanded quietly. "Aryael, I know what you're thinking—and you and I both know we cannot risk it."

"I *can* risk it," she ground out, flame dancing in her eyes. "I can, and I *will*. No one can stop me," she hissed. She made to push past him, heading to her war room.

Symon turned as she passed him, taking a slow, deep breath. "Aryael, you cannot." His voice was quiet but resonated with power. "If you go, you risk the safety of your people. You are Queen, now. Not a vigilante."

The truth of his words held her as if he'd enchanted her. Yet a single tear rolled down her cheek as she thought about what it would mean to leave Suda to his torment, to wait for more information. Her back went rigid.

"We will send our people out, people we can trust," Symon continued. "We *will* figure out a way to save your brother, but you have to trust me." He turned her back to face him, laying his hands either side of her face, framing her in so she had nowhere else to look.

"What if we're too late?" she asked, her voice was barely above a whisper.

He pulled her in, crushing her in a hug. "Then we will burn all of Speridisia to the ground. We will break the wards we've built, and I will join you on the battlefield so I can watch you torch the whole goddess forsaken land. And I will laugh at the razed ruins. I promise."

Aryeal marveled at her mate's ability to bring forth so eloquently the vision she so desperately wanted to realize. The promise of harsh and irreversible retribution on such a grand scale soothed the rage that burned within her a little but it did nothing to calm the roiling anxiety. She closed her eyes, breathing slowly to become grounded once more, clutching Symon's jacket.

A few moments passed, and they stood, locked together. Gripping each other as if nobody else in the universe could possibly offer the salvation they were so desperate for.

Once she felt like she could speak again clear and strong, hear her brother's name without wanting to burst into flames, she asked, "What time is our next council meeting?"

Symon answered in a whisper, his chin resting atop her head. "This afternoon, we have about two hours before they gather."

Aryael released a heavy breath, a soft shudder following it. "Then we should prepare."

Symon kissed her forehead. "Agreed. Let's discuss our plans over lunch in my study. We can ask the council to advise us on how to proceed in rescuing your brother."

Aryael gave him a final, tight lipped smile, then lifted her chin to walk regally from her personal chamber. She would not allow herself a moment of visible weakness in public.

Nor would she let herself look back at the box that would haunt her until her brother was returned.

Chapter 1

❧ ✳ ❧

Sage sat along the creekside, listening to the soft murmur of water gliding over rocks and mud. The wind danced through the tall grass surrounding her and an orchestra of bugs sang their praises to the full moon overhead. The noise was shrill, but not unpleasant.

Absent-mindedly, she picked at one of the fast healing scabs from the week's trials. She still sported a few scrapes to her face and arms, and there was still a blister that occasionally throbbed.

Her body warred between grief and relief. Unsure of how to feel, sitting securely next to a creek in Mystaira, the weight of truth thrumming through her with urgency.

Her journey to Mystaira, alongside Gavin, had ended three days prior. For three days she'd slept, only waking to eat whatever food had been slipped into the room where she slept. Someone must have carried her to the room when she and Gavin had finally arrived at his family's home. All she could recollect was dozing off, nestled in the back of a mule-drawn wagon, watching the passing scenery. Motifs of rolling hills and orchards had lulled her exhausted body and mind.

She wasn't sure when her sleep had changed from sound-less and hollow into the montage of destruction that her mind insisted she dwell on. At some point, nevertheless, images of Ian's prone body, the sound of Hyacinth's final breath, and the feeling of blood splattering her feet began to repeat themselves through her sleeping mind.

Finally, she had flung the blankets off, fought the urge to shiver back into them, and dressed hurriedly in the over-sized tunic that had been hung in her room to use as a nightgown. Barefoot and unsure, Sage had crept through the small home, aiming for the sanctuary of fresh air. The warm, humid night soothed her cramped muscles, and she'd soon found herself wandering through the tall grass, onto a well-worn trail that led her to a creek.

She'd lost track of time staring at the bright, round moon that hung in the sky. Its light refracted off the creek like shards of crystal spearing through the darkness. Her cheeks sticky from tears, a strange sense of calm—which had been missing since she was fifteen years old—stole through her body. It was as if a piece of a puzzle had been ripped from her beating heart that first night she'd escaped captivity. And somehow, Gavin had found that puzzle piece and of-fered it to her by vowing to help fight back. It felt as if that missing piece had begun to wiggle itself back into place.

She would make her way back home, somehow.

She would free the magical creatures the tyrants of her world had captured.

And she would repay the man that had taken everything from her, from her family, from her world.

A quiet thrill of vengeance slipped through her body as the last shudder of grief left her, and she found herself tossing rocks into the creek, naming the people on her list who were owed pay-back. She used her magic to raise several rocks at once and launched them into the creek, their noise creasing the night air with a sound of finality.

"That was impressive," a wispy voice scoffed.

Sage turned, eyes narrowed at the blue woman with wild braids standing at the end of the path. Before Sage could acknowledge her presence, the goddess of water, Allyra, strode towards her. In the past Sage would have been shocked at the appearance of a goddess. But tonight, somehow, she was unsurprised. The goddess's appearance seemed normal, almost as if Sage had been waiting for her arrival.

Sage shrugged. "Just biding my time." She turned away from the approaching goddess, focusing on the creek's lively banter instead. "How are you here?" The question floated from her mouth before she realized her curiosity. But with it out in the open, she angled her attention to the imposing goddess beside her.

"That's not important, and I don't have much time to discuss it." Allyra's voice was bright, somehow mimicking the creek next to them while still sounding human. There was an urgency in her voice that was unmistakable.

"Well, get on it with it then. What have you come to tell me?" She hadn't meant to sound so standoffish but despite the rest, bone-weary exhaustion bloomed within her at the sudden appearance of the goddess. Sage suspected a visit from Allyra would have some sort of consequence on her journey home. It didn't seem she could catch a respite from the deities even in a different world.

"Sit. I have much to tell."

Sage complied and waited for Allyra to elaborate. Moments trickled by like the creek while Allyra sat, staring at the moon, shredding a long piece of grass. Abruptly, she began, "Were you aware that I haven't always been a goddess?"

Sage's mind had begun to wander while she waited for Allyra to speak, but the question sent her plummeting back into focus like one of the rocks she'd tossed into the creek. "What do you mean?"

Allyra shrugged, an oddly mortal gesture on the goddess. The tattoos on her arms rippled with the movement, and a breeze lifted a stray hair from her braid as she peered across the creek. Sage wasn't sure the goddess would answer, but softly, Allyra began to speak.

"A long time ago, I was just a mortal girl, searching for the right path. A lot like you." A wan smile graced her lips. "My brother and I, we were both elementals. Back then, it wasn't an uncommon trait. That was how our people learned magic."

Sage nodded silently, waiting for Allyra to continue. Allyra propped a leg up, wrapping her arms around the knee and resting her chin upon it. She looked almost childlike. Sage wondered if appearing like this was meant to put her at her ease, as if she would forget that this creature in front of her was a powerful, immortal being capable of destroying cities and annihilating entire peoples if she so chose.

"I was a bit of a troublemaker, always wielding my magic when my emotions got the best of me. My brother was more grounded. Ironic, really."

"Therisyd is your brother, right?" Sage asked, but she was sure she remembered that part of the story correctly.

"Ah—good. You're not completely dense then," Allyra replied, bumping her cold shoulder into Sage's. "I wasn't very good at making friends. But then, a great evil invaded our world. Magell had never been threatened like that before, and the destruction at the hands of our enemies was catastrophic.

"I became a warrior. I found my place on the battlefield. I found Cerridos, my love. And Brighid found us all. Together, we four led the way to end the one who sought to trap us and enslave us. The one who wanted to bastardize our magic and take it for his own use."

Allyra paused and stared up at the moon, going as still as Gavin whenever his memories became distant. Sage understood, had seen and felt enough to know that memories were as real as the world around her. Allyra's braids shifted as she dropped her head, and Sage couldn't help but wonder what evil it was that she and her kin fought all those years ago.

When Allyra didn't continue, she asked, "So, how did you defeat him?"

"We trapped him. Beyond the reach of anyone he might harm. But there's always a risk of evil rising again." With that, Allyra looked at Sage squarely, her playful demeanor evaporating like rain from a hot road. "I've come to remind you of something, Sage Brennan."

Sage's stomach twisted. "The bargains?"

"No! Though that was a foolish move on your part."

Sage scoffed, "Like you lot gave me much of a choice!"

Allyra threw her head back, laughter twinkling through and around her at Sage's remark. "Fair enough," Allyra said, composing herself. "That's not what you must remember. The answers you must seek will eventually lead you to TupaGuara. There's a reason why we told you to go there in the first place."

"TupaGuara. What will I find there?" Sage's voice was quiet, barely a whisper, joined by a ripple of quiet that seemed to hover around the creek before dissipating back into insect song. A nameless power that inexplicably swelled then fell away.

"That is not for me to tell, unfortunately." Allyra said. Remorse shone in her eyes, and Sage knew the goddess was restrained by a fate of her own. "That is not all. You have to be watchful of your enemy's plans." Allyra's eyes sparkled, and Sage sensed a flood of rage pulsing like waves of heat from the goddess.

"Ranquer?"

Sage watched as Allyra tensed at the name and clenched her jaw. The creek vibrated. "Ranquer..." The name slipping from Allyra's lips caused a surge of power, and Sage scrambled back as the creek began to take the form of a water dragon. Allyra muttered to herself, her eyes glowing, "Of all the stupid names he could choose..." Sage could barely register Allyra's words as she staggered beneath the rising form of the water beast. "I can't wait to rip out his throat—"

"Allyra?!" Sage squeaked as the dragon turned to look at her.

With a shake of her head, Allyra's eyes cleared, and the water crashed back into the creek bed.

Sage put a hand on her chest, her heart hammering. Taking a soothing breath she sank back to Allyra's side. "What do you know about Ranquer?"

"Another great question, my girl. Another one I am unable to answer on this night." Allyra's head snapped to the side, her attention snagging on something as if she'd heard a whisper on the breeze. She tilted her head, listening acutely. What Allyra detected remained a mystery to Sage, there was nothing that reached her ears beyond the bubbling creek, crickets, and wind running its tendrils through the grass.

"My time is drawing to a close, my girl, there is just one more thing we must discuss," Allyra continued, standing gracefully. "I sensed your guilt and shame. The feelings overcame me a few nights ago and I've been preparing to visit you ever since. Tonight has been my first chance."

Sage nodded, tears prickling her eyes, knowing exactly the day and events of which Allyra spoke. "I can't help but feel responsible for all that's happened to everyone. It's my fault that people have died."

Allyra nodded. "I had my suspicions you were feeling this way. Sage, listen to me." The goddess grabbed Sage by the shoulders, compelling her to look into her eyes. "You mustn't fret over your man, Ian. He made his choices long before he met you."

"What do you mean?" Sage asked, once more reaching for answers, and hoping these were some that Allyra could shed light on.

"Ian had already been working against Ranquer. Think about it. How else would he have known to have the Egress Key made? To have invented all those spells? I wouldn't put it past him to have developed a few other tools that will aid us in times to come."

The information washed over Sage like a bucket of icy cold water.

It was as if a veil had been lifted from her eyes. Ian had been working against Ranquer before they met. Of course he had been. Why else would he so readily want to rescue a girl squatting in a vacant building? Why else would he be so ready to help her escape Techeduin? All of the inventions, all of the knowledge he was so ready to share with her. And the fact that he never questioned her, never once acted with disbelief when she shared her story. Looking back on it, she should have known there was more to his story all along.

"Chin up, my girl. There's much to do." Allyra smiled, grazing Sage's chin with her forefinger, then before Sage could respond, the goddess shimmered into mist.

Moments ticked by as Sage sat, rooted to the spot.

Ian had known the truth. He'd known what evil Ranquer had been up to, and had been plotting to overthrow him all along.

Sage wasn't sure how that made her feel. A small part of her felt betrayed. Betrayed that she had shared so much of herself, but Ian had never shared his truth. Another heinous part of her felt relief: she wasn't solely responsible for his death, then. She allowed her sorrow to roll over her like a tidal wave, pinning her to the ground she sat upon. When she finally felt the weight of her grief shift from her shoulders, the moon had begun to sink into the horizon. Sage finally stumbled out of her daze, pushing herself back onto tired legs.

Slowly, she made her way back to Gavin's family home, tiptoeing along dark corridors, her eyes straining against the pitch black. When she'd shut the door to her room, she had pulled all the pieces of her mind back together. Enough so to realize that she'd never gotten an explanation of how a mischievous girl-turned-warrior had become a goddess.

Suddenly tired again, Sage slipped back into her bed and decided she didn't want to know the answer after all.

It might make her second guess her next course of action.

⚘✳⚘

After a slightly more restful sleep, Sage took a deep breath to steady her nerves before rounding the corner of a curved, stuccoed wall that led from the hallway into the kitchen and sitting area. A female with springy, black curls bustled around a sink and counters, cleaning fruits and vegetables before setting them into various baskets or jars. Morning light poured through the window perched above the sink.

Her encounter with Allyra the night before had left her feeling watery and disoriented, but a dull hunger had urged her to finally end her sabbatical and rejoin the world around her.

Sage waited a few heartbeats before clearing her throat, not wanting to startle her.

"I knew you were standing there. Could hear you walking down the hall," the female called over her shoulder, not bothering to look up from her washing. "Well—you going to continue standing there, or do you plan on having a seat and sharing a meal?"

Warily, Sage approached the oversized butcher-block island that dominated the kitchen space. She took a seat at a backless stool and waited quietly as the female continued washing carrots in the washbasin. Looking around, Sage took in the stuccoed walls, a large brick oven with embers smoldering at the bottom, and a countertop covered in dark green tiles. The space was small, nearly cramped, and yet incredibly cozy. Something about the space felt so familiar. She realized with a start, it was because it was a space she'd always envisioned Gavin being comfortable in. Another realization sprang to her mind. The female at the sink was not just anyone, it was likely Gavin's sister.

Swallowing hard, Sage mustered the courage to ask, "Where's Gavin?" Her voice felt scratchy and soft, and she cleared her throat once more.

The female with curls turned, quickly grabbing a dish towel off the counter, and began drying her hands. Sage took in hazel eyes and a face that looked so much like Gavin's her heart squeezed. Her hair curled wildly around her face, and there was an intensity to her that was different from Gavin's. There was no doubt she was a strong female, and her generous build was not softened by the cream and brown homespun skirts fluttering by her feet. Sage squirmed under her stare, feeling more exposed with every passing second.

"My name's Delphia. You must be Sage, it's very nice to meet you."

Sage shook her head, clearing her thoughts and realizing she had been rude. "I'm sorry. I've heard so much about you."

Without acknowledging Sage's attempt to placate, Delphia placed a platter of various stuffed rolls in front of Sage, then filled two glasses of water before taking her own seat at the island. Sage sat uncomfortably on her stool. Delphia's gaze was inscrutable, and Sage couldn't figure out if she was being judged. Finally, after Sage reached out to grab her glass and take a sip, Delphia placed a cheese stuffed roll onto Sage's plate.

"Gavin is away. Been gone nearly two days now."

"Oh," was all Sage could manage to say. He'd left without saying goodbye, and after everything, the news felt heavy and foreboding. She had assumed he would include her in whatever trials he faced now that he'd exposed himself. She knew that meant he would be duty-bound to whatever role

Lord of Mystaira required. But if she was honest, she didn't expect to be without him so soon.

"He was called away early in the morning," Delphia continued, speaking around a small bite she'd taken from her own pastry. She looked up briefly from her plate, her bangs partially hiding her gaze.

"I see."

Sage was no longer hungry. She'd taken a small bite of her pastry, which on any other day would have been delicious, but now it felt leaden and dry. She chased it with another sip of water. An awkward silence descended as Delphia chewed her pastry and Sage played with hers, Delphia stared at Sage, and Sage tried to stare anywhere but at Delphia. How had she wound up alone with Gavin's sister already?

"Right. Well—you know Gavin told me plenty about you. I didn't peg you as the sort of female to sit around and pine after someone like a lost pup. With as much as you've been through, I expected a bit more grit out of you."

Sage's wits snapped back to her, her eyes darting from a shelf of ceramic mugs and plates sitting on a floating shelf to Delphia. She had her elbow resting on the counter, leaning towards Sage with an intensity she hadn't quite experienced before. Delphia's words replayed through her mind: *I expected a bit more grit.*

"You're right. I'm being stupid." Sage pushed her plate away. That seemed to spark something in her opponent. Delphia straightened as well, brushing her hands on the apron sitting across her lap. "Can we start over?" Sage asked, her wits now fully returned to her.

What did it matter that Gavin hadn't bothered to say goodbye? She didn't need to be included in everything he did; he was *Lord* of Mystaira now, afterall. Undoubtedly he'd be called away frequently from here on out.

"That's more like it," Delphia said, picking up the plates and grinning. "Grab those dishes and we will finish the washing. There's plenty to be done today."

Sage grabbed her glass and the bowl of pastries, following Delphia to the sink. "Do? What do you mean?"

"Well, this is an estate. It doesn't run itself," Delphia explained, rinsing their plates off in a tub of water. "Or did you think your stay here would be a leisurely stop over?" Clearly, Delphia was not one to mince words, even by Sage's standards. She was quick to chide, and even quicker to act. Sage could only imagine what it would have been like to be her younger sibling.

"To be honest, I didn't know what to expect," Sage answered while drying the plates Delphia handed to her.

"No matter. We will catch you up in no time." Delphia turned as she spoke, flicking water from her hands. Sharply, she gave Sage a nod, as if she had decided something. Sage was unsure what verdict had been passed in Delphia's mind, but she set down her dish towel and followed as Delphia led her out onto the property of the new Lord of Mystaira.

It had been four days of following Delphia around the estate. Waking early to bake bread and pastries, cleaning up after the morning rush to feed the farm hands, feeding animals, cleaning up after animals. Each day was a relentless flow of chores that demanded their attention. Sage found herself exhausted and ragged at the end of every day. And yet, she had never felt more free, more alive.

She used her magic freely, calling forth water to replenish the wash tub after it was emptied. She raised fire
from embers each morning as they prepared breakfast. She
used wind and earth to sweep away mud trails left by Levi,
Gavin's brother, as he ran through the family home, searching for a book on breaking colts. As her magic grew stronger,
she felt as if she could burst with contentment.

At the end of each day after the evening meal, Sage
sat in the family sitting room listening to Lydia and Jethro,
Gavin's parents, tell embarrassing stories of Gavin's childhood and adolescence. Sage grew more eager to see him
with each new nugget of information gleaned. She missed
Gavin terribly, but she was growing incredibly fond of the
estate, the people who ran it, and the animals in their care.

Delphia turned out to be excellent company, adding her
own versions of childhood stories when they were alone
doing their chores that revealed a fierce protection for her
brother, hidden by a healthy dose of spirited teasing. Sage
had had to stop work several times as she held her sides
with laughter at Delphia's deft retelling.

She'd also learned that it was due to Delphia that she
now felt so well rested. Gavin had wanted to wake her to say
goodbye and explain why he had to rush away, but Delphia
had insisted that he let Sage be.

"I suspected you'd insist on heading off with him. And
he wouldn't have been able to say no. It was clear you were
done in. And frankly, we need you whole and ready for
action." Delphia had explained with a wry smile.

Sage had nodded in agreement. This was sound, practical
advice and made sense. She had begun to feel more whole
than she had in the decade since she began her voyage. And
the additional control she'd developed over her elemental

powers was, she had to admit, invaluable. They now felt so much a part of her, she didn't even have to think about them. They'd become as natural as breathing.

That morning, Sage was helping Delphia move a water trough. She had opted to help move the sloshing monstrosity by hand after Delphia had teased her about using her magic so often. As the two women heaved the half barrel on its side, spilling the old water onto the ground, Sage tripped over the boots that were slightly too large for her. Sage struggled to release her hold of the trough to break her fall, landing heavily on her side, her head banging painfully on silt, hay, and wet mud, making her ears ring and stars flash in front of her eyes.

Delphia dropped her side of the barrel, rushing over to help Sage stand. Grunting, Sage slapped the muddy water as she pushed herself to standing. "These blasted boots!" She shrugged Delphia's helping hand off her shoulder, flinging mud and water off her hands as she walked away from the pool they'd just created.

"The boots don't fit properly?"

"I'm grateful to Gavin for finding them, and his guess of size was close. But no, they do not fit, and I keep tripping on them."

"So you need new boots," Delphia said with a shrug. "I'm sure we can scrounge up a pair—"

"No!" Shame immediately reddened Sage's cheeks at her outburst. She took a breath, clenching her fists and jaw to get a hold of her emotions. "I mean, no...thanks, but no. I don't want to scrounge up boots. I don't want to wear anymore borrowed clothing. I've been wearing borrowed clothing, sleeping in borrowed bedding, and living a borrowed life. I just don't think I can do it anymore!"

Sage reached as if she could grab something and whipped her arm through the air. Tiny pebbles slashed through the pen, pelting the fence across from where she stood. Her pulse throbbed in her neck from the sudden outburst, and she exhaled sharply to try and gather herself.

She turned to face Delphia. Her pacing during her tirade stirred up the dry, dusty ground in the animal pen. Delphia looked on, waiting for her to continue, clearly sensing that there was more for Sage to spill than the water on the ground. "I spent a long time on my own. I stole, I bartered, and traded to get what I needed. Even when Ian took me in, I worked. I just..." Sage sighed once more, grappling for the words to carry the weight of the feelings that had been swelling inside her since arriving in Mystaira. "I know I've been pitching in around here, but I need to do something for *me*."

"Like, earn your own coin?"

A wave of relief settled over Sage. She hadn't realized how much the constant charity was beginning to weigh on her sense of self. It'd only been a matter of days since she'd recovered the rest of her memories, lost Ian for the second time, witnessed the horrific murder of her dear friend, and escaped capture once again. But continuing to be at the mercy of those helping her was too much to bear.

"Exactly," Sage breathed.

"And what skills do you possess?" Delphia questioned further, sitting down on a bale of hay. "You can't earn coin without having something to offer."

Chewing on her lip, Sage thought about her options. "You know, in Thuledain, I always felt I was horrible at spellcast-ing, but in reality, I was pretty accomplished with casting protection and disguise spells. I had to hide for so long, and did a pretty damn good job of it." Ideas began running through her head as she took a seat next to Delphia. "Now that I can use my elemental magic without fear, I suppose I could cast quite a few defensive or protection spells."

Delphia nodded. "I see. Let me send a letter tonight. I think I know someone that can get the word out. With the raids that have been going on I expect we'll have a few buyers for your little spells."

Chapter 2

❧❋❧

It had been a week.

A horrible week on the road, on the run, in the woods—chasing raiders who seemed to disappear like phantoms as soon as they'd ransacked a village.

His body was as bruised and scratched as his ego after trying, and failing, to once again track down the raiders. He was exhausted, cranky, and very close to the end of his rope. After barely escaping the Dark Born's clutches, Gavin had hoped that he'd be given some time to rest and replenish himself and his powers at his parents' home. But the raiders had other plans. Things were escalating fast, leaving Gavin feeling like he was losing control of the situation.

And worst of all, he was stuck with Seth, who refused to leave Gavin with the problem alone and insisted on griping about the raiders and Gavin's handling of them at all hours of the day. Gavin wasn't sure what he'd expected when he and Seth had drawn their truce at Aryael's reception, but he had thought the old male would have lightened up a little.

Things hadn't been quite so easy. Gavin was forced to spend his mornings and evenings over-explaining his plans to the tiniest detail to appease Seth's caution as they'd chased the bandits across the hills of Mystaira. Yet still they'd come up short of finding the raider's headquarters.

Just this week alone three villages had been ransacked. The attacks were coordinated, precise; pre-dawn attacks, conducted under the cover of darkness. Completed quickly and efficiently, in under an hour, which was impressive considering how thoroughly each homestead was stripped of all its assets. Thankfully, the bandits seemed content to loot the quiet villages of food and valuables, but leave the people mostly unharmed, other than shaken from being held hostage.

No lives had been lost in the attacks. Yet. And Gavin's fury at not being able to catch them in the act battled with his anxiety over the wellbeing of their people.

He'd only been Lord of Mystaira for a handful of days, and already, things seemed to be falling to pieces. Sure, the raids had begun before he'd been officiated as Lord of Mystaira, and Seth bore a great deal of culpability for how bad things had become. Still, he couldn't help but feel immense responsibility and shame for failing to solve the problem quickly.

Now, Gavin was ruminating on what a mess everything was, simmering inside a canvas tent he and Seth had pitched after finishing what they could to help the villagers.

A couple of thankful citizens had loaned them a few meager furnishings, including a small table upon which a cloth map of Mystaira was draped. They each sat upon crates they had overturned in order to inspect the map. Bedrolls lay on either side of their makeshift planning area, scattered with the paraphernalia of battle—his sword and dagger, waterskins, and a pad of enchanted paper.

Outside, the sounds of livestock being regathered, shuf-fling of feet, and calling of voices had begun to quiet as night drew near.

"I think it is only fair that we *demand* the King and Queen send back the reinforcements they'd intended to help pro-tect our trade routes." Seth jabbed the makeshift table with his finger to emphasize each point, making it wobble. "That they pulled them back to Veritasailles so quickly just proves how little they think of our province." Lord Seth was as much on edge as Gavin, his words laced with ire. Yet, Gavin found himself empathizing with the old Lord.

"Seth, it's frustrating, I'll grant you that, but we both know that's not the reason they pulled the troops back. The Dark Born have their sights on Veritasailles." Gavin raked a hand through his hair before scratching the stubble growing at the back of his neck. "Besides, these are our own people we are struggling against. We should be able to handle this ourselves."

Seth huffed, leaning away from the table and rolling his eyes. He muttered under his breath, just loud enough for Gavin to pick up something about being young and naive.

A tightness gripped Gavin's chest.

This was a test. And if he failed, Seth would never look at Gavin as more than a pup who'd wasted an opportunity. He *had* to find the headquarters, and it needed to happen fast.

He leaned back on his crate, snagging his dagger to give his hands something to do besides throttling Seth like he wanted. He flipped the pommel of the blade around and around in his hand, staring at the map while simultaneously ignoring Seth's huffing. The old male leaned down, reach-ing for his waterskin and bumped into the table, knocking a stack of notes off. Gavin dropped his dagger on the ground, saving a sealed letter from hitting the floor.

As he tidied the letters back into order, lining them up to tap them into a pile, something about the clean line of cream paper connecting two raid sites made him look closer. He suppressed a bubble of anticipation. Tracing his finger along the route of the attacks a pattern began to emerge, an idea taking form in Gavin's mind.

"Seth," Gavin said quietly, hesitant to voice his thoughts. "Do you notice anything about where the attacks have taken place? And when?"

Seth dropped his waterskin onto his bedroll and straightened to look at the table, drawing his focus back to the map. Villages that had been attacked in the last week were marked with circles. Gavin watched Seth as he took in the three circles, all falling along the valley of foothills of the southwestern border. The foothills rose into forested peaks, growing into mountains along the border of Borea, an unpopulated province north of Mystaira.

"They're using the forests as cover," Seth said, noticing the same pattern that had caught Gavin's attention.

"And they've bypassed the larger villages, favoring these here," Gavin noted, pointing at the smaller, less protected villages that had been attacked. "What do you think the probability would be that our raiders will strike here next?"

Gavin pressed his finger to a small village, lying just outside of popular roads and passageways. The village was a quaint, quiet community, consisting of people who would often move to large estates during harvest time as extra labor was needed, and sell blankets and clothing in the winters.

Gavin continued, excitement building in his voice, "We already know the raiders aren't the same group each time. But if we're prepared we might be able to capture someone willing to give up where their headquarters are located."

"And you think we can accomplish this on our own?" Seth asked, hesitantly. Gavin could tell Seth knew the plan was good, but he agreed with his wariness. Two lords against a horde of raiders. Gavin didn't like those odds, despite how powerful he and Seth were.

"No. But I think I can get us some extra help."

Without wasting any time, Gavin took out the stash of enchanted paper he'd become accustomed to taking whenever he traveled. Scratching out a quick note, Gavin hoped King Symon would answer his call and send the weapon he knew would grant him success.

Two days later, the hush of approaching dawn wrapped itself around Gavin in his white hawk-eagle form. He'd hidden himself in a corner between two commonhouses, their roofs merging to form a crook which he fit himself into, perching atop a roof tile. The moon shone overhead, occasionally hiding behind passing clouds.

The small village of Texeri slept lazily through the late spring night. The village sprawled across the middle of one of the foothills, a small vineyard rolling down one side of the hill and houses dotting the landscape. The village's people had erected long rows of houses connected to each other, each with its own porch in the front, and charming courtyards to the back. Families worked together to maintain gardens edging the village's borders and raise livestock to produce the fabrics at the center of their economy. Gavin's sense of anxiety spiked as he thought of all these people stood to lose if he failed them.

Gavin's watch post overlooked the village center where the markets were held. Across the cobblestoned street, Seth hid behind a smallish grain silo. And Meliza, Goddess bless her, had arrived just in time to take up her position hidden in the brush beside the road that led back into the forested foothills.

It was their plan to herd the raiders along that path for Meliza to capture them.

They'd opted to discuss their plans with only a handful of the most senior town leaders so as not to alarm the townspeople and give away their presence. Gavin was sure the raiders had insiders reporting back to the group and he wanted this opportunity to catch them off guard. Gavin remained alert, every sound and movement registering as he waited for the attack to come.

The night yawned as it approached its depths, darkening in the way that indicated dawn was just about to begin its triumphant arrival. The air stilled, even the crickets quieted as they settled into their nests. This was it. Any moment now the bandits would make their appearance, laying siege to the peaceful village. Time slowed, the seconds crawling by as Gavin waited. The skittering of a mouse caught his attention. He took advantage of his bird form, inhaling deep to take in the scent of the critter. Not fae. A simple mouse then, and Gavin turned his focus back to the southern road where he expected the intruders to arrive.

A rustling along a window box lined with flowers followed by a foreign wisp of wind alerted him. It was time. Three slight flashes of light, and Gavin saw the outlines of newcomers casting into the village.

As Gavin lifted off to swoop down to meet them, a winged fae sparked a fire to one of the townhouse porches. The timber lined roofs quickly ignited followed quickly by the sound of a tocsin ringing urgently through the small community by one of the village leaders given the role of raising the alarm. A gust of energy, and a hoard of twenty fae poured up the hill, swarming the village center, ready to ransack.

Gavin landed, shifting into his fae form, sword already in his fist. He met the winged fire wielder and simultaneously ripped the air from the fire crackling along the rooftop. Nevertheless, smoke and screams filled the air, as panicked citizens fled their homes. Two of the leaders ushered children to places of safety while the adults were hurried into bucket lines to quell the flames or given weapons to use upon the attackers.

Gavin's chest swelled with pride at the fight these simple people were putting up. The raiders wouldn't get their trophies so easily this time. Metal clashed, and he heard the whoops and calls as the village leaders led the counterattack, chasing the would-be intruders down the road, right into Meliza's waiting trap.

Gavin fought, striking the winged fae with quick precision. The fire wielder was untrained, and Gavin quickly disarmed him. He reached to pin the male to the ground, hoping to trap him so they could question him about the raiders' headquarters, but the male quickly shimmered into light, disappearing into nothing.

Gavin casted, landing further down the road to put out fires that had sprung up along the village square. He could just make out Meliza through the smoke at the end of the road, trapping fleeing raiders in cages of stone while knocking others out with the blunted end of her spear.

The raiders were becoming desperate. Some of them grabbing sacks of food already packed for market day, others simply giving up and running to save their lives. It was of no matter, now, they'd find them when they had knowledge of their headquarters.

Gavin gritted his teeth, a surge of protectiveness for these people—his people—rising through his body.

One fae sprinted by him, jewelry clutched in his hand. The cry of a woman chasing after the raiding fae ringing out around him. With the fires all smothered, Gavin lashed out with a rope of wind, snatching the jewel thief back to his waiting hand, catching the fae by the throat. He bared his teeth at the fae before slamming him down to the ground, the fae's head cracking against the cobblestone road.

Gavin lashed out with his wind, casting with speed and accuracy from raider to raider, rendering them each unconscious. The need to protect his people crying out as they desperately tried to save their livelihoods pushed him onwards.

Many who could casted away, abandoning their brethren without the power to do so. But others seemed unwilling to give it up. Seth battled against two dagger wielding raiders, and Gavin had half turned to assist when he heard screams tumble toward him from above the village square.

Just above them, near the top of the hill, Gavin could make out three raiders chasing after a female struggling to stay ahead of them as she held a child close. One raider leapt, knocking her to the ground while another snatched the child from her grip. The third stood over her, pressing his foot into the soft flesh of her unprotected wrist. Gavin casted, rage pummeling through him.

He landed mere yards away, a sword in one hand, his dagger in the other. "Stop!" The command ripped across the hilltop, dominance and fury thundering through the air. The fae dragging the child obeyed, submitting to the command of a more powerful fae. The third raider turned, smirking at Gavin.

"Son—go!" The female shouted, and before anyone could react, the child shifted into the form of a songbird, flying quickly away to safety. The female sobbed as her captor pressed his weight onto her arm.

"Come to have some fun, Lordling?"

The raider kicked the female towards his comrade, who grabbed her round the waist, hauling her up to standing, a leer on his face. Turning fully towards Gavin, he pulled a sword from his own scabbard.

These raiders possessed a different demeanor than the others. Gavin had experience with males like these, those who used chaos and tragedy as fodder for their dark desires. The males were greasy, grimey and disheveled. The stink of stale ale clung to them, wafting through the breeze towards Gavin. No doubt they'd grabbed the female and her child with intentions to harm them. Memories of males like them raced through Gavin's mind. Oh, yes. Gavin knew exactly what kind of males he was dealing with now. And as far as he was concerned, Mystaira had no place for the likes of them.

Amusement lit two of the raiders' faces as the sun finally slipped above the hilltops behind them. The other raider, who'd had the sense to obey Gavin, tore across the hilltop, making his escape.

"Call me that again." Gavin's voice came out as a growl, and the fae gripping the female faltered slightly before pulling her to him, pressing a dagger to her throat.

"Take one step closer, and I'll slit her throat, *Lordling*," the raider called.

"Very well," Gavin rumbled, not moving an inch. Slowly, not taking his eyes off his two opponents, Gavin called to the wind. Little by little, Gavin drew the wind to his side, stealing the air from their lungs. He watched as their eyes began to dim, eyelids fluttering as they fought for consciousness. The female also succumbed to his powers.

"Stop that," the taller, sword wielding raider croaked, his hands grabbing his throat as the air became thinner.

But Gavin would not. His outrage at the months of ill treatment towards the people of Mystaira at the hands of these brigands overcame him. Wind began to whip around the hilltop, snagging dust, dirt, and leaves spiraling upwards. All the while, air continued to leave the attackers' bodies. The female crumpled to the ground, her attackers unable to support her weight as she fainted.

Gavin took the opportunity, and struck. He casted once, grabbing the female, then casting her to safety. Before the weakening raiders registered what had happened he was back in front of them, ready to seal their fate.

Gavin casted at the speed of light, slashing through the two raiders. Light sparked as he cast. Again. Again.

Everytime he reappeared, his sword and dagger ripped through a part of the raider's flesh. His rage fueled his speed, his accuracy, the song of death rang through him as he sliced through the males whose malice had led to their demise.

In a matter of moments, the males had been reduced to nothing more than fleshy ribbons. Gavin's leathers were soaked with blood, seeping through the sleeves of his shirt that lay against the skin of his arms.

A gasp sounded behind him and Gavin turned to find Seth, a look of awe on his face.

Whatever Seth beheld caused the older fae to cower. Seth dropped to one knee, bowing his head low. "My Lord."

Another shimmer of light, and Meliza was on the hill, sheathing her sword. "Gavin?"

Challenge hummed through Gavin. Meliza stood tall, meeting his gaze. Something urged Gavin to fight, to boast, to force those around him into submission. The need for dominance was foreign, but it sang with a fierceness that made him grit his teeth. Meliza cocked a brow, spiraling wisps of hair jutting out from her braid. She tossed her spear to the side, lifting her hands up, palms open in a sign of peace and good faith.

Still, Gavin could not suppress the urge to challenge. A growl rippled somewhere deep within his chest. Seth, still on one knee, tilted his head to address Meliza. "Do you recognize what is happening?" he asked in a whispered voice.

"It's the Signum Dominari—" Meliza answered, a half-smile on her lips, "the Seal."

At the answer, Seth inhaled sharply, his eyes lifting just high enough to look at Gavin before lowering back to the ground. Sound drifted into nothing as Gavin and Meliza eyed each other.

Gavin's heart thundered, his body craving a battle between him and Meliza, the only other fae there that could challenge his strength. "What's the Seal?" Gavin asked between clenched teeth. He knew, deep down, he didn't want to fight Meliza, didn't *need* to fight her. But something else in him was demanding it.

"It's an ancient power. It's what used to declare the rightful leaders of our lands, back when we were tribes and not nations. It hasn't surfaced in our people in many centuries."

The words drifted through the air, settling onto Gavin's shoulders. *The Signum Dominari.* The words felt familiar, like they were a missing piece of him. A part of him yearned towards it, welcomed it. He resisted. He didn't want this kind of power, he didn't need that kind of responsibility. And yet—

Slowly, Gavin breathed until calm began to make its way back into his body, and Meliza's shoulders relaxed some. Seth remained kneeling, seemingly content to wait for a command to rise.

"Things are about to get interesting," Meliza mused. "I think I might stick around for a while longer."

The ghost of a smile played on Gavin's lips as he turned to survey the village beneath him. Yes, things were becoming interesting, indeed.

Chapter 3

⚜❋⚜

Gavin walked out of the prisoner barracks, hastily constructed and guarded by the villagers of Texeri and some of Seth's tenants who arrived as extra help. In the past week, Gavin had interrogated the prisoners taken from the attack on Texeri, stopped another attack from taking place, and interrogated the additional prisoners gained from that. And as a result, he'd learned excruciatingly little about where the raiders went after their attacks.

What he had learned was that whoever was in charge was very powerful. Powerful enough to cast hordes of fae in just a few short jumps. That meant the raiders knew very little about where the actual location of the headquarters were located. A clever trick, Gavin had to admit.

In addition to managing rebuilding efforts for the five villages that had been raided, overseeing the prisoners, and gathering information, Gavin was having a hard time managing himself. The Signum Dominari was proving to be a powerful opponent.

Meliza had found some material for him to study on The Seal so he could better understand his new power. From his brisk reading, he had learned that The Seal provided powerful fae with inherited dominance, which would allow him to better command lesser fae. It also intensified one's powers and battle skills, making those under its possession more adept fighters with greater perception and instincts. In the beginning months and years of its development, The Seal had the potential to cause a fae to act more animal than fae, which would explain the tumultuous feelings he constantly battled. He woke up every morning at war with himself, torn between allowing the dominance to overtake him, or staying true to the values that had always guided him.

Never before had Gavin been the sort of male to challenge another fae simply because of the way they looked at him. He simply hadn't cared before. And truthfully, he didn't care now. But the Seal was causing him to weigh each and every fae whenever he walked into a room.

More disturbingly, he found himself looking for a challenge, seeking it out. Twice Meliza had to drag him out to the stables into a training ring used to break colts and challenge him to a fight. Just so he wouldn't hurt someone with an unpleasant attitude. And twice, they'd called a truce, something that had never occurred before. Part of Gavin was thrilled with his improvements in the training ring, the other was frightened by what it all meant.

All of these thoughts were swirling through Gavin's mind as he walked through the village square. He'd thankfully only been a witness to the last interrogation, something he insisted remained as unviolent as possible. Which meant he was not the best candidate to perform them. In his present state he was likely to rip someone's head off. But taking a back seat did allow him the opportunity to sit and listen. Another advantage of the Seal was that it had made him even more aware of body language and scents in fae. It was turning him into a hugely effective supervisor to those who questioned the prisoners. He still wasn't as keen as Meliza, a thought that somehow brought him some relief. Her Truth Teller power had been irreplaceable over the past few days. Interrogations had kept her busy, and he was happy for her to take the afternoon off. And while he'd been working just as hard, he still couldn't allow himself the same privilege.

"Ah—there you are." Meliza's light voice caught his attention, and she smiled as she approached him from the porch of one of the townhouses lining the street. He nodded in greeting but continued down the road in search of food.

"Here I am."

"Well, since I have your full attention," Meliza continued, matching Gavin step for step, "perhaps you care to share your plans for the rest of the evening."

She was baiting him, he knew it. She walked with her head held high, and spoke without the same deferential tone most of the other fae had begun to use when addressing him. Being unable to subdue her in combat meant she had every right to walk without bowing to him, logic told him that. Instinct, however, began to rear its annoying head and urge him to challenge her again.

"What's your business, Meliza?" Gavin asked, not wanting to submit to the urges that were washing through him.

"You need to take a break. One day off won't ruin the campaign you've set for yourself." Meliza stepped in front of Gavin, blocking his way down the path. "If you keep pushing yourself, the next time you lose control could be worse."

Gavin glared at Meliza, even as her words rang true. He'd lost control the night before and had thrown one of the prisoners through a wooden door. The male was okay, nothing a healer couldn't mend, but the outburst had frightened Seth's men.

"If you keep down this path, you are more likely to encourage *someone* to look for different leadership." She crossed her arms, giving him a direct look.

"Which would mean another bloody fight on our hands," Gavin growled. He exhaled strongly through his nose, trying to encourage his heart to stop racing.

"Exactly."

"What do you suggest?" Gavin asked, some sense of control filtering back through his body.

"I think there's only one place, one *person*, who can help you take that edge off," Meliza answered, smiling as if she knew a joke he didn't.

"No." Gavin pushed his way around Meliza, stomping his way toward what had become a food hall for those visiting in the village. "I don't want her to see me like this," Gavin's answer snapped out of him. It had been two weeks since he had last seen Sage. He didn't want the first time they saw each other again to include a visit where he was more animal than fae. He couldn't bear it if she thought of him as a brute. He hoped Meliza would drop it

Naturally, she would not. "Oh, but she wants to see *you*." Meliza said the last word with a bump to his shoulder. Gavin staggered slightly, stopping to glare daggers at Meliza. "You want to see her, too. Even just talking about her I can sense your body unwinding."

She was right, of course. Meliza was almost always right. In a way, it reminded him of his sister. But that wasn't who he wanted to think about right now. No, right now, a different female was dancing through his mind. A female with cinnamon colored hair and sparkling green eyes. A female with soft skin, a petite frame, soft curves, and—

"See! You *do* want to see her, and badly from what I can gather standing next to you." Meliza chuckled and Gavin fought his embarrassment, and another urge to strike her.

But she was right. If he couldn't figure out a way to get a grip of himself, his people might start turning on him. And what would he do then? Would he hurt his own people because they recognized him as a threat? Would he prove them right? That made him no better than the Dark Born, or the mysterious being who was orchestrating the raids. No, he'd better listen.

"Fine. We'll go back this evening. But only for tonight. Tomorrow, we are back here with Seth, coming up with a plan for finding the headquarters."

Gavin pushed past the smirking Meliza once more, making his way to the food hall. He would eat, then he would bathe, then...he would go and find *her*.

༄ ✳ ༄

Sage and Delphia rode down the bumpy trail back toward the family's home. They had spent the last few days making the trek from the small house to a neighboring town not far away.

Delphia had been correct. In a matter of three days, her friend Lily had spread the news that The Realm Leaper was in Mystaira, and offering her services to those looking for extra protection. Sage's notoriety and the increased raids had worked in her favor. Already, Sage had earned half of what she needed to purchase her own wardrobe, and have a little left over. By her estimate, she'd only need to ward two or three more houses to begin placing her order with the local clothier in the village.

It might be silly, but Sage had eyed a soft robe in the clothier's shop window. For some reason, a robe felt like something so adult, so...well-adjusted, and Sage longed for the garment. Its soft blue silk seemed to fall like water around the mannequin's shoulder. Without meaning to, Sage began imagining what it would feel like to have Gavin's warm hands race along her shoulders, pushing the cool material from them.

Delphia coughed, clearing her throat in a way that told Sage that her thoughts were a little too obvious for the fae sharing a wagon bench with her. Sage smiled with thin lips, shrugging in apology.

It had felt like ages since Gavin had gone away. She'd enjoyed her time with Delphia and the rest of his family. She'd enjoyed the space his absence had given her to gain confidence with magic, to grow stronger and more sure of herself. But she missed him dreadfully. At night, she had to force herself not to imagine him with her, afraid that any sounds, or scents, might be cause for an embarrassing breakfast the next morning.

And during their separation, Gavin had only had time to send two notes. The first, detailing the trials he'd faced tracking down the raiders, and how he'd figured out the patterns of their attacks. The second note had been different...*so* different. It'd been a rambling mess.

He'd started with a quick account of what happened in a village called Texeri, which she had immediately found on a map in his room. Then, the note devolved into admissions of how much he thought of her, *how* he thought of her, and what he needed to do when he thought of her. Reading the note had forced her to escape down to the creekside to avoid any prying fae from sensing the note's effect on her, especially when she got to the part where he detailed what he'd like to do to *her*.

"If you keep thinking about my brother like that, I'm going to toss you in the back of this wagon."

Sage chuckled. "Sorry. But if you must know, he started it."

"I would not like to know, thank you very much. I'm happy for him, and you, but I'd rather imagine that things are more innocent than...*that*." Delphia emphasized her last word, casting a glance up and down Sage's body which sat bouncing on the wagon bench beside her.

"Well, friend, I'll do my best. But I make no promises once he's finally back."

Delphia snorted in disgust, and Sage laughed, the sound bright and cheery to her own ears. She'd noticed the change in her laugh over the past few days. It was genuine, and light.

In the past weeks she'd had moments of intense grief. Times when she thought of Hyacinth, wishing to write her friend a note, then remembering she was gone. There were times when the truth of her reality seemed in such stark contrast to her day to day life in Mystaira, it felt almost unreal and a sense of panic crept back into her veins.

Then there was the intense rage. The vengeance that bubbled up beneath her skin when she thought about Ranquer wickedly secreting himself into this world, to bring his own version of evil to this peaceful land—it left her trembling and nauseous.

But those moments drifted by. She let them wash over her as she acknowledged the truth in them, but refused to let anything rob her of the moments of joy she was blessed with currently.

The wagon continued bouncing over the gravel and dirt pathway, taking the gentle curve that led to the family's stuccoed house. Smoke rose merrily from the chimney, despite the increasing heat of the season, a sign that someone had already begun preparing for supper. Sage saw Levi chasing after a colt in the training pen, and laughed as he had to jump the fence to avoid being kicked by the troublesome youngster.

As they drew closer, Sage noticed a familiar form standing alongside the drive they would eventually park on and dismount the mule pulling them. Springy, golden curls waved in the breeze as Meliza smiled and waved. Sage's heart skipped. If Meliza was back, did that mean—

"Who is that?" Delphia whispered.

"Meliza," Sage answered, almost as quietly as Delphia asked.

Delphia cleared her throat. "Right, the Head of the City Guard. Wonder what she's doing here, then?"

"She's been helping Gavin, over in Texcri."

The wagon grew closer, and Sage's heart leapt into her throat. Gavin's absence on the driveway strained something in her stomach, and Sage almost fell out of the wagon to greet Meliza.

"Meliza, it's good to see you," Sage panted as she quickly strode over to the warrior. She was tall, much taller than Sage, and her figure was formidable as always. "Why are you here? Did something happen?" Gavin's absence suddenly seemed ominous, and Sage's palms grew sweaty.

In the distance, Levi's shouts disrupted the moment of silence before Meliza answered. "I'm here because I thought it would be good for Gavin to take the night off. I pretty much had to kidnap him to get him here."

"That makes sense. I know he's worried about Seth's opinion of his handling of this whole thing," Sage said, waving her hands to indicate the whole of Mystaira, not just the capture of the raiders.

"Oh, I don't think that will be a problem anymore." Meliza's answer caught Sage off guard. There was a smirk of knowing on the fae's face, and Sage couldn't help but feel slighted at the response.

"What do you mean? Where is he?"

"He's waiting for you," Meliza replied, dropping her voice as Delphia began to unhitch the mule from the wagon. "He's in the big house—" Meliza grabbed Sage's arm before she could turn and look for Gavin, "but there's something you should know before you find him."

"What's happened?" Sage whispered. Delphia, clearly overhearing the conversation, arrived next to Sage, crossing her arms and staring at Meliza.

Sensing her ire, Meliza turned her attention to Delphia, a spark lighting her eye. "You must be Delphia—"

"Aye, and I want to know what's happened to my brother," Delphia said, interrupting Meliza.

Meliza nodded, looking back at Sage. "It's called the Signum Dominari, also known as The Seal."

"The Signum Dominari? But that's ancient power. We haven't seen the likes of *that* in what... close to a thousand years?" Delphia said, rearing back as if she'd been hit in the face.

"You know it?" Meliza asked, her eyes drifting back to Delphia.

"Yes. I can read, you know, and I do...read." Delphia crossed her arms, glaring at Meliza.

"Stop—what does this mean, Meliza? Why are you telling me this?" Sage said, stepping between Meliza and Delphia.

"It means, he is going to be a little different when you go see him," Meliza answered, then nodded, jutting her chin out in the direction of what was commonly referred to as "The Big House" by Gavin and his family.

Sage had never ventured down the path that would lead her to the house, but suddenly felt like the gravity of a massive planet was pulling her there.

"He's waiting for you in there." Meliza's voice had dropped low again, but Sage was already walking towards the house.

It didn't take long to walk to the large, multi-storied house. Terracotta tiles lined the roof, and happy, round archways dotted a breezeway along what she might have referred to as a basement. A double staircase encased the front entryway fading into a grand porch, adorned with black iron railing.

The whole house looked imposing yet cozy. By a count of windows alone, Sage guessed the house contained ten rooms or more, making it larger than any place she'd ever stayed—at least, when not counting derelict buildings in Thuledain or the Obelisk in Veritasailles. Or the palace. Okay, so she supposed she'd stayed in some pretty large abodes before. But never a *house* so grand.

Sage climbed up the staircase, reaching the large, dark wooden door. Feeling self-conscious suddenly, Sage took a moment to smooth out her hair in the reflection of the window gracing the center of the door.

Gods, on second thought, Sage wished she'd taken the time to bathe, maybe even change clothes before seeing Gavin. It's not like spellcasting was strenuous work, not compared to the chores required to keep his estate running, but riding behind a mule certainly didn't make one smell like roses. Her mouth started to feel grimey, and she ridiculed herself for being so self-conscious. Rolling her shoulders back, and lifting her chin, she turned the knob and pushed open the door.

Dust motes danced through sunrays, and Sage walked quietly through the tiled foyer. A sitting room sat to her left, while what appeared to be an office sat to her right. Further into the home, she could make out a dining room and a hallway that she guessed would lead to the kitchen. In the dining room, darkened as the sun set to the front of the house, she found what she was looking for. Her breath caught as she took in the sight.

Hunched over the table, Gavin gripped the side of it, his head hanging between his shoulders. "Gavin?" she asked in a whisper.

"I could hear you approach, I heard you hesitate, and I wondered if maybe you had changed your mind." Gavin's voice was rough, weathered sounding. And there was something else that laced his voice, too, something Sage wasn't sure she could place.

"I was only thinking I should have cleaned up a bit before I came here."

Gavin lifted his head, turning to face her as she fully entered the dining room, passing through the curved archway that separated the room from the hallway. The light of the setting sun turned the windows silvery, and it only served to intensify the look that radiated from Gavin.

"So you weren't second guessing me? I'm assuming Meliza told you what has happened." His voice had that strange sound to it again, almost menacing.

Sage approached Gavin, dropping the tension that had been held in her shoulders as she finally reached him. "She told me that you've changed somehow, but none of it made much sense to me." Sage smiled, reaching up a hand to place it over his heart. *Finally,* her body seemed to breathe as he covered her hand in his. He stared at her hand, and she expected him to drop his shoulders. But there was little change in his posture as his eyes met hers once more.

"I have changed," Gavin answered, pulling her to him, then pushing the back of her legs against the table. "You might not want to be with me once you know how I've changed."

"Don't be stupid Gavin," Sage said, rolling her eyes. "With everything you know about me, there's no way you becoming Lord of Mystaira is going to drive me away, now."

She looked up sharply, Gavin squeezing her hand, his other hand grabbing her waist in a tight grip. His jaw flexed, and he spoke around clenched teeth.

"Don't—" he said, "don't make promises like that when you don't know the full story."

Sage reared back, looking at Gavin as he squeezed his eyes shut. His heart raced so much even she could see the pulse throbbing in his neck. And beyond that, she could feel the effect her presence had elsewhere in his body. As he opened his eyes, she noted the blackened pupils, an almost feral energy to his stare. "You might not want to be with someone like me, Sage. I don't know what's happening, but I feel out of control, out of my depth. I don't know if I can master this, so you can't promise that this is what you want."

Wind began snapping through the dining room. Old shreds of wallpaper that had begun to peel from the walls whipped like flags as the wind picked up speed. Dust motes swirled around her and Gavin as he squeezed her tighter.

"Gavin, what are you saying?"

"I know I told you not to leave, not to run, but now..."

"Are you saying you don't want *me*? Have *you* changed your mind, Gavin?" Sage's questions were sharp, flung back at him like daggers thrown at a target. She tried pushing at him, tried pulling her hand free, but he squeezed tighter, almost to the point of pain.

"No," Gavin replied. A growl started low in his chest, and she felt it now. Felt the animalistic thrum beneath what she'd always known as Gavin. "I want you, Sage," the admission slipped from him like it was painful, like the words were hot embers slipping through his throat. The wind whipped harder, pulling the hair from Sage's face. The chandelier above them swung wildly. A whistle began to howl as the wind wrapped itself around the room, threatening to burst through the windows.

That was enough. He was doubting himself, and in turn, doubting her. And Sage was past doubting. Shoving with all her might, Sage pushed Gavin back. He staggered, something registering in his eyes. Before he could react, she flung out her arms. "Stop!" she commanded. The wind died immediately, dust dropping to the floor, wallpaper slapping back against the wall. The chandelier screeched as it dropped back to its home.

Gavin stood a foot away from her, panting hard. He glared through his eyelashes at her. Slowly, Sage lowered her arms, placing them on her hips and lifting her chin.

"Stop that Gavin. Remember what you told me? We are not running anymore. *You* are not running, and neither am I. Neither of us know where all of this is going to take us, but we won't run from it either. So stop throwing a fit, and tell me what you need."

Time crawled by as she waited for him to react, waited for something to happen. But a stillness had fallen across Gavin, and she couldn't even tell if he breathed as he continued to glare, his head dropped, and his eyes turned toward her.

A slow smile spread across Gavin's mouth, and for the first time since she'd seen him, a small feeling of intimidation sprung up inside her. Slowly, so slowly it was nearly painful to watch, Gavin knelt, placing one knee on the floor and bowing his head. "What are you doing now?"

"I'm bowing, to my Lady."

"Your....your lady?" Sage stammered.

"Yes. You will be Lady of Mystaira." Gavin lifted his gaze, catching her in it so she couldn't look away if she tried.

"I can't be a Lady, Gavin." Sage scoffed. The idea was ridiculous. She would have to leave, eventually. There was no way for them to make the arrangement work.

"If you are not my Lady, I will have none. There is no one else who can stand by my side, who can command me like you. From here on out, I will only kneel for my King, my Queen, and *my* Lady."

As improbable as it sounded, and though there were a thousand or more reasons for it not to work, something about his words resonated with Sage. Something about them fit, like a piece of her soul. "Gavin," she whispered.

He moved, his hands reaching for her, then skating up the backs of her legs. They stopped when they reached her hips, and he pressed his face between them, breathing deeply. "Gavin," she whispered again, "what are you doing?"

"You asked what I need from you. But all I need *is* you." He said the words with his forehead pressed below her belly button. Then, he let his nose rest against her soft leggings. Before she could register what he was doing, he began tracing his nose upward, up against her stomach so that the tunic she wore bunched below it.

She'd never thought of noses as being erotic, but as he dragged his across the plane of her stomach, then up between her breasts, slowly across the soft slope of her chest then her collarbone, before finally sliding up the side of her neck and stopping behind her ear, she had never been more turned on. Her center turned molten, her knees quivering with need as he brushed the curve of her ear with his lips and whispered, "I need you, Sage. I want you, but more than ever, I *need* you." His hands gripped her hips as he pushed her against the edge of the table.

"And what if I ask you to stop," Sage asked, barely able to form the words beyond the breath catching in her chest as her heart hammered the same rhythm taking hold deep below her belly.

"You know that I would," Gavin answered, his breath fanning out against her neck like a phantom kiss. "But I might combust if you do, so please don't."

A whimper escaped her lips, and she knew Gavin noticed as she rubbed her thighs together, an involuntary action that betrayed her own want. Though she was sure he could smell the pulsing need growing in her with every breath. With eyes closed, her breaths short and hot, she nodded. "Yes," she said.

In a blur, Gavin had her lying on the table, her tunic bunched up by her neck. Without warning, he splayed kisses across her chest, stopping to lick her sensitive nipples already peaked from his earlier torture. She lifted her legs, wrapping them around his torso, scraping her fingers through his tangled hair as he kissed lower and lower. "Gavin," Sage commanded. He stopped, looking up at her face, giving her the moment she needed to pull her tunic up and over her head, tossing it to the side.

He took the meaning, removing his own shirt. She might have been embarrassed by the panting that shirtless Gavin caused in her, but his own lust drowned out whatever self-consciousness she could have possessed.

Wildly, they each unbuttoned their own pants, Sages's slipping off easily as they'd been a borrowed pair from someone in the village.

Gavin flung off his pants, his erection bobbing slightly, and Sage leaned back onto the table as he covered her body in his, kissing her hard on her mouth. The sensation of his lips on hers, finally, nearly sent her over the edge.

There would be no need for foreplay. She'd been ready for him long before he actually began to touch her. A whine hummed in the back of her throat as she felt his head graze her entrance, and he made no move to go further. Gripping his shoulders, she pulled him in tighter, pushing him to go.

Gavin pulled away from her. "I want you to say it, Sage. Tell me you want this."

Sage shook her head. "No. I need this, Gavin. I. Need. You."

That was it. It was all it took and Gavin was crashing into her. He kissed her ferociously as he barreled into her center, parting her and claiming her in one swift motion. She cried out into his mouth, pleasure flooding her body with sensation sweeter than she'd ever felt.

"Yes, Gavin," Sage cried, and he groaned, his mouth pressed against her neck. She wrapped her legs around his back, using her own strength to pull him in tighter, deeper. He plunged into her, kissing her deeply, and she'd never felt more cherished, more at home than in that moment.

"Oh—Goddess," Sage called out as the intense pulse at her center grew.

"Say it again," Gavin growled.

She recognized it then. Sage had called out for his Goddess, not the Gods of her home. "Goddess," Sage whispered, and she felt him grow within her. Her need intensified, and he matched her, pace for pace. He kissed her again, his hands draped across the sides of her face, cradling her as he hammered home.

The pulsing within her grew, faster, more intense, and she arched her back as everything exploded. Worlds collided, stars went out, time ceased as she met her release. Seconds later Gavin joined her, crying out as he dropped his head to her chest.

They lay there for minutes, catching their breath, and Sage realized the wind had begun dancing through the room again, vines crawled up the walls, and the soft trickle of water could be heard down the hall.

Sage glanced down at Gavin, who had lifted his head, resting his chin between her breasts. "Oops," she said, a new blush creeping across her cheeks.

Gavin breathed deep, kissing her sweetly between her breasts. "It's okay. This place is a dump anyways. It needs a good washing."

Sage scoffed, but Gavin continued, "In fact, I had been contemplating getting rid of this table. But, come to think of it, I'm quite fond of it now."

"Very funny, Gavin," Sage said, running her fingers back through his hair, "but we are not feeding your family on the table we've rutted on."

"If you say so, my Lady." Gavin rose, offering his hand to her to help her off the table. "Meliza forced me to take the night off. I had planned to spend the night here." Gavin pulled Sage close to himself, their naked bodies' heat twining between them. "Would you stay with me? Please?" Gavin asked, dropping his voice to a whisper, then kissing her forehead.

"Of course," she replied. "But you'll have to feed me. I'm starving."

⚜ ❋ ⚜

Meliza waited on the road until she was sure Sage was safe within the walls of the big house. It wasn't that she thought Gavin would actually hurt her, but the Signum Dominari was something no one of their time had experience with. She had no way of being sure what Gavin would do.

Aryael and Symon had agreed that Meliza was better off staying in Mystaira until The Seal had become permanent and Gavin learned to control his new powers. In addition to growing more powerful with his wind control, he'd increased in speed and strength. The first time she'd dragged him into the training ring in Texeri, she was caught off guard by the strength behind his blows, the accuracy in his strikes, and the ferocity with which he fought. He was a different opponent than the youngster she'd trained in Veritasailles.

Still, she had faith that if anyone in this world were marked with The Seal, Gavin was the best candidate. He had a good head on his shoulders, and was a compassionate, eager leader. He didn't actually want people to bow to him in submission. She was sure that as time went on, the same laid back demeanor that drew people to him would make its way back.

The sun began to make its loping descent, sinking beyond the dirt road that led away from the estate and into the rich agricultural land that lay beyond it. Meliza turned away from the big house, making her way back to the family home. She was sure Gavin would spend his evening away there with Sage, and assumed he wouldn't mind if she used his room in the smaller house for the evening.

Her stomach gave a low rumble as she opened the front door and stepped into the welcoming scent of supper wafting through the air. Following the scent, Meliza turned the corner and stepped into a cozy sitting room and kitchen.

At the counter stood Delphia. Her back was turned and she was busy airing the flames that worked below a grate. With the embers glowing to her specifications, Delphia raised her head to stir a pot, something aromatic bubbling away within. Meliza walked closer, leaning against the counter with a hip and waited for Delphia to acknowledge her presence.

"Are you just going to sit there and stare?" Delphia said, her face still looking in at the soup she stirred.

"I'm enjoying the view," Meliza said sweetly.

Delphia huffed what could have been a laugh below her breath, but refused to acknowledge the warrior leaning against her counter. Meliza took the opportunity to take in the female more fully. She liked that Delphia's hair was wild and curly, similar to her own. And her arms showed a sinewy strength beneath tanned skin. She'd always found herself drawn to females with formidable builds like her own. Better that than some waif like her own sister, a female who couldn't put up a fight if she'd needed to. She supposed that made her a bit conceited, but that idea had never bothered her before. She enjoyed the reputation that preceded her, and fought to keep it intact.

"I suppose you'll be needing to be fed," Delphia asked, turning from the soup and grabbing a spiraled sausage that had been secured with roasting pikes. Deftly, she grasped the ends of the pikes and placed the meat atop the grates. A lively sizzle erupted as the sausage began to cook over the bouncing flames below.

"If you can spare a meal, I'd like that very much," Meliza answered, smiling. Delphia turned, looking acutely at her. Deciding to push her luck, Meliza grabbed a plum that sat on the counter, polished it on her sleeve, and bit into it. She tried not to smirk as she noticed Delphia's gaze dart to her mouth as she licked away a stray bead of juice, then snap back to her eyes.

"I suppose we can spare a meal for my brother's friend," Delphia said.

"Delphia!" cried a voice, "I said I'd be right back!" A fae woman slightly older than Meliza entered the room, walking briskly with a cane.

"I know, Mama, but you've traveled far today. Go take a rest, and I'll finish up," Delphia said, ushering her mother to a chair before kissing her on the head.

"And who's this?" asked Delphia's mother. Lydia, that's what Gavin said her name was, thought Meliza.

"Mama, this is Meliza—"

"Truth Teller! Of course," said Lydia. "Welcome to our home! I'm Lydia, but perhaps you knew that already. Does that mean Gavin has come for a visit?" Lydia asked cheerfully, looking at Delphia for the answer.

Delphia shot a glance to Meliza, unsure of how to answer. Choosing to spare Delphia the discomfort of how to broach the subject of Gavin and Sage, Meliza interceded. "He's in the area for the evening looking for a solution to one of the problems we are facing in Texeri. He's spending the evening at the big house, looking for answers possibly left by the former Lord of the province."

The answer had been close to the truth, but the last little bit had stung; one drawback to her truth power was that telling untruths was uncomfortable. The bitter taste of deceit clawed at the back of her throat, and Meliza hastily took another bite of her plum to wash it away.

"Gavin suggested I rest here tonight, and I gladly took his offer. You have a very nice home," Meliza continued around her bite of plum.

"Oh, thank you," Lydia replied, smiling sweetly.

Without further conversation, Lydia turned, picking up a book and opening to a dog-eared page. Meliza took the action as her cue to leave, and turned back to Delphia, glad of an opportunity to get to know her a little better.

Meliza tossed the pit of her plum into a bowl, the contents of which was plainly destined for compost, and approached Delphia.

"Is there anything I can help with?" she asked, leaning her elbows on the counter.

"No," Delphia answered sharply.

A tingle raced along Meliza's fingertips. She grinned broadly as she stood back up and whispered playfully, "Liar."

Delphia stopped picking apart the newly washed greens destined for a salad and blew a stray curl from her forehead. "Fine. If you'd like," she said sweetly, batting her eyelashes mockingly, "you can slice the bread sitting on the island there."

"It'd be my pleasure to slice your bread," Meliza answered.

Her voice dropped as she said it, and she knew she'd hit her mark as a faint blush swept across Delphia's cheek, even as the younger female stifled a laugh.

Without further remarks, Meliza stepped to the island and began slicing a loaf of bread warm enough to suggest it had been freshly baked.

As Meliza arranged the bread in a bowl, Delphia quickly removed the sausage from the grate it had been cooking on, transferring it to a large plate. Skillfully, she removed the pikes, and sliced the meat. Without saying a word, she served two plates of greens and sausage, then fixed two bowls of white bean soup.

"Mama, supper's ready when you are. I'm taking Meliza to the back for a visit." Delphia grabbed a tray she had placed the meal atop, then said to Meliza, "Grab that bottle and two glasses, would you?"

Meliza quickly complied, then followed Delphia down a hall to a dimly lit door, an arching window gracing the center. She managed to open the door, balancing the tray, without dropping anything, then walked briskly out into the golden evening to a cast iron table sitting behind the family home. The yard beyond sloped downward just enough that Meliza could make out a creek running the length of the property, all the way down to where the Big House sat beyond where they could see.

Meliza took her seat across from Delphia who placed the plates and bowls on the table, then set the tray aside. Meliza poured them each a glass of what turned out to be red wine.

"Well this is nice," she said.

"Don't get it twisted," Delphia said. "I just thought it'd be better to avoid Mama with Gavin's current situation. I could sense how the deceit in your explanation affected you. Consider this a gift." Delphia ripped a piece of bread from its crust and dipped it into the stew. She inhaled and exhaled deeply, closing her eyes as she chewed. "You are in luck. Mama makes the best white bean soup. It's not often she fixes it now with how much she travels to tutor."

Meliza followed suit, dipping a piece of her own bread into the soup. Savory, rich flavor flooded her mouth. "Mmm —I'd have to agree," she finally said. She took a few more spoonfuls of the soup, savoring each taste. "This is excellent."

Delphia smiled, setting down her own spoon, then taking up her cup and sipping. As she set it down, she looked toward the creek, the sky ablaze in orange and pink as the sun set behind them. "Does it ever strike you as strange? Moments like this?"

Meliza took her meaning. She imagined it would be incredibly strange for someone born into the camps as she and Gavin were. "Sometimes. Sometimes the years in the camps seem like a fever dream. Sometimes it feels like I must have been in a coma, the horrors of Rankor and his rule just a made up story my brain used to occupy itself. And then other times..." Meliza trailed off, not sure she wanted to talk about the nights she woke up in sweats, screaming for her brother and sister as she was ripped away from them.

"Sometimes the dreams feel more real than when you're awake?" Delphia asked.

Meliza nodded. "Sometimes they do," she whispered.

"Cheers," Delphia offered her glass.

As they clinked their cups together, Delphia raised hers again to add, "To lives that feel like a dream after surviving what could only be explained as a nightmare."

"Here, here," Meliza agreed and felt her heart swell as she looked at the land stretching beyond them, the rich meal at her elbow, and the beautiful female that sat across from her.

Chapter 4

◈※◈

Gavin crouched in the crook of a tree branch, huddling next to the trunk jutting into the dark sky. Crickets still chirped in the distance beneath the waning crescent moon. His hawk-eagle vision caught each rustle of branch and brush, the soft song of a creek below the hill he perched atop fading to background noise as he surveyed the forest floor in the dwindling night.

Two days prior, Seth had received information from an associate about how and where the raiders would escape to after their attacks. According to the witness, a hooded, male fae met groups of raiders beneath the overhang of a great boulder.

This corroborated information collected through weeks of interrogations: the hooded fae would meet his colleagues beneath boulders, in the mouths of caves, or deep within canopies of tightly woven forests. It appeared the raiders had a preference to hold their rendezvous in darkened, shadowy areas.

Gavin had mulled over the information for several days, yet again something tickling his mind about familiar patterns. The connection remained unresolved, however, and Gavin set it aside as they prepared for the ambush which would take place within the next few hours as dawn approached.

His days and nights for weeks had led to this moment. When he hadn't been planning with Seth and Meliza, he'd been building respect and loyalty with the people who had arrived to help their cause. When he wasn't doing that, he was helping rebuild the villages that had been attacked, or meeting with various other towns and villages he and his council had estimated would be most in danger from the raiders. And when he hadn't been doing either of those, he'd been writing Sage.

Leaving their bed that next morning after his only night off had felt like dragging his body across blazing coals. She, on the other hand, seemed to fare just fine. She'd practically pushed him out the door, mentioning something about an appointment in a village outside their estate.

He would have been offended had pride for this tiny female and all she was accomplishing not blossomed within him. Sage was headstrong, and more cunning than she realized. She had a way of endearing the people around her, even when they didn't want to appreciate her. She was full of contradictions: impulsive, yet steadfast; emotional, yet reserved; a smart mouth combined with an ability to read her opponent. She was exactly who he needed next to him as he stepped into his role of Lord of Mystaira, and took full control of his new powers as The Seal embedded itself into his body and soul.

The fact she would be required to return to her world to fulfill the bargains she'd made would be a problem they could solve later. Perhaps there was some way to break the soul contract. It was something they could research together, if they ever made it to Shiphrah and the Rafalatriki.

These thoughts, and a hundred others, ran through Gavin's mind as the night stilled before him. He shifted slightly, tucking his wings closer, leaning tight against the tree. In the distance, he could just make out the form of Meliza hidden in the shadows of two fallen trees, joined together to create a makeshift lean-to. Shadows yawned from the structure, deepening just as the world began to lighten ever so slightly. Dawn was now approaching, triggering his anticipation like a spring. Slowly, like the first drops of rain in a thunderstorm, fae began to make their way through the pine forest.

His instincts urged him to swoop down and confront the fae creeping toward the village lining the creek at the foot of the hill lying below them. But his role was not to apprehend the footmen. No. He, Meliza, and Seth lay in wait for the dark-hooded fae who would arrive soon after the attack began.

One fae stepped on a twig, snapping it loudly. He cringed, another fae shushing him, her finger pushed against her lips, ire written across her face. Then her focus changed, whipping up into the tree where Gavin perched. Her brows squinted as she peered into the tree.

"What?" whispered the male.

"Hush," she answered. "Something doesn't feel right."

The female inhaled deeply, trying to scent whatever it was that had alarmed her. Gavin pulled in his head, trying to blend into the tree even more. He could sense Meliza pull further into the shadows. Their plan hinged on the foot soldiers attacking the village, ultimately to be captured by the forces hidden in the village houses. Then he and Meliza would swoop in to capture the dark-hooded fae who could somehow cast a band of raiders in one jump.

After what felt like countless heartbeats, the female below shrugged. "Come on," she said, again in a whisper. "Let's catch up with the others."

Quickly, she pulled free a dagger, and nimbly sprinted down the hill, barely making a noise. Her male counterpart was less coordinated, clearly younger and less experienced.

Gavin loosed a breath through his beak, his heightened vision and sense of smell returning to the surrounding forest. Further in the distance he heard shouts and the clashing of metal as the raiders breached the outskirts of the village. An explosion sounded, and Gavin's heart pounded as he resisted the compulsion to race down to the village to ensure the safety of his comrades. But he had faith in the leadership he'd chosen, proven warriors and sentry members with battle experience and discipline to boot.

As the fight rang through the forest, echoing in the treetops, Gavin's attention snagged on a soft ripple in the distance. A tall figure stood on the ledge of the path that dropped into the steep hill rolling into the village. The draped outline of a black hood stood out in sharp contrast against the fragmented beams of light that had only just begun slicing through the forest canopy. The figure stood, unmoving, as he watched the fight below unfold. Gavin could hear shouts of panic as raiders fell into trap after trap, his own forces executing their roles flawlessly.

A burst of movement through a tangle of brush broke the stillness of the path. Three raiders crashed through the brush, two of them half carrying, half supporting a third, clearly injured, a leg dragging beneath him. With lightning speed the hooded figure cast to the trio.

"You have to get us out of here!" one raider yelled, dragging her partner as they continued toward where Meliza waited.

"It was a trap," moaned the injured fae.

The trio and the hooded fae reached the fallen trees, the hooded fae whispering to his companions. As they walked, Meliza stepped into their path. This was it, this was their chance to capture the mastermind behind the raids.

With a flash, Gavin cast behind the trio, blocking their escape behind them. Seth stepped out of his hiding spot, unfolding from where he'd crouched on the slope above the path. The two raiders supporting their friend gingerly laid him on the ground, the female whispering for him to press on the gash that ran the length of his lower leg.

"Your friend should really have that wound seen to. We can guarantee his safety," Meliza brokered. Her enchanted spear still rested in her palm, no longer than a dagger in its undrawn form.

With deliberate, slow menace, the dark hooded fae lowered his hood before drawing two short swords from his belt. His companions followed suit, drawing daggers and swords.

Their leader, now hoodless, turned to face Gavin, a wicked smile stretching across his face. "I've been waiting for a chance to challenge you," he answered, pointing one sword at Gavin.

The earth seemed to pause. Birds stopped singing, the sun ceased rising, and Gavin's heart slowed as recognition took hold. He knew the fae standing in front of him. And suddenly, everything made sense.

Instincts kicked in, and time caught up with the moment. Gavin blocked the slashing sword hurling toward him with his own sword. Black swirled around Gavin as his opponent's cape billowed around and between them as Gavin blocked swing after swing of each sword. The two fae beyond began their battle against Meliza and Seth.

The deathly song of sword and spear flooded the forest, drowning out whatever creatures had begun welcoming the coming dawn. The sun crept higher, and still they fought.

A scream wrenched through the air, and Gavin saw the female raider drop to the floor, Seth's sword pointed at her throat.

"Stay down," Seth growled, even as she grunted in defiance.

Meliza laughed as her challenger tried to catch her off guard, easily stepping to the side as he charged her. Swiftly, she swept out the blunted side of her spear, efficiently knocking him unconscious.

Gavin's foe was more evenly matched. Gavin found himself on the defensive, caught off guard, as his opponent met him blow for blow. The male anticipated his every strike, and moved with a swiftness surprising to even himself. But in fact this didn't surprise him. After all, this had been the first fae to teach him any self-defense, to notice a warrior spirit within him, to recognise the raw, untamed power simmering below the surface.

As the sun continued its ascent, the dawning shadows stretched out around them. Realization clawed through Gavin.

"Shit!" he whispered. "Grab them!" he yelled, pushing his advantage against the cloaked fae. He pushed, harder, harder, harder, trying for the opportunity to grab the male, pin him to the ground.

But the fae was wily, twisting and dancing out of Gavin's grasp, his eyes alight. Too late, Gavin realized his foe had maneuvered them right into the shadow of the fallen trees. Shadows yawned out to cloak the three fallen fae.

With a booming laugh, the cloaked fae threw a short sword at Gavin like a dagger. But it has simply been a distraction, catching him off guard for a few precious moments so the cloaked one could make his move. Whipping his gaze back, Gavin watched, helpless, as his opponent flung out his cloak, the garment billowing and stretching with an ethereal enchantment Gavin had never seen before. The shadows pulsed, throbbing with power, making his ears pop painfully. With a groan, reality expanded, then contracted like a heartbeat. Gavin struggled to draw breath, Meliza grimaced. Then, a loud implosion punched through the forest, leaving their ears ringing.

The raiders had disappeared, the shadows that had clawed across the path shriveling back to their rightful positions.

Panting, Meliza asked, "What the hell was that?"

Gavin pointed his blade to the overhang. "That, was Micah."

"And who is Micah?" Seth said. "You recognized him?"

"Yes. And that has just made our situation much more difficult."

✧✦✧

Aryael peered down at the map in her war room. With each passing day vast forces gathered along the Spearsan Pass, the only gap in the mountains that separated Nysa from Speridisia. Reports of metal beasts roaming the forests and snatching hunters had grown so widely that Nysa had put an embargo on all hunts moving forward, a blow to the country's traditional rites of passage for younglings stepping into their majority.

Staring at the map, she allowed herself one singular tear, wiping at it before it could reach the bridge of her nose.

Aryael slammed her fist on the table.

The gathering forces she could understand; clearly, Abbadon and Apyllon planned to invade Nysa at some point—probably fairly soon by the numbers they already had.

What was less clear was the purpose of the metal beasts and the abduction of elemental blessed fae. From Sage's story, Aryael knew that elementals were critical to some part of Ranquer's plan. But exactly what that was and how it benefited him was proving a challenge to unravel.

That one little unknown warred within her mind, plaguing her with doubts she wasn't used to having and preventing her from determining any sort of clear strategy.

It was infuriating. And costing her people dear.

Furthermore, Suda was not an elemental blessed. His powers made him impossibly fast. What could the Dark Born and Ranquer want with him, beyond a bargaining tool aimed at her? Yet they hadn't brokered any sort of negotiations.

None of it made sense. And not much angered the queen more than mysteries.

She banged her fist on the table again, squeezing her hand closed until her nails dug into her flesh.

No word since the insult of Suda's severed finger had been delivered. Aryael had burned the box, and Suda's finger, as an offering to the Goddess. She'd prayed for protection, prayed for guidance, and prayed for the opportunity to burn the Dark Born twins when the time came.

And still, no word from the Goddess had come either.

Nothing.

That's what Aryael had. No plans. No guidance. No clues, no ideas, no certainty.

Nothing.

Fingerprints singed themselves into the wooden table, and Aryael jerked her hands back.

Symon opened the door, sniffing the air. Then quirked an eyebrow at her.

"Not now, Symon," Aryael growled.

"I was coming to see if you'd like to spar," Symon squared his feet beneath him, "but if you're too tired..." he trailed off.

"Too tired?"

"Or maybe too sore from yesterday. I mean, I'd understand." He grinned widely.

Aryael knew his game. That he was trying to distract her from the pain of not knowing what was happening to her brother. And she loved him for it.

Without a word, she cast into their private training ring. He appeared immediately after her.

"No powers?"

"No powers," she nodded, then charged at him, her fist raised. In that moment, she thought, no other male was more beautiful than Symon, as he smiled widely and squared his feet beneath him.

He dodged her blow, knocking her fist out of range, then sidestepped before she could strike again. Quickly, he grabbed her arm, yanking it so that he pulled her backwards, his arm reaching around to grab her in a headlock. Before he could cinch his forearm too tightly, she spun in his arm, pulling him to her. Understanding what was happening, Symon released his grip slightly, but still wrapped his arms around her. Aryael looked up at him, her chin resting on his chest. "I love you," she whispered.

"I know," he replied.

Sweetly, he pressed his lips to hers. She would never be able to understand how after everything, and amongst the chaos they faced now, she'd been blessed with such a love. A male who saw her for everything she was, and loved her despite it. Someone who challenged her when she needed it, and had her back at every moment. She knew, no matter what faced them in the coming trials, they would enter eternity together before they'd let the Dark Born win. It was a balm to her soul, to feel his love and his certainty.

Before he could break their kiss, Aryael swept one leg between his, pulling it sharply forward. Symon hit the ground with a loud thud, a gasp escaping him. "Urghh..." he groaned, still smiling. "I saw that coming, and you still got me."

"That's one for me," Aryael teased, walking back to her side of the ring. "Ready to go again?"

Symon stood, hands on his knees as he shook his head and breathed through the pain radiating from his core. Then he stood tall, walked back to his side of the combat ring and rolled his shoulders. Then bouncing on his toes and smiling like an angel of war, purred, "Always."

Chapter 5

❧ ✳ ❧

Sage squinted as she finished engraving the final runes on the wooden border of the door jamb. Her wand sparked as she maintained her spell, one that allowed her to burn protective runes into nearly any surface she wished. With her elemental magic flowing freely, the process of enchanting the house had gone seamlessly.

The corner of her bottom lip slipped between her teeth as she focused on the last few swoops, critical to solidifying the intent of the wards. She sent another grateful wish to Donn, that he would send her thanks to Ian, wherever in the Otherlands he had ended up. It had been his spells she'd used on the houses and businesses the last four weeks, and with an increase of attacks from rogue raiders, she'd been busier than she ever expected to be. So far, the wards had proven effective in at least one attempted break-in.

With a final arched line, Sage finished warding the entryway. She had already warded the windows, a plus for the parents of two adolescent fae who had already been caught sneaking out of their rooms once. Now came the final touch, a process that usually made her customers wary, but was absolutely necessary to complete the spell.

"Alright, that just about does it. There's one final step, but I will need everyone in your family here for the process," Sage explained, turning to face the matriarch of the home.

"Boys! Come down here please!" The fae mother cupped her hand around her mouth, yelling up past the rafters of the first floor where her two sons were probably...wrestling? Sage assumed that must be what they were doing while she worked below, based solely on the noises that periodically rattled the walls and furniture. She grinned as they thundered down the wooden steps, lined with rough timber posts.

The father of the family stepped blearily out from the couple's bedroom tucked behind the stairs, adjacent to the combined kitchen and sitting room. The small house was crowded with the wares of a busy family home: pots and pans hung above a wooden counter, what looked like clubs for some sort of sport lay haphazardly behind a reclining chair, and parchment, blankets, books, and crafts lay scattered across tables and ledges. It was clear that the boys were a handful; hopefully, Sage thought, her wards would give the parents a little peace of mind.

"All finished then?" the father asked, scrubbing his face from falling asleep as Sage had worked in the other rooms.

"Just about," Sage answered. "There's one final thing to complete and the wards on the front door will be set. All I need from each of you is a small bit of blood to seal the spell."

"Blood?" The mother gasped, laying her palm against her chest. That had been the usual response when her customers found out about this part of the process. Sage had learned to leave it until the end, having experienced one family outright refuse to let her ward their house from fear of Blood Sorcery.

"Yes. It's just a tiny little pinprick, then we place it right here on these runes, see?" Sage indicated the runes she'd drawn around the door frame. "These here—" she pointed at the last four runes on the right side of the frame "— each represents one of you. It lets the door know that you are always welcome to enter, without special permission. Without the combination of the rune and your blood, the spell can't work."

Sage waited, allowing space for the information to make its way through the small family.

"And does this Blood Spell do anything else?" the father asked, stepping forward just a bit so he could shield his wife. This was also a usual reaction.

Sage tried her best to smile serenely. She understood their hesitation, especially after meeting Apollyon and witnessing the devastation of his blood sorcery. "The only thing it does is give you each full control over who comes into this house. Without your permission, no one will be able to get into this house, I guarantee it."

The mother reached a hand out, placing it on her husband's shoulder. "I think we should do it," she whispered to her husband. "Sylvie had her home warded not long ago, and—"

"I don't care what *Sylvie* does or doesn't do," the father snapped. "But I do care about this Sorceress possessing us with her Blood Sorcery."

"Papa, she's not a *Sorceress*. She's the Realm Leaper!" one of the boys said, rolling his eyes at his father.

The older brother, standing closer to their mother, seemed to be a harder client to convince than his younger sibling. She tried not to grin as he crossed his arms, empha-sizing the developing biceps of a late-stage adolescent boy.

"Thank you," Sage said, nodding her head toward the youngest boy. "Let me clarify a bit. My magic is different from the powers fae wield. While some of it looks similar, specifically my elemental magic, my spells and wards come from a different source of power. Everyone born in my homeland has access to the power, and we train at schools to learn how to use the magic. We use materials around us to help strengthen our spells, in this case, I am hoping to use your blood. Although, if it truly makes you too un-comfortable, I could modify the spell by using locks of your hair. That would make the spell a little unstable, however, and I might need to come back a few times a year to check the integrity of it. Which will cost more."

"I still don't like it," the father said, turning fully to his wife.

Sweetly, his wife cupped his face with her hands, looking up at him in the way that only couples who had seen more life together than apart could look. "I know. But would you rather a raider break into the house and take our savings?" She cocked an eyebrow, a look of triumph gracing her face. "Let's get on with it then, I've got washing to do." Sliding her hands from her husband's face she approached Sage, holding out one of her hands.

Sage pulled out a neat packet from her bag, extracting a small bottle of clear liquid and a thin, gleaming pin made of solid gold. She wiped the pin with the astringent, always sure to keep the tool clean and protected.

Gently she took the female's offered hand and ran her finger down the pinky finger of her client.

"Deep breath," she said, preparing the pin, "this only hurts for a second." Quickly, Sage pricked the female's finger, squeezing so that a rotund, bright bead of blood formed.

Stepping to the door with the female's hand, Sage muttered the incantation as she swabbed a rune with the pricked finger. As the last edges of the rune were coated in blood, a light sparkled within the grooves of the rune. The mother snatched her hand back, startled by the effect. As the sparkling finished, she gasped, leaning closer to gaze at the brilliant turquoise lacquer that filled the rune.

"Very pretty," Sage commented. "Would you like to stay close as I do the rest of your family? To see what color their rune will be?" The mother nodded, smiling at the pretty adornment now gracing her door frame.

"Yosef, come here," she called, waving over her youngest son. "You next."

The boy beamed as Sage took his hand. She repeated the process again, the boy only hissing when she pricked his finger. When his rune sparkled, he laughed, then fist pumped the air when his rune shined a bright, bold red—his favorite color. Sage finished the rest of the family, the eldest son's rune shining royal blue. The family all joked when the father's rune sparkled to reveal the dark gray of cold iron, befitting a fae so stern and steadfast.

Reluctantly, the father of the home pressed four coins into Sage's palm. She shook his hand, said her thanks to the rest of the family, accepted a hastily made sandwich, then said her farewells.

After leaving her last appointment of the day, Sage stopped into the village's local clothier. There, she made her final payment for the order she'd placed two weeks earlier. Accepting the wrapped package, Sage beamed as she exited the shop. Nestled in the parcel Sage carried two sets of leggings, soft and *not* made of leather, three tunics, a few pairs of undergarments made to her specifications, and the robe she'd eyed all those weeks ago. She was tickled, smiling broadly as she walked down the now familiar path, ready to begin the eight mile trek back to the homestead.

Sage was still beaming, humming to herself as she entered the short forested part of her journey. Tall pines yawned up to the sky like pillars. In the weeks Sage had been traveling around the area, she'd made a game of counting how many different types of animals she could spot. Rodents with chubby cheeks raced along the branches above her, birds camouflaged to look like the shadows of the forest floor flitted from nook to nook, and once, she'd spotted a red stag before he'd bolted away, bounding for a deeper corner of the forest.

A loud rustle of brush behind her alerted Sage, and she wondered if it was the stag again, or maybe some of the large ground fowl she had seen the week prior. On stealthy feet, she crept to the side of the path, hugging close to a massive pine. She hoped fortune continued in her favor for the day and she'd be blessed with another exciting animal sighting.

She was left disappointed at the sound of cursing followed by a loud snap as a branch was broken, two males stepping clumsily out of the overgrown ferns. The cursing one was rubbing an arm while his companion wiped his dirty face on his sleeve. Twigs and leaves stuck to their pants and shirts and mud streaked both of their faces. They brushed their arms and legs, trying to dislodge the hitchhiker seeds that clung to them.

One of the fae bumped into the other, and his companion shoved him roughly aside with a string of expletives. Their hair was greasy and unkempt, and Sage wondered how long they'd been lost. By this point, she knew her way around the area fairly well, and could at least point the two wanderers in a direction that could help them.

"Hello," Sage called, stepping out from behind the tree. "You two look a little lost. Can I help?"

The two wanderers stopped bickering to look over at Sage with a startled expression. A look of realization washed over the burlier of the two and he straightened. His dark clothing was partially covered by scraps of leather armor at the shoulders and chest. Dark, scraggly hair dipped towards his eyes and his skin was slick with sweat. His pointed ears were pierced with silver hoops at the tips. He swatted his friend, who promptly stopped gawking.

An easy smile spread across his face, something that didn't quite reach his eyes. "Oh, and who do we have here?"

A thrill of alarm ran up Sage's arms and settled in a pit in her stomach.

"Just someone offering help," she responded, quickly adjusting the parcel so one hand was free. She slipped her now free hand toward her pocket, her fingers wrapping around the wand resting securely in its place. The bag resting across her body suddenly felt burdensome, and she shifted her shoulders to swing it out of her way.

"What's that?" asked the second male, pointing at Sage's parcel. "Do we find ourselves in the presence of fortune?" He wore similar dark clothing, though Sage noticed he lacked any leather protective gear. He stepped toward Sage and she sidestepped, away from the tree and back onto the path. A breeze wafted across the pathway, rustling her hair.

"Look at her ears. She's a mortal! In Mystaira?" The male pointed at her worn soft leather boots, which creaked as he stepped closer to her, his eyes drawn back to the package tucked under her arm. "What've you got in that package there? I'd like to see what's in that." He was mere yards away from her now. Sage took a step back.

Two thoughts barreled into her at once. One, these males could work for the Dark Born. Two, they were rogue raiders, escaped from Gavin's traps and looking for something to steal. From where she stood, she couldn't detect any redness around their eyes, but they weren't quite close enough for her to be sure. The male further away withdrew a slender dagger from a holster she hadn't noticed.

"Who are you?" she asked.

"Us?" the armorless male asked. "*We* are Mystairans. *We* were born here. The better question is, who are *you?*"

He had stopped advancing on her when she asked her question, but Sage supposed it had been the wrong thing to ask based on the intensity that followed his answer.

"You don't know who I am?" Sage asked, perplexed. She had been recognized so often his response caught her off guard.

"Why would I recognize a puny mortal?"he scoffed. His response elicited a chuckle from his compatriot, and Sage glared at them. "Now, don't make me ask again. Be a good girl and give me that package." A wicked gleam entered his eye.

Sage squared her shoulders. "No."

"What?" the male asked.

"I said no." Sage didn't know who this male was, but it was clear he truly didn't know who she was. She was *The Realm Leaper*. She had taken on drones and monsters and a bitch of a government agent that couldn't seem to die. She wasn't afraid of two washed up fae thugs.

"You just made a very big mistake, mortal," the male in the back spat, chuckling.

"I think you underestimate me." Her statement caused both males to go very still. That strange fae stillness Sage first learned about months before became overwhelming as she and the raiders stared at each other.

With all the speed she could muster, Sage whipped out her wand, a defensive spell on her lips. Before the words could even form, the male in front had transformed. Wings like a dragonfly's burst from his back and he was over her. She didn't even have time to react before the second male was barreling into her, knocking her package from her hands and sprinting off with it. She twisted, trying to catch herself, but ended up face planting painfully into a root, an explosion of stars bursting behind her eyelids as blood gushed from her nose.

"No!" she cried out. A snap rippled out from the air. Above her, the male with the dragonfly wings laughed as he dropped the two broken halves of her wand. "No," she whimpered.

The world turned red. Reality stopped making sense. Something feral coursed through her body, like when she'd fought Apollyon's possessed. A drumbeat thrummed inside her.

Gathering herself, Sage rolled onto her back, making a whipping motion with her hands. Vines burst up from the earth to chase the fae who sprinted down the forested path with her package. A thud, then a scream told her she'd hit her target, but she glared at the fae above her.

He dove down to her, baring his teeth in a growl. Sage simply pushed out with her palms, sending him hurtling through the air with her wind magic. She stood, planting her feet below her. Slowly, she wiped the blood from her nose. Turning, she took in the fae who'd tried to run, now dangling above the path, suspended by her tame vines. She could snap his ankle with a snap of her fingers, and he seemed to sense her power as he swung, his struggles ceasing.

She twisted her upper body, then threw both arms out toward where his friend lay, gasping for air after belly flopping to the ground. A meaty bounce sounded as one fae collided into the other, the one with wings having just made it back to his feet before his comrade came flying through the air, pummeling into him.

Sage stalked over to the two fae, sprawled on the ground, groaning. Her face throbbed and she absently wiped her nose with her sleeve again, barely noticing the pain over the pulsing rage that had taken over her body.

"You broke my *fucking* wand."

"A sorceress. She's a sorceress..." muttered the wingless fae. Fear emanated from him in waves, she could feel utter terror gripping him. But that wasn't all that'd grip him before this was over, thought Sage.

"You tried to steal my package," Sage growled.

Both males scrambled to their feet, but Sage splayed her hands and roots shot from the ground. Before they could react, the roots entwined themselves around and above them, encasing them in a prison.

"Do you have any idea how fucking hard I had to work for that?" She had stalked forward, about halfway to where her prisoners now waited.

"Please, please...let us go," begged the wingless raider. He at least had the sense to fear Sage, had the sense to understand who was in charge now. The fae with wings glared at her, boring into her with his fury. But his fury was nothing to match her own.

"And what? Let you go rob other innocent folk?" Sage spoke softly, now just outside their root prison.

The winged fae lunged forward, snapping his teeth at her. With a wave of her hand, she ripped the air from his lungs. His eyes went wide, bulging with the realization of what she was doing. She let him turn purple before releasing him again.

"Who are you?" cried the begging one. Sage almost felt bad for him. Almost.

"I'm the Realm Leaper. And I warned you that you'd underestimated me."

Sage stomped her foot, slicing down with one hand. In one motion, she had turned the ground beneath the two males to quicksand and pulled the roots back into the ground, sucking the struggling fae down until just their heads and shoulders were visible. Her other arm drove up to the sky, palm facing upward. She clutched her hand into a fist, and the quicksand hardened into stone, trapping the would-be robbers.

"Now," she said sweetly, walking right up to where both fae struggled in the unforgiving stone. "I think both of you should take some time to think about what you've done."

Sage patted both males on the head like they were school children, and stalked to her package, scooping it up before walking toward the estate.

She'd walked another twenty or so minutes of her journey before the reality of what had taken place fully hit her as the adrenalin that had been coursing through her body wore off.

Her wand.

Her wand was gone.

She'd had it for such a short time, and now it was gone again. And so soon after she had finally figured out how to wield her magic effectively.

Tears sprung into her eyes, prickling at the corners. She squinted her eyes tight, clenching her fists and screamed. A deep, guttural, animal scream, like something wounded and hurt, but that promised trouble and danger.

She was so angry. So mad at herself. She'd let those two fae scare her into forgetting how powerful she was. Instead of relying on her wand, she could have stopped them with her elemental magic. She should have been able to block them, to defend herself easily against their relatively puny attack.

What if that happened again? Or her magic powers were unavailable? Then what?

All these thoughts and more were pummeling through her as she walked, hot, angry tears streaming down her face.

As she rounded the last bend in the path she glared at what she saw ahead.

Meliza and Gavin stood along the drive, talking about something and looking off in the distance.

Sage tucked her head, and walked as quickly as she could, making for the creek behind the small house.

If she had her way, she could avoid them and her embarrassment at failing so miserably at protecting herself.

She made her way to the path that led to the creek, taking a shortcut through the grass.

She was nearly beside the house when she walked into something solid.

Chapter 6

❦ ✳ ❧

He had caught her scent as she walked down the drive, pulling him away from the report Meliza was giving him on the latest happenings in Veritasailles. At first the scent had been comforting, wrapping itself like a scarf around him, warm and soft. But then...the metallic tang of blood grated on his nerves, the soothing sense of her evaporating. Meliza must've picked up on it too, trailing off mid-sentence.

Sage hurried past, her head hanging low, her body hunched and tense. She clutched something wrapped in cloth hard against her, a cross-body bag slung across her torso.

Scanning from this distance he couldn't see any wounds on her. But the smell of her blood still vibrated through the air. And her lack of eye contact or greeting him told him all he needed.

Gavin cast onto the path that led to the small creek running behind his family's home. Sage, head still down, ran smack into him.

"Uph!" She rubbed the spot on her forehead that had collided with his chest.

But Gavin didn't budge. The animalistic side of the Signum Dominari surged through his body as he took in the dried blood crusted beneath her nose, the darkening bruise forming under her eye.

His heart thundered in his chest.

"Who did this?"

Sage wiped a hand beneath her nose, trying to rub off some of the blood and winced. "No one. I tripped." Her eyes slid away from his.

"Don't lie to me," Gavin clenched his jaw. "I can smell something around you, on your clothes. So tell me what happened."

She rolled her eyes, huffing through her bottom teeth. Crossing her arms, the parcel in her hand hanging from a crooked finger, she slowly brought her eyes to Gavin. "I took care of it, okay?"

"Okay? No, it is not okay," Gavin said, leaning toward her. "Tell me what happened."

"Fine, jeez," she said, tossing the parcel onto the ground. "I was walking back from the village, and these two fae guys stopped me. They tried to rob me, and..." her voice quieted. She closed her eyes and clenched her mouth. A lone tear trickled down her cheek. Gavin gently brushed it away with his thumb. "They broke my wand," she said in a whisper.

Sage broke away from his touch, shaking her head rapidly and inhaling deeply. "It's fine, though. I took care of it. I trapped them in stone back in the forested part of the road. I suppose I should ask Meliza to go free them at some point, but—"

Gavin had heard enough. He was pretty sure he could find the two bastards that had hurt Sage. Without saying another word, he casted to Meliza.

"What was that about?" she asked.

Gavin grabbed her hand, and used his power once more to cast into the forest. He stood listening for a moment, then two voices crying out for help carried to him through the trees.

"What is going on?" Meliza asked again, pulling a dagger from the sheath on her belt as Gavin stalked off in the direction of the voices.

Gavin tried to summon his voice, to find the words to explain what had happened to Sage. He'd brought Meliza to release the fae that had attacked Sage, but now as he approached the males the last thing he wanted was to see them walk free.

One of the males saw Gavin and Meliza's approach, fixing them with a malevolent glare. His companion still looked around wildly, calling out for help. Sage had done well, Gavin thought. They were each encased to their shoulders in stone, the road around them fading into dirt. They each struggled, trying to pull themselves free from their entrapment, but the stone held firm.

Still, they had hurt what was his. *Mine*, his blood hummed.

"Look what we have here," Meliza mused as they approached the trapped fae. "A pair of lonely raiders."

Her voice seemed to snap the second male out of his panic as he swiveled his head to look up at her. The other male, the one with shorter hair, continued to glare daggers at Gavin, not taking his gaze from him for even a moment. Gavin returned the look.

"If it isn't the little Lordling that could," said short-hair.

"Said quite confidently from a male trapped in stone," replied Meliza, grinning. She turned to Gavin, "I take it Sage is responsible for this?" She waved the pointy end of her dagger at the pair of thieves. Gavin gave a sharp nod, his voice still not able to beat through the thrumming blood-lust building in his bones.

"Shall I release them? Maybe they would like to join their brethren in the Texeri prison?"

"If you can catch us," Short-hair said. Despite facing Meliza, notorious in Felysia for her battle prowess, the prick had the nerve to speak as though she were a peasant.

Gavin took in the male, the drooping, iridescent wings behind him. A vein pulsing at his temple, partially con-cealed by hair matted to his head by dried sweat. The other male had gone completely still and compliant, head bowed. Sensible.

Meliza, ever the professional, replied, "Look, make this easy for us and we will guarantee civilized treatment. I'm assuming you both escaped from the last raid where we trapped the rest of your party. Cooperate, and you can join them until we figure out what to do with you."

Short-hair scoffed a laugh, but Meliza continued on, "Three hot meals a day, supervised time outdoors, clean water, and a place to sleep. Sounds good, right?"

The quiet one nodded, keeping his head down.

"I want to hear him say it," Short-hair said, jutting his chin at Gavin obnoxiously. "I want *him* to guarantee my safety."

Gavin's voice finally decided to reappear. "You hurt her," his voice a low, guttural growl.

"Who? The girl with the package? So what if I did?" The short-haired male didn't seem to understand the danger he faced, even while his companion seemed to cringe beside him. "She's just some trumped up, mortal sorceress. Some-one ought to grab her and teach her a lesson or two."

"Let them go," Gavin ground out to Meliza.

"Gavin, I'm not sure that's a great idea. Why don't you let me handle this."

"Yeah, Lordling. Let the General handle this." Short-hair seemed to lack even basic intelligence.

"Do it," Gavin commanded.

Meliza blinked, the stone turning to sand. The males both struggled, pulling their bodies from the slippery grit, then crawling on their bellies to escape the pit.

"Now... *Run.*"

Something in his voice had both fae looking sharply up at him. Short-hair losing the color in his face. Without more than two heartbeats between his command and their realization of who they now faced, both took off past the pit of sand.

Short-hair ran fast and hard, trying to flap his wings so he could take off into the sky. Gavin let them go just a few moments, just enough to let them think they'd escaped.

But it wouldn't be that easy. No. They had hurt *his*. They had put her in danger. This was his home now, and he could not allow that kind of danger to continue existing.

Gavin's body sang, *now, now, now...*

He cast directly into their path. The quiet one screamed, both turning to run the other way, into the path of Meliza.

But Gavin was there again, right in front of them. No weapons in his hand, just his body and his power.

Both males turned in unison, heading for the overgrown forest bracketing the road. Gavin reached with his wind power, yanking both males back onto the road. They scrambled to their feet, running again. Gavin shifted, wings bursting from his back. He flew low to the ground then scooped up Short-hair beneath his arms, spearing up towards the sky. Gavin heaved once, tossing the male upwards then grabbed his wings, letting gravity take hold.

With a crack, the wings dislocated from their joints before Gavin released him. He screamed in horror and pain, blood pouring from an open wound where a wing had partially torn free. Gavin let him fall for several feet before casting again, catching the male in mid-air.

"You hurt what is mine," he growled, flying over the forest. "I should let you fall to your death here."

The male yelled beneath him.

"Enough of that," Gavin ripped the air from his lungs.

He flew high, holding Short-hair by one ankle as the male clawed at his throat, struggling to draw breath as Gavin forbade the air to re-enter. When the male's face had turned purple, Gavin relented. He heaved again, hoisting the male up so that he flew out in front of him. His back bled freely, raining down onto the forest below.

Gavin caught the male by the throat. "Tell me again. What is it you think about my sorceress?"

Short-hair clutched Gavin's arm as he squeezed, then seemed to sense his fate, all physical fight draining out of him. He looked into Gavin's eyes, "I said, someone should teach that bitch a lesson."

Gavin's shoulders tensed, his lips clenching to a thin line before he plunged down towards the waiting forest below. Still holding the male by his throat he hurtled towards the canopy, angling for a tree with the right kind of jagged branch pushing into the sky...

With the *thunk* of flesh meeting wood, Gavin flapped once, staring at the male impaled on the branch, sightless eyes staring up vacantly.

Casting again, Gavin appeared beside Meliza who stood over the quiet one, now cowering and muttering in front of her. The air stank of piss.

"I'm sorry, I'm sorry...we didn't mean it." The male pressed his face against the dirt, groveling and cowed, the crotch of his pants wet.

Gavin kneeled, bringing his face close to the male's ear. "You will go to the prison in Texeri with the rest of your miserable crew. And let it be known, The Realm Leaper is mine, and *your* future Lady. Nod if you understand."

Frantically, the male shook his head. "Good. You will tell your fucking useless comrades what your new Lord will do if anyone so much as touches a hair on her head."

The male nodded again, still fawning in the dust. Gavin stood, towering over the male.

He looked at Meliza. "Take him to the prison, then meet me back at the estate."

"If you say so," Meliza raised an eyebrow, looking him up and down. "I suggest you walk the rest of the way back, though. You'll need to sort yourself out before talking to her."

Meliza was right. He nodded once to her before soaring into the sky above the forest canopy.

He'd patrol the skies until he felt in control of himself again.

❧ ✳ ☙

She wasn't sure when it had happened, but the creek had become a familiar friend in the past weeks. Something about the rustling, tall grass and the smooth pebbles that lined the brook was calming for her. Even if it brought back memories of her visit with Allyra.

Sage's tears had dried up, the lingering feeling of embarrassment had lessened sufficiently that she didn't constantly wish the ground would swallow her whole. But she couldn't shake the feeling of uselessness.

What good was she to the gods if she couldn't defend herself against a pair of thieves? Sure, her elemental magic had swelled to great proportions over the last months; and her ability to enchant had never been better. But her instincts? She knew how to run, but that time in her life was over. Done. Now was the time to face her enemies.

How would she meet Nehalennia, the great wolftress from Thuledain, "on the battlefield" once she was back home? Remembering the Wulver's words in Therisyd's temple pitched her stomach into flips and dips, and Sage shook her head to dislodge the memory. She would never be able to fight next to the Wulver, not in her current state.

And now she didn't even have her wand. It was like half of her worth had been stripped away from her in an instant.

Anxiety was just beginning to bite again when two booming whooshes of air beat against her back. She didn't know how but as Gavin had left the estate a short while ago she'd felt his absence inside her soul like a vast lake had been emptied inside of her. She wasn't sure how long he'd been gone, but she wasn't confident she was ready to face him just yet. Hugging her legs tight to her chest, she muttered against them, "Go away."

He didn't.

Of course he wouldn't. She knew Gavin could be stubborn. She just wasn't ready to analyze what had gone wrong today. Not yet.

He stood behind her, not moving. She could feel his stillness, and it was unnerving.

"Please go away?" she tried again.

Still, he stood there, not saying anything. Sage huffed, picking up the rag she had used to clean beneath her nose then stood to face him. "Fine. I suppose you want to talk about it?"

"No," Gavin said, his voice rough.

She looked closer at him, taking in his darkened eyes, the clench of his jaw. "Why not?" Sage asked warily.

"I took care of it." Gavin's reply was short, as if whatever happened meant nothing.

"No, *I* took care of it. I'm assuming Meliza is taking them to wherever the others are imprisoned?"

"One of them," he said. He still barely moved, and Sage got the feeling there was much more to the story.

"What do you mean, 'One of them'? Did the other escape?" Sage's voice hitched slightly. She couldn't have botched that, too, could she?

"He didn't escape. I killed him."

The answer was sharp, hurled slicing through the air at her.

"You did *what*?"

"He hurt you," Gavin growled.

"So what! I took care of it." She threw her hands in the air and began to pace on the narrow path that led to the creek. "I had it under control, Gavin. Why did you kill him?"

"I needed to send a message. That you are *mine*, and I will protect what is mine."

"*Yours*?" Sage asked. "Oh-ho...let's get one thing straight. I am *nobody*'s. I am my own," she said, pushing at her chest with an extended finger. "I can take care of myself, and I *do not* need someone to fix my problems."

"He hurt you. You are under my protection. How do you think it will look to other fae if they discover I don't protect the ones I love?"

His confession startled her, but she chose not to acknowledge it, deciding instead to push the issue to where she needed it to go. "And how do you think your people will react when they find out their new Lord is a bloodthirsty misogynist?"

"Misogynist?" His question seemed to awaken something in him, his eyes clearing finally.

"Yes. An alpha-prick who thinks his solutions are better than everyone else's. That's the way you are behaving right now." Sage turned from him, muttering to herself. "'Mine...' What a crock of shit..."

She took a deep breath before turning back to him, then spoke very slowly. "Okay, let's hash this out. Right here, right now.

"When I say 'I've got this,' I mean it. If I say 'I don't need your help,' I don't need it! I agreed to let you help me before, but that does not give you permission to decide when—and if—I need it." Gavin remained still, impassive. "The only one that gets to kill in my name, is me."

Unexpectedly, a slow smile overtook Gavin's face.

"What?" Sage demanded, crossing her arms in front of her.

Whatever she had expected from him, this wasn't it. Instead of arguing with her, or putting up a fight, he took a step closer to her. His heat radiated from his body, and she fought the urge to lean into him. Instead, she hardened her face, lifting her chin so it looked like she was looking down at him, instead of the other way around.

"Spoken like a true Lady of the Province," Gavin said, stepping closer still.

"I never agreed to that," Sage replied, a shade coyly.

"Nevertheless, if you keep it up, you'll have the fae bowing to you in no time."

Sage huffed, rolling her eyes again. "Well, before that ever happens, I need to be sure we don't repeat today's occurrences."

"Agreed," Gavin said.

"I just wish I felt more confident. I could have easily taken those two, but I froze in the moment."

"Sounds to me like you need some training." Meliza's voice bounced from behind Gavin as she walked down the gravel path. She nodded to Gavin as she joined them.

"What kind of training?" Sage asked.

"The fun kind," said Meliza.

A buzz ran through Sage, equal parts thrilling and terrifying, as Gavin and Meliza grinned at each other, Meliza waggling her eyebrows as if they shared a joke.

This was either the greatest idea ever, or the dumbest thing Sage had ever agreed to.

✧✦✧

"After the smoke had cleared, the whole city erupted in screaming. They say a massive shadow had laid itself over the city. Homes burned, crops withered, livestock dropped dead where they stood, and..." Epyllo's voice tapered off. He swallowed hard before he continued, "any children caught within the shadow, died."

He paused for a moment seemingly stunned by his own words as his audience murmured among themselves, shock and fear registering behind whispered comments. Symon cleared his throat, indicating for Epyllo to continue. "The only good news was that since the attack happened at midday, some of the civilians noticed the roiling shadows approaching and made it safely within the Senate Fortress."

The council finally grew quiet. Stunned silence ringing deafeningly through the room. Raphael squirmed uncomfortably in his chair as counselors on both sides of the court looked at each other furtively.

Meliza, Gavin and Petra's presence were missed from the round table, Raphael reflected. One sister was away helping with the troubles in Mystaira. The other sister... Well, she was somewhere else. Captured deep within her own grief, Petra hadn't been seen since she'd moved back into the Obelisk. He hoped she would let them in soon; he worried for her health. And, selfishly, he wanted back into his medical ward.

Seth sat at the round table instead, filling in for both Meliza and Gavin. His turn to share news would come soon. But it was Epyllo's last statement that had filled the room with quiet.

Symon was clearing his throat. "If the Dark Born have truly found a way to break through the enchantments protecting the Nysan capital, what is our counter move? What will they be expecting us to do, that we are able to deliver upon? "

The question was a tricky one. For one thing, Nysa and Felysia were allies—of course— together, both nations were all that stood between Speridisia and the rest of the world.

The other half of the question centered around what forces Felysia would be able to spare. Their troops were stretched thin, fighting off their own in Mystaira while still providing reinforcements at the capital city.

"The Senates are holding strong within the walls of their fortress," Acantha interrupted. "They have a large number of civilians within the walls, but they will be starved out before too long."

"They have plenty of reserves. They are better equipped within the fortress than anyone would expect," Aryael countered. "The fortress was designed for that very purpose. It took the entire force of Speridisia and Rankor to break in last time. I suspect the enchantments and defenses are even stronger now."

"It wouldn't be a smart move to spread our troops out even more," Zeke said. It seemed everyone was in agreement not to send help. Yet.

Raphael nodded his agreement, then, "I suggest we provide relief at our border." He leant forward in his seat. "The last report counted over two hundred refugees making camp along the nation lines. And we need to relocate them somewhere safer."

"Jordynia is a possibility," Seth offered. "The province is not overly populated, and it's on the coast. Or, perhaps we can convince Maracadia to harbor the refugees?"

"Unlikely," Aryael answered. "The cowards have yet to reciprocate any correspondence since the Dark Born began this conflict. Again, it seems, the Maracadians are happy to watch the rest of the world burn while they sit back in safety."

Raphael didn't miss the clenching of Aryael's fists. Dark smudges marred the skin beneath her eyes and he wondered how much sleep she'd been getting since her brother's capture. Added to that, the sacking of her home city must be almost too much to bear, even for one of the strongest females Raphael had ever encountered. But despite her pain, she'd shown up for every meeting, and given brilliant insight and strategy for every qualm. He just hoped she would be able to sustain her efforts through the inevitable dark times to come.

"Perhaps I could lead a group of healers to the border," Raphael offered. "We could at least heal those who are wounded and sick."

"Agreed," Aryael said. "Raphael, send word to Shiphrah and have her select which healers she thinks would be best able to help. Once they arrive in Veritasailles, we will provide a guarded convoy to the border. From there, we can escort refugees to Jordynia for the time being."

Symon nodded once in agreement. "In the meantime, I think it is best we bring in more enchanters. If the Dark Born were able to break through the wards guarding Nysa, we need to look to strengthen our own."

"I've already brought in a few more to help repair the wards broken during the attack," Zeke answered. "I'll have them double their efforts."

Zeke's lips pressed together tightly, a line appearing between his brows. Despite being a fae without much interest in romantic relationships, Raphael knew being kept away from his mate would be taking its toll on Zeke. Yet he also knew the warrior wouldn't allow that burden to be shared. In Zeke's eyes, his relationship with Petra was his responsibility alone. Her self-enforced imprisonment in grief and anguish, day in day out, had to be wearing on the male. And yet, he remained as stoic as ever, tending to his duties with the utmost diligence.

Not for the first time, Raphael considered leaving a sleeping tonic behind for both the Commander and their Queen. But they wouldn't take it, their sense of duty and fear for their people should an emergency happen while they slumbered would prevent such self care.

Raphael sighed, catching the attention of Aryael. He waved her off with a shy smile. He would need to ask Zeke's help gathering his supplies from the Obelisk, but that could wait until they heard back from Shiphrah.

Seth leaned forward, tapping his fingers on the table. "Does that mean we are ready to discuss the conflict in Mystaira?"

Symon rubbed his fingers over his eyes, stopping to pinch the bridge of his nose. "Proceed, Seth."

"Well—it appears that the problem with the raiders may have become more problematic." Seth spoke softly, more warily than Raphael had heard him before.

"Of course it is," muttered Symon.

Zeke chuckled, evidently surprised by Symon's candor. Aryael even cracked a smile, and a moment of brevity settled around the table.

"The leader of the raiders is the last remaining relative of the former Lord of Mystaira, a first cousin of the family," Seth explained.

"Who?" Aryael demanded. "We had no knowledge of an heir. When Gavin was given the title, it was on the basis that there were no more remaining living relatives. Or none that had made it out of the camps."

"He escaped from the same camp as Gavin, which adds another layer of difficulty to the situation. He was a sort of mentor to Gavin, before Gavin left to fight against Rankor. The heir didn't join the fight, instead fleeing Felysia via the sea at Jordynia."

Seth extended his palm out across the table, as if he'd just laid out the chess pieces, and awaited his opponent's move. Only, his opponent wasn't present in the room. He was somewhere in Mystaira, raising a force to overtake their province.

"And let me guess, now he believes he has some claim to the lands?" Aryael raised an eyebrow.

"Correct. Not only that, but a strong majority of his followers are in similar situations. Property that should have been passed down to them has been granted to followers of the crown, those who fought in the battles against Rankor."

"I find it mighty convenient that so many apparent heirs have suddenly decided to resurface, when they were nowhere to be found when we were fighting for our freedom." Symon rapped his knuckles against the table. "Who is this supposed heir to Mystaira?"

"His name is. And he's a shadow master."

"A shadow master? In Mystaira?!"

Raphael's shock leapt from his voice before he could check himself. Shadow masters were rare amongst the fae, at least outside of Speridisia. It was a power that had lain dormant since the ancient times when travel across national borders had been frequent and tribes had mingled—and interbred—more.

There were rumors that Petra's power came from Speridisia, but it was different from those of shadow masters. These power wielders could manipulate shadows for protection. More than that, they could transport anything within their shadows at will.

"That explains how the raiders were able to get away so quickly," Aryael said.

Seth continued, "And why it is so difficult to find their headquarters. The raiders have no clue where they are actually transported to. Micah has concealed the location to even his most trusted advisors, many of whom we have imprisoned in Texeri."

"And what does Gavin suggest?" Symon questioned.

"Well, he's been trying to find a way to make contact with Micah. He hopes their former relationship will be enough to broker an agreement."

"And what if Micah's only desire is to regain his position as heir?" Finally, Zeke's question had probed the great beast lingering in the room.

"Micah is no longer eligible," Aryael replied.

"The Signum Dominari will not allow it," Seth continued.

Zeke quirked an eyebrow, the ghost of a grin dancing beneath his stoic demeanor.

"But if enough of our people rose up against Gavin..." Raphael suggested.

"Then it is Seth and Meliza's job to see that that doesn't happen." Aryael's reply was sharp, unyielding. "Tell us the rest of Gavin's plan."

"Well," Seth began, almost hesitantly, "there are areas of Felysia that are underpopulated. They are still rebuilding, and could use leadership. He is under the impression that those areas are ripe for new Lords and Ladies."

"Which areas, to be precise?" Symon asked.

"Jordynia?" Aryael suggested.

"Or Borea." Acantha suggested. Her answer caught several of the council off-guard, but Seth nodded once. Borea was a cold, unforgiving land. It had once been populated by an industrious people, but they had migrated to warmer parts of Felysia, becoming farmers and sailors. There were rumors of secrets that lingered in the area, but no one had been daring enough to risk exploring the land.

"Goddess save me," muttered Symon. "I suggest we table the discussion for now. Tell Gavin I need a convincing reason to send a group of angry fae to Borea as Lords and Ladies. But we will consider it when the time comes."

The rest of the council agreed, standing and stretching, then walking out of the meeting space in small groups.

Raphael pushed himself slowly away from the table, a troubled frown creasing his brow. The world felt like it was tilting away from him, so many questions and problems gaped out in front of them. At least now he had a sense of purpose. Helping the people of Nysa heal and find safety was something he could manage. He just hoped it would be enough to stave off the impending trials that were barreling their way.

Chapter 7

᪥✳︎᪥

Sage's breath heaved out of her in hot, heavy blows. A long wooden sword drooped from her clenched fists. Meliza stood on the far end of the ring, twirling wooden batons in her hands as if they weren't fighting for their lives in this godsforsaken ring. Sage supposed it didn't feel that way to Meliza. She, on the other hand, felt every muscle in her entire body quiver, her sword arm cramping and tingling from the repeated impact of Meliza's batons. Even the muscles that wrapped over her skull pulsed with fatigue.

"Goddess, Sage," Meliza drawled. "How long are you going to make me wait over here?"

Sage whined, heaving with her arms to lift the heavy sword. "Okay," she huffed. "Again."

Without warning, Meliza charged at Sage. Sage blocked one blow with the sword, batting away the baton. Before she could even celebrate the minor victory, Meliza whacked her in the side with the second stick. With a whoosh, Sage's legs were swept out from beneath her. The world spun, and Sage landed with a thud on her back.

Sage sucked in hard, the breath knocked out of her. Stars prickled the sides of her vision. "My fault," Meliza murmured, offering her hand to Sage. "I keep forgetting how delicate you mortals are."

"Yeah," Sage gasped. "So delicate." She hunched forward, hands braced against her knees and spat dust onto the ground. She was on lesson five with Meliza, all back to back. Everything in her body hurt. She suspected she hurt worse now than when she'd fallen from the sky. She was sure of it. There was no way that her body could have ever hurt more than in this very moment. Breathing hurt. Blinking hurt. Thinking hurt.

"Again?" Meliza asked.

Sage answered with a sound that sounded pitifully between a groan and a whimper. Meliza laughed, which would have made her angry, except having any sort of emotion was also painful. Sage wondered if maybe there was some sort of muscle attached to emotions, too. Days and days of running, jumping, lifting barrels of sand to build muscle, followed by training with a sword had left Sage completely wrung out.

On top of that, Sage had been pushing herself to finish cleaning out the Big House. She'd used her magic to sweep away the old dust and cobwebs, and wash away lingering grime before collapsing into the big squishy bed in the bedroom she'd claimed there. Delphia must have taken pity, because every morning she found a tray of breakfast sitting in the dining room and a packed lunch. In the evening, a bowl of soup sat in the same spot after she'd bathed. She hadn't the faintest clue where Meliza had been staying, but honestly, there wasn't an ounce of spare energy left for her to care.

"I take that as a no," Meliza declared. "I'm giving you the next two days off," she finished, tossing the batons into a bucket in the corner.

Sage nearly cried from relief. "Thank you," she muttered.

"Make sure you are eating plenty, and drinking extra water. We need to strengthen your body, beyond whatever strength you gained in Veritasailles. You're not weak, but you definitely could use some...bolstering."

Sage wasn't sure she'd survive long enough to see the results of Meliza's training. What good would training be if she died in the process? Sage stayed glued to her resting place, staring at the open gate of what had become their training pen. Meliza walked out, leaving the gate ajar, but Sage remained.

She would have sold the remaining parts of her soul in that moment for the ability to cast, or maybe for another Egress Key. Anything to keep her from having to walk back to the Big House. It was so far away. Her muscles screamed at her just for standing. But even getting herself into a sitting position would require her muscles to bend in ways that would surely kill her.

Then, like an angel, Gavin waltzed into the ring. "How's the training going?" he asked cheerfully.

Sage clenched her eyes shut. She actually might cry.

"That rough?" he asked. She nodded in answer. "I think I have something that might help," he whispered, now so close to her that she could feel his body near hers, even with her eyes closed.

Gently, he wrapped his arms around her, and she felt the tell-tale shift of reality as he cast them someplace new.

The sounds of songbirds trickled around her. She opened her eyes, taking in the new scenery around her. To the side of them, a gentle waterfall broke over the surface of a crystal clear pool. On the other side of them, milky pools with steam scattered the rocky floor of what could have been described as a plateau. Sage could see a pine forest reaching out in the distance, below where she and Gavin stood.

"Hot springs," Gavin said, pointing to the pools where steam waved in the evening breeze. "They're great for sore muscles."

Sage whimpered. "I love you."

"Are you talking to me, or the pools?" Gavin asked, a chuckle rumbling deep in his chest.

"Both," said Sage as she carefully shed her tunic and made her way to the springs.

❦

Meliza, done with training for the day, made her way to the room that had become hers. Gavin had stopped staying in his family's house, taking up residence in Texeri while he ensured its safety. But from what she understood, he would be moving into the Big House once he felt like the small village was completely secure.

Gavin had found enchanters who could ward specifically against Shadow Masters and their powers. It hadn't been easy, but the two fae seemed competent enough to create the wards necessary. Meliza had wondered why Gavin hadn't simply opted to have Sage ward the prison that had been built, but then she supposed it would be difficult now that she had no wand.

Meliza's thoughts whirred as she walked, only stopping when she heard a grunt come from a shed. She turned the corner, taking in the sight within the small building.

Delphia heaved, picking up a heavy bag of what must have been grain of some sort. With a grunt, she moved the bag into a wagon. She paused, wiping her forehead with the back of her arm. Her hair curled so wildly around her head, only the very tips of her ears poked through the dark whirls of hair.

"Again with the staring?" Delphia called, not turning to face Meliza.

"I was just wondering if you'd actually take my help if I offered it." Meliza had barely broken a sweat during her training with Sage. She still had plenty of energy to use before the sun went down.

"Actually, yes. I had hoped Levi would be here to help, but Mama's taken him to a healer. That colt finally got a piece of him; broke his arm."

"How inconvenient of him," Meliza mused, rolling up the sleeves of her tunic.

"Agreed," said Delphia, smirking. "I've got to move all this grain to somewhere more secure. It seems we've acquired a family of mice."

Meliza nodded once, then began grabbing sacks of grain and putting them into the wagon. Delphia paused to take a sip of water from a jug that sat atop the lone windowsill in the shed. Once she'd refreshed, Delphia joined Meliza, each grabbing bags and hoisting them into the cart. Once full, Meliza grabbed the handles and lifted the cart so she could wheel it to the cellar behind the house where Delphia had cleared a temporary space for the feed.

They emptied the cart, then returned it to the now empty shed. "That's enough for today," announced Delphia, hands on her hips. "Come. This deserves a drink."

Meliza followed Delphia to the stone border that lined the estate. They each climbed atop it, and Delphia reached into one of her pockets. "Swiped this while we were in the cellar."

"Is that moonwater?" Meliza asked, eying the blue bottle.

Delphia nodded. "One of the many skills Levi's learned from his books." Delphia took a swig, grimacing at the strong liquor. "Of course, I had to supervise to be sure he didn't blind us in the process."

Meliza laughed before taking the bottle offered to her, taking a swig of her own. The liquor scalded her throat as it slipped down. "Hauaghhh..." she groaned, beating her chest.

Delphia laughed, a boisterous sound as Meliza sputtered. "Not for the faint of heart." She grabbed the bottle and took another sip. It was Meliza's turn to laugh as Delphia screwed up her face and shook her head.

Meliza was preparing to take the bottle when she was struck by how the sunlight wrapped around Delphia. Beams of light seemed to frame the female so it looked as if she radiated from within. Not wanting to spook her, but also unable to stop from touching, Meliza brushed a stray curl from Delphia's face, hooking it behind her ear. "There," she said softly.

Delphia looked down, a soft smile on her face. Meliza's heart beat quicker. She wanted to kiss her. Her hand brushed Delphia's as she took the bottle, bringing it to her lips, even though what she wanted touching her lips sat across from her. She let the bottle sit there for just a moment as a breeze blew from behind Delphia, ushering her scent to Meliza. Sweet hay and apple blossoms. That was the scent Meliza caught above the stinging smell of moonwater.

Before Meliza could take her next sip. The booming sound of hooves echoed behind her. Meliza set the bottle down and jumped off the stone wall they sat upon. In the distance, a rider bounded towards them on a horse, dust curling behind them.

"Lily?" Delphia asked.

Meliza palmed the dagger on her hip, but made no move to grab it. It appeared as though Delphia knew the rider.

"Lily!" Delphia exclaimed again. The rider, a broad shouldered female with a long, flaxen braid to her hip jumped off the horse. The females bounced toward each other, wrapping the other into a tight embrace.

Delphia smiled broadly as they hugged tightly, her arms around the blonde female's neck. Meliza tried not to acknowledge the jealousy she felt at *Lily's* arms around Delphia's waist, a palm splayed across her lower back.

Meliza cleared her throat, merely trying to dislodge the moonwater that wanted to claw its way back up. The females pulled away from each other, Lily peering around Delphia to look at her.

"Who's this?" she gestured with a chin.

"Lily, this is Meliza." Delphia stepped to the side, opening her arm to indicate Meliza.

"The Commander of the City Guard? What's she doing here?" Lily's question seemed impertinent, almost accusatory.

"Minding my own business," Meliza replied, not particularly caring for Lily's tone.

"She's helping Gavin," Delphia answered, sidestepping the discomfort brewing from the new intruder.

"I see." Lily walked to the wall, grabbed the bottle of moonwater, and lifted it in question to Delphia.

"Of course," she replied. "Now, it's your turn, Lily; what are you doing here?"

Lily's attention turned from Delphia to Meliza as she took a sip of the moonwater, not grimacing in the slightest as she drank. "I suppose, if you're here to assist Gavin, I've come to speak with you. Unless he's here." Lily looked around them, as if Gavin would pop up from behind the stone wall.

"He's not on the property at the moment," Meliza answered. Even if he was, there was no way she was leaving Delphia alone with Lily, not after the moment they'd shared earlier.

"Well, tell him he was right."

It took a moment to understand what she was referring to. Meliza's apprehension dropped as she realized who Lily must be. "He visited Amos?"

Lily nodded. "Just like Gavin expected. Micah visited today. Amos gave him Gavin's letter, and then Micah left."

"What did he want when he visited?" Meliza asked.

Lily shrugged. "I expect you already know that," she replied, taking another swig of the moonwater. "He was trying to get us to join him. Seems he's down quite a few good raiders."

"So you think Micah is willing to meet with Gavin?"

Again, Lily shrugged, looking toward the family home where smoke was beginning to rise from the chimney. "Maybe."

Meliza's fingers tingled. "Try that again, little Lily." Meliza tried not to grin as she saw a blush of embarrassment creep along the bridge of Lily's nose.

Delphia grunted. "Lily, you know what Meliza's powers are, don't you?"

Lily rolled her eyes. "Fine. I expect he will meet Gavin."

"Then why lie for him?" Meliza's question was out of curiosity, but she felt Delphia stiffen.

"He was a friend, a long time ago before he went into hiding. Don't want to see him taken advantage of."

Truth rang from her words. "Well, then. Let's hope he agrees to what Gavin's got planned."

Not wanting to linger between the energy of Lily and Delphia, Meliza turned on her heel and made her way back to Gavin's, no—her, room in the house. She'd write a letter to Gavin and Symon, letting them know their plan was a go.

Chapter 8

◆◆◆◆

Dark brick walls lined the room, curving so the room formed a circle. Chains hung from hooks, and despite the alchemists' best efforts, stains clung to the bricks in curtains. Abbadon stood leaning in the arched entranceway, where a thick iron gate stood ajar, staring at the subject lying comatose on a padded table. What Abbadon had learned were called machines beeped quietly in time with the heartbeat they monitored. Tubes ran from Suda's still form, filtering fluids and drugs through his body.

The months had passed by in a frenzy of plans and subterfuge. When *Ranquer* had suddenly appeared in the stone fortress he and his brother called home, the twins had been perplexed with their father's new appearance, and how he'd been reborn. The truth of their circumstance had been stranger than anything Abbadon could have ever predicted. With Ranquer came answers to some of Abbadon's most secret questions. Questions about their origin and their father. It'd been no secret that little was known about the Dark Born's mother, and the truth had been incomprehensible. But Ranquer had been patient as he explained the depth of their true power.

The one truth that was easiest to understand was that he and his brother had been destined to rule this world. They would scourge this earth of the weak-hearted fae who resisted the idea that mortals should bow to them. Starting with that bitch of a queen, Aryael.

Abbadon pushed off the wall and stalked over to Suda. Punching a button, Abbadon smiled as the slow drip of lunastium ceased. The elixir, made from the moonflowers of Ranquer's world, kept the patient in a deep, unfeeling sleep. But Abbadon needed Suda awake for this next part of his plan.

Checking that the straps were taught against Suda's biceps, Abbadon waited for the male to wake. Slowly, Suda's eyes began twitching. His mouth grimaced, and a groan began deep in Suda's throat. Excitement bloomed within Abbadon; he always liked this part of the process. The part when his captives truly learned the depths of his power, when they discovered who was in control.

Abbadon walked to the opposite side of the table, the place where a forearm used to rest, but no longer existed. Without much force at all, he squeezed the nub that used to connect to an elbow. Suda's eyes flared open and a jagged, hoarse scream wheezed from Suda. Stringy saliva clung to his mouth, and Abbadon felt his own mouth part with fascination. That hadn't been difficult at all. He was surprised at how tender the wound still was for their patient. Perhaps he could use that to his advantage a while longer.

"Good morning, handsome," Abbadon purred.

Suda panted, shock and horror making his eyes wide. His head turned and he looked at the location of Abbadon's hand, hovering just above the bandaged nub. Suda screamed again as new shock flooded his system. Abbadon laughed, the feeling of despair flowing from his victim feeding into the euphoria of control that always took over in moments like these.

"I'll tell you, that never gets old," Abbadon said, stepping closer to Suda's side. "Tell me Suda, do you dream about using that hand when we put you under?"

Suda didn't answer, his eyes still glued to his missing forearm.

"That's rude, you know, to ignore a question when someone is trying to make polite conversation." Abbadon picked a stray piece of grass from the lapel of his jacket, likely left over from his morning ride around the fortress.

Suda, seeming to grasp the situation, understanding falling back into his mind, grit his teeth. Around clenched jaws, Suda growled, "Get fucked, you Dark Born piece of shit." Spit frothed at the edges of his mouth.

Abbadon tsked, "Now, Suda. That's no way to talk to your host." To emphasize his point, Abbadon squeezed the nub once more. Agony poured from Suda as he writhed under Abbadon's control. "That's more like it," he whispered into Suda's ear. "Sing, Suda. Sing!" Abbadon squeezed harder.

Piss began to trickle onto the floor. Abbadon inhaled deeply. Oh, yes. This was the best part. "Would you like me to stop, Suda?" Abbadon added more pressure to the wound.

Suda nodded, "Yes."

"Yes?" Abbadon squeezed again.

"Yes. Please, yes." Suda's voice slipped into that perfect whimpering sound that would almost always give Abbadon that euphoric feeling he looked for. But he held himself on a tight leash today. Today, he needed answers.

"I'll let go, sweet Suda, but you have to give me the answers I'm looking for." To demonstrate, Abbadon released a little bit of the pressure he held on the nub. "Nod to let me know you understand." Suda nodded, and Abbadon wiped his brow with the handkerchief he kept in his front pocket while keeping his other hand on the wound.

"Now, you know what I'm going to ask. Do you remember the last time we spoke?" Suda nodded, his eyes closed, tears spilling from the creases. Darkness, Suda strapped to the table was such a beautiful sight, Abbadon thought. "We are looking for the insignia. The ones that came with The Realm Leaper."

A whimper escaped Suda, and Abbadon's stomach gave a pleasant flutter at the sound. "Tell me where they are," he whispered in Suda's ear. "Tell me where they are, Suda, and I can make this all go away."

Another whimper. Oh, Darkness, he sounded so good. Abbadon brought his mouth even closer, so that his lips brushed Suda's ear. "Tell me where they are, Suda. I can make this pain go away. I could make you feel so much better."

"I don't know where they are," Suda croaked. Abbadon squeezed, hard. Suda thrashed, screams bouncing from walls around them in a sweet symphony. "We never found them! She didn't have them when they found her," Suda screamed, his knees flexed, trying to pull his back from the table. Bound by thick leather straps, Suda was constrained to Abbadon's will.

Abbadon grabbed Suda's face, squeezing his cheeks as he forced Suda's head to the side so he had to make eye contact. "Tell me again. Look at me!" Suda's eyes focused on Abbadon. His chest rose up and down with every heavy breath.

Tears trickled again as Suda's pupils dilated. "She never had them after she fell."

Disgusted that the same old lies were being told, Abbadon pushed Suda's face away. Perhaps he would need to think of a better way of questioning the male. He wondered what kind of information he could get if he flipped the male over and—

Cian, Ranquer's assistant, marched into the room. "Have we got any new information?" the beaky mortal asked.

Abbadon growled, "I would, had you not interrupted. What have I told you, mortal, about disturbing me?"

Cian pushed his square glasses up his nose. "Have you considered the possibility that the patient has shared all he knows?"

Abbadon growled again, ready to rip the mortal to shreds with his bare hands. But this was no mere mortal. Green glowed around Cian's irises, a warning to Abbadon that he would do well to remember just who he was dealing with. It seemed, from what Abbadon had gathered, that Cian was more like himself and Apyllon than he would like to admit. At least as far as their origins went.

"Why are you here, Cian?" Abbadon asked, straightening the cuffs of his sleeves as he walked away from Suda's side. Cian stalked to the machine beeping above Suda's head. Suda muttered, pleaded as Cian punched a button, sending a trickle of lunastium through a tube connected to Suda's remaining hand. Without acknowledging his patient, Cian turned back to face Abbadon.

"The experiment was a success," he announced. "Your brother has full control of his shadows, and it seems the speed and agility gained from the patient has become permanent." Cian pushed his glasses up his nose again.

Intrigue replaced the disdain Abbadon felt. "And?" If Apyllon had fully mastered his shadows, that would mean they were one step closer to taking over Panchia. Not even Maracadia would be able to stop their advances. Then, Ranquer would have what he wanted, and he'd leave the twins to their own devices.

"I think it is viable to complete phase two of the mission. We will need to prep the patient for operation, then we can perform the ritual on you. Everything should be in order for you to go under by tomorrow evening."

Abbadon smiled, Suda whimpered softly as he finally fell under the spell of lunastium. "Can you use this?" he asked as he ran a finger up the upper arm of Suda's nub.

"I don't see why that would be a problem. Scans report that power is entwined with all of the subject's DNA. It doesn't seem to be location specific."

"Good," purred Abbadon, leaning down to peer across Suda's sleeping face. "Let him know that it was me who saved his other hand. I'll have him think of me every time he goes to use it."

Chapter 9

✧◆✧

Raphael and Zeke landed heavily on the balcony of the Obelisk. Raph hadn't been back to the tower since the attack on their city. Despite the balmy afternoon, the balcony felt wintry and foreboding. Stains and debris littered the floor, collecting in the corners.

Raphael cringed at the sight of his beloved Obelisk.

"She's refused any attempts to clean up this mess," muttered Zeke. "At least she's gotten rid of the bodies. They were starting to stink." Zeke didn't bother waiting for Raphael. Instead, he walked straight for the stairwell that led into the complex.

Raphael followed, hoping his presence wouldn't upset the precarious balance of Petra's mourning. Stepping carefully, Raphael attempted to walk without making a noise, lest he disrupt the vigil taking place within the Obelisk's walls.

Breaching the stairwell, Raphael blinked in the sunlight streaming in through the windows. If he could just make it across this room without encountering Petra, he would gain access to his medical ward. He could be in and out in thirty minutes if he was quick...

"What...are *you* doing here?" a raspy voice caused a shiver to run down Raph's spine like a chilled finger.

A lone chair Raph had failed to notice sat facing the wall opposite the floor to ceiling windows. The crown of a head peeked over the chair's back, and Raphael only knew one fae with thick, black locks coiled into a tight bun.

Petra sat in the chair, not bothering to turn and greet Raphael or Zeke, her partner...her bonded. She sat rigid, unmoving. Ice ran through Raphael's veins seeing her like that.

"Raph needed supplies from his ward," Zeke replied gently, but neutrally, not moving either. He stared at the chair's back, as if he was debating whether he should approach her or not. His fists clenched and unclenched, and Raph's heart broke for the male, for them both. Petra had isolated herself in the tower since the day of the attack. She'd thrown her shadows at Meliza when she'd tried to check on her, and not even Zeke had been able to convince her to leave the tower or let anyone come and help her.

"Fine." Petra's answer was as cold as a dagger's edge.

Not waiting for further conversation, Raphael tucked his head and walked briskly to his ward. His powers surged, wanting to check in on Petra, sensing her pain. Logic told him there was very little he could do to heal the wound that festered within her.

Losing the battle against his powers, Raph reached with his healer's sight while he simultaneously began furiously cataloging and packing his supplies. His healer's sight raced through the hall, allowing himself full access to the conversation that continued in the dining room.

"Petra," Zeke's voice had grown hoarse, breaking as he said her name. "Please, come back with me."

"I can't," Petra said, her words hard and unfeeling.

"Yes, you can," Zeke said. It sounded as though his teeth were clenched, and Raphael hoped he'd be fast enough to avoid witnessing a full fledged fight between them. "Just come back with me. Let me take care of you. We don't even have to stay in Veritasailles. We can go to Jordynia; I'll convince Symon to let me go scope it out for the refugees."

"No, I can't," Petra said again, Raphael could almost feel the rigidity in her spine at her frustrated refusal. "I can't bring myself to face you—any of you. If it hadn't been for Symon and Aryael—and *you*—Hyacinth would have never been killed."

"That's ridiculous," Zeke replied. "You know as well as I that the Dark Born have been chomping at the bit to attack us, to get revenge."

"Yes," Petra said, the legs of her chair squalling. She must be standing, Raph thought as he stuffed gauze into his travel chest. "And if we'd just let the Realm Leaper die, you wouldn't all have been so distracted. We would've had more time to prepare. It was *her* arrival that prompted them to attack us now. And *you* would have been able to stop the attack."

The proclamation was sharp, and outrageous. "You can't possibly mean that," Zeke's voice wobbled on the edge of control. "Petra, your hatred of that girl is clouding your vision. You are being unreasonable."

"Unreasonable?" Petra's voice was low, almost a growl. "I'll show you unreasonable."

"Please," Zeke whispered. "Please, Petra. Just come back to me. Don't leave me here alone."

"You need to go. Now."

"I love you."

"Get. Out."

There was a pregnant pause. Raphael imagined the two mates facing off against each other. It was heartbreaking. Raph hung his head, surprised at the ache in his heart and tears prickling behind his closed eyelids.

He was snapped out of his grief by the sound of a foot scuffing in his room. He looked up to see Zeke standing in front of him, the pain etched in his face unmistakable. He tried not to stare at the hardened general, but it was hard seeing this genial, strong male almost completely unmanned in his grief.

Raphael reached out with one hand, placing it gently on Zeke's shoulder. The other male nodded, breathing deeply.

"I'm sorry," Raph whispered.

Zeke didn't answer. He just looked away.

The moment passed, and Raph snapped his travel chest shut. Together they heaved it up from the table and casted. They landed in the foyer of the castle. The chest lurched and smacked the ground as Zeke let go of the handle, then walked quickly away. Pain wafted through the air behind him, jeering at Raphael and his powers. Raph very rarely felt helpless, but sensing the pain from trauma and heartbreak seemed to plague him everywhere he went.

Watching as his friend disappeared down the halls of the palace, Raphael wondered if Petra was lost for good this time. He turned, looking out the window of the palace towards the Obelisk where a dark shadow swirled around the top of it.

Quietly, he asked nobody in particular, "Have we already lost?"

Chapter 10

꩜ ✳ ꩜

Gavin woke suddenly.

Sheets tangled around his legs, and he flailed in the bedding as he tried to remember where he was. Moonlight streamed through the open window, humid summer air flowing in on a breeze.

The heavy timber bed post creaked softly as he pushed himself awake. He'd been dreaming of the Dark Born and watching them drain a boy of blood. Rather than the memory happening as it had in life, this time, Apyllon's face had whipped to the window where Gavin peered in. Hands had reached up out of the dirt and held Gavin's feet in place so that he couldn't run as the Dark Born advanced, knives and needles in hand. Their teeth had grown into sharp points as they approached him, and try as he might, no sound escaped Gavin's screaming throat.

Gavin groaned, running his hands down his face. Leaning back on his hands, he realized something was missing.

Sage's side of the bed lay empty, the mattress cold where his hand sat. He looked at the sheets, flung back from where she should have been. The robe, which usually hung on a chair in the corner, was missing.

Deciding he wouldn't be able to fall back asleep, Gavin pushed himself out of the bed, pausing to tighten the laces that held his breeches in place. On quiet feet, he walked through the Big House.

Reaching out with his newfound power, Gavin searched the hallways and rooms for Sage, searching for her presence. Downstairs, in the far corner of the house. He could feel her whirring mind, restless and working.

Gavin padded through the house, noting the soft glow that flickered in the hallway outside of the home's library. Pausing at the threshold, Gavin peered in as Sage ran her fingers across dusty books. He'd been moved that night after he'd taken her to the pools when she showed him the work she'd done on the Big House. She'd spent her spare time cleaning and rearranging everything so it felt less like a mausoleum and more like a house he could actually picture himself in. His own father had put in countless hours repairing broken windows and building furniture for the place. Even Levi had contributed.

Now, Sage pulled down a heavy book, bound together with leather lacing and wooden covers. She walked the tome over to the lone desk which sat near the far end of the room. Peeling back the front cover, Sage bent over the desk as she looked through the contents.

"Couldn't sleep?" Gavin asked, pushing off from the doorway.

"No," Sage answered, not bothering to look up from the book. "Something occurred to me as I slept, and I couldn't stop thinking about it."

Gavin walked over to where she leaned onto the desk, and peered over her shoulder. His body gave a tight squeeze at the bruise that graced the slope where her neck met her shoulder, but he forced himself to unwind. She was bound to be bruised training with Meliza, and he needed to be grateful she was getting such great tutelage. It would make caring for her that much easier.

Sage's lower lip slipped between her teeth as she looked at the contents of the book. Tearing his gaze away from her, he looked at what she read.

"Ancient Fae and Their Tribes?" Gavin, perplexed, tried to connect the dots of what had preoccupied Sage.

She nodded, not bothering to lead him to any answers. He waited, reading over her shoulder as the book introduced the varying tribes that used to populate the continent of Panchia. "What are you looking for?" he asked quietly.

"I was just thinking about your plan for Micah. You need a convincing reason to send him to Borea, and I thought there might be answers somewhere." Sage still focused on the book, her eyes moving with the words she read.

"So, you think the answer might have to do with Tribal Fae?" Gavin still couldn't connect the dots.

"Well, something had to keep the people of Borea there. There had to have been plenty of game in places like Mystaira. And, according to this, Jordynia was rich with precious metals and fishing. There had to be something that kept people in Borea for so long."

Gavin nodded. "Okay. Can I help you?"

Sage sighed, more out of focus than frustration. "Sure. I'm not sure the answer will be in a home library, but I figured why not start here."

"I was actually thinking about that," Gavin said. "Well, not about researching Borea, but Symon has told me that you've been invited to the Rafalatriki by Shiphrah. I'd hoped to have the situation with the raiders finished before bringing you there." He walked over to the wall of shelves Sage hadn't already checked.

Sage perked up, her attention not fully focused back on Gavin. "The same place Raph went?"

Gavin dipped his chin in answer, then turned to scan the bookshelves. "Raph will actually be there later this week. He's been asked to choose some healers to help him with the refugees from Nysa."

Sage's lips thinned. "Oh," she said quietly.

She had cried when Gavin explained what had happened in Nysa's capital city. He knew she still wrestled with feeling responsible for the conflict that had arisen in Panchia since she arrived. But Gavin knew, deep down, the Dark Born were always going to try and retake the continent. If not to avenge their father, then to satiate their own dark desires.

"We can go to the Rafalatriki tomorrow," Gavin answered.

"What about my training?" Sage asked, head still dropped to the book in focus.

"I'll talk to Meliza. I think you've earned a few days off."

Sage laughed. "I'd like to see how that goes."

Gavin brought a different book titled *A Complete History of Panchia* to the desk. According to his mother, many of the history books in this home library were likely biased, written to favor the families that eventually became political leaders in Felysia. They were better off waiting to look once they got to the Rafalatriki. He opened the book, scanning through the introduction that rambled on with semicolons and dashes interspersed through every sentence. He peeked over at Sage, her eyes moving as she read, her palms flat against the desk as she leaned over it. Taking her lead, he tried to focus on the book he held, but his eyes blurred, and he felt himself erupt into a wide yawn.

"You don't have to stay up with me," Sage said, still looking down.

"I know," Gavin replied, moving over to a chair in the far corner. Sinking into the cushions, Gavin readjusted the book, opening back onto the page he'd stared at previously. The rustle of pages turning became a lullaby, and Gavin exhaled a deep breath as something tight in his chest unwound. Sage's murmuring, the scratching of a pencil against paper, faded into the back of his mind, and Gavin felt himself smile as he drifted back to sleep.

❧✳︎☙

Meliza stood across the ring. Dust from their sparring danced in the air in big, playful clouds. Sage's chest heaved with painful breaths as her heart thudded heavily, but she'd blocked the last advance Meliza had made, and she felt the ghost of a smile on one corner of her mouth.

Two wooden daggers, longer than any knives Sage had seen before, were gripped tightly in her hands. One dagger jutted out from her hand in the reverse angle so that the daggers pointed in the same direction, something she had discovered made her reflexes quicker and offered her the option to punch at her opponent if necessary. Fighting with two separate daggers had proven much more effective for her. Swords were cumbersome, and fought against her reflexes. The spear was a laughable attempt that Meliza hadn't even given a full lesson. Meliza had offered Sage a battle-ax to try, but Sage's instincts told her that wouldn't go any better than the spear.

Daggers, on the other hand. Oh, Sage had enjoyed the last week of lessons with the daggers. She might have bruises all over her body, but Sage had blocked more of Meliza's blows, both with a sword and a spear, than she ever had before. Perhaps it had come with the consistent training, but Sage couldn't help feeling she had found her weapon of choice. A song blossomed within her as she fought with the daggers, and she'd been surprised to find at times she enjoyed the tune.

Meliza sprung forward, her feet striking the ground hard, her body tilting forward as she ran. Her wooden sword was raised high to one side. Sage's heart gave one hard *thud* before she reacted. Running forward a few steps, Sage planted her feet and braced herself. Meliza's sword arced toward her body and Sage ducked, reaching to strike with a punch at Meliza's open side. Meliza's elbow came down in a sharp blow, deflecting Sage's punch. The hit rang through Sage's knuckles, but she didn't slow as she stepped back and struck with her second dagger. The blade of her dagger met the joining of Meliza's sword and hilt. Sage pushed down, trying to move the longsword so the tip pointed at the ground.

Sage thought she was making progress, the feeling of victory dangling just away from her, when Meliza's arm flexed. The sword swung high, Sage's dagger caught in the momentum. Sage just barely gripped her dagger enough so that it didn't fly out of her hand. Before she could counter-act, Meliza's foot flew from the ground, striking Sage in her stomach. She flew back, her backside hitting hard on the dirt floor. Air evacuated her lungs, and she gulped.

Quickly, Sage pushed herself back up to her feet, but Meliza was nowhere to be seen. No magic, or powers. That was the rule in the training ring. So where Meliza had gone was a complete mystery. Sage's heart thundered. She raised her daggers, spinning around to see where Meliza could be. The ring was empty, devoid of anything to hide behind.

A flash of light in the corner of her eyes alerted Sage, but not before Meliza struck her in the stomach again. Meliza disappeared, then another flash of light. Again, she struck Sage and disappeared.

Sage gasped. No fucking powers or magic. That was the rule! Frustration bubbled up in Sage's chest. She pushed herself back up onto her feet, raising her wooden daggers in the defense position Meliza had taught her.

Questions trickled through Sage's mind as she whirled, reacting to every sound and rustle. Could Meliza have been possessed? Was this some attempt to kidnap or hurt her by the Dark Born?

A flash of light, and Meliza appeared beside Sage, dipping low and sweeping her feet from under her. The sound of hitting the ground was a boom that echoed in her head, but she scrambled back to her feet.

Sage's breath raked out of her. She heaved, but not just from the pain of being knocked down again. At this point, she was beginning to lose her cares about why Meliza was casting in the training ring. No. At this point, she was beginning to feel pissed.

Another flash of light, this time arcing around her sides, and Meliza reappeared behind Sage. Strong arms wrapped around her chest, Meliza's forearm squeezing her throat.

"This is what you face when you fight against fae," Meliza said, her hot breath pelting Sage's face.

Sage couldn't breath as Meliza squeezed tighter. She reached up with her hands, dropping one dagger and using the other to try and pry Meliza's arms off her. Meliza was so tall, Sage's legs flailed in the air, kicking uselessly as Meliza siphoned away any chance of breathing. Her heartbeat became a sledgehammer in her temple, and Sage felt her skin begin to tingle with the lack of air, the lack of blood flow. Spots began to speckle the air around her, and just as she thought she'd pass out, Meliza released her.

Sage gasped, turning to face Meliza. But she'd already cast again. "Bitch," Sage whispered, rubbing her throat. Grabbing her dagger from the ground, Sage ran forward a few steps, trying to come up with some sort of plan.

Again, Meliza appeared, hooking Sage around the waist with her muscled arms and slamming her to the ground. Meliza raised a spear over her head, aiming for Sage's chest. Without thinking, Sage rolled out of the way and crouched on her feet. She aimed a kick at Meliza's feet, but Meliza whacked her with the end of the spear. The strike ricocheted through Sage's shin, and she screamed in pain and frustration. Sage barreled forward, attempting to grab hold of Meliza. But as she ran, Meliza disappeared again.

"Come on!" Sage screamed. "Fucking fight me, fair and square!" A drumbeat had begun in Sage. Rage, hot and oily, coursed through her veins as she spun, trying to anticipate Meliza's next attack.

The next shimmer of light, Sage was ready, abandoning her daggers, Sage reached out with her magic, grabbing Meliza in a grip of stone. The stone covered Meliza completely, molding over her like clay. Before Sage could react, Meliza broke free from the stone, sending pebbles flying.

Meliza released her power, sending stone after stone flying at Sage like shrapnel. Sage used her wind and earth magic to disintegrate the stones and blow the dust away.

Shit. She'd forgotten Meliza's powers included earth wielding.

Meliza ran forward, the sharpened end of her spear aiming for Sage's heart. Without thinking, only feeling that rage that had taken over, Sage whipped her arms in a circle in front of her. A massive ball of water erupted from the ground right in front of Meliza, and she stepped right into it. Sage focused her energy on the creature within the ball of water, stacking her arms in front of her with clenched fists. The water churned, fast as a water devil, and Meliza thrashed within. Flashes of light within the water indicated that Meliza was trying to cast out from the water, but Sage held firm, clenching her fists so tight her nails bit into her palms. She held Meliza there, the female thrashing, pushing within the churning water ball.

Sage pushed down harder within her own magic, ready to crush her opponent. A ripple of movement to her side barely registered as she pulled harder, constricting the flailing fae within her water prison.

"Sage—" Gavin's voice broke through the chaos. She looked from the water ball, her blood cooling instantly. Gavin stood at the entrance of the training ring, looking at her. Then his attention snapped to the waterball. "Meliza?"

"Shit," Sage whispered.

Instantly, she released her hold on the water ball, Meliza slapping the ground with a wet smack. Gavin ran to her, but she was already turning over onto her stomach. Mcliza propped herself onto her forearms and retched as water forced its way out of her body. "Oh, gods. Meliza!" Sage rushed to her side. "I'm sorry. Shit, Meliza, I'm so sorry."

Sage reached Meliza's side, looking for any way she could help, forgetting the frustration from before. Gavin knelt beside them both, asking something about what was happening. Meliza finished retching, then rolled onto her back, taking in heavy gulps of air. A slow smile spread across her lips, then a giggle. Gavin sat back on his heels, shaking his head. Before she could ask what was going on, Meliza burst into a full fit of boisterous laughter.

"Okay, well, you could have warned me," Gavin whispered, more to himself than to Meliza.

"What is going on?" Sage asked, a note of panic to her voice as Meliza continued bellowing with laughter.

"That was a test," Gavin muttered, pushing up to his feet.

Meliza wiped her eyes, seemingly pulling herself back together, and nodded. She pushed herself up so she sat outright. "Congratulations, Realm Leaper. You can defend yourself." Another chuckle escaped Meliza.

"Yeah, but only with my magic," Sage retorted. "You're supposed to be teaching me how to fight."

"No," Meliza replied, still smiling. "I'm teaching you how to survive. In a fight, you use everything you have to your advantage. Your magic, your skills," Meliza said, pointing to Sage's daggers, "your wits. Everything. Nothing is off limits when someone is attacking you. Got that?" Meliza's demeanor had sobered some while she spoke, and she looked at Sage. "You reacted quickly once you realized I wasn't playing by the rules anymore. Not quick enough, but you'll know better next time."

Sage sighed. "Gods, Meliza. I thought you'd been possessed or something."

"Good. That means you haven't let your defenses down since you got here," Meliza said, wringing out some of the water from her hair.

Gavin, who had walked a slow circle around the ring while Meliza spoke, made his way back to the pair. He offered his hand to Meliza, pulling her up by her forearm. "So does this mean she's ready?"

"I suppose. But I'm still coming up once a week for training. For you both," Meliza answered, pointing at Sage and Gavin with the hilt of a wooden dagger she'd snatched from the ground. "Now, if you don't mind, I'm off to find myself some moonwater." Meliza sauntered out of the ring without a second glance, leaving Sage and Gavin behind.

Sage stood, rooted to her spot. "What does she mean, I'm ready?"

"It means, we're going to see Shiphrah," Gavin said as he draped an arm around Sage's shoulders.

Attention of Her Majesty:

Dearest Aryael~

I always forget how stunning your country is. The abundant rivers and forests are like gems that sparkle in the early morning light. I'm struck by how spectacular the sight is.

And the people?

Oh—the people are divine. I especially love the females. Their voices as they run for their lives, scooping up their precious younglings as they sprint for what they imagine to be safety. Oh, yes, a male could get used to that.

By now, you should be fully aware of the powers I wield. My brother and I are beginning to see the benefits of our alliance with our father's look-alike. He came to us with the most interesting toys.

I have devoured your homeland. The country you rule with your mate is next. Unless, that is, you'd be interested in a trade. I would be willing to talk with my brother and convince him to stall our attacks on your country- and trust me, they are coming. All you need to do is provide us with the girl.

Give us the Realm Leaper and the insignia she fell with, and you can save your country. And your precious females and their younglings.

You have exactly one month to make up your mind. By that point, my brother will have joined me, and his shadow is bound to be insatiable.

Choose wisely,

Apllyon

Chapter 11

✧◆✧

Raphael wiped sweat from his brow. The midday sun was brutal, beating down on what had become a refugee camp along the border of Nysa and Felysia. Tents rustled in the meager breeze, and the chatter of healers and patients hummed through the camp.

Raph had been ready to return to the castle to give his reports directly to Aryael and Symon. But then fae had started pouring into the camp in droves. Some had casted directly into the camp, others arriving on foot dragging loved ones on makeshift stretchers.

But it was the females, dead younglings in their arms, that had nearly been Raph's undoing.

He'd never seen anything like it. He'd examined several of the dead children, and from all that he could sense, their hearts had just...stopped. One female, so distraught from the loss of her child, had grabbed a short sword from one of the sentries and ran herself through. Raphael had cast to her side, attempting to save her from her self-inflicted wound. But the female had encased his feet in quicksand with the last vestige of her powers. He watched as the blood spilled from her body and the light went out of her eyes.

Raph shook his head, trying to dislodge the memory. Whatever power the Dark Born had found was devastating, otherworldly. How could someone float along the land and decimate so many people? Control so many shadows at once? That kind of power was unheard of.

Raph pushed aside a tent flap, greeting the patient who lay on a cot inside. "Good afternoon, Zuri. How are we feeling today?"

Zuri pushed himself up on his cot, nodding. "Much better, thank you. That fever was a bitch," he muttered.

Raphael was relieved to see the lightheartedness return to Zuri's eyes. Despite everything, Raph was always amazed at the fae's ability to continue on even in the face of such darkness and despair.

"Good. And you're right. That fever *was* a bitch."

Zuri laughed, a booming sound that reminded Raph so much of Suda's boisterous laugh. His heart squeezed, leaving him distracted for a moment by thoughts of his friend. He wished he knew something about the male, where he was, if he was alive. Aryael hadn't sent any news on her brother, so he was left to worry.

He swallowed down his thoughts, plastering a forced smile to his face before turning his attention back to Zuri.

"It seems as though quite a few of you have come down with the same fever. Do you think it could have something to do with the shadow?"

As a town leader, Zuri had orchestrated the escape of many of his people. Allowing dozens of families to cast to safety before the shadow had reached his town. Zuri had stayed behind to help in the aftermath. Those who'd remained after the shadow had passed were all struck down with various ailments.

Zuri's fever had taken three days to pass, and despite his talents as a healer, it had taken every ounce of that talent and almost all of his power for Raph to save the male. Other healers had nearly burned out trying to save their wards, and a few patients were lost before they were able to break the fever. It was the kind of illness that came so fast, and so intensely, no one had had time to prepare.

Then there were the ulcers. Giant pustules filled with putrid liquid that covered other patients' bodies, riddling them with such acute pain they were left thrashing in their beds. No other symptoms accompanied the illness, but Raph and his fellow healers had yet to discover a remedy for the boils, the only comfort they could provide was sedating the patients so as to numb their suffering. One of Raph's patients had gotten so bad, the growths covered the inside of his mouth. If they didn't find a solution soon, the male would die of thirst.

"I'll send someone in later today, Zuri. We need to get you out of that cot and moving around." Raph patted the male on the shoulder, then moved toward the exit of the tent, passing by two empty cots of patients who'd been lucky enough to regain strength enough to finally walk on their own.

Heading toward his own tent, Raph ran through the options of tonics he could create to help with the boils. He still had a strong supply of valerian and elm's root. Both were exceptional at reducing inflammation. Perhaps he could create a salve that they could dab on the abscesses, and a tea for drinking. They had already tried garlic paste, the traditional treatment for boils, along with a litany of other treatments. Their efforts had little to no effect on the patients, and Raph and the other healers had been perplexed. He also needed to make time to visit the healers recovering from burnout after trying to heal the ulcers with their powers. Raph had gotten the sense these ailments would resist their healing powers, which meant his knowledge of mortal medicine was more in demand than ever.

Raph was deep in thought when he nearly ran straight into someone. Thick leather armor blocked his vision, Raph quickly looked up.

"Ionus!" Raph beamed a genuine smile at the sight of an old friend. "How good to see you!"

"You, too, Raph," Ionus replied. A mop of wavy blond hair crowned the male's head, and sunrays danced amongst the whirls and waves. Ionus's bright blue eyes twinkled in the sunlight, and Raph had to take a step back to fully take in the male's form.

"What are you doing here?" Raph asked automatically, then caught himself. The spy wouldn't be able to discuss his business in the middle of the camp. "Hold that thought," Raph said, holding up a finger and moving by Ionus. "Why don't you join me in my tent for some tea."

"That'd be great," Ionus replied, following.

Raph gestured for Ionus to sit on the spare cot he kept made up in case a healer needed it with the influx of additional refugees. He poured two glasses from a pitcher of iced tea, enchanted by a grateful refugee to stay cool.

"So, Ionus, what brings you to the border?"

Ionus looked around briefly, then with a wave of his hand, Raphael felt the tell-tale pressure of a sound barrier forming.

"This is confidential," Ionus said, giving Raph a penetrating look, "to the greatest degree. What you hear in this tent goes nowhere. Understand?"

Raphael nodded. "Of course. Ionus, has something happened?"

Ionus shook his head in response. "It's the lack of something happening that has caused my deployment. Amare and I are headed into Speridisia."

"Through Nysa?!" Raphael exclaimed.

Nevermind the peril of actually crossing into Speridisa. With the attacks occurring throughout Nysa, Raph was momentarily bewildered by the immense peril that would face the spies. But, he supposed, any information that the spies could gather about the enemy would be invaluable. This was war, and however distasteful he found sending members of their community into such danger, Ionus knew the risk when he answered the call to serve Aryael. Raphael trusted that Aryael's strategist's mind had a plan for getting the spies in and out safely.

Except...a thought occurred to Raphael that made him question Aryael's motives. He looked hard at Ionus. "You're going to try and find Suda." Raph bowed his head. They all wanted to find Suda, but this was risky.

A heavy quiet descended in the tent, Ionus not offering a reply, his silence answer enough. He and Amare were being sent into Speridisia not to conduct surveillance but to try and find—and rescue?—Suda. Despite the dangers, despite the fact that if they were caught national secrets were at risk if the Dark Born and their generals decided to torture them for information. Of course, Ionus and Amare both had the capacity to withstand torture, but Raph had seen the destruction wrought at the hands of the twins. He wasn't sure anyone was capable of withstanding their base cruelty.

"Aryael has arranged an escort through Nysa. The Sekiri will guide us through the forests and get us to the border.

We're saving our energy to cast back from the border once our objective has been met."

The Sekiri were an elite tribe of warriors who operated within and outside of Nysan politics. They were both part of Nysa, and apart from it; their ancestry reached far back in time to when fae were ruled by more primal foundations.

"And...this mission. Is it reconnaissance or...rescue?"

Ionus offered a grim smile. "Reconnaissance—for now."

Raphael was beginning to question Aryael's strategy. Surely, she couldn't think it was a good idea to risk Ionus and Amare just to find out *where* Suda was being kept.

"Once you've crossed their borders, you won't be able to cast back to us."

"No, we won't."

Raphael ran a hand down his face. Ionus' grim acceptance of what this could mean for him and Amare thundered through Raph's body, jolting against his instincts as a healer, as a fae who would rather choose anything than this path. He had a horrible feeling about the whole expedition.

But, he also worried for Suda. Many a night he'd lain awake into the early hours wondering if his friend was still alive. And whether that would be a miracle or a curse. There was no telling what the Dark Born had subjected Suda to in the months of his captivity.

"Well, Goddess speed, my friend." Raph raised his cold glass in the air in a symbol of salute and fortune.

Ionus responded with his own glass and a tight lipped smile. "I'll stop by on my way back. This outpost is about as far as I can cast from the Spearsan Gap."

"I look forward to your return." Raphael reached into a satchel he'd stashed beneath his cot, pulled out a bottle and poured a liberal amount of lilac liqueur in his and Ionus's tea. "Until then, I drink to you and Amare."

Chapter 12

ᨶ ✳ ᨵ

Sage craned her neck back, trying to take in the massive complex before her. The Rafalatriki was a sprawling building that sprung upwards from the ground, stair-stepping its way into one great pillar that reached for the sky. Beneath the rectangular, blockish segments, a breezeway lined with arches adorned the massive building. The structure reminded her of the University in Techeduin with its sleek, sharp lines.

According to Raphael's stories, relayed what felt like ages ago, other buildings out of sight from the entranceway dotted the campus. But the majority of training and healing took place in the main building. A thrill ran through her in anticipation of being in the presence of so much knowledge. A piece of her from school days which had prided itself on being an excellent scholar nearly squealed with delight at the prospect of doing actual research again. She might not have been officially enrolled at the University, but working in the library in Techeduin had fed a piece of her soul she hadn't realized had gone dormant when landing in Felysia.

Gavin squeezed her hand. They'd only landed on the gravel drive that led to the complex moments earlier. Casting with Gavin, she was coming to understand, was different from casting with others. Instead of feeling like she was being squeezed through a vat of molasses, it was like becoming mist, her body expanding and stretching in a pleasant yawn before being whisked off to someplace new. The sensation left her with less vertigo, something she was glad for as Gavin gave her hand a tug and they began walking toward the main entrance of the towering building ahead.

Fae dressed in various colored robes seemed to float through the breezeway, walking from one end of the open-aired tunnel to the next. Their robes were highlighted in contrast to the dark gray stone of the building. Some carried stacks of books, others pushed carts of supplies which rattled as bottles clinked against each other. Some of the healers moved purposefully at a near run, while others chatted merrily to companions. The variety within the breezeway was somehow uplifting, causing some of the nervous tension to melt from her shoulders.

As they entered the breezeway, Sage took a second to take in her surroundings. Small doors dotted the stone wall, and archways led to what could have been courtyards or gardens. Directly ahead of her and Gavin were a set of towering double doors, made of wood and iron.

"Are we supposed to enter through those?" Sage whispered, leaning against Gavin as they walked. Gavin nodded, not taking his eyes off the doors. He'd been quiet since before they departed. A letter from Seth had arrived shortly before and she'd sensed his increased anxiety ever since. "Seems a bit overkill, if you ask me," Sage said, still glaring at the tall doors.

Gavin cracked a smile, and she couldn't help but feel satisfied to have lifted his mood even for a moment. "Just wait until you meet Shiphrah," Gavin said, a chuckle evident beneath his words.

"What does that mean?" Sage hissed. If she'd learned anything in her time amongst the fae, it was their enjoyment for dramatic reveals. She would rather be prepared for what she faced, but had come to accept their penchant for surprises. Sage rolled her eyes as Gavin's grin grew, refusing to answer her question. "Fine. Just don't blame me if I say anything embarrassing."

They walked on passing what appeared to be sitting rooms, lecture halls, and staircases on either side of what might have been called a foyer had it not been so grand. The ceiling loomed high overhead, and the width of the space gave it more of the feel of a ballroom. At the end of the cavernous space yawned a wall adorned with portraits, while small, cut out windows flecked the stone wall, providing a glimpse to the winding stairs within. Occasionally, a body scurried past the windows, but no one exited any of the three archways that punctuated the behemoth wall.

With a flourish, a tall, thin fae swept from the center archway. The gray stone contrasted sharply with the tan skin and warm cream robes. Black hair cut to stubble skated along a sloping scalp, feeding into sharp, high cheekbones and eyes that seemed to dance with mischief. Rosy cheeks chased a sharp nose, and Sage was reminded just how stunning fae could be. The female seemed to trot toward them, and Sage leaned into Gavin, making to move to the side so the healer could get quickly by.

"It's about time," a spritely voice spilled from the healer's mouth. Her arms reached forward, and Sage struggled not to look behind her, to scan for the recipient of such a warm welcome. Before she could react, Gavin dropped her hand

and clasped his with the healer. Her eyes shone as she looked at Gavin, and Sage felt a pang of...jealousy? Curiosity? Some cacophony of emotions that made the scene in front of her hard to decipher.

"I was beginning to wonder if the Goddess had told me true," the healer said, her voice ringing with maturity that grated against her youthful appearance. If Sage had to guess, the female couldn't have been more than seventeen years. But, of course, appearance was not usually the truth in the world of fae.

"I'm sorry to keep you waiting," Gavin offered genuinely. "I'd like to introduce Sage Brennan." He stepped to the side, releasing the female's hands and gesturing to Sage.

"Oh, I had no doubt who stood next to you, Gavin," the healer replied. Eyes both dark with wisdom and bright with empathy landed on Sage. She felt herself straighten under the scrutiny of such a gaze. "How far you have traveled. You must be bone weary."

"It's been a time," Sage admitted. "But, I feel better than I have in ages." She felt herself grow lighter, the truth of her words ringing like music in her ears.

"I'm sure you do." Some sort of knowing danced within the healer's eyes, and Sage wondered again at who it was she spoke to. "Now, without further ado, let us make our way to my office. There is much to discuss."

Gavin winked at Sage, who simply shrugged back. What more could she do? It wasn't like she knew anyone in the complex, nor could she figure out where she was meant to go. Only that she was there to research Borea and how its history *might* provide something useful to Gavin in his attempt to assuage Micah.

As they passed through the centered archway, the portrait of an elderly fae came into view. Pointed ears reached up and accentuated the shaved head of the female in the portrait. Something in the fae's eyes, their skin, even the playful smile seemed painfully familiar. But that was ludicrous, as Sage knew very few fae. "Who is that?" Sage asked Gavin as they passed the painting, following the healer ahead of them.

Stopping abruptly, the healer turned. A playful smile punctuated her answer, "Would you believe me if I told you it was me?"

Sage frowned, looking closely at the fae standing above her on the steps, then turned to look again at the portrait. The painted fae was clearly lined with age, gnarled hands clasped at the base of the portrait before falling beneath a gilded frame. "That can't be you," Sage said, leaning closer to inspect the portrait. "I mean, I can see a resemblance. Perhaps a relative?"

The healer laughed. "So you truly didn't tell her, Gavin? You rascal!" Sage looked, perplexed and exasperated at Gavin and the healer.

"I told you to just wait," he said.

"You're Shiphrah?" Sage asked. "But then..." Quickly running the two steps past Gavin and back to the portrait, she leaned in close to inspect the brass plate attached to the frame. Shiphrah's name was etched into the tag, along with a string of numbers that must have indicated a date that Sage hadn't taught herself to recognize yet.

"But you—" Sage looked back at the fae on the stairs.

"I, am Shiphrah. Head Healer and Provost of the Rafalatriki."

"But you—" Sage stammered again, pointing at the healer on the stairs, then to the portrait and back again. "How?"

"That is a story, and a long one at that. Perhaps I can tell it to you as we make our way to my quarters?" Without waiting for a response, Shiphrah turned, swishing her robes, and began climbing the stairs once again. As her steps echoed around them, Shiphrah spoke in a clear voice that tumbled back to Sage and Gavin. "You know, many fae don't even remember that I started out as a warrior." She hummed to herself, almost as she was reminiscing, before continuing. "Felysia and I shared a girlhood," she explained chuckling, "or, more like, what we consider a nation now, was still in its burgeoning era as I developed from girlhood and was commissioned as an enlisted warrior. My family had hoped I would find a bonded partner of some wealth, but I had my sights set on travel, on glory even."

Sage and Gavin continued walking behind Shiphrah, Sage fighting against the urge to pant as they climbed and climbed upward. A soft hand settled on her lower back, and she felt a bolster of energy from Gavin's proximity. How was it that such a gentle touch could muster the butterflies now pinging around her stomach? Finally, they reached a landing that faded into a sitting room, the walls decorated with paintings, knicknacks, and four separate closed doors.

Taking her seat behind a wooden table turned desk, Shiphrah gestured to a pair of chairs facing her. "I explain all this to lead you into a brief overview of how I became a healer. You see, the powers I was gifted at birth made me an exceptional warrior. I was fast, and not just with a sword, but with strategy. I could watch an opponent for just a few sparse moments and know exactly where their weaknesses lay. I rose quickly through the ranks, becoming a lieutenant in just four short years."

Gavin let out a short whistle. "That's right," Shiphrah nodded, grinning. "By the age of twenty-four, I was lieutenant of a troop that hovered around...oh, that was so long ago," she muttered, leaning back into her seat, "I believe it was a troop of eighty soldiers."

"So how did you become a healer then?" Sage asked.

"Love." Shiphrah's answer was simple, her smile still present, though her eyes seemed to be ringed with an essence of grief. "I fell in love with a healer. Being young and reckless, I conscripted her into the service of my troops. She followed us, along with other medics, as we battled. We were blessed with fifty years together in that manner. I would ride into battle when required, and she would stitch up my warriors, and occasionally me." Shiphrah laughed then, as if a particularly fond memory had made its way to her. Her youthful skin glowed with vibrance, and Sage caught sight of freckles dancing across the healer's cheeks.

"And then," Shiphrah continued with a heavy sigh, "my recklessness caught up with me. I was away on a campaign, camped along the Nysan border. You see, at the time, we were not on friendly terms with the Sekiri tribe. They were still rambling freely through Nysa, and our Queen was agitated by their recent advances along our borders. So we engaged them. We battled on and off for three bloody months. One of their spies found out about Lilit, my love.

"They knew that if they distracted me, they had an excellent chance at defeating my troop. I caught them before they could attack Lilit in her sleep, but it cost me. I fought, ten against one, and killed at least eight of them."

Shiphrah raised an eyebrow at Gavin as if in question. He responded with a nod of appreciation. "But one of the devils had managed to make a swipe at me with their spear, slicing open my abdomen. He and one other managed to escape, but I was left bleeding out on the perimeter of the camp. By the time Lilit found me, I was walking along the path to Eternity."

A solemness settled amongst them, the shadows in the room seeming to darken. Shiphrah, a predatory stillness wrapping itself around her, continued. "I could just barely make out the cries of my love. And then I heard the whispering. She prayed to the Goddess, asking for her to save me, promising to trade anything. That was the last thing I remember, hearing her prayer to the Goddess."

Shiphrah inhaled deeply and stood from her chair. She walked to a large window that anchored the room.

"So, what happened?" Sage asked.

Shiphrah turned, smiling sweetly. "You know, the bond is a powerful thing. It enhances the natural powers of fae. But I also believe it gives us a special connection to the Goddess. She's benevolent, nurturing, even. When I woke, I was shocked to find that my powers had changed. Where I had been gifted with intuition and speed, I suddenly had a gift for healing."

"And Lilit?" Sage asked, pushing again for the answer Shiphrah seemed to dance around.

"Lilit got her wish. She traded my place in eternity for her own. So now, I honor her sacrifice by leading the Rafalatriki. I was among the first fae to petition our Queen to have it built. I spent my youth building this complex, and establishing the basis for our academies. Eventually I aged, and then...a peculiar thing began to happen to me. Rather than dying, shortly after that portrait had been painted, actually, I began to grow young again. I was already passed my five-hundredth year when that portrait was painted."

Sage shook her head slightly, trying to rattle the story into place. She was looking at someone who had not only been alive for over five-hundred years, but simply...reversed in age. Not only that, but the tragedy of Shiphrah's origin felt familiar in some ways. She wasn't sure how she felt about Lilit's decision to trade her life for her lover's. "So, when you said Lilit traded her spot in eternity for yours, does that mean..." Her voice trailed off, unsure about the intimacy of the question.

"Does it mean I am immortal?" Shiphrah finished Sage's question with a wry smile. "Your guess is as good as mine," she answered with a grin. "But, nevermind all of that. Sage, it is an honor to host you at the Rafalatriki. Please, do not hesitate to call on me for whatever you need."

"Thank you," Sage said, understanding that the time had come to change topics.

"But that does bring me to what I really brought you both to my office for. I wasn't terribly surprised to have you call on me, Gavin, but I'm not sure how we can help you with your current circumstances."

"Actually, it started with an idea I had," Sage interjected, even as Gavin leaned forward to speak. "I was hoping to access your libraries. We're looking for anything relevant to the people who used to live in Borea."

"Our hopes are to relocate the displaced rebels to Borea, but we need a good reason, something to offer them," Gavin continued.

"There must be something useful in the mountains if there were tribes who used to live there and built a culture there at one point," Sage mused, already anticipating the thrill of researching and problem solving again.

"I see," Shiphrah said, leaning on her desk. "Well, I might not have any scholars to spare in your efforts, but I can inform our historians and make sure they check in on you from time to time, to answer any questions you may have."

"That is very generous, thank you," Gavin answered, pushing himself from his seat so that he stood. With disappointment, Sage also rose, wishing she could spend the rest of the day talking to this unusual and spirited female.

Shiphrah smiled again, a bright, genuine smile that warmed Sage through her soul. She wasn't sure she'd ever met someone so radiant before. Unlike Queen Aryael, who seemed to radiate magnetism, Shiphrah's warmth came from the authenticity of someone who has accepted life for the balancing act it was, someone who could accept hardship without it weathering them. Perhaps that was the lesson of immortality; perhaps her heart had out maneuvered hardship.

"There is an attendant just outside my quarters, waiting to show you both to your accommodations. Take as much time as you need, and if I can be of any service, be sure you send someone to find me." She walked around her desk, and grasped Gavin's hands once more. "It's good to see you again," she beamed at him, her eyes taking on a shine that reminded Sage of her long-gone grandparents, such a striking contrast to the freckled cheeks that Shiphrah bore now.

Without any further discussion, Shiphrah dropped his hands and moved back to her desk, ruffling through some papers. As they walked toward the staircase, Shiphrah called out, "Good luck, Realm Leaper. I get the feeling we will all be thankful for your efforts."

꘍ ✳ ꘍

Gavin had accompanied Sage to their room. Perhaps he had been a bit gruff with the apprentice who had been elected to show them the way when she had announced they'd arrived at their *rooms*.

Rooms. Plural. As if he and Sage weren't going to be sharing the same living space. He'd tried, and failed, to keep the edge from his tone when he informed the poor healer that they would only be needing one room. Sage had scoffed at him, and generously thanked the young female for her help.

Shortly after, they'd received their baggage, sent via an enchanted crate Meliza had dug up in the Big House. Sage had taken no time throwing back the lid and finding her notebook, already tabbed with notes to be cross-referenced in the massive libraries of the Rafalatriki. Gavin had unpacked his bag, then given Sage a quick kiss on the cheek before answering to the letter that had been slipped beneath their door just a few moments after they'd entered their room.

Sage had given a simple "hmmm," when he told her he was stepping out for a little bit and would be back shortly. She was still sitting cross-legged in a chair, pencil between her teeth and gaze locked on her notebook, when he closed the door.

Now, he stood in the open air of a balcony high above the Rafalatriki grounds. He'd exited through the front, taking the opportunity to fly in his bird form. Shiphrah was already waiting for him when he landed, shifting back into his fae body. She chuckled as he turned, and gave her an assessing gaze.

"Shiphrah," he nodded in greeting.

"*Lord* Gavin," she responded. "I'm not sure how long it will take me to actually get used to that."

"I share the sentiment," Gavin replied warmly. His demeanor dropped, however, as he pushed to the topic of why he'd really come to the Rafalatriki. Sage might be under the impression it was just to find a solution to Micah and his campaign for Lordship, but Felysia desperately needed answers to how the Dark Born were getting their new powers. "I need to ask you some questions, better in person than by letter," he explained.

Shiphrah nodded. "The burden of old age is knowledge," she said, a lopsided grin to her mouth. "I'm guessing this has to do with Speridisia and the Dark Born?"

"Yes. What do you know about the twins and their Blood Sorcery?"

"Ah—" Shiphrah's face clouded and she walked towards the edge of the balcony. Gavin followed, giving her the mental space to sort through all she could remember. "They were not the first to experiment with it. From what I can recall, the demons that rose up through Speridisia came with special knowledge. It's not known for sure, but I suspect Blood Sorcery is part of that knowledge." She took a long inhale. "King Rankor defeated the previous rulers of Speridisia through bloody combat, and I'm not convinced he didn't use Blood Sorcery himself."

"So, what exactly is it?" Gavin probed, looking for specifics. Perhaps, if they knew how the sorcery worked, they could fight against it more effectively.

"Well, it's a way of siphoning magic from one fae, and transferring it to another. It also, used in just the right circumstances, can be used to control another. But, you already knew that." She eyed Gavin closely.

He nodded. "I saw the twins drain a boy of his blood. Apollyon drank some of the blood, and he gained fire power. But it was very brief."

"And that," Shiphrah said, wagging her finger in the air, "is the only thing keeping the Dark Born from draining every and any fae within their clutches. It would do them no good to siphon away the power of everyone when the power is so fleeting."

"But now," Gavin pushed, "they've got some new power. You can't tell me that isn't Blood Sorcery at work."

"It could be, but from the letters you and the Crown have sent my way, it could be a result of their new ally. Could it not?"

Gavin had thought about that. Aryael seemed to believe it had something to do with Suda's disappearance, but Symon insisted the two occurrences weren't necessarily related. Gavin scrubbed his hands down his face. "I don't know. And that's what bothers me most."

Shiphrah nodded in agreement. "It is truly vexing, isn't it?" She looked at him, her smile almost watery. "To not be able to fix the problems of the world?"

Gavin nodded. Vexing. What a great way to describe the jumble of emotions that seemed to chase him these days.

"And how are you doing?" Shiphrah asked, sharply.

"I'm doing fine," Gavin answered breezily.

Shiphrah's mouth turned down slightly, and she bobbed her head side to side as she weighed his answer. "The Signum Dominari," she said, finally. "That's a burdensome fate."

He shrugged. So what if it was. He couldn't change the fact that a long-dormant trait had sprouted within him, but he could manage its side effects.

"There were still a few fae gifted with The Seal when I was a girl. Enough, back then, that we knew the signs to watch for." Shiphrah began speaking, almost as if she were simply reminiscing. Gavin continued to lean against the bannister, crossing his arms to match her. "Some of the fae who manifested The Seal went mad with the power. They, ultimately, either killed themselves with their madness, or had to be put down by their own people."

"That won't be an issue," Gavin answered quickly. By this point, he already had a grasp on the primal urges that had ravaged him only a month before. He'd hardly lost his temper since moving onto his estate. He'd even allowed himself to question one of Micah's elite raiders, and had done so with quiet command. The interrogation had been a success, allowing them to learn more about Micah's ultimate motives than they had since Gavin had first arrived in Mystaira.

"Ah—I see," Shiphrah nodded. "And what about a partner? Have you considered seeking out a fae that might be suitable for the bond?"

"That won't be necessary," Gavin answered, again, quickly.

His tone seemed to alert something in Shiphrah. "And why not?"

"I'm not interested in partnering with any fae."

"Because you think the Realm Leaper is a suitable match?" Shiphrah's question was acute, and he realized this had been the sole purpose of her check-in with him. Gavin remained quiet; he wasn't sure how she expected him to answer. "You do realize, young Lord, that a bond is one of the most significant ways to increase your power, and your ability to manage The Seal, don't you? By refusing to search for a suitable partner, you are also refusing your people the opportunity for the most capable Lord they might have."

"They have already been blessed with that," Gavin quipped, causing a wry smile to appear on Shiphrah's face. Gavin pushed off the banister, walking toward the center of the overlarge balcony. He turned quickly to face Shiphrah, jabbing a finger into his own chest. "I am the first fae lord with The Seal in millenia. There are no other Lords or Ladies with the power I am growing now, and that may be the least humble thing I have ever muttered. But I say it because I know, deep within my bones, that the only thing that could make me more powerful, more stable, is the mortal girl with magic sitting in a room six floors below us."

"And what will you do when that security you are so sure of leaves this world to go back to her own?" Again, Shiphrah's words were accurate. Acute. Biting, even. Her voice may have held an edge of coldness, but Gavin sensed the kindness in the undercurrent of her questioning.

"I haven't figured that part out yet," Gavin admitted, running both hands through his hair. "All I know is that there is no one else for me after Sage. And I've made my peace with that."

"Okay, then," Shiphrah announced, leaving the bannister and dusting off her hands. "Then when the time comes, remember the words you have spoken this night. It will not be easy once you have friends and family clamoring for you to bond. Take it from someone with experience." She reached Gavin, placing both hands on his cheeks.

Softly, he grabbed her wrists and closed his eyes. "What if this is all a fluke? What if I wasn't the one that was supposed to have this power?" His voice was soft, but he felt the weight of the last ten years melt away as he asked the healer for guidance.

"The Goddess herself has blessed you with this power. There's no other way to explain how such a thing could reappear so suddenly, and at such a time as this. You've been chosen Gavin, and we chosen get very few choices of our own. But when you are faced with a choice, a true choice that is *yours* to make, make the choice. Lean into it with your whole heart. You cannot go wrong if you do."

She patted his face gently twice, then walked away, leaving him alone on the balcony. It would seem that while trying to save his land, his old mentor, and his people, he would also be trying to save himself.

Chapter 13

Attention of Her Majesty:

Today marks the beginning of the third week of refugees pouring in from the Nysan border. Day after day, thousands seek safety. At this rate, Jordynia does not have enough space to house all who are looking for safety. Perhaps it is time to reach out to Maracadia again. I realize the effort is likely futile, but things are desperate.

Reports of multiple shadows engulfing towns and cities throughout Nysa are becoming more concerning. The refugees have come to call the strange power The Shadow of Death. Not only are the Dark Born killing the younglings as their power runs through the land, but sicknesses I've never seen the like of are rampant.

We are in dire need of more supplies, more healers. Many are suffering under the weight of work and lack of progress. One or two are succumbing to despair. It hurts me to see my fellow brethren so beaten down.

At this point all the tributes we can spare to the Goddess herself must be made. I beg of you.

Additionally, I had the pleasure of intercepting your package as it made its way to its destination. I'm hopeful it will meet the appropriate recipient. I would request an update on the package's outcome if you are able to forward any news.

Please send Symon my regards. I will continue correspondence as circumstances develop.

All my best~

Raphael

✧◆✧

Aryael stared at Raphael's latest report. More refugees. More death. More illness. More problems.

And more than the fact that every waking moment was an opportunity for greater problems to pile upon them, Raphael's momentary slip from his usual formality to beg for offerings to the Goddess left Aryael disturbed.

Standing up, she scrunched the missive in her fist and strode to the window. Here in Veritasaille all was peaceful. Quiet. Too quiet. Aryael needed action.

Her heart ached for her homeland, for her people. Providing relief at the border didn't feel like enough. But with the deployment to Mystaira, Felysia lacked the troops at the moment to send a full force to help defend them. Besides, how exactly would they fight a shadow?

Sick of her own company, she left her apartments to make her way to Symon's war room.

It seemed as though the Dark Born had burned the last vestiges of their souls, turning themselves fully—and seemingly with great glee—into the corrupt darkness she'd always associated with them. Their murky devilry fueled her preoccupation with the issues in Mystaira, the rising conflict in Nysa. The gnawing worry about Suda.

How, exactly, had they been able to manifest the powers they now possessed? According to Apyllon's letter, it had something to do with Rankor's look-alike. And that provided little to answer the questions that hounded her and Symon.

Stalking down the palace halls she stopped abruptly, an eerie shiver running across her shoulders. Looking behind her she half expected to see if her problems had actually acquired corporeal shapes and become monsters that lurked in her peripherals. But the hall remained quiet, and she rolled her eyes at the ludicrous idea that anything could follow her in her own palace.

The palace had been enchanted within an inch of its foundation. Some of the enchantments included the ability to bar entry from anyone she or Symon considered an enemy. Another tricky enchantment forbade either her or Symon from leaving the city boundaries at the same time. The idea had been that it would protect the city from both rulers leaving or being captured, ensuring one of them remained in place to guard their people. With no current heirs, it was an idea they'd had early in their marriage. Now, it felt like a mistake. They would need to track down another enchanter in order to break the ward.

The chance that they'd all end up on the battlefield was beginning to feel more and more like the most probable outcome. All this, and more, was swirling through her mind as she pushed open the doors into Symon's war room. The setup was nearly identical to her own, but Aryael admired the cozy additions Symon always seemed to make time for. Velvet cushioned chairs dotted the room. Books stacked on tables pushed against the walls, and Symon had even had the foresight to add a wet bar to one corner.

That was what had driven Aryael to seek out Symon now. If there was anything she needed right at this moment, it was a drink...and...well, a solid night in bed with her husband.

Aryael walked by Symon, who was peering across the circular map of their continent, small figurines dotting various points on the image. Tossing the letter from Raphael onto the table, she walked straight to the bar, calling over her shoulder, "What are we drinking tonight?"

"Good news, then?" Symon asked, a wry note to his question.

"Well, Raph is still alive, so I suppose we rejoice in that." She hadn't meant to be so dejected in her reply, but something of the underlying tone of despair in Raph's letter had her on edge.

"There's narresh liquor sitting on the bar top."

"Mmm...you know me too well, King." Aryael poured herself and Symon each a generous glass of the cinnamon flavored liquor, a favorite with deep ties to her homeland. Taking a sip, she relished the burn of the drink before walking back to Symon and placing his glass on the table next to him. "I've been thinking," she began, Symon remained staring at the map. Had he blinked since she'd entered the room? "I think it's time to find an enchanter to change the wards." She knew he would know exactly which wards she spoke of.

That got Symon's attention. His posture snapped upright. He grabbed his glass and he turned to face her. "For what purpose? So we can both go into Speridisia?"

"It will likely come to that anyway, Symon. Perhaps it's time we take the offensive stance instead of planning on the defensive." Her palms prickled with anticipation. She knew Symon wouldn't agree with this, but it was time they began considering it.

"Look, I know you want to go and find Suda. I understand. I would want to burn the whole damn country down if it was either of my siblings. Zeke, even. But strategically...you and I both know it puts our country at too much risk."

"Not if we catch them off guard!" She'd thought of this. Thought of the outcomes. "The fact is, the Dark Born are both aware of our wards. We don't know how, but they know. They won't suspect us both to be there on the attack." She heaved a breath. "We are capable of casting a troop apiece. That is more than enough to take the Dark Born's fortress if we are strategic about it."

Symon stared into her eyes. His blue irises were like chips of an iceberg, so deep, so crisp, so cold. She'd always felt like he could read her, with or without his mental powers. He sipped from his drink. "No."

The wards required agreement from them both to change. "Damn it, Symon!" Aryael slammed her glass on the table, sloshing amber liquid. "You and I both know we are going to end up over there. Why not do it now?!"

"Because I'm not ready to risk you!" His fist clenched his glass, and his voice echoed around the spherical room. "I'm not ready to lose the only constant in my world, Aryael." His voice dropped to a whisper, and she hated herself in that moment. Had the roles been reversed, she was sure she'd be saying the same thing.

But that was her brother over there, her last remaining blood. "Can you be certain you won't, if we don't act soon enough?" She wasn't sure exactly what her question meant, but it was the only words she could fathom.

Symon exhaled hard, setting his glass on the table, then pulling her into an embrace. "I don't know," he said quietly, brushing his lips over her forehead, "and that might be the scariest part of all."

✧✦✧

The court was gathered in the council room. The advancing summer would have made the room sweltering with the floor to ceiling windows encasing one wall. But Aryael had made it a point to have the whole castle enchanted so that it remained comfortable year round. A merciful coolness wafted through the room, and she could sense relief on more than one fae Lord and Lady assembled on the chairs facing her and Symon.

They'd gathered as many Lords and Ladies as they could at such short notice. The only three nobles from Jordynia that had managed to make the meeting at the last moment coming to the council room directly from their journey. Casting all the way from the province would have been too much for even Symon. Instead, it appeared the noble-fae had casted as far as they could, then hired wagons to escort them through much of Mystaira. But they sat with straight backs and chins lifted high, any signs of weariness vacant from their demeanors.

Mystaira representatives outweighed those of both Jordynia and Veritasailles. Then there was the province of Bithnia, but no nobles had been sent there. Bithnia sat to the west of Veritasailles, a natural buffer between Felysia and Nysa. It served as the nation's greatest collective of war camps and training complexes. Zeke had redesigned many of them himself, along with input from Meliza, and oversaw the operations of the province alongside his commanders and lieutenants. Many of the residents of Bithnia had become wealthy merchants, practically noble-fae in their own right, from the trade that had proffered between Nysa and Felysia. The additional business from sentries and young soldiers had to be a boon as well.

Aryael blinked once, dislodging all the rampant thoughts swirling through her muddled mind. A slight throbbing had begun behind her eyes, and she inhaled sharply to keep the pain at bay. Perhaps she should have allowed Raphael to leave behind a bit of that sleep tonic. Months without a proper rest were beginning to take its toll.

Symon opened the meeting, his strong voice rolling through the throne room with ease. "Lords, Ladies. We are thankful for your attendance on such short notice. We have a lot to discuss, so we will jump right to it. Once we've closed this meeting, rest assured, you are welcome to spend as much time in our palace as you need before departing back to your estates."

He paused. The mood in the room was somber, news of the calamities in Nysa having reached even the far reaches of Jordynia.

Ayrael picked up the address, "We are especially grateful for the representatives of Jordynia, as our news pertains especially to you."

Symon turned, addressing Zeke who sat in a lowback chair at the foot of the stairs below the thrones. "General Zeke will begin with an explanation of the conflict in Nysa."

"As many of you know by now," Zeke began, "Nysa has been invaded by the Dark Born. The specifications of exactly *how* the Dark Born are attacking are...confusing." Zeke bobbed his head a little from side-to-side, as if trying to parcel out which parts of the reports were most critical to give to the masses, as whatever was said in the throne room would undoubtedly become gossip across the country. "Accounts from survivors indicate that the Dark Born twins have developed some sort of power, or weapon, able to surpass Nysa's usual enchantments. Their attacks have left their victims with lingering illnesses, and Nysa has suffered the casualties of a large portion of their young.

"Even so, the Nysan capital still seems to hold its leaders within its fortress walls. News, obviously, is coming slow, but we all hope that the fortress will continue holding strong. We are actively working with enchanters, both civilian and enlisted, to reinforce our own borders and strongholds."

"Yes, we've heard all of this already," Megara, Seth's wife, interjected, her voice piercing the room. Seth didn't budge, his gaze remained forward, unblinking, as if all his energy were focused on not responding to his wife's words. "What does this have to do with the Council?"

Aryael had to hand it to the female, she had a warrior spirit, even if she were untrained in battle. Indeed, this was a woman whose battleground lay firmly in politics and strategy. What a boon The Seal had been to them, to force Seth out of the way as an obstacle, and into their pockets as an ally. Megara would be a fierce addition to the Council should they succeed in swaying her to their side.

"Excellent question, Megara," Aryael said. "Part of this council meeting is to formally notify all noble-fae that we are now on high alert. You should begin researching ways to strengthen your wards and enchantments, double check your own strongholds and supplies, and remind your hands to remain vigilant. Mystaira, especially, should be wary of attacks along their border."

"If the Dark Born are surpassing Nysa's enchantments, how are our own enchantments supposed to stop an attack?" Megara replied sharply. Aryael could see it wasn't in disrespect, the gears churned in Megara's mind.

"Perhaps we ask the Realm Leaper."

Aryael sought out the identity of the speaker, Tylia of Mystaira. She was one of the few who had fought against the raiders, alongside those who lived on her estate as hired help, and won. The female was a power unto herself and Aryael was grateful to see her present for the council meeting. "I, myself, had the Realm Leaper visit my estate recently. She was able to provide several wards to my home, but also along the grounds. They've been effective thus far." That explained her victory against Micah's bandits.

"Her magic is strange. Do we think it would be impenetrable to the Dark Born?" Megara asked, turning toward Tylia.

"We think so," Symon replied. "The use of Sage's magic has already been discussed. Unfortunately, it may be some time before she's able to help. She's currently occupied at the Rafalatriki—" mutters erupted within the throne room "—I'm afraid it *is* imperative she remain there for the time being."

"I think that brings us to the next point of business," Zeke spoke over the whispers that continued through the room, holding up his hand for silence before continuing. "Representatives of Jordynia, the next part of this meeting pertains mostly to you." He let the proclamation settle before continuing. "We are in the process of assisting refugees from Nysa. It has been suggested that Jordynia could be a safe place to house those who've escaped Nysa, until we can figure out further plans."

The three representatives of Jordynia, Iris, Tallum, and Rashim, stood as one and without hesitation. Iris, the only born noble-fae, spoke for the collective. "It would be our honor to provide sanctuary—"

The doors at the back of the room burst open. Raphael, grimey from his time at the refugee camp, came stalking into the room, his face grim.

"Raph! You're back," Aryael began, pushing up to stand even as another throb behind her eyes threatened to topple her over.

Raphael continued walking forward, followed by two fae carrying something between them. Aryael made it two steps before stopping.

"We've been sent a message," Raphael announced, stopping halfway down the long aisle that would bring him to Aryael.

Raphael jerked his head to the side, gesturing to the fae behind him to continue in front of him with the heavy package they carried. It was large and bulky, Aryael realized the two fae were sweating from the effort of carrying it.

Streaks of some liquid oozed through the burlap from whatever was inside. Aryael watched as Raphael clasped his hands behind his back, the muscles in his jaw going taught as the two fae set down the bundle reverentially in front of Ayrael and began slowly unwrapping it, their hands shaking.

Eventually, his eyes met hers. "You had to have known," Raphael ground out. "You knew the danger, and yet..." His voice cracked.

Aryael, frozen, tore her gaze from Raphael's glare, feeling his anger thrumming from him, mixing with her own increasing heart rate. She sensed Symon joining her.

The burlap wrapping, being so carefully unraveled by the fae in front of her, was stiff and scraped as it was unfolded. As the layers were removed, wavy tendrils of hair the color of ripe corn began poking up. As the final layers fell away, Aryael gasped. "No!"

"Yes," Raphael seethed.

The throbbing in her head increased, pulsing against her skull as through blurred sight she took in the horror that lay in front of her.

Ionus's beautiful golden waves fell against a scarred and pitted face, marred by a grimace of pain that revealed the atrocity of his last moments. But as her gaze roved onward, she recoiled at the stitches that ran around the base of his neck. The glow of his fair skin contrasted sharply against the rich dark brown of a female warrior's body. Amare.

The Dark Born had removed Ionus's head and attached it to Amare's body before shipping the abomination back to them.

The deep silence at Raphael's entrance seemed to explode into a thousand conflicting voices as the stench of fear and rage flooded the throne room, beating against Aryael's head. Her knees buckled, forcing her to the floor.

You sent them into Speridisia? Symon's voice pierced her mind as Aryael continued to stare at the evidence of her recklessness, unable to tear her eyes away. *Aryael. Look at me.*

Blinking back her tears, Aryael gathered herself to look up at her husband. Shame warring with her innate need to protect her own. Tearing her gaze away from the punishment that lay on the floor at last, Aryael turned. Cold blue eyes held her gaze, even as she inhaled hard to suppress a sob. There was an edge of pity to Symon's gaze, which made the reality that much worse.

Aryael balled her fists next to her side. Using her fire power, she heated her skin, singing away the tears that hovered against her eyes. Focusing the ache of shame and despair into a heated ball of rage. They would pay.

She turned back to Raphael, silently demanding an explanation.

"They are coming, Your Majesties. And we'd best get prepared."

The world erupted around her.

Heartbeats melded with loud voices.

"Pull everyone from the border!" Zeke's booming voice reverberated through the room.

Snatches of orders given and scraps of sound wavered around her as Aryael gazed upon what was left of her fallen friends. Fallen and maimed because of her and her desperate need for news of her brother.

Placing a soft hand on Amare's chest, she drank in the sight of the broken body, intent on feeding the rage that was now simmering inside of her. Her eyes fluttered closed. "I'm so sorry," she whispered.

Amare was missing several fingers. What looked like manacle scars blistered her wrists and ankles. Lash marks warped the female's torso, visible through the slashed muslin of her undergarments.

A bloody slice down the length of Ionus' face severed the flesh of his forehead and eye, down to the corner of his nose. Dried spittle crusted the corner of his mouth.

Something caught her eye. A pale sliver of what could be material poked from the corner of Ionus' mouth.

With quiet precaution, Aryael touched it.

It was cloth.

With a grimace, she tugged on the material. A square piece of fabric unraveled, soaked in the fluids that had been slowly drying, reeking of death and despair.

At the center, in what could have been blood or charcoal, was one word.

Alive.

Chapter 14

14

◆◆◆◆

Apyllon seethed as he passed the barriers of his fortress. The sound of his brother's heavy steps in the squelching mud and the feel of his ire radiating off him in waves indicated that neither of them were impressed about being *summoned* back to their own territory.

They'd just been terrorizing the pathetic inhabitants of a nice little town on the coast of Nysa. Really, why hadn't they explored that area more in the days of their father's rule? They'd had their fun in Nysa, for sure. But now they had time to linger, to savor their time there. Yes, now, they got to take their time and caress the coast of Nysa with their attention. Stroking the fear and despair from the inhabitants of Nysa was so much better than the ram-rod, militant style of their father, who'd only cared about bringing the continent to heel as quickly as possible. The thought brought a brief smile to his lips, but he quickly lost it as he shook the dark hair from his eyes and glared at who waited for them on the steps of the stone walls that stretched into the sky.

The noisy flap and crack of flags ricocheted from the top of the battlements, playing against the sounds of metal clanging as the brothers' smiths continued laboring over their guests' orders. Cian, the self-important assistant to Ranquer, stood on the steps scribbling on something attached to a board. The man had the gaul to complain about the lack of "accommodations" they'd provided him, even after they'd handed over their entire smithery and unlimited access to their stationery. It appeared Cian was used to more advanced *technology*, whatever that meant.

Abbadon adjusted the cuffs of his black shirt as they passed Cian, neither of them acknowledging the man's presence.

"What took you so long?" Cian fizzed as they walked into the dark corridor, escaping the light that dared to peek through the clouds overhead.

"Not that it concerns you," Abbadon answered, "but it does take time to travel the length of the Nysan coastal panhandle."

"Even in our shadow form, we cannot be here in the blink of an eye," said Apyllon.

"Well, you're in luck. Our master has yet to arrive, but he would have been none too pleased—"

"*Your* master," Apyllon hissed, whirling directly into Cian's face. "Remember whose world you are on when you speak to us." The little twat didn't even have the decency to cower. Apyllon's irritation simmered below the surface of his skin. If he wasn't careful, he was liable to boil the imbecile where he stood, consequences be damned.

Cian, mere inches from Apyllon's face, pushed his spectacles up the bridge of his beaky nose, his eyebrows twitching slightly. "Yes, well, it would serve you right to remember who *you* serve. Need I remind you who Ranquer is in the grand scheme of things."

Abbadon stepped forward, slapping a hand onto Apyllon's shoulder. Apyllon still writhed inside with the impertinence of the birdlike alchemist, but Abbadon's presence was enough to reign in his ire. "Come brother, the sooner we see to these summons, the sooner we can get back to our own machinations."

A brittle chuckle chased after them as Cian muttered, "Hardly."

Apyllon had mistrusted Ranquer on his first visit, but he had to admit that already they were seeing benefits to their alliance. That, coupled with the revelation of the truth of their origins, had found him feeling obligated to support the duplicate's ambitions.

Nevermind all of that. Abbadon was correct: the sooner they answered their ally's summons, the sooner they could go back to what he loved best—torment. A slow smile broke across his face as they passed through the damp stone hall.

Their fortress had the benefit of tunneling deep into the ground, keeping the halls and rooms chilled. The one complaint he had about Nysa was the damned heat. And the humidity? Darkness, if he could change one thing about the land east of the Spearsan Gap, it'd be the fucking humidity. It amplified the heat. No bother. With his new strength over shadow, he could fix that issue once he and his brother finally laid waste to the snivelling bastards ruining this continent.

The hallway emerged into a rounded gathering room which had been turned into a laboratory of sorts for Cian and his ilk. Two other alchemists muttered to each other in a corner, looking at what might have been a map for all the scribbles Apyllon could make out on the papers. Machines, something Apyllon and Abbadon had had to become familiar with, littered the room. Wires, tubes, things that beeped and buzzed spanned the circumference and filled the air with a humming energy that was warm and restless. On the far side sat a cylindrical, glass encased machine that Apyllon could hardly tear his eyes from.

Months ago, a rip in the sky had jolted him and his brother from their drunken slumber. Out of it, Ranquer and his assistant had come hurtling directly into their fortress. Somehow, the self-proclaimed President had managed to land unscathed. But Apyllon had watched in fascination as the beaky Cian had reformed under Ranquer's magic wand. The sound of bones popping back into place had been intriguing enough to force the twins from drowning themselves in self-pity night after night. If there was one thing he could be grateful for, it was the wake-up call that had accompanied the man who looked like his father. In hindsight, Apyllon supposed the sorcerer that had landed in their midst *was* his father, in some regard.

A faint light began to emit from the glass tube, and the silver rods affixed to the top of the machine began to whir, spinning excitedly as the light grew. The humming of machines intensified to a wail, and Abbadon raised his arm to block the light as it cascaded through the room. Apyllon continued watching, refusing to look away as two forms began to coalesce within the glare.

As the light ebbed, four long, lean legs materialized from the glow, coalescing into two thin torsos. Finally, Ranquer's round head appeared upon one trunk, accompanied by the face of a woman with slicked back, dark hair on the other. A mischievous smile danced on her face, and Apyllon thought she looked like a woman who knew how to bring a peasant to their knees. Perhaps there would be more to be grateful for before the day was through.

The whir and buzz subsided sharply, and Ranquer tapped the glass door. Cian, the petulant mortal, shoved one of the alchemists forward, who rushed to open the door for Ranquer and his new addition.

The woman stepped forward first. Her long legs were bound in black, cloth pants that fed into a crisp buttoned shirt and black coat. Her devilish smile mirrored Apyllon's own as she scanned the room.

"Cian," she said, with a tilt of her head.

"Dullahan," Cian answered.

Apyllon couldn't be sure, but he thought he detected some tension between the two, something he'd enjoy exploiting, given the chance.

"Ah, I see we've all been gathered," Ranquer announced with a clap of his hands as he exited the glass tube.

Week after week, Ranquer had flitted back and forth between dimensions, sometimes bringing alchemists with him, other times leaving with a Dark Born soldier or two. For what purpose, the twins hardly cared, as long as the alchemists continued their research and tests on increasing their powers. Already, the manifestations of new powers had grown with their experiments.

Apyllon only concerned himself with whether those experiments continued. Ranquer had also had the two alchemists send dozens and dozens of elemental-blessed fae through the glass encased machine. Again, Apyllon could hardly care less what happened to the peasants once they left his sight.

Finally, Apyllon tore his gaze from admiring Dullahan long enough to take in Ranquer, his pseudo-father. Vicious marks ran beneath an obsidian eye patch, clashing with Ranquer's tidy, combed hair and staunch suit.

"Ran into a bit of trouble, I see," Abbadon said, clearly enjoying seeing their ally facing some sort of trouble. It seemed the man got usually everything he wanted, except for the Realm Leaper.

"Yes, well," Ranquer answered, adjusting the long piece of material tied under the collar of his shirt. "I had hoped to find a shortcut to our little problem with Sage." Ranquer stalked to the alchemist holding what Apyllon assumed was a map. Holding it away from his face, he peered at the markings and continued, "Not to worry. I'll have the dog put down once I'm back in Magell." He smacked the map and its clipboard against the alchemist's chest and walked toward the twins. "How's the progress on your mission?"

Abbadon, who leaned on one leg the other crossed over it, studied his nails as he answered, "Progressing."

"And that means?" Ranquer asked.

Apyllon raised his eyebrows in delight as his brother shook his shoulder length black hair from his face and looked around the room in boredom. "It means that we will complete the mission once we've got Nysa under our thumb. You may have your priorities, but we have our own as well."

Faster than was possible, faster than any fae should be able to move, Ranquer was in Abbadon's face. With impressive strength, Ranquer grabbed both Abbadon's shirt collar and Apyllon by the neck. Apyllon struggled for air around the hot fingers clasped around his throat as Ranquer pulled them both close.

"Listen closely, *boy*. I have opened the world for you with the truth of who I am. Do not forget that you are on this world only because of me." Ranquer shoved the twins away, continuing his rant as he turned away. "I should send you both back to Inferna to incubate until you've remembered who you are. And why you are truly here."

Apyllon massaged his neck, soothing what felt like scorch marks. Still, he straightened his spine and glared at Ranquer and his brood. "If you hadn't been so careless in your other form, perhaps you would have two bodies to facilitate your plans." His voice was icy, smooth, like his father—the version he still associated as his true father—had taught him.

"You two have been on this world for far too long. It's a common side effect in this place to become *slack*. *Lazy*. I should have propagated you years ago, and let my other children take your place."

Abaddon bristled. "You mean the child who had the Realm Leaper in her grips and allowed her to escape." Dullahan's eyes snapped to Abbadon, then slid to Cian who seemed rather amused himself. "That's right, lovely. Your brother there shared that little story with us."

Dullahan shot forward, and Abbadon met her. They exchanged quick blows, neither of them landing any successful punches, each of them ducking and blocking with expertise.

Ranquer exploded. "ENOUGH!"

Blue flame crawled along the wall, incinerating one of the alchemists where he stood. The other ran for cover in the glass enclosed tube. A horned shadow stretched along the wall and Abbadon and Dullahan were blown apart from each other. Muscle and tendon bulged from Ranquer's neck as he wielded cold flames, whipping each of his offspring. Apyllon was struck across the face, and he careened back against the wall, head ringing.

Ranquer's form rippled, and Apyllon—for the first time in his life—felt fear. Ranquer's voice grew so that it permeated through their bodies, vibrating within the stone walls and their minds. "All of you are a disgrace. The process has already begun, and if we are to be truly freed, I must depend on you."

The flames dissipated. Released, Apyllon slouched down the wall, sweat beading his entire body. Dullahan's head lolled to one side and Abbadon was similarly slumped on the floor.

Ranquer's steps clicked as he approached Apyllon. He squatted so they were nearly nose-to-nose. Ranquer grabbed Apyllon's cheeks and squeezed. "You will retrieve the insignia by the Harvest Festival, or I will end you." Apyllon's head cracked against the wall as Ranquer roughly pushed him back. "When we have the insignia, *before* the Harvest Festival, that will give us enough time to travel to TupaGuara and finish what we've started."

"We?" Abbadon croaked with disdain.

"Right," Ranquer replied, turning to face Abbadon. "Cian, Dullahan, and myself will travel to TupaGuara. You two can stay here and rot for all I care."

Dullahan gathered herself from the floor, dusting her jacket and cracking her neck in an unsightly angle. Without further word, she followed Ranquer into the dimension traveling machine. With a shove, she dislodged the frightened alchemist who still crouched there. Cian, who had already pushed to his feet, began pushing buttons and pulling levers.

The whirring and humming were a dull irritant compared with the thoughts thundering through Apyllon's mind as Ranquer and Dullahan disappeared from his world.

Chapter 15

❧ ✳ ❦

Sage looked up at the swish of robes to see Shiphrah approaching the table where she was hunched, showing Gavin the result of a week's research. She sat up straight, massaging a crick out of her neck from being bent over her notes and fresh texts for hours.

After more than a week of diligent study, Sage was disappointed by the lack of progress, seemingly unearthing more contradictions than anything else. So far, very little had popped up about the history of the Borean tribes. It was looking more and more likely that the viable option would be to establish more estates in Jordynia. But with all of the new refugees relocating there, Gavin had raised legitimate concerns about the sustainability of the plan.

"So what exactly is it that you two are looking for?" Shiphrah asked, placing a satchel on the table before perching on its edge. She hadn't visited much since they'd arrived. In addition to bringing refugees to the shores of Jordynia, many had arrived at the Rafalatriki for healing. Shiphrah had been kept busy overseeing the operations of the complex. Even now, Sage could make out the telltale signs of a bag full of tonics and potions by the way it clinked as she'd put it down.

"A miracle," Gavin answered, plopping into a seat he'd dragged to the table moments earlier.

Sage, looking back to her notes, hummed her agreement."It's taken nearly this entire week just for me to understand your dating system," she said. "You'll have to thank Daveed. He's an excellent scholar, and was exceedingly patient with me. I think I finally understand how your culture has categorized dates."

"You know, I had never considered that would be a challenge," Shiphrah mused. "So, what have we found?" She pulled up her own chair and sat close to the table, eyeing a timeline that Sage had sketched on a roll of paper, which now sprawled across the surface.

"Well, I think I've got a grasp of the schism between tribal fae politics and what later became nations. Daveed has an excellent theory, which other historians seem to agree with, that there was both a dwindling and a refinement of power in the fae people. That, and humans removed themselves from the mix—" Sage pushed several papers of scrawled notes toward Shiphrah "—I'd actually like to learn more about that some other time, *but* more importantly, we learned that Borea hasn't always been so cold.

"That's important, because it does imply that some sort of cataclysmic event caused the change in environment. It also indicates that tribes in Borea had survived much the same way other tribes did. What I also found interesting," Sage continued, shuffling through a stack of papers, "is that very little has been recovered of the Borean tribes. There's very few artifacts, which is just fascinating, if you think about it—"

Shiphrah held up a hand, halting Sage. Chuckling, she said, "My, you have learned a lot in a short time."

Sage took a long breath, and then laughed at herself, pushing the hair from her eyes.

Gavin quirked a smile, unable to stop himself from admiring Sage's passion for problem solving. But that smile slid away as he turned his focus back to Shiphrah. "Sage's research has given me some thoughts on how to solve what could become a very dangerous problem, but we've yet to find anything promising. If I can't convince Micah to move, and take his horde of angry fae with him, Felysia will have two fights on their hands. And neither fight would be an easy one to win."

Shiphrah nodded. "So, what's the timeline?"

"Next Firstday," Gavin answered.

"Firstday?" she asked, her head cocking to the side in perplexity. Then, a knowing smile spread across Shiphrah's face, and she broke into laughter. "Oh, that's clever Gavin. I assume you've picked a barren, flat piece of land?" Gavin nodded. "So, a moonless night, without anything to cast shadows. Very, very clever Gavin. Can he shift?"

"He cannot, at least, not to my knowledge." Gavin leaned back in his chair, crossing an ankle over his other knee. "At least this way, I know he can't use shadows against me."

"Except, if the moon is dark, that's just one giant shadow," Sage murmured.

"Shit," Gavin muttered, stilling with the thought. "I don't think it works that way."

"Let's hope not," Sage retorted, still looking down at her notes.

⚜ ❋ ⚜

Meliza swiped a sword across a dummy propped up in the ring. With her other hand, she threw her spear, hitting another dummy dead in its gut. She'd spent the afternoon swapping her sword and spear hands so that both were equally trained. A good warrior was always balanced, and she practiced as hard, if not harder, as any of the sentry under her command.

She ran forward, practicing the movements that had been ingrained in her as a youngling. As second born, she had always known it would be her job to protect her older brother once he became King, something he immediately terminated when he made her Commander of the City Guard. Still, she took her training seriously, especially with the disasters taking place in Nysa, and all the trouble that had followed Sage into this world.

As she finished her final strikes with her practice sword, an enchanted note flitted to the ground at her feet. She stooped to scoop it from the ground, noting the curling script as Symon's neat handwriting.

Meliza~

I'd hoped to hear from you about the progress of Gavin's situation with Micah. With the lapse of communication from him, I expect we are still at an impasse. Unless you have any new information you'd like to pass along?

In the meantime, Zeke has been busy securing the border of Bithnia, but the City Sentry have been holding their own. The Royal Guard has been operating smoothly, and the enchantments have been updated to the highest degree. I'll admit, I'm surprised you've allowed your lieutenants to take on such responsibility. Yet it seems your training has prepared them well for your delegation—which is a credit to you.

I can't help but think though, my dearest sister, that this is most out of character for you. You've not taken a day off in ten years. So perhaps on your next visit, we can chat about what's actually been keeping you in Mystaira. It couldn't be a certain someone keeping the Truth Teller from the city, could it?

Also, I should let you know that it seems Petra has attempted to sever her bond with Zeke. We should be on guard in case he is unable to perform his duties should she be successful. I wish there was more we could do, but she nearly killed me the last time I tried visiting. I am truly at a loss at what more can be done for her.

Be safe, sister.

-Symon

Meliza folded the note, shoving it into her pocket. There was a lot to unpack in such a short message.

She allowed herself a wry twitch of a smile at the thought of her ever astute brother being so close to the mark about her true reasons for lingering in Mystaira. Was he ever wrong? There *was* a certain someone who had kept the Truth Teller in the countryside and away from the City Guard she commanded. And, despite her reluctance to do so in the past, she knew her lieutenants were well trained for the delegation she'd bestowed upon them over the last few months. They'd done a fine job of providing top notch security for the capital, and would continue doing so until she returned.

The other part of Symon's missive was far more burden-some. Petra, it seemed, was getting worse. For a fae to sever the bond from their partner was rare, and it seldom worked out for those involved. While it was entirely possible for a fae to survive the breaking of a bond, it was not without debilitating consequences. If Petra succeeded, Zeke would likely be bedridden for a very long time, leaving a gaping hole in their team. A situation Meliza wasn't prepared to accept.

If Meliza thought she'd have any chance of escaping the Obelisk with all of her body parts intact she'd have left Mystaira to try and reason with her sister. Remembering the last time she'd tried to tell Petra to "sober up and move on" had been enough to keep Meliza at bay. An annoying scar still lingered on the inside of Meliza's upper arm where one of Petra's shadows had snapped at her. Petra had always been more prone to intense emotions than Meliza. It was likely what had caused such a rift between them at an early age.

Heaving a sigh at the thoughts and *feelings* that swirled through her, Meliza turned to face the open gate that led into the training ring.

"Are you just going to sit there and stare?" she asked, throwing the words back at Delphia, who stood between the walls of the ring with wary eyes.

Shaking her curls free from her eyelashes, Delphia backed up a step. "No, I just..I was just—"

Meliza laughed, tossing her blonde braid behind her shoulder. "It's okay," she said with a cock of her head, "I don't mind an audience." She punctuated her remark with a quick wink that seemed to snap Delphia out of whatever stupor she'd been lulled into.

Standing taller, Delphia balled her fists and lifted her chin. "It's not that, I just came to ask you something," she said, rigidly.

There was a tingle in Meliza's fingertips that suggested there was more to the statement, but she let it slide. "Mmmkay—ask away."

Delphia tilted her chin, jutting it out slightly in a way that would have seemed comical if Meliza hadn't found it so dang cute. "Well," Delphia began, squeezing her fists tightly at her side, "Well..." her voice faded, and she looked away.

Quickly, she shook her head once more, straightening her spine and looked at Meliza directly in her eyes. "Well, I was thinking that it might be beneficial for me to have some training." She gestured with her hands at the equipment hanging in the ring, "You know, similar to what you taught Sage."

"And why would you need that?" Meliza asked, walking to a rack that held wrappings. Carefully, she unbound the cloth she'd wrapped around her knuckles earlier.

"Because, in case you haven't noticed, I'm kind of important to this estate. And, if anything were to happen here...I just...I just think it would be wise for me to be able to defend my home...my family."

There was tremor somewhere deep within Meliza when Delphia explained her questioning, but another part of her body answered with the clanging feeling of pride. Yes, Delphia should know how to defend herself, and she'd be more than pleased to teach her. "What about your brother?" Meliza pushed.

"Gavin? Well, he's always off dealing with one emergency or another—"

"I meant, Levi."

"He can hold his own. He's been grappling with Lilly since he was a tot, and since we've moved here, he's actually practiced with some of the farmhands in the area. But if it came down to a fight, I won't leave my family vulnerable. Better to have us both work side by side."

"Good. That's good." Meliza rolled her shoulders, ideas running through her mind about where to start Delphia's training. "Do you have the proper clothes for training?"

Delphia scoffed. "You mean you expect me to run out and get a whole different outfit just to train in? No. I'll train in what I'll most likely be fighting in, skirts and sandals."

"Excellent point," Meliza said, beaming at Delphia. "You know, you'd make an excellent strategist."

"I don't want to be a strategist. I just want to run this estate and keep my family safe." Delphia squeezed her fists again, bringing tension to her shoulders.

That this really mattered to the female was obvious, but asking for help like this was totally out of Delphia's comfort zone, thought Meliza. Okay, enough playing. "Alright. Go ahead then, take your position over there, in the center of the ring."

"What, now?"

"Why not?" Meliza said. "You've clearly got time in your schedule if you came all the way over here to ask. Why wait?"

Delphia's face fell, and Meliza half expected the female to find some excuse to turn down the offer. But, as if she'd given herself a mental dressing down, Delphia shook the curls from her face, lifted her chin in that endearing way again, and strode to the center of the ring.

"Alright, then." Squaring her feet beyond the width of her shoulders, Delphia bent her knees and lifted her hands, hands curled into fists.

"Your form isn't half bad," Meliza said, striding over to her new pupil. "Bring your feet in just a little." Delphia did, her gaze focused on a spot on the distant wall. "Go ahead and show me what you know."

Delphia's fists dropped slightly, and she cut her eyes toward Meliza. Furrowing her brows, she brought her fists back up and gave the air a few hesitant punches.

"Come on now, you can do better than that."

Huffing, Delphia began again, this time striking with a little more fervor, but still not anything Meliza would qualify as skilled.

"Okay, that's enough."

Delphia dropped her hands, glaring at Meliza. "If I wanted to be teased, I'd have just gone and found Levi."

"I'm not teasing," Meliza said gently, a placating hand held out towards the female. "How am I supposed to teach you if *I* don't know what *you* don't know? Now, fists back up."

Delphia complied, although her facial expression held an edge of bitterness, which had Meliza swallowing a smile. She didn't want to upset this female, but she was utterly captivating when provoked.

"If you ever do get in a fight, start by using your palms," Meliza reached over, flexing the fingers that Delphia had been squeezing shut. "You are fortunate that your hands are not soft. Your years working the farm have made your hands tough, but fists are rarely as strong as we think they are. Instead, I want you to practice striking with the heel of your palm, moving your weight from your back foot to the front."

Meliza demonstrated by reaching up and guiding Delphia's hand through the motion. Then she gestured for Delphia to try on her own.

"Good!" she felt genuinely pleased as Delphia practiced the strike three times in a row. "That's very good."

Meliza grabbed Delphia's hand as it was still outstretched, holding it in the air. Standing in front of her, Meliza had to use every ounce of her professionalism to stay focused. Delphia had already developed a sweaty glow that complimented her dark hair and hazel eyes so perfectly, she could hardly tear her gaze away. A stray bead of sweat was making its way towards the dip between Delphia's breasts, which did little to stay Meliza's concentration.

Meliza pulled herself together, intent not to make Delphia uncomfortable. It wouldn't do for her new pupil sense where her thoughts had nearly drifted. "When you strike, you want to strike here—" she placed the heel of Delphia's palm square on her nose, "here," she said, moving the palm to her mouth, "here," her windpipe, "or here." She moved Delphia's palm to her sternum, where a tiny joint was located. "Remember, as you strike, you want to continue the hit *through* their body. Don't pull away once you've made contact."

Delphia's breathing ticked up a notch. "Am I supposed to hit you now?"

Meliza chuckled. "You sound so eager."

"No, I just—"

Without answering, Meliza stepped to the side, reaching within her earth power to create a dummy of semi-soft clay. The clay shivered and grew until it had taken the form of the merchant who had tried to cheat Delphia of the full invoice he owed the week prior. "There," she grinned, "that looks like a worthy opponent."

Delphia let out a low growl, and Meliza felt her face split into a bright smile. "Have at him."

With vigor, Delphia began striking the clay dummy, denting the figure with every hit she dealt. Meliza, pleased with how quickly Delphia had taken on her training notes, nodded with each satisfying punch. When she'd run the path from his nose to his chest, Meliza reformed the figure and commanded Delphia to switch sides.

"Again."

Strike. Strike. Strike. Strike.

"Again."

Delphia repeated the exercise until her skin shimmered with sweat and her breaths came out hot and fast. With every move, Meliza was given a clear picture of Delphia's strong muscles. Meliza ran Delphia through several more movements and strikes, including a forward kick aimed right at the dummy's groin which Delphia practiced without even attempting to hide her glee. Meliza's fingers itched to run themselves through the dark curls that bounced with every move, even as they became damp with sweat.

The sun had begun to set. The time had run by faster than Meliza realized. "Brilliant! That's enough for tonight."

Delphia let out a satisfying groan as she let her arms fall, her head dropping back. Meliza couldn't help but chuckle as the ever so assiduous Delphia stood so relaxed and even a bit disheveled. The sight made Meliza shiver, and when the most brilliant smile broke across Delphia's face, Meliza knew then and there she'd seen the most beautiful sight she would ever see.

Clearing her throat when Delphia cut a glare, noticing her attention, she grabbed a tin of salve she'd taken to storing on the racks by the gate. "Come here," Meliza gestured. "This will help with the soreness."

With the slightest tinge of wariness, Delphia adjusted the sleeve of her homespun chiton and walked over to Meliza. The looseness in Delphia's muscles now, compared to the start of their training session, was marked. Having a moment when the tension could be expelled from her body seemed to be a rarity for the female who bore the burden of her family and her brother's estate.

Delphia reached Meliza's side and gave a long, free inhale and exhale that Meliza could feel through her own abdomen. How long had it been now since she'd walked around without a knot in her own stomach?

Meliza took one of Delphia's hands, scooping a dab of salve and rubbing it along Delphia's palms and wrists making small circles with the salve until it was absorbed into the thick skin and calluses.

"Do you give such attention to all of your sentry?" Delphia asked, a smile evident in her voice.

Meliza looked up to see a gentle smile playing around Delphia's lips, making her even more beautiful. She smiled in return, saying nothing.

Grabbing another scoop of the salve, she began rubbing it into Delphia's other waiting hand. As she used the pads of her thumbs to knead the paste into Delphia's skin, moving to sweeping motions with her palm up the sides of her arm, Delphia stiffened.

"Is that sore?" she asked.

"A little," Delphia replied, air hissing between her teeth.

"Here," Meliza said, pushing against the tightly knotted muscles that ran up Delphia's forearm.

Delphia exhaled sharply as Meliza continued to work, but stood stoically, accepting the discomfort in a way that impressed Meliza—she knew how painful massaging a sore muscle was. Delphia really was a contrasting mix of a fae female; she had an inner strength and worldliness Meliza had rarely witnessed in any fae, male or female, yet was so vulnerable and soft...

Through her wandering thoughts, Meliza realized Delphia was now very close to her. Close enough that she could feel her breath on her shoulder and the heat from her body. Delphia's arm extended along Meliza's waist and a trembling thrum of tension blossomed between them.

The tell-tale mark of arousal mingled with Delphia's usual scent, and Meliza knew Delphia could smell it on her too.

"Better?" Meliza asked, carefully releasing Delphia's hand but not stepping away. She wanted to hold this moment close to her. This female did something to her she'd not experienced—ever.

"Yes," Delphia whispered, leaning so close now, Meliza could feel her answer. A tingle crept through Meliza's fingers.

"Liar," Meliza teased, just as quietly.

This close, Meliza could make out the flecks of amber in Delphia's eyes that sparked in the sunlight. A breeze fanned across them both, sending their curls dancing across their faces, entwining briefly with each other. Images of being entwined around Delphia flicked across Meliza's mind, and she knew Delphia could sense her own arousal heightening as her breath hitched.

"I suppose I should go," Meliza said, not breaking eye contact or making a move to actually leave. She itched to reach out and pull Delphia to her. Even as she could feel Delphia's breathing increase, a yearning clearly written across her face, in her body language, in her scent.

Even so, she would go. It was the right thing to do, not muddying their friendship. She wouldn't push—

Delphia pulled Meliza into her. The electricity of their lips touching tentative and then more passionate ran right through Meliza's body. Delphia pushed her hand into Meliza's hair, tangling in her blond curls.

Giving herself up completely, Meliza matched Delphia's intensity, any considerations of complications flying out of her head. It felt so right, Meliza couldn't fathom how they'd resisted this for so long. She pulled Delphia in by her waist, her hands moving down to her hips as she staggered back into the wall. Delphia wrapped her arms around Meliza's neck, pressing herself tightly against Meliza in a way that made her head spin, her breath coming in short gasps, their lips racing across each other at a feverish pace.

Their hearts thundered against each other, bodies writhing as they wrung themselves out, exploring and tasting. Meliza wrapped her hands further around Delphia's waist moving down until she found the muscular slope of her backside. With strong hands, Meliza pulled Delphia in until she straddled her thigh. Panting, Delphia's legs parted, never once releasing Meliza's mouth.

Without needing any prompting from Meliza, Delphia began grinding her hips against Meliza, her center warm against her thigh. Meliza reached up with one hand and took a fistfull of hair, pulling her head back to reveal the delicate skin that skated down Delphia's throat. She ran her tongue down Delphia's throat, tasting her salty sweat.

A gasping, delicate, perfect moan tore from Delphia's throat, making Meliza's knees weak, her core heating up to boiling. The smoky sound filled Meliza with such satisfaction, she repeated the movement up the other side of Delphia's throat. Meliza could feel Delphia's want through the layers of her skirts and her own leggings. She was close, and damn if that alone didn't have a similar effect on her.

Meliza gripped Delphia's ass firmly, pushing her to continue riding her leg as she released Delphia's hair and pushed her hand up Delphia's waist until it found her breast. All the while, Delphia clung to Meliza's neck, her neck arching back, little moans escaping her. Meliza swept her mouth down, finding purchase at Delphia's breast. Through her dress, Meliza bit gently as she found Delphia's nipple. With a cry, Delphia's body found its release, shuddering and shaking with the force, bringing Meliza almost to the point herself.

For a moment, they remained against the wall, clinging to each other. Meliza nuzzled Delphia's hair, relishing the scent of apple blossoms and arousal that danced around her. Slowly, Meliza straightened, supporting Delphia as she regained herself, but glad she had a wall at her back as her own body yearned for more.

Meliza cleared her throat. Her core throbbed with desire as she took in Delphia, her cheeks rosy, her eyes glazed with satisfaction and unfettered desire.

"I suppose I should go now."

They remained locked together, smiling into each other's eyes. Slowly, Meliza let her arms fall away from Delphia's waist. She wouldn't push for more than Delphia was ready for. But if anything was certain, Meliza *would* be back for more. This female enchanted her. Especially now. Her core gave another throb of desire and she knew that Delphia could feel it, too. There was such intensity in the way their bodies had responded to each other. This wouldn't, couldn't, be a one time thing.

Nevertheless, she had never been one to push herself into someone else's life if she wasn't wanted. She took a deep breath, straightening to her full height, only an inch or so taller than Delphia.

She was just getting ready to side-step, to leave the training ring, when Delphia reached back for Meliza's hand. "Don't," she said quietly.

Arching her eyebrow in question, Meliza let the statement hang in the air. Everything suspended around her as if time itself had stopped. Meliza had watched as those she cared for had given themselves over to the bond that tied fae partners together. It wasn't that she'd taken such a thing lightly. On the contrary, she'd long ago decided that romance would only hinder her from the duty she'd been born to bear. Now, she was wondering if she'd been mistaken.

"Stay," Delphia whispered, stepping up close to Meliza again so their lips nearly met, and pressing herself against her again in that way that had her heart rate picking right back up to where it had been only moments before.

"Where?"

"With me."

Searching her eyes, Meliza could see the conviction and knew in that moment that Delphia felt exactly the same for her as she felt for Delphia. She reached forward, wrapping

Delphia in her arms, and casted them both into the room that had become her own.

Lips locked, hands frantically pulling at shirts and skirts, Meliza walked until Delphia's knees collided with her bed. Before Delphia could sink onto the mattress, Meliza asked, "You want this?"

"Do you think I'd let you get this close if I didn't?" Delphia's answer held the slightest bite of humor to it.

"Excellent point," Meliza said, before ripping her own shirt off her body.

Goddess, bless it, she thought. Today had finally given her something to be thankful for.

Chapter 16

Tick, Tock...

Fucking Tick, Tock.

That had been all that was written on the simple note delivered to her along with the robes she had last seen Suda wearing. A gash had been torn through the back of the garment, stained, presumably, with Suda's blood. The Dark Born were taunting her. They knew she was powerless to their demands. And yet, they held onto her brother, doing Goddess knew what to him. She had escaped to the gardens to try and clear her mind, but every step seemed to echo the note.

Tick, tock.

Tick, tock.

Tick. Tock.

Tick.

Tock.

They were running out of time.

They were running out of options.

What were they going to do when the Dark Born and their Shadow of Death were on their doorstep? What were they going to do when their wards failed? What were they going to do when everything fell down around them and they all ended up prisoners again?

A vice wrapped itself around Aryael's heart, and she sank to the white gravel ground, a hand thrown incautiously out to one side in an attempt to catch herself. She'd ended up in the rose maze, hardly noticing the blood trickling down her wrist from the hand that had grasped at the roses as her knees had crumpled beneath her.

Breathing was impossible. Her inhales were too short. Her exhales, non-existent. Her fingers buzzed with painful tingling as her body filled with too much oxygen.

The world blurred, tipping in and out of focus as that sound followed her. Sweat dripped down her back, coated her palms, mixing and stinging with the thorn cuts. Her heart spasmed, and she thought it was possible it might explode inside her chest. A deep pain radiated down both sides of her neck, and she had to clench her teeth through it.

Tick.

Tock.

Tick.

Tock.

Tick tock tick tock tick tock tick tock tick tock ti—

"Breathe." The command broke through the clearing with such force and dominance it shattered the rattling in her body. Warm hands pulled her up, and though her legs felt like wet paper, she allowed herself to be propped up. Hands grasped her by the head, forcing her to look.

Symon's cold blue eyes pierced through her, and he spoke into her mind.

"In through your nose. Good, now hold." She did.

"Exhale. Slowly through your mouth." She did, though her lip quivered.

"*Again.*" And she did. "Again," he said, this time aloud.

Once she could feel the air return to her lungs, she asked with a quavering voice, "What if we can't do it?" Her voice, barely a whisper, felt like betrayal.

"We can. We just have to have faith," he answered. But she felt the lie. He was worried, too. Symon gave her a watery grin, and she leaned into his chest.

"I'm afraid," she sobbed, tears like acid running down her face.

"So am I," he said. "But when have you ever let fear stop you from what must be done?"

She laughed then. He was right. It was nearly fifteen years ago that she first hatched her plan to get herself into King Symon's sights. She hadn't thought he would end up being her lover, much less her husband, but she'd known their alliance could end their suffering. She'd gotten herself into so much trouble, the Regent of the sector had been forced to send her to the maximum security work-camp. The only reason they'd kept her alive was because the Dark Born had their sights on her. Thankfully, she never discovered why the Dark Born had been interested in keeping her alive. But she'd been scared then, too. She had thought there was no possible way she could ever lead her people to freedom. She felt as hopeless then as she felt now, but that hadn't stopped her.

"There's my girl," Symon breathed, an unsteady smile on his lips.

"Thank you," she said, squeezing the lapels of his jacket. "What do we do now?"

"I think it's time we get our people involved." Symon answered as if it were obvious what he was thinking, but Aryael hadn't a clue what he meant.

"How so?" she asked, pulling her head back so she could see Symon more fully.

"I think it's time we make a sacrifice."

A sacrifice to the Goddess could be made in dire times. It required deep intention, and it had to indeed be a sacrifice. The only thing Aryael could think of were the stores she and Symon had facilitated building in the case the Dark Born did attack. Those reserves of food and water could last their people a month, best case scenario. Without the reserves, they would be risking the safety of thousands of people. "You can't be serious," she asked.

"I am. Already, the Goddess has come to you *and* Gavin. Don't you think she's invested in the outcome?"

"Symon?" Aryael wasn't sure if he was serious. That kind of risk wasn't something to be taken lightly.

"If we do it during the waning moon, we might have our answer by Firstday," Symon continued.

"You mean to complete a city-wide sacrifice by tomorrow evening?"

"I do." Symon stepped away, shoving his hands into his pants pockets. "And I think you know that is our best option as well."

Aryael breathed heavy, the tightness in her chest returning. This couldn't be happening. This couldn't be the answer. She thought the one thing she could control were the reserves; *that* was the one thing in their power. And he wanted to throw it all away.

"Faith, remember?" Symon's voice slipped across her mind like a silk sheet.

Her breathing slowed, and she nodded, keeping her eyes shut. She breathed deeply, willing herself to stop panicking.

"Faith," she repeated. "Okay. We will send out the word this evening."

"I'll get Zeke to use the sentry."

Aryael squared her shoulders, and looked behind her. Without realizing it, she'd run herself to the center of the maze, where a rotating statue sat. As it turned, Aryael looked at the three forms of the Goddess, and wondered if she'd been running this way for some greater purpose all along.

The sun set behind the palace gifting the city with a blessed reprieve from the sweltering heat. Summer had hit its highest peak and was now in its decline. And yet, the heat and humidity clung to the city like a lover loathe to retreat.

The word had raced across the city of Veritasailles that a mass sacrifice would be made in honor of the Tri-Goddess, a plea for sanctuary from the devastation that the Dark Born had reigned in Nysa. Already, reports of Dark Born forces laying siege to townships and villages that had been ravaged by the Shadows of Death had burned throughout Felysia. Panic had become a tangible thing in marketplaces and the temple.

Aryael stood on the bottom step of the white, looming temple before her. A large, golden-crusted bowl of fire was ablaze on the top stair. Further beyond, the marble pillars billowed into the sky like the masts of giant ships, support-ing the squared ceiling of the temple. Behind her, fae from all walks of life gathered with their own offerings, all to be burned at the feet of the rotating statue depicting the Tri-Goddess's three forms.

Haestas. Goddess of Day. Ruler of wisdom and inno-
vation.

Anthephone. Goddess of marriage and fertility, granter
of growth and profit.

Dianis. Goddess of Night and the hunt.

Aryael had been born on Haestas day, fitting as she was
gifted with such a strong affinity over wielding flame. But
she'd been feeling drawn to Dianis. She wondered if the
Goddess of the Hunt could protect them from the darkness
that seemed to be looming over all of their fates, creeping
closer with every rotation of their world, Panchia.

Flanking Aryael and Symon, sentries loaded with reserve
goods lined the stairs. Aryael, carrying a sealed clay pot of
honey, walked up the stairs, Symon accompanying her with
a vase of oil. As they approached the flames, they both
began muttering their prayers beneath their breaths.

Symon, dressed in his temple clothes, raised the jar of oil
above his head as he finished his prayer. The simple white
muslin somehow made him appear more regal than any
finery he wore in the palace. His silver circlet resting atop
his head glinted with the dancing flames before he dumped
the oil into the bowl of fire. Fire erupted, sending plumes
of white smoke into the air. The smoke swirled as Aryael
stepped up to the bowl, Symon shifting to the side.

She wore the temple clothes of her girlhood: bold red
fabric draped down her body, embossed with gold embroidery depicting the symbols of each of the Goddess's forms.
Draped across her head was a long headscarf that flowed to
her mid-waist, covering her hair completely. As she finished
her prayer, asking the Goddess of the Hunt for her protection and guidance, pleading to Haestas for wisdom, and begging the Goddess of profit for security, she lifted the jar of

honey toward the sky. Her sleeves drifted down her arms as she squinted against the sunbeams spearing high above the temple as it sank beneath the horizon. "Please, Goddess, do not forsake us yet," she whispered before tossing the honey into the flames.

The crackling of burning sugar and splintering glass followed her as she took her place next to Symon. Black, swirling smoke erupted as soldiers stepped up to the bowl, tossing in the stores that she and Symon had acquired over the last years. All that hard work, forfeited to a Goddess who may or may not answer their call.

Symon's hand squeezed her, "Faith," he whispered.

"Faith," she answered back, and she felt the squeeze of hope around her heart. Tears rimmed her eyes as her people continued up the stairs, adding to their sacrifice: grain, paper, medical supplies, bounties galore, even a few toys contributed by the sparse youngling of their city. All thrown into the fire and accompanied by pleas for sanctuary.

Aryael stared across the steps of the temple, her eyes rimmed with tears she couldn't let fall while she stood stoically for her people. Zeke, Meliza, and even Gavin stood across from her, having already given their sacrifices. A hole seemed to pulse between where Meliza and Zeke stood, a space where Petra should stand. Against her better judgment, Aryael's eyes slid back to the Obelisk where the faint swirl of shadows could just barely be made out. If she squinted, Aryael thought she could make out the stark figure of Petra, now more phantom than fae.

Aryael prayed quietly to the Goddess, "Anthephone, please watch over Petra. Bring her home, Goddess. Let her come home." Symon squeezed her hand once more, and she looked over to him in time to see a faint shudder as he held back his own tears. How cruel could fate be? To make her love watch as his sister ripped herself away from those who loved her, just as their enemy had once done.

Darkness settled, but the fire raged on. One of the many priestesses who presided over the temple stepped forward. As one, the people below the steps dropped to their knees, bowing their heads. With a clear, ringing voice, the priestess began singing. The song cascaded across the crowd, weaving its way through the temple's campus. As she finished singing, she began a chant, a common call and recall prayer that everyone would be familiar with.

"May your hunting for profit lead to wisdom; May the light of wisdom lead to growth; May your growth guide you as you yearn for night."

The circular flow of life created by the Goddess seemed everlasting in that moment as Aryael gazed out across the crowd, all gathered to worship together. In that moment, a fluttering ember of hope blossomed and she allowed herself a moment of gratitude. She only hoped, this one time, the Goddess would spare them all the cycle of despair they'd experienced before.

Perhaps, maybe this time, their hunt for wisdom would lead to bountiful sanctuary.

Chapter 17

❖❖❖❖

Abbadon followed the sounds of shrill keening echoing along the hallway.

A lesser male may have felt the sounds shivering through their skull, causing a frisson of fear and loathing to creep up their spine, a jellying of the legs as delicious adrenaline coursed through their veins. But the twins weren't lesser males. Pain and suffering were their joy. The screams and pleading of their captives the fulfillment of their spirit.

He'd been waiting over an hour for his brother in the courtyard, desiring conference with him before they had another meeting with Cian and that irritating female, Dullahan, Ranquer's agent who had recently become a fixture within their stronghold.

An hour of waiting hadn't done anything for Abbadon's mood, which was surly at the best of times. Finally, he'd asked one of their legion if they'd seen Apyllon. The male, a hulking beast with barbed points protruding from his eyebrows, grunted, saying that the twin hadn't been seen all morning.

The news had grated Abbadon so much he'd finally begun his quest to track down his counterpart himself.

It wasn't that Apyllon's absence was unusual; it had long been a habit of his twin's to venture off on one of his little —side sports. Apyllon's bloodthirst was notorious in Speridisia, there'd been plenty of times Abbadon had walked in on his brother satiating himself with a member of their own legion. This in itself was fine with Abbadon—until it began to affect their numbers.

Now was not the time to chance their strength on foolish whims. They needed to focus on finding those damned insignias *before* Ranquer's henchmen, in order to secure their power on Panchia.

The wailing was coming from their key prisoner's cell. The Queen's brother had given them both hours—weeks— of sport. He. Just. Would. Not. Die. It had amused Abbadon at first, but then became boring. His twin's fascination with continuing to torture that battered piece of meat became redundant. The door was shut fast, blocking his entrance, the keening growing louder before Abbadon could burst through. It wasn't the sound of Suda wailing, that sound hadn't been heard for some time.

No...the sound came from Apyllon.

Abbadon's power slammed from him, shattering the door as he breached the threshold. The sight on the other side caused the anger that always seemed to simmer beneath his skin surge to life.

"Are you fucking mad?!" Abbadon shouted, throwing a bowl of used dressings at his brother.

On the floor, next to a motionless Suda, sat Apyllon. Gore spilled from Suda's face, Apyllon's own face smeared with blood. Their captive's eye had been crudely removed. There was a wild look to Apyllon, the sound coming from him a mixture of glee and hysteria.

"We're expected to meet with Cian and Dullahan upon the hour, and here you sit, entertaining your fucking fancy."

A sharp inhale, a wheeze of excitement peeled from Apyllon. "We shall consume all the power from within brother. Come!" He rose from the mess he'd created on the floor, his black clothes shining with blood. "Join me, brother!" Apyllon made to reach again for Suda's prone body, but Abbadon whipped out with his shadows, constricting his brother.

"Enough," Abbadon growled. "Your *obsession* will lose us the continent."

Apyllon struggled against Abbadon's shadows, his own shadows growing thicker. "Release me," Apyllon hissed.

But Abbadon did not. If his brother could not control his whims, he would. Reaching into the Darkness, Abbadon let his shadows roll through the room, climbing up from the seams of the floor and the walls. Still struggling, Apyllon let his own shadows begin joining the fray.

"Release me, brother. Or perhaps you have come to finally find out which brother is the strongest." Apyllon's serpentine voice raced through the shadows, seizing Abbadon. Cackling, Apyllon wrenched himself free from Abbadon's grip, disintegrating into smoke and reappearing behind him.

Abbadon felt the prick of a blade at his throat, his brother's breath hot against the side of his face.

"Maybe, after I've finished you off, I will go after those wretched mortals." The wetness of his twin's spittle as he spoke churned Abbadon's ire.

Apyllon clearly believed he had the upper hand, but his bloodlust had always dulled his wits. With breathless speed, Abbadon reached up with a taloned hand, his brother missing the shift, and sliced at the arm holding the knife. The blade clattered to the ground, and Abbadon whirled to face his brother.

Apyllon was waiting. He struck out with a fist, aiming for Abbadon's nose. But Abbadon fought with more finesse. He easily ducked out of range, coming up on the other side. Quickly and efficiently, Abbadon grabbed his brother's arm, then struck him once in the face then the ribs. Finishing him off, Abbadon swept Apyllon's feet from beneath. He still gripped the offending arm, causing Apyllon to spin in the air. Apyllon landed with a meaty thud, his face and stomach meeting the floor with added force as Abbadon followed, digging his knee into his brother's back.

Abbadon knelt, his hair sweeping the floor as Apyllon struggled to break free of his hold. Abbadon brought his face close to his brother's ear. "We both know I've always been the better fighter," he said through clenched teeth. "If it's Darkness you seek, just say the word and I can rip your heart out through your back." Abbadon's talons reformed, pricking Apyllon's wrist and back for emphasis. "Or, if you'd like to join me in meeting with Cian and Dullahan, perhaps we can get back to our true purpose."

Apyllon stilled, stopping his struggle beneath Abbadon. "Or maybe I'll just wait and slit your throat while you sleep."

"Even better," Abbadon hissed. "We both know you'll never be able to best me."

A manic laugh rumbled from Apyllon his body going limp, the signal that his bloodlust had run its course. As he stood, Abbadon grinned as his brother rolled onto his back, the eyes no longer rimmed with the wildness that had been there before. Abbadon reached out, offering a hand to his brother and pulling him to stand. "Please, brother, save your next venture into insanity for when we face our enemies."

Apyllon dusted his shirt, grimacing slightly at the blood that coated it. "And what would be the fun in that?"

"Excellent point," Abbadon laughed. "Come, let us get cleaned up, then we can go find out what this hellhound of a woman wants from us."

Abbadon slung an arm around his brother's shoulder, adding pressure to keep him from turning back to the body that had so preoccupied him earlier. In truth, Abbadon couldn't give a damn what Apyllon did with the body on the floor. He did, however, want to get Ranquer and his agents out of his stronghold. The sooner they found the insignia, the sooner they could do just that.

A short while later, Abbadon and Apyllon walked into the room containing Cian's beeping, buzzing, whirring machines. Apyllon was now dressed in a clean black shirt with deep blue embroidery lining the collar and sleeve hems. His brother had opted to pull his hair away from his face, and only a few rebellious curls dared to escape the hold of the leather band.

Dullahan leaned against a shining silver machine with bright, bulbous buttons scattered across its surface, one booted foot tapping, inspecting her nails. Her hair was also tied in a slick ponytail, tight as ever. "Why set a meeting time, if everyone intends to arrive late?" she side-eyed the brothers as they entered the room.

"I've wondered the same thing," Apyllon replied, stalking toward the agent. "Good to see you, too, Dullahan. You're looking...sour as ever."

Dullahan rolled her eyes, scoffing to herself.

"Where's Cian?" Abbadon asked, taking the seat the alchemist usually occupied.

Dullahan shrugged, returning her focus back to her nails. Abbadon spun in the chair, peering at the notes that lay scattered across the table. Some of the forms and figures were unrecognizable to Abbadon, while others were easily deciphered. It appeared the alchemist had some theories on where to continue their search for the insignia. There was no question that they hadn't fallen in Nysa. They'd already searched, using several flying machines operated by Cian, Dullahan, and a handful of other alchemists brought through the tube just for the event.

Cian had practically vibrated with frustration when not a single insignia was found. It appeared the beaky little alchemist was counting on finding them for his own motives. The alchemist's trembling frustration had been a source of humor for the twins for days after.

Just then, Cian bustled through the doorway, muttering to himself, his cheeks splotched with pink.

"Nice of you to join us," Apyllon said, mischief in his smile.

There was a gleam in his eye that made Abbadon stiffen. It would not do for his brother's bloodlust to resurface, not in front of the agents who could use that information against them.

Huffing, Cian glared at Apyllon. "Well, if you must know, I am late because I had to clean up a mess left behind by *someone* else." The implication was clear. Cian had been in Suda's cell, cleaning up after Apyllon. "Need I remind you that this space is a laboratory. We require a level of *cleanliness*."

Apyllon pushed away from the wall he'd been leaning against, coming close to Cian. "And need I remind you whose home you're staying in. Whose food you've been enjoying all these months."

Cian had the good sense to blanch slightly, breaking eye contact. Abbadon took the opportunity to stand.

"Now that we are all here, why don't you fill us in with what you've discovered, Cian." Abbadon could tell the squat mortal still seethed, wanting to lash out against Apyllon with the strange magic that writhed beneath his miniscule frame. Abbadon assumed it was the same magic that made the Realm Leaper so powerful, by mortal standards, at least.

Cian continued glaring at Apyllon through squinted eyes, but he began speaking. "I believe I've calculated the most likely region to search for the missing insignia." Dullahan sharply pushed away from the machine she'd been lounging against, her focus now fully on her peer. Cian pushed his glasses up on his nose, turning to face Abbadon, also eager to hear more about what Cian had to say. "I've used micro-drones to record storm patterns across the oceans. Unfortunately, I appear to have lost any that flew into Meropoli territory—"

"That'd be the mortal defenses. They don't even allow birds to pass from the sea to their borders, too afraid of shifters potentially crossing over unknown," Abbadon provided. And he was likely correct.

The mortals had discovered weapons that worked against even the strongest of fae. Elm proved especially fatal to fae, and the trees only grew on the Meropoli continent. The mortals had discovered ways to create arrows, swords and spears with the material. They'd even developed explosives they could fire en masse which would release hundreds of barbed elm projectiles at a time. If they were nothing else, Abbadon found mortals to be especially cunning. Maybe even a little vicious. He liked that about them.

"Interesting," hummed Cian, his gaze becoming briefly clouded with thought. Abbadon had no doubt the alchemist was wondering what kind of discoveries he might find on the continent. "Nevermind that," Cian continued, shaking his head. He grabbed a clipboard from the table. Clipped to the top sat a map of the Meropoli continent, notes scratched across the front. "I've calculated—based on the shape and assumed weight of the objects— that they've landed along the east coast of Meropoli. If we can get our drones on the continent, we will have the insignia well before the Harvest Festival."

"What does your President want with those trinkets, anyway?" Apyllon asked, settling into Cian's chair and kicking his feet onto the alchemist's work table.

"That's none of your business," said Dullahan, smacking the Dark Born's feet off the table. "What matters is that he's likely to send us all back where we came back from if we fail him." Her words were sharp as iron. "I prefer not to be returned to ash."

"Fair point," said Apyllon. "Well, I can tell you one thing, Cian, you won't be getting your little buzzing discs over on the mortal continent. Leave it to us," he said, standing. "We have a contact on the Eastern border."

"A mortal contact?" Dullahan asked.

"Oh, yes," said Apyllon, leaning back in his chair with his hands behind his head, "a very wicked mortal."

Two weeks later, Abbadon stood next to his brother on the prow of a ship. In the distance, a stone fortress rose from the precipice of a bone-white cliff face. A fine layer of grass blanketed the ground around the stronghold, but little more life dared to take root around the area. The treacherous mountains, which made stealing onto the continent doubly dangerous, speared into the sky behind the fortress. The sharp, rigid outlines of peaks spanned the horizon before the Dark Born in both directions, north and south.

In front of them a ship with grand, navy blue sails made its approach. The sails stood out against the painfully white cliffs as men rowed the boat closer to their own. Abbadon peered through the hazy sun, a slippery grin stretching as he spied the mortal they'd come to visit.

Once the approaching boat finally made its arrival, the two ships were fastened to each other, a long plank stretched out so that Abbadon and his brother could board the mortals' ship.

Standing in the center of the main deck, surrounded by men wearing military garb, stood the man they'd come to see. Sahl was regal. In the sunlight his white robes hanging below his knees shimmered as bright as the cliffs behind, a purple cape fixed to his shoulders. His hair was meticulously styled in the way that was popular in Meropoli—curls plastered to his forehead so they all swept in the same direction, mimicking the motif waves painted on the border of the ship. A thin, gold circlet spanned the man's head, emphasizing the manner in which he held his head high so that he looked down his nose at everyone, no matter their height.

"Abbadon. Apyllon," Sahl greeted, one hand perched on his hip, the other held effeminately bundled with the thick train of his cape. "It's been an age. I was surprised to receive your letter."

"Oh, dear Sahl," Abbadon began, "you sound as though you've missed us."

"I was under the impression you two were no longer interested in the products I have to offer."

Sahl looked questioningly between the two brothers. For years, when Sahl was just beginning his political climb in Balam, a city on the Eastern front of Meropoli, the man had supplied the twins with a steady stream of slaves. Some of the caged men and women had become fodder for Apyllon's bloodlust, others had become entertainment thrown to their soldiers to do as they pleased. But even that had become dull and boring to the Dark Born, and eventually they'd ceased doing business with Sahl. Based on the fine robes and golden circlet, the man had done just fine for himself.

"You always had such a fine selection of goods," Apyllon crooned as he caressed the railing of the ship. Abbadon caught a glint in his brother's smile as his teeth elongated into sharp points, another improvement that came from Suda's sacrifices.

The soldiers, who moments before had appeared idling around the ship doing nothing much, hadn't missed the pointed teeth, responding instantly to defend their leader. Spears with sharpened elm points were pulled back, archers perched on the mast drew their bows. Apyllon chuckled darkly as he took in the soldiers surrounding them, pacing slowly in a little circle around the deck. His insolence only proved to wind the soldiers even tighter, spears inching further back, bows drawn more taut.

"Now, you wouldn't want to do anything reckless, Sahl. If your men kill us you'll never hear the offer we've come all this way to bring you." Apyllon's words snaked through the crowd, his staccato voice breaking through the tension mounting throughout the ship.

"By the look of things, it is not *I* who is acting recklessly," Sahl replied, eyeing Apyllon's teeth, his voice oily with contempt. He may not refuse the Dark Born's coin, but it was clear he did not approve of their existence or their amusements.

"We've come to offer you an alliance. You get us what we want, and you'll be a King among your people." Abbadon grinned widely, slipping his hands into his pockets in a show of disregard. "Just imagine—you and your people reigning over all those in Meropoli. Your financial empire would become a physical empire."

As Abbadon spoke, he stepped closer to Sahl, watching his expression as visions of power played across his mind. The licking of the lips. The quickly darting eyes of a man calculating exactly to the penny how much additional wealth this deal could get him. The man was greedy—*ravenous* for power. He'd excelled at building an empire of wealth for decades, dealing in both legitimate and black market business holdings. And yet still the man wanted more. He yearned for the entire continent, a continent which prided itself on its egalitarian government. A government which scorned those who desired might over others.

And where there was this level of desire, Abbadon knew he could find that little chink that would get him exactly what he wanted. Whether or not the partners in his dealings ever got what they wanted wasn't Abbadon's concern.

It mattered not to him that agreements made in greed and in haste often turned sour for the recipient.

"All you have to do, Sahl, is find something for us. Then, when the time is right, we will back you as you take over the continent. The Dark Born and Balam will become allies, and together, we will conquer the world."

"What is it that you seek?" Sahl asked, an irritating shrewdness coming into his expression

Careful, Abbadon thought to himself, don't scare the sheep.

Apyllon reached into his pocket, pulling free a square piece of parchment before passing it to his brother. Abbadon, in turn, passed it to Sahl, who unfolded it and stared at four drawings, precisely rendered by one of Cian's clever machines.

"We are in need of four medallions. What you hold are the specifics of each. They must be the real thing, not replicas. It's likely they fell from the skies roughly six months ago. Have you heard of anything similar?" Sahl's answer would determine Abbadon's next move.

His bushy eyebrows pinched in a rigid V, Sahl inspected the drawings. "No," he answered, "I can't say I have." Quickly, Sahl handed the parchment to one of his attendants, "But we hear there was news of a strange occurrence of weather along the East Coast, followed by a freak meteor shower. I'll have my diplomats look into it."

"So we have a deal, then?" asked Apyllon.

Sahl nodded. "On one condition."

Abbadon carefully arranged his features into a look of polite enquiry, quashing down the rage that filled him at this mortal's audacity. "That is?"

"You seal the deal via a bargain."

Oh...the clever mortal, thought Abbadon. "Fine, I bargain with you, on pain of death, that we will fulfill our side of the bargain. I promise, by the Darkness, that if you provide us with the insignia, we will provide Balam, and you—Sahl —assistance in conquering Meropoli."

"And," Sahl added, "you will commit yourselves to being allied to me and my heirs."

"Agreed," Abbadon and Apyllon replied in unison.

Sahl extended both hands, shaking each of the Dark Born's outstretched hands at the same time. Abbadon watched with glee as the mortal pulled a face, signaling that the bargain was in place.

"We'll see you soon," Abbadon said as he stepped back.

With a rush of power, the twins exploded into shadow, sending the soldiers rushing Sahl back to his ship. Elm arrows fired after the swirling shadows gleefully dancing through the air, out of range of the missiles.

Once Sahl and his ilk had retreated, and the ships had separated, the Dark Born both landed back on the deck of their ship. Apyllon waved mischievously as their ship pulled away.

"What a shame," Apyllon mused. "The poor mortal was clever in making us make that bargain."

"Yes," said Abbadon, smirking with glee. "It's a shame bargains only work on those who have souls to offer."

Apyllon's crackling laughter raced along the boat as the sails cracked in the wind, their ship heaving back towards Speridisia.

"I can't wait until he finds out," Apyllon shouted.

Chapter 18

❧ ✳ ❦

The door creaked open as Sage pushed against it with her shoulder. Her arms were laden with notebooks and scrolls she'd borrowed from the archives. She'd have to return the scrolls by morning, but needed a change of scenery.

She'd hardly left the archives all week. Only three days remained before Gavin's meeting with Micah, and she felt no closer to finding a solution to his problem. Perhaps she'd been kidding herself into thinking she could actually help. It wasn't like she'd been some sort of genius academic back in Techeduin. She hadn't even finished secondary school. Any research experience she had came from her time in the library with Stiofanie and Ian.

A familiar pang rippled through her chest. Grief had been fleeting lately, but spending so much time in an academic setting had caused her to feel sharp stabs of sadness more often. Allyra's words kept flitting through her mind, and she couldn't shake the feeling of intense curiosity about what the goddess had meant about Ian's rebellion against their government.

If only she'd had more time with him to discover the truth.

Sage made her way to the table that sat on the far side of the room. In her world, she would have described the room as a studio apartment, complete with a small kitchenette with space to store baked goods, beverages, plates and glasses, and other knick-knacks that made their stay a little more convenient. While they couldn't actually prepare any meals, it was nice to get away for a bit to the quiet of their own room and snack on fruit and crackers, or maybe a nice glass of wine.

That was what she wanted. A big, full glass of wine.

Sage tossed her work on the table, then grabbed a glass and bottle from one of the small shelves. She'd just finished pouring herself a glass when Gavin cast into the room, plopping into one of the wingback chairs next to the fireplace. It'd been far too hot for a fire, but the chair was set within the pathway of the open window, allowing occupants to revel in the evening breeze wafting into the room.

"Good evening," Gavin said with a smirk. He'd left to travel back to Veritasailles when he found out they were making a sacrifice to the Tri-Goddess, and Sage hadn't expected him to arrive back so soon.

She took a sip of her wine and walked to the chair next to him. "Hello?" she asked, noting the playful grin on his face, the slumped nature of his shoulders. "And what have you gotten yourself into?"

"Mmm...cards. Meliza was back from Mystaira and was playing Zeke, but I hadn't taken any coin with me. So, we made the wagers drink." Gavin shrugged his shoulders as he spoke, and a playful giggle followed his explanation. "It was good to see him smile for a bit," he said, nestling into the chair.

"Gavin?" Sage asked. "How long did it take you to cast here?"

"Hmm?" he asked, opening his eyes that had begun to drift close. "It was just a short little jump. Just here to there," he explained, clapping his hands.

That didn't seem right. As far as she knew, the journey was too far for a fae to cast from the palace in Veritasailles all the way to the Rafalatriki. Even Raphael had taken a full day, with a large meal and a rest between casts. It took Meliza one stop in between to get to Gavin's estate from the palace. But Gavin was clearly drunk, so perhaps he could give her more detail in the morning.

"I just missed you," he muttered, still smiling, but eyes definitely closed.

"Alright, flyboy," Sage said, setting her wine on the side table. "Why don't you go lay down in the bed before you pass out on the chair?"

Gavin chuckled. "Are you trying to sleep with me?" As she leaned in, he tapped her nose.

"I think actually sleeping is all you're going to do," she said, grabbing his hands and pulling him up. He barely budged. "Come on," she grunted, trying to heave him out of the chair.

Without warning, Gavin disappeared, leaving Sage plummeting onto her backside. "Ow!"

Gavin reappeared in the bed. "Oops...next time you should just cast with me," he chuckled.

"Gavin, I can't—" snoring interrupted Sage's attempt to remind him she wasn't fae, and could not, in fact, cast. "Whatever." Slightly annoyed, but mostly relieved to have him back, she gave him a soft kiss before draping a blanket across his prone body.

Suddenly feeling rejuvenated, she grabbed her wine and headed back to her notes. Perhaps a fresh perspective would help jostle something in her mind. The sweet taste of berries and citrus played against the scrawling notes filling her notebook. She unwound the scrolls, scanning through them for anything that might be new information.

After two glasses and four scrolls, Sage sighed, huffing a stray piece of hair from her eyes. Nothing. Not one iota of information seemed compelling. Sinking into the chair at the table and crossing her arms, she glared at her notes.

There had to be something, she thought for the umpteenth time as she snagged her glass and drained the remaining wine from it. A strong breeze rustled through the open window, chilling the room, and Sage hummed in relief. It was becoming hotter by the day.

A loud snore from Gavin punctuated the sound of paper rustling in the breeze, making Sage jump. A strange sensation crept through her body. Something akin to whispers—she couldn't tell if they were around her or inside her mind—tickled her senses. Could Ranquer have found her again? The thought chilled her to the bone.

The breeze whistled in again, this time winding itself around her ankles, which was in itself strange. A momentary cocoon of security settled around her, stilling her fears. Whatever this was, it wasn't Ranquer. The strangest sensation, like a tug around the center of her spine, pulled her to her feet. Without thinking, she walked from the room, leaving the door wide open behind her.

A part of Sage's mind questioned why she was obeying strange compulsions to walk around the building by herself late at night. The little voice wondered how she was remaining so calm. She hadn't the faintest clue where she was headed as she walked, down, down, down. Back into the archives, but past the books, tomes, and scrolls she'd been pouring over for days. Fae light twinkled in glass and bronze lanterns as windows became more and more scarce.

As she descended, the archives changed from books and scrolls to tapestries. Beautiful woven tapestries clearly depicting events from Panchia's history, some of which she now recognized. Several edges were burned and torn. Some looked brand new, and she wondered if they were recreations made after the conflict with Speridisia. Others were missing whole sections, and Sage pondered at what great efforts it must have taken to preserve such grand pieces of history.

The tug grew more intense, yanking her past the tapestries and down a narrow side passage. The fae lights grew more and more frequent, becoming the only source of light as she reached a section of the archives dedicated to artifacts. The upper recesses of the walls grew dark and shadowed the further she walked.

A chill grew, laying heavy on her shoulders and raising goosebumps on her neck and arms as she continued. For the first time in ages she wished for a shawl to cover her bare shoulders. The muslin of her skirts felt too thin and flimsy against the cool of these deep catacombs of knowledge.

Glass cases holding weapons on one side, and medical instruments on the other, ran the length of the hall she'd entered. Dim light flickered in the distance, and she turned to peer back across the expanse she'd traveled so far, the hallway seeming to disappear in the fluttering lights.

Sage stepped up to a case holding wicked looking curved swords. The swords boasted large, scooping guards that flowed from the broad, swooping blades. The handles twisted into emerald encrusted pommels. Beneath, a placard glinted in the fae-light: *The Swords of Artemia—Felysia's First Queen*. Sage shrugged, moving away from the case. From her research, she knew that Artemia had been a fierce warrior queen. She'd nearly conquered the entirety of what was now considered Nysa, but had acquiesced at the request of her youngest son who had fallen in love with a Nysan-tribal prince. Their union had fortified Nysa as a nation of its own, and solidified Nysa and Felysia's long reaching alliance.

The tug at her spine grew more insistent, and Sage muttered, "Okay, okay."

Something about the power being wielded to get her to wherever she was going didn't feel malicious or dangerous. Perhaps she would be caught out as a blindly trusting fool, but logic told her, once she'd had time to consider it, that the Rafalitriki was probably the last place in Panchia that Ranquer could attempt to control or track her. In fact, as she walked, she noticed that the power that pulled at her had the distinct feeling of belonging to this world. Not only that, it lacked the bite that had followed whatever possessed the Dark Born and their power. This insistent, nagging power was new to her. In some ways, it reminded her of Gavin, but that thought was fleeting as the power gave her another nudge to continue walking.

Crossing the hallway, Sage stopped in front of another glass case, this one filled with vials that had been sealed and labeled, alongside what could be a primitive syringe and needle. She peered up at a portrait hanging above the shelves depicting a male and female clasping hands. The female held a silver rod topped with a lotus. The male grasped a hazel branch, blooming with flowers.

Beneath the male, hazelnuts scattered the ground and two serpents, one green and the other blue, wrapped themselves around his arm, their expressions somehow joyful. Sage tipped her head to one side, becoming oddly fixated with the serpents when she started, a jolt running through her body. The male's ears were clearly rounded, and the arm that clasped the female's hand had oddly familiar blue tattoos spanning up onto one side of his neck.

"No, way," Sage breathed, looking closer.

The placard beneath the portrait was titled *Portrait of Amare and Eron, Heroes of Healing*. Eron...Eron with the rounded ears. Eron with the tattoos that looked nearly identical to those worn by a certain Goddess of water. Sage stepped back, looking at the portrait with awe. Was it possible that Eron was from her own world? Her mind raced with questions, scrambling for any information she could recall about the couple.

Before she could gain any traction, the tug that had brought her this far yanked hard, nearly sending her off her feet. Stumbling, she continued down the darkened hallway. She tried clearing her mind, to get her brain to focus on whatever intuition was controlling her as she walked briskly, further and further away from Amare and Eron's piercing stare.

Her feet faltered as the tugging changed, seeming to pull downwards for a moment, making her stop. On one side of the hall stood a glass case holding what Sage was positive was a dried and ancient corpse. Scaly lips peeled away from browned teeth. Tightly bandaged arms lay bound against the chest of the corpse. A hard shudder skittered down her spine as she stepped away from the macabre sight.

"Ow!"

She hit her head hard on another exhibit on the wall behind her as she'd backed away, the sound of her exclamation bouncing around the room.

Sage rubbed her head gingerly, softly cursing as she looked at the offending shelf lined with rudimentary tools. Bright white stone carved into a variety of tools—arrowheads, axes, spear tips—shone within the display.

The shelf stretched on and on as she walked down its length. Something in her gut told her this was why she'd been brought here. A little ways down a label detailed what was inside: *Weapons from Tribal Borea, circa 400 B.N.*

B.N....Before Naissance.

That was the schism that tore the fae people out of tribes and into nationalities. The time when humans had fled the continent of Panchia to populate their own continent, safe from the powerful beings that often enslaved them.

As Sage continued down the row of weaponry, the exhibit changed slightly. Where the weapons had all been startlingly white, the shelf became dotted with smooth, black orbs. The stone shone with penetrating brightness, reflecting back into Sage's face.

The placard on this section read: *Borean stone orbs: Uses, Unknown. It is theorized the orbs were a source of currency amongst many tribes. Research suggests that the two popular stones were the result of a fallen star that struck Borea hundreds of years prior to any evidence of Borea being populated. The white stone is a result of the intense heat generated from the blast which occurred after impact. It is unknown where the fallen star originated.*

The orbs buzzed with familiarity. There was only one other place she'd seen such a stone. Memories of Ian flashed back to her as he'd handed her the Egress Key. There in the center of the clock-like device had sat a round, black stone. There was no denying these two were related. It had been flat in the center instead of spherical like those on the wall. But Sage was positive they were the same material, wrought by the same galaxy.

Ian had often droned on about alchemical properties. Hadn't he told her about how he built the Egress Key? If she were honest, she often tuned him out, but this seemed important. This seemed relevant to something.

The tantalizing, ethereal whispers flooded through her mind again. This was something, this was something! If she could just remember what he'd said.

Something about...about its magical properties. It was like...a...

Oh, what had he called it?

A conduit!

Realization pounded Sage's body as she finally grasped the significance of what she stared at. Borea had to be a hub for this material. This stone could act as a conduit for magic, or for power. And what they needed now, more than ever, was a conduit for power.

She turned on her heel and ran back the way she'd come. She had to get Daveed. Maybe he could fill her in.

"Thank you, Ian. Once again, you've saved me."

Her whispered prayer seemed to dance around her as the force that had guided her released her from its grasp. She ran through the halls, a smile playing on her lips as she bounded through the archives.

Maybe this would all work out. Maybe, just maybe, she'd done something to help.

Questions and doubts weaseled themselves into her mind as she ran, but she was done with that. After all she'd been through, she'd proven she could overcome the challenges she faced. And even now, she wasn't playing the victim to those who'd have her against her will. As questions tried to wrap themselves around her mind once more, she slammed them firmly down, building a stone wall in her mind, forcing them to remain at bay. Everything else could wait. She just had to finish this one thing, and then the next part of her journey could begin.

A sweet sadness built in her as she thought of what came next.

Next... she would begin the journey to discover her way back to her own world.

Next... she would have to say goodbye to what had begun to feel like home.

Next... she would have to prepare herself to say goodbye to the fae male who slept in her bed, and who had grown to embody everything that she'd ever dreamt home would feel like.

Where would that leave her then?

Chapter 19

❦✳︎❧

The hallway felt stuffy with so many bodies crammed into it, all of them staring at the shelf on the wall.

In a matter of hours Daveed had taken Sage to Shiphrah, who had sobered Gavin very quickly. Enchanted notes were then sent to Symon, Aryael, Meliza, Zeke, Raphael, and Delphia. Only Aryael and Delphia hadn't made the journey.

Symon, attending as his specter-self, crossed his arms, squinting at one of the larger black orbs on the shelf. "Somebody, please explain to me again what exactly this material is supposed to mean."

Shiphrah gestured for Daveed to speak.

Daveed adjusted the collar of his robes as all eyes turned to him, a tick Sage noticed became more prominent as more people focused on him. The scholar was soft-spoken, but his gentle demeanor hid a talent akin to wizardry when it came to locating hard to find resources. She could kick herself for delaying his suggestion to peruse the artifact's wing days ago. She'd wanted to be thorough and logical in her examinations, but her approach might have cost them precious time.

Tiny beads of sweat dotted Daveed's forehead, and Sage detected a tremble in the scholar's hands. She gently squeezed his arm beneath his robes, giving him an encouraging nod.

"W-well," he stammered, seeming to shrink in upon himself under Symon's imposing stance even as a bead of sweat decided to roll down his temple. He distractedly swiped it away.

Sage's heart squeezed for him. She wished she could have sheltered him from presenting to this august group of fae, gathered in his domain, whose presence only seemed magnified in this tiny space. But they needed his expertise.

The scholar stalled, licking his lips as his eyes swiveled from one fae to the next. "Go, on Daveed. We wait with bated breath." Raphael's encouragement reached Daveed with a hint of familiarity, a teasing nudge toward someone who was clearly considered a friend. Daveed responded with a wobbling smile before hefting a heavy breath.

Finally, Daveed continued. "This material was found shortly before the occupation of Felysia. It was discovered within a deep, clefted valley, along with the white material. We believe the shape of the valley suggests a fallen star made impact with our continent."

Moving toward the shelf, Daveed lifted a trembling hand to indicate the white material. "These weapons are actually made of a rare type of topaz. It's hard enough to withstand hand to hand combat, and as you see here, this spear may have even been used to hunt ice-leviathan before their extinction."

"I've not heard of topaz weaponry before," Raphael mused aloud. "You would think there would be more of it across the continent if it were so strong."

Daveed took a shaky breath, adjusting his robes once more. "What's actually interesting," he said, continuing to gesture at the spear, "is this specific metamorphic mineral could have only developed under the immense force and pressure caused by the falling star, which makes it incredibly rare as we have no evidence that it has been found in other parts of Panchia."

Sage grinned, she could tell that Daveed's immense knowledge and interest in his subject were winning against his nerves. She gave a discreet lift of her eyebrows to Raphael in silent thanks, knowing he had stepped in to ease Daveed into his lecture. Her friend shot back a conspiratorial wink as Daveed lifted his hand to gesture to the exhibit.

"And this," Daveed continued, stepping over to the shiny black orbs, "this is where things get especially fascinating. It's theorized that these orbs were used for currency, but there is no evidence that the Borean tribes used any sort of currency. In fact, it seems more likely they relied on a service-trade based economy. So the presence of these orbs is perplexing." Daveed pulled at his robe once more, loosening the collar as he took a deep breath. "These specific orbs were actually found placed around the only remaining structure erected by the Borean people. Many of them were laid out along tables, and others were arranged in a pile in what looked like a fireplace."

"Which," Sage interrupted, "leads us to what *I* am suggesting." Sage stepped next to Daveed, facing the row of fae who now stared at her, giving her an uncomfortable inkling of what Daveed must have been feeling. Gavin tilted his head with a grin, urging her to continue.

"You all might remember learning about my friend Ian," Sage began. Meliza coughed roughly, then covered her mouth as she tried to hide her outburst. Sage cleared her throat. "Right, well, he used a material called orichtium in his inventions." Sage paused, waiting for the crew to catch on. "This," she gestured at the orbs, "is orichtium."

When the faces of the gathered fae remained blank she shook her hands in frustration. "Okay, again...orichtium is a material that Thuledain has mined for—a century at least. It came from a distant planet in our solar system that had been broken apart. Pieces of that planet struck our world at some point in our ancient history and were buried in the crust of our earth. Eventually, alchemists discovered the material and found ways to use it."

"And how did they use it?" Meliza asked, arching an eyebrow.

"It's a conduit!" Sage replied.

"And?" Meliza said, one palm extended in front of her.

Sage resisted the urge to huff in frustration. "It channels magic, or in your case, power. I bet the Borean people used the orichtium to enhance their control over their powers. At least until their powers began to wane and they had to leave the north and join the tribes to the south."

"So, that means we could potentially have access to a material to build weapons *and* increase our powers?" Zeke said.

Symon turned to Sage, his eyes almost boring into her, not mind-reading, but searching her face. She could almost feel his thoughts racing as he pieced the information together. "Okay," he hummed, nodding as he thought, then turning back to the others. "I suppose we don't have very many other options. And we are running out of time to think of an alternative. Do you think Micah will go for it?" Symon looked at Gavin, his question hovering between them.

"If there's a chance for him and his raiders to profit, I think he might. What would Veritasailles be willing to invest for the materials they mine?"

"The Crown would be indebted. I'm not sure there is a number that could adequately define our willingness to come to an agreement."

"So add glory to profit," Gavin said. "I can't guarantee all of the raiders will agree to the offer, but I think Micah would."

"Then make it happen," Symon said. "Daveed, thank you for your expertise." With a wave of his hand, the spectre of Symon dissipated.

Stuttering, Daveed said his quick goodbyes before shuffling back into the safety of the archives.

"When do we meet?" Meliza asked.

"No 'we'. Just me," Gavin replied. When Meliza began to protest, Gavin held up both hands. "It was the only way I could guarantee his audience. He won't show if I'm not alone, and trust me," he continued when Meliza tried to interject, "he will know if I'm not alone."

Sage stepped to his side. "I still think Meliza's right. You should have someone go with you." Gavin shrugged his response.

"This is truly a dangerous position to be in, Gavin, can you trust him?" Zeke asked.

"What's done is done," Meliza huffed, pulling her hair back into a ponytail. "I'm heading back to your estate if you don't need me. Sage—I'll see you next week for training."

Sage groaned, making Meliza laugh.

Meliza, Zeke and Gavin began to walk away, the Commander still nagging Gavin about attending the rendezvous.

Raphael gave Sage a sweet smile. "Well done, my dear. This is an excellent discovery. You and I must talk about that compulsion you felt sometime, it's an interesting phenomenon and I'd like to learn more about it." He took a step toward the healer, "Shiphrah," offering a bow, his hand on his chest, before turning to follow the others.

Sage began to follow, but turned at the last second, grabbing Shiphrah's arm before she could leave, too, as a thought raced across her mind.

"Yes, Realm Leaper?" Shiphrah asked, eyeing Sage's hand.

"Sorry," Sage said, quickly removing it. "I just wanted to ask you something before you go."

"I'm listening," the healer said, a playful smile gracing her face.

Again, Sage was struck with her youthfulness, despite knowing the truth about the healer. "I was just wondering, do you know anything about Realm Leapers? Like, how they managed to move between worlds?"

Shiphrah adjusted the sleeve of her robe, pulling at the embroidered cuff. "Back in the earliest days," she began, "Realm Leapers arrived through a singular portal. No one is sure how it came to be, but it's what Maracadian society built itself around."

Shiphrah began walking down the hallway, continuing her explanation. Sage followed, eager to hear any information Shiphrah might have first-hand knowledge of. "You see, our world had begun changing rapidly. Nations were forming, societies advancing quickly. And during this time, Speridisia was experiencing strange phenomena. Word of fae-like creatures clawing their way up from the depths of the ground spread across our continent. It was like a plague. None of us sure at the time if they were summoned or just

—appeared. And if that were so, why they chose Speridisia as their invasion point.

"Felysia and Nysa allied themselves to stop the creatures from invading our nations, but Speridisia was lost to the demons who overran their land. That was how the Dark Born were created."

Sage nodded, familiar with that piece of history. "So, the Realm Leapers came because they sought to destroy the Dark Born. I've learned that already. But how did they travel? I have to assume the Gods from my world couldn't have stayed here for too long."

Shiphrah nodded. "Correct. From what I remember, Maracadia was the first portal that appeared. While the islanders never joined the fight against the Dark Born—insisting on remaining neutral—they did assist the Realm Leapers with accessing the portal. Eventually, the Realm Leapers were able to create other portals. The Rafalatriki is built upon one of them, actually." Shiphrah raised her eyebrows, anticipating Sage's interest.

Sage jolted. "So, it's possible I could realm leap from here?"

"Sadly, no," Shiphrah continued as they breached the artifacts hallway and continued into the archives. "Over time, the only portal to have remained intact is the temple in Maracadia. I'm not sure what sort of magic was lost, but the main island is the only place I'm aware of that still remains active. And by that, I mean the enchantments that protect the island came from the Realm Leapers."

"Which means I'll eventually need to find my way to Maracadia."

"Which means, you'll need to figure out how to cross through the wards protecting the islands, surpass the guards which undoubtedly protect the temple, and power the portal before leaping. I assume you still have the keys?"

Sage's shoulders dropped. The only thing Shiphrah could possibly be referring to were the Gods' insignias. And those were lost to time and space as far as she could tell. "Nope."

"Then I would suggest starting there."

⚬✳⚬

Short, dry grass brushed Gavin's feet, crunching slightly as he walked to the center of the field. Firstnight had arrived, the night of the rendezvous with Micah.

Not long ago, lilting hay had filled the field, but now it was clipped short after the harvest. Sage's outline stood out against the stark, moonless night. As much as he'd tried, she'd refused to concede when he told her he would be meeting Micah on his own. "He'll assume I'm a petty human at first scent. You need someone there to watch your back," she'd argued.

He had to admit, trusting Micah after all these years to follow through with his own demands had unsettled him. Gavin fully expected him to arrive with at least one fae as back up, even if they remained nestled in the hills beyond. Having Sage there put him a little more at ease. Not that he worried he wouldn't be able to hold his own against Micah and another fae. No. Sage's presence would help assure that he didn't completely lose his shit and do something stupid, like kill them both in an unnecessarily gruesome way.

Even as he thought that, a surge of power ran through him. He took a deep breath, instead leaning into the grounding feeling of Sage's presence, her arm brushing against him. A thrill of energy hummed between them, and he resisted the impulse to grab her hand. A soft breeze played against his skin, cooling his forehead where beads of sweat had just begun to form. The quiet felt hollow compared to the staccato of the last few weeks, and he rolled his shoulders to ease the growing tension.

Sage leaned in close, strands of her hair brushing his arm beneath the leather armor he wore. "He's late, isn't he?"

Gavin cleared his throat, nudging her playfully even as he stared across the field. A faint ripple of light disturbed the air against a hill rising far in the distance. It was the only surface that offered a hint of a shadow, and would require Micah to either cast or walk the several hundred yards to the meeting point.

"Oh," Sage muttered, catching the faint outline of a body in the distance.

Micah.

The Shadow Master began walking toward them, his approach slow, and deliberate. Sage blew out a quiet whisper. "That's Eshamel?" she asked sharply. Gavin nodded, not wanting to lose his focus. "Wow. I mean, don't get me wrong...but...wow."

"What do you mean, 'wow'?" Gavin hissed, still eying Micah's approach.

"I don't know," Sage said, her voice up an octave as she teased him. "Just, you know...you might have a run for your money." Sage hip bumped him, and he glared at her.

"Take it back," he hissed. Sage laughed, the sound startling the quiet night, and he caught her wink.

The figure disappeared, reappearing in front of Gavin and Sage. Standing taller than Gavin, and clad in black leathers with a cloak draped over one shoulder, Micah smirked at Gavin. His shaggy, sand colored hair was tousled by the breeze. Gavin was just able to make out markings along the column of Micah's throat and across his knuckles. Tattoos; tattoos that weren't there the last time they'd seen each other in the war-camps.

The same easy-going stance Gavin had admired as a boy preceded the Shadow Master, and Gavin grew more anxious to get their meeting going as the night stretched out around them.

"Your human friend has an interesting sense of humor," Micah said, his gravelly voice breaking through Sage's playful banter. "Whatever happened to coming alone?"

"My human *friend* insisted," Gavin shrugged. "You're late."

"Yeah. You chose the hardest fuckin' place for me to shadow jump in all of Mystaira, and on the darkest night. I had to cast twice just to find a place with enough shadows to jump." Micah stood squarely on both feet, both hands on his hips. "Not a bad strategy, runt."

"It's Lord Runt, now," Gavin jested.

"Yes, well, I suppose we should get to business, then." Micah rubbed the stubble growing at his chin. "Although it would only be polite to introduce me to your *friend*. She seems like someone I'd like to get to know a little better." A gleam entered Micah's eye, and Gavin balled his fists to avoid striking the male who once mentored him.

"His *friend* can introduce herself," Sage interjected. "The name's Sage, and I'm just here as a witness to your negotiations."

Gavin wasn't sure where she got that line from, but he was thankful for her quick thinking. He hadn't yet decided if it would be wise to trust Micah with information on who Sage was, and what she meant to him.

"Ah, well, can't blame a male for trying," Micah winked.

"Do you want to hear what the Crown is offering, or not?" Gavin said, cutting Micah and his impertinence off. Goddess, maybe Sage was more of a distraction than help.

"Not really, but I suppose you're going to tell me anyway."

Gavin sighed, rolling his shoulders once more. "Micah, I'm trying to do the right thing, here."

"Oh, goody. How about you give back what was meant to be mine then?" Micah spoke lightly, but there was an unmistakable challenge in his voice and stance.

Gavin scoffed. "You mean the title you left behind when you abandoned Felysia as we fought our way back to freedom?"

"Just because I didn't fight in what anyone else would have considered a suicide mission, doesn't mean I deserved to have my titles and lands stripped from me." Micah leaned forward, the challenge unmasked.

"It was the King and Queen's choice, Micah. Their prerogative when you disappeared and left us in the shit. We could've used your strength and cunning. But instead you left us to the wolves. " Gavin looked deep into Micah's eyes, pinning the male to the spot. "We got out of that prison, and you left, Micah. We lost good people who may have survived had you been there. Where have you even been all of these years?" The barest hint of hurt was evident in his tone, and Gavin cleared his throat to dislodge it.

"I got out!" Micah cried, slapping his hands to his legs. "I made it to Jordynia, and boarded a ship. I got off this forsaken land and tried to make it into Maracadia." Micah's voice wavered.

"So why did you come back?" Gavin asked. His body trembled. Facing Micah took him right back to the war-camp, pulling him back to the hopelessness of oppression and despair.

"I might have gotten kicked out of a harbor town or two," Micah muttered as he picked at one of his fingers. "But I didn't expect to come back to Felysia and find my entire inheritance given to someone else."

"Wait—" Sage said, "I thought you looked up to this guy? You spoke of him like he was a hero..." She looked at Gavin, confusion evident on her face, the words left unspoken echoing his own thoughts. The male he'd once idolized, who'd been his mentor for years in the camps had changed. Or maybe it was Gavin himself who had changed—he'd grown up.

Micah's attention whipped to her. "Hush, mortal." Faster than Gavin could anticipate, Micah shot forward, dagger in hand. But Sage was faster. Vines erupted from the ground, snaring Micah's outstretched hand and binding his legs. Apprehension flooded Micah's face as he looked from Sage to Gavin. "A sorceress?"

"Sort of," Gavin shrugged. Sage waggled her eyebrows, grinning with delight. "It doesn't matter why you've come back, Micah, or how the tables have turned for you. *I* am Lord of Mystaira now. The King and Queen decreed it. And the other properties and titles have been passed on, too."

"Then prepare to—" Micah began.

Sage flicked her wrist, and another vine stuffed itself into his mouth. "Shh...he's not done."

Gavin cleared his throat to stop himself from outright laughing. He'd never seen Micah so out of sorts, and Sage's unwavering support gave him the nudge he needed. "If you abandon your people, there has to be consequences. But, those consequences don't have to be permanent—*if* a fae can become loyal again.

"Like I said, the properties and titles are not up for negotiation...in Mystaira." Micah, eyes wild, looked at Gavin sharply, interest obviously overcoming him. "The Crown and I would like to propose another option. An option that would include property, titles, and an investment opportunity."

The vine in Micah's mouth slipped away, and he coughed. Sage leaned in to whisper, "I'm going to let you go now. Be a good boy." She gently patted him on the cheek, stepped back, and made a gathering motion with her hand. The vines slowly unwound from around Micah, slipping back under the ground to Goddess only knew where.

Micah took a moment to compose himself, rubbing his wrist and righting the leather tunic that had bunched up around his waist. Taking a wary step away from Sage, he peered at Gavin with sidelong eyes. "I'm listening."

"Have you heard much about the new threat Felysia faces with the Dark Born?" Gavin offered the question lightly, testing Micah's pulse on what was happening across the continent.

"No."

"Basically, they've discovered a way to wipe out whole villages in one fell swoop," Sage said.

"And how does that affect us?" Micah asked, looking at Sage.

"Besides your own potential doom?" Sage asked.

"It affects you because Felysia is in need of a weapon to fight back," Gavin said, putting an end to their quarreling before it could begin. "And *you* are going to get it for us. And earn your way back to the right side of history, with your fealty to your nation." Gavin paused, allowing Micah time to fully comprehend the demands this agreement would require of him.

"Go on." Gavin could see Micah begin to sway to his proposition. Whether he wanted to admit it or not, the male had a sense of vainglory. A chance to clear his reputation wouldn't be taken lightly.

"There's a material in Borea that can enhance and funnel power. The Crown is offering you, and your followers, the chance to go to Borea, mine the material, and profit from it in the meantime."

Micah adjusted his stance. He crossed his arms and looked from Gavin to Sage, and back again. He turned, paced a few steps, then stopped back in front of Gavin. "So let me get this straight: we agree to move to the frozen north, do manual labor for you, and that's supposed to be our consolation?"

"It's better than being thrown in their dungeons," Sage said. "You do realize Symon can control minds, right?"

"Only if he can catch me," Micah quipped, clearly unable to stop himself from engaging with Sage.

"You'd be Lord of Borea," Gavin said, "And the savior of Felysia. Not to mention the profitability of a substance that will literally change how our society operates."

Micah hummed, rubbing a hand across his chin then his lips as he thought. "And who decides land ownership?"

"I suppose the Lord of Borea would," said Gavin. "You know your people best. I've vouched for you to the King and Queen, and they've agreed you'd be the best candidate to decide who gets which parcels. There's also an option for anyone who doesn't wish to relocate to the north to move into Jordynia, but as citizens."

Micah looked at the ground, and Gavin hoped he was putting serious thought into the proposition and not stalling.

"That's the offer," Gavin said. "You'll have until sundown tomorrow to make your decision." Gavin thrust a slip of enchanted paper into Micah's grip. "Respond via writing, and I will coordinate the finishing touches."

"I'd take the offer, if I were you," Sage said, grabbing Gavin's hand as he stepped back.

"Make the right choice, Micah." Gavin nodded to the male he'd once admired, hoping he'd made a compelling enough offer as he and Sage shimmered into nothing, casting back to the Rafalatriki.

Chapter 20

✧✦✧

Queen Aryael stood at the round table looking down her nose at the male who'd attempted to pry Mystaira from her and Symon's control. Regardless of what Gavin said about Micah, a thrill of anger rushed through her as he fairly glided into the council room of leaders gathered to finalize his ascension to Lord of Borea.

She stared at Micah through narrowed eyes. It didn't feel right that Gavin had not received the same pomp and ceremony they were bestowing on this—ruffian. The day's events seemed trumped up. Or perhaps it was his swagger— akin to that of a pirate lord with the social graces to match.

He stood taller than Gavin with narrower shoulders. His face was covered in stubble, which only added to his mischievous air. To any other female, Aryael supposed, he would be attractive. Instead, she imagined that plenty of other fae would fawn over his toned, leggy physique and all-black ensemble. Her eyes tracked him as he came towards her and her mate with a sinuous, graceful walk. Even his tattoos, which ran up one side of the column of his neck and across both sets of knuckles, didn't detract from his rugged features.

I can't decide if I should be jealous of the male or not. Symon's voice broke through her own thoughts.

Aryael scoffed. *I was only thinking he's probably arrogant enough to have used his looks to persuade others to join him.* She cast a quick look at Symon and noticed a quick smile as he took his seat next to her. *Are we sure this is a good idea?*

Having a Shadow Master become Lord of Borea? Not at all, Symon answered. *But, he is one of the few of us who can transport weapons directly to us as we need.*

And that is not an advantage we can lose. Aryael's statement felt sour in her stomach as she sent it down the link connecting her and Symon's mind. "Let's get this over with," she whispered in his direction.

In the corner of the room, Acantha and Epyllo stood tall and silent, watching over the gathered council. Their welcome home from Bithnia had been full of relief, but rushed. Symon had ushered them into the council room just in time for these ridiculous, preening proceedings to begin. Ayrael clenched her teeth, breathing deeply through her nose.

Symon reached for the parchment sitting atop the round table. "If everyone could please gather round." As everyone took their seats, Symon continued. "This document will serve as an official record of what occurs in this room today. Gathered in this room are the required members to serve as witnesses as we bestow the title of Lord of Borea upon Micah." Aryael took a deep breath as Symon paused. "Before we begin, Micah, you are required to declare your fealty."

Aryael's chair scraped the floor as she stood, pulling her long sword free from the sheath that rested, propped against the table. The large ruby on the hilt glinted in the sunlight as she and Symon approached Micah's side of the table. Gavin stood at the same time as Micah, followed by Zeke, Meliza, Raph, and Seth. Iris, Jordynia's attending representative, slowly stood, holding her chin high as Micah knelt.

"Do you have the oath memorized?" Aryael asked as Micah bowed his head.

Gavin nudged Micah in the side with his knee when there was no answer. Micah grunted, then nodded his head, clearing his throat.

"Yes, I've got it," he responded in a surly tone.

Well, that's a good sign, Symon's voice whispered in her mind. Despite herself, Aryael felt the ghost of a smile as she placed the sword, balanced on its tip, in front of Micah.

"Go on, then, Shadow Master. Pledge your loyalty." Her voice was bright, victorious, and she almost hoped he would be tempted to stand and fight. The arrogance of others was always satisfying to conquer.

With an unwavering smile, Micah raised his head, locking eyes with her, then began his pledge. "I, Micah, former heir to the lands of Mystaira and as a citizen of Felysia, hereby pledge my fealty to Queen Aryael, Flame Wielder of Felysia, and King Symon the Destroyer and Lion-Born. I pledge my loyalty to my King, Queen, and Country. I pledge the support of my lands and the faithfulness of my people. I pledge my life to the honor of my Queen and King, from hereon until the Goddess of Three claims me once again."

A ripple of anticipation danced through the room as Aryael glanced at Gavin who gave her a knowing smile. That wasn't the oath she'd expected Micah to give, and she wondered what Gavin was up to having the male recite the same oath he'd given on her birthday.

None of that mattered now as she brushed off her questions and continued with the ceremony. She lifted her sword, tilting it so that it angled toward Micah's face. Rather than flinching like a civil fae, he smiled boldly into her face, still maintaining eye contact before leaning forward to place a kiss on the blade. She stared right back at him, forcing herself not to roll her eyes or react to his insolence at all.

Yes. This male was arrogant. Vain. Conceited to boot. But it appeared he had a strategist's mind. The kiss to her blade probably looked like a grand gesture of fealty to the Council who sat as witness. It would go a long way in reassuring those in Mystaira, and now Borea, that she and Symon had a grip on things.

"We accept your oath with gratitude, Micah." Aryael's voice rang with confidence, the tone still echoing through the room even as Symon's followed.

"Stand."

Micah did as he was told, and Symon gestured for the male to add his signature to the parchment. Once he'd scratched his name with the ink pen, they all took turns shaking hands and congratulating him.

"Tell me," Meliza's voice rang out as she approached the throng that now gathered around the new Lord of Borea, "was your change of heart made out of honor, or a love for profit?"

Micah pulled his hand free from Seth, who had just been welcoming him back into the fold of nobility. Aryael exhaled sharply to avoid scoffing out loud as the male cocked a half-smile. "And why would I answer the Truth Teller when I can simply keep you guessing?"

Meliza tilted her head in acknowledgement. "Well, at least your oath was spoken true."

That caught Aryael's attention. She'd like to hear more of this banter between Meliza and Micah. The luncheon that was to follow shortly would be the perfect opportunity to watch Meliza pick him apart.

"In honor of Lord Micah's fealty and our newfound advantage, please join us in the banquet room for luncheon," Aryael called out to the room.

Symon looped his arm around her waist as they led their guests down the hall and into the banqueting room. Where the full expanse of the room had been used for her birthday, a curtain had been pulled across one half of the room to create a more intimate setting, better suited to a small gathering. Along the long table centered in the middle of the space sat platters of fresh fruit, pickled vegetables, fried bean cakes, and baked fish. One of their attendants finished placing baskets of flatbread within easy reach of the group as they found their places at the table.

No seats perched either end at the head of the table, instead, Symon and Aryael sat across from each other at one end. Gavin took his seat next to Aryael, while Micah took the honored position next to Symon, and Meliza next to him.

Zeke was not in attendance and his absence stung Aryael, even causing a heated argument between her and Symon only the previous night. The ongoing malaise surrounding Petra was becoming seriously problematic and Aryael felt Symon, as Petra's brother, should intervene to support his friend and brother in arms.

Poor Zeke was a broken male. Each time he returned from his attempts to reconnect with his mate he came back looking utterly forlorn. But this last time had been truly haunting. He'd looked as if his soul had been forcibly ripped from body. Aryael couldn't imagine the emotional turmoil Zeke must be experiencing, and a part of her raged at Petra for putting him through it.

Taking in the table and those who sat around it, Aryael noticed that Symon's spies had disappeared again, and she wondered at where they'd been sent now. Not knowing vexed her. Of course she trusted that Symon would fill her in once they had a moment. But he could, of course, have simply whispered it to her through their mind-link. And yet, he'd chosen not to. The thought irritated her more than she cared to admit, particularly on top of the anguish from Zeke's absence.

Shaking her thoughts free, Aryael lifted a glass of wine newly poured by Symon's hand in a toast. "To Felysia," she called out to the table, "may the Goddess continue to find us in her favor."

"To Felysia!" the table exclaimed, everyone raising their own glasses. One by one, they sipped and as Symon lifted his fork and took his first bite, the table broke into side conversations.

"Micah, I'd like to thank you for your quick action and response to our offer," Aryael said. The words sat like lead in her stomach, though she was careful her tone did not betray her reluctance to offer gratitude.

"Yes, what a sacrifice he's made," Meliza quipped before lifting a forkful of fish and vegetables to her mouth.

"Well, I'm nothing if not magnanimous," Micah replied with another disarming smile.

"Hmm," Meliza hummed, clearly unconvinced.

"That's not the word I would have chosen," Gavin said, quirking an eyebrow as he raised his glass to his lips.

"I'm surprised you didn't bring along some of your own people," Symon said. "I would have thought they'd like to see their new Lord receive his title."

"Yes, well, it was decided that it would be a better use of their time to focus on the construction of our new homes," Micah replied smoothly around a morsel of food. "You see, although we've just been gifted a beautiful piece of land with unsurpassed views, unfortunately, there's not a lick of infrastructure."

He said the words lightly, the pleasant look on his rugged face still firmly in place. But there was the slightest bit of scorn to his words that Ayrael could see by the stiffness in his shoulders. Meliza hadn't missed it either.

Yes, thought Aryael, this male could be both useful and incredibly dangerous. A risky mix.

"You will let us know if you need anything," Symon continued, gesturing with his fork.

"Actually, I could use some enchanters," Micah said quickly. "Fortunately, two of my best leaders are master-ful earth wielders. We've developed plans for building and should be able to complete our housing project quickly." Micah paused to wipe his mouth with a napkin—he might look like a rogue but he was still very much a noble—before leaning back in his seat and eyeing Gavin. "However, we lack enchanters. And we wouldn't want anyone working for those blood-sucking abominations getting their hands on our product, now would we?"

"So you seek safety for your mines, and not your people?" Aryael asked, a slight acidic tone punctuating her words.

"Some might say those mines *are* our safety," Micah said, not missing a beat. "I'm sure the Crown would look much less favorably upon us if we had neither weapons nor magic baubles to offer." As if his brashness weren't enough, he added a rakish wink at the Queen.

Aryael found herself huffing another strong exhale. *Why did this male get under her skin so badly?* Of course, what he said was true, partly. It would be much easier to just imprison the former rebels if there were no orichtium. That said, a part of her railed against the action. She supposed it was because fae life had become so precious after the occupation; and now, with their new conflict with the Dark Born and President Ranquer becoming more dire? Well, it would be best if it was them that held all known sources of orichtium. Not the enemy. Goddess knew this was going to be a hard enough fight as it was.

"Excellent point," Meliza said, cutting in. "The city has contracted the best enchanters in Felysia. Provide me the date and time, and Gavin and I will escort them to you."

Micah nodded. "And what about you, runt?" he asked, gesturing to Gavin. "Have you nothing to say about all of this?"

"We have spoken," Gavin replied coolly, setting down the glass he sipped from. "You know what I think."

"You've always been a male of few words." Micah smirked, a devilish glint to his eye. "My father always said it was the quiet ones you had to mind. It seems he would have been correct on that front."

Aryael found Micah's confidence both loathsome and intriguing. The contradiction made her uncomfortable; she did not like being so unsure about herself, or someone else, for that matter.

"One would think that would have influenced you to talk less." Gavin's eyes sparked, and Aryael could see it written plainly on her friend's face that he felt very much the same as she did. Despite himself, he could not help but be pulled in by the rogue sitting at their table.

"Yes, well, my father was a pig-headed bastard. He did us all a favor by siding with the Dark Born and getting himself killed."

"Oh, so you've got daddy-issues," Meliza chirped, lifting her glass in a salute. "Welcome to the club."

A bark of laughter rang from down the table, and Aryael was surprised to find Iris choking on her wine. Slowly, the amusement rippled down the table, until several more noble-fae were laughing at the joke. Welcome to the club, indeed. All those gathered at the table had some sort of injury or strong feelings tied up where family was concerned. If nothing else, they had that in common.

Eshamel smiled broadly, and Aryael thought it was the first genuine reaction she'd seen from the male. "Nothing like trauma to build a bridge."

"Here, here," called Symon, raising his glass high.

Iris, eyes sparkling lifted her glass high again, "May we have the fortitude to withstand where our parents could not."

Aryael saluted the noble-fae down the table with her own glass, took a deep sip, and sent up another silent prayer to the Goddess that their manifestations would ring true.

✧◆✧

Gavin walked down the pristine white hallways of the palace. He'd intended to have a word with Epyllo, but the spy had disappeared before he had the chance to get him alone. Instead, Gavin found himself making a stealthy exit before he could get drawn into a lengthy debate with any other fae nobles. Things had been awkward with Seth since

The Seal had made itself known, and Iris had a reputation of trying her hand at matchmaking. The Lady had six daughters, all eager to find a partner.

No, thank you, Gavin thought as he turned a corner, the ivory inlaid front doors coming into view.

Before he could make his departure, a figure shimmered into existence, blocking the exit. "Leaving so soon, Lordling?" Aryael asked, a knowing smile on her face. "I'd hoped you would at least stay for a drink."

"The last time I drank with the likes of you, I required Shiphrah to sober me. She's still giving me crap for it." Despite his playful reply, a pea-sized pebble of guilt had dropped itself into his gut. It was possible he'd made his getaway in haste. How long had it been since he'd visited with his friend?

"Pfft," Ayrael replied with a waft of her hand. "I only meant come and join me and Symon. Something quiet and refined, not drinking games and cards with Meliza. She can drink anyone under the table."

Aryael looped her arm around Gavin's and pulled him in the direction of Symon's study. Her ruby dress swished as they walked, and Gavin's guilt pebble grew into an uncomfortably large stone as the heat of her hand warmed his arm through his shirt sleeve. Yes, he decided, he had neglected his friend these past months. He wasn't completely to blame of course. With all that they'd been facing it was no wonder he'd been absent from her. But now that he'd resolved things in Mystaira, he could offer Aryael his attention, at least for today.

"I'm proud of you," she said as they approached the double doors that led to the study, the warm oak contrasting with the bright white walls. "You've handled a situation with subtlety and aplomb that could've easily gone horribly wrong. Even with the rise of The Seal and all the added challenges that brings. A lesser fae would have killed the rebels and been done with it."

"I thought we all agreed: Felysian lives are too precious for that kind of behavior." Gavin wondered if Aryael might be leading into a lecture of sorts, wondering if perhaps she disagreed with how he'd handled Micah.

"More now than ever, I think," she replied, her voice becoming a near whisper. She stopped outside the door to the study, turning to face him. "The fact is, Gavin, you've proved yourself beyond the limits of others. Because of you, we now have a fighting chance against the Dark Born and that evil man that followed Sage."

"You'll have to thank Sage as well. I hate admitting this, but I was nearly ready to give up there for a moment."

Aryael nodded, opening the door before abruptly stopping on the threshold.

Aryael's eyes took on a confusing glint as she pushed open the door. Inside sat Symon, sitting comfortably in the chaise that looked across the room towards his desk, which sat in front of the expansive windows that overlooked the gardens. And across from Symon sat...Micah. *Great*, thought Gavin. He should have led with his Maracadian goodbye-not acknowledging anyone and just leaving as he pleased.

Gavin stalked into the room, his shoulders immediately rolling as he tried to ease the tension now crawling over them. He considered Symon's relaxed posture, but he figured the King could be relaxed. Gavin would probably feel the same if he could read whomever's mind he wished.

"Symon," Gavin greeted with a deferential nod. Walking past the other couch and heading for the table acting as a miniature bar, Gavin called over his shoulder, "Micah."

"So she caught you after all," the Shadow Master hummed.

Not acknowledging his former friend, Gavin reached for the decanter sitting on the table as Aryael took her place next to Symon. "Narresh?" Gavin asked Aryael, Symon gesturing with his own cup by way of urging him to partake.

"Yes, please." Aryael's voice was light, but Gavin didn't miss the tightness beneath it.

He poured them both a healthy dose, and brought the crystal glass to the Queen. "Ah, I'll take one myself, thank you," Micah said, sinking deeper into the crook of the couch where he sat.

"That's nice," said Gavin, handing the glass to Aryael then taking the chair on the far side from where Micah sat.

"So it's like that, is it?"

"Well, you're just so good at helping yourself with what isn't yours." Gavin noted the twitch of Micah's lip, one of his few tells when he was truly irritated.

"Excellent point."

As Micah gracefully stood and swaggered to the bar, Symon urged him, "Help yourself."

"I intend to."

Not willing to spend any more effort focused on Micah, Gavin decided to change the subject. "I'd hoped to speak with Epyllo before I left. I was surprised he didn't attend the luncheon."

"He's been called away," Symon said, setting his own glass of amber liquor on a side table. "He and Acantha are assisting Raphael on a voyage."

"Voyage?" Gavin asked, surprised. Raph couldn't be going, not at a time like this. They still had no idea what kind of illness the Dark Born could bring, and Raphael was one of the most trustworthy healers in all of Felysia.

"You should ask Sage for the details when you make it back to the Rafalatriki," Symon answered. "He insisted on visiting her before he departed." Symon's gaze flitted to Micah as the male drank deeply from his own crystal glass, then refilled it. Gavin took his meaning; this was not information they were ready to divulge to the new Lord of Borea. Not before he could prove his loyalty.

"I'm sad to have missed Raph," said Gavin.

"So..." Aryael interjected, "you and Sage?"

"Me and Sage."

"What is that all about?"

Aryael had a habit of playing coy when she wanted to, and Gavin felt as though he were being set up in a trap. "I'm not sure what you mean," he replied smoothly.

"She means, what's your endgame with the sorceress," Micah said, sloshing his drink as he sank back into the couch. He grinned wickedly, knowing he had interrupted both the Queen's game of cat and mouse, and Gavin's attempt to avoid whatever conversation they were wading into.

Gavin let the others sit in the uncomfortable silence that bloomed, contemplating whether he deemed the question worthy of an answer. Aryael, not one to wait patiently for answers she craved, broke through the silence. "What's your plan once she leaves?"

"I'll go with her."

Symon pitched forward. "You cannot be serious, Gavin." His cold blue eyes burned into Gavin.

"I am." There had never been a question in Gavin's mind as to whether he'd stay or go. If Sage left, so would he. It was as simple as that.

"First, need I remind you it is impossible for our kind to realm leap?" Aryael added, leaning forward, mirroring Symon's posture. "Second, do you truly value your place in Mystaira so little?"

"Yes, you might come back to find your titles bequeathed to another," said Micah. Oh, the smile on his face spoke volumes about the delight he was getting from witnessing this conversation. Not for the first time, Gavin wondered at why the King and Queen had even invited the rogue turned Lord to the study. And why wasn't someone, anyone, else there? He wished Meliza were with him. At least she would support him.

"We don't know that it's impossible," said Gavin, rolling his shoulders as that primitive part of his power began to wriggle beneath his skin. The dominance radiating from Aryael and Symon was tempting his own power to respond. But he refused to fight his friends, especially in front of Micah. "And Delphia and Seth are plenty capable of leading Mystaira in my stead. They did it for years while I trained."

"Yes, except now we have the Dark Born on our doorstep," Aryael hissed. He'd never been the target of her frustration before, and he found it uncomfortable. Tossing her red braids over her shoulder, she stood and stomped to the windows overlooking the gardens. "I can't help but find it a little hypocritical that you are so willing to shirk your duties *again* after lecturing Micah for doing the same."

"I never asked for these duties." Gavin's head began to throb from the effort of keeping his powers from taking over. "All I know, Aryael, is that my place is wherever Sage is. I can't explain it, but my heart tells me that once she's fulfilled her bargains, she will come back. Her place is here, her final place. And I'm meant to help her."

Aryael whirled, her eyes bright with firelight though the fireplace remained unlit. "Your place is here, with your people." Gavin felt Micah squirm, the male obviously cluing into the fact that a battle of wills had begun brewing.

"Do you think history will take kindly to the young Lord who abandoned his people to follow a Realm Leaper?" Symon asked in his usual calculating tone. It grated on Gavin, tearing at his resolve.

"Your people have waited, *I* have waited for you to fulfill your duties. I said nothing as you dallied the last ten years, wanting to give you a chance to grow up, a chance to fall in love with what this nation stands for. And this is your response?"

"Enough!" Gavin's voice boomed through the room, blowing like a cyclone in one short burst. Papers flew, curtains rocked, and time stilled. Gavin watched as trinkets flew from their shelves, toppling onto the floor and shattering. He was standing, not really meaning to, but the power had taken hold. "I never wanted this," he yelled back to Aryael. "You never asked me if I wanted to lead Mystaira. I was fifteen!" Aryael had been pushed back into the windows, unharmed, but shocked. He could feel Symon on his feet behind him, his glare boring through his head.

Be very careful how you choose to respond next, Symon's voice slithered through Gavin's mind.

Exhaling through his teeth, Gavin continued. "I am not asking for permission. I am going with Sage, with or without your blessing."

Aryael was panting with frustration now, and he felt no small amount of distress as he watched tears begin to rim her eyes. "So I was a fool?"

"You aren't listening." Gavin paced toward the door, unsure if he meant to leave or just needed a moment to collect his thoughts. Power still pulsed in his palms, throbbing from his chest into his arms. "I am going with Sage. And when her mission is complete, we are *both* coming back. Don't ask me how I know this. I'm just asking you to trust me, just like you asked me to trust you when you decided I should be Lord of Mystaira."

"For what it's worth, I believe you," Micah's voice cut in. All three fae's attention snapped to him.

"I'm afraid your vote of confidence might be detrimental to my cause," Gavin muttered, clenching and unclenching his fists.

"Well, count it as my good deed for the day, anyway," muttered Micah, dipping back into his glass for another sip of liquor.

Despite himself, Gavin felt a traitorous tug to his lips, and felt relief as he saw the same response from Symon. "Aryael," Gavin began, "please understand that I don't do this to hurt you, or anyone. I didn't want to be born in a work camp, but I was. I never desired to be a warrior, to be battle tested, but I was. I picked up every weapon I was asked to along the way. I never dreamed of leading a province, or being nobility. But when you asked it of me, I accepted it. And while I may have 'dallied,' as you like to call it, I did so under your command. I went where you asked me to, trained with who you chose for me. All my life, I've been under the rule of someone else's whims."

Aryael's eyes remained trained on him, boring into him even as he could feel the tension ease from Symon. It'd seem that he'd made his point to the King at least. "Let me ask you," Gavin tried, with the last straw he could grasp to convey to her the importance of his quest, "if you were asked to leave Symon behind, could you?"

Aryael released a sharp breath, her eyes cutting to her partner, her soul-bound love. Slowly, she returned her gaze back to Gavin. "Is that what she is to you?"

And this was the test. Gavin knew, without a doubt, that Sage was it for him. He'd been saying it all along to anyone who might ask. He'd told Shiphrah. He'd told Sage. He'd told his mother even, and had to suffer a multitude of hugs and questions. All that was left was to convince Sage that they were a match, that they were equals in all the ways that mattered. "I can't reason away the fact that she fell from the sky and landed so near to us instead of Maracadia–"

"–But that could have just been because that awful agent of the President interrupted her leap," Aryael interjected, brushing away his reasoning.

"It could have been," Gavin acquiesced, "but it wasn't." He shrugged, walking back to the table where he'd set down his drink. Stalling for time, he sipped deeply, trying to untie all of the knots that cinched themselves around his thoughts. Finally, he found a loose thread and tried again. "You know that feeling of wrongness? The one that follows us around when we think too hard about what's happened to us?" He looked at Aryael, then Symon, and even caught Micah as they all heaved a breath and nodded. It was impossible for them not to understand. Living so long in captivity would always leave its mark. "The only thing I've ever found to chase it away has been Sage. It's like...it's like there was a piece of my soul that I was born without. And she's brought it back to me."

His words fizzled through the room. He felt the electricity in them, the power behind his statement. And acknowledging just *how much* this mortal girl from another world meant to him filled his center with the greatest feeling of peace. It didn't matter what anyone else said. The Goddess herself couldn't keep him from her; not anymore.

"Then it is settled," Symon said, patting his knees and standing. "You will go with the girl, and come back when it is done." Symon said the words to Gavin, but his eyes were trained on Aryael. Gavin supposed if anyone knew what he felt, it must be the King.

Quietly, Aryael closed her eyes, and then nodded. When she re-opened them, she looked to Gavin, "Yes, it sounds as if you must." Her voice was soft, her words slipping to him as if they danced through velvet.

"Time for me to throw my own coin into the circle," Micah declared, standing. "Gavin, brother," Gavin winced at the endearment, but Micah waved it off. "Truth be told, I'm somewhat grateful to you for taking that estate off my hands. In all honesty, I never wanted to inherit my father's lands or title. I meant it when I said he was a pig-headed bastard." Gavin nodded. He remembered hearing about Micah's father, who had sided with Rankor, then sold his own son into the work-camp so his title wouldn't be threatened as his progeny grew in power. Micah had been born a few years before Gavin, on the outside of the work camps. As Micah began showing his power, his father had become paranoid that the youngling would challenge him for his lands and power. There'd been many beatings and "lessons" before the boy and his mother were thrown into the work-camp. Gavin had only been six years old when that happened.

"After going to Borea, seeing our people working to create something beautiful, I'll admit...I've fallen quite smitten with the place." Micah paused, setting his glass down, then walking toward the fireplace, pinching the bridge of his nose. It seemed the male was struggling with something. "Och...fuck it all to Darkness...what I'm trying to say, is that I have no desires to challenge you for your titles. And if you ask me of it, you'd have the support and protection of Borea while you're away."

Gavin was stunned. He'd come to think of Micah as a conceited fae with elaborate designs of power. He looked to Symon, who responded with a shrug. *I detect no warring thoughts*, came Symon's smooth voice, colliding against Gavin's own thoughts.

"I might require you to make that speech for Meliza before I believe it," said Gavin, walking to the male, his hand extended.

"You rob a few villages and suddenly your name is sullied," protested Micah, even as he grasped Gavin's forearm.

"It's good to have you back, brother," Gavin said smoothly.

Finally, it felt as if his world were tilting back in the direction it should. All he needed now was to convince the other half of his soul that he was correct.

Chapter 21

A cool breeze danced through the window of Sage and Gavin's apartment. The fresh air whispered against Sage's skin, chilling the areas that had begun to bead with sweat.

Mystaira, even this late in summer, was balmy to put it mildly. The Rafalatriki remained mostly cool due to its large stone walls, but the exterior rooms, she found, tended to become muggy as the day wore on. Thankfully, their temporary apartment faced eastward, where a pleasant breeze almost always seemed to blow across the hills and into the upper rooms of the complex.

She flipped a page of the book that had vexed her for the past several days, trying to bide her time as Gavin spent the night in Veritasailles for the ceremony that would officially acknowledge Micah as Lord of Borea. In her lap rested a memoir that served as an eyewitness account of realm leapers jumping to and from Panchia. Some of the details seemed...hyperbolic. Part of her doubted Cerridos would arrive on the back of a dragon, though she wasn't sure she'd put it past the playful Allyra. Scanning the pages she'd already read twice over, she hummed as a gentle knocking came from her door.

Her heart skipped, stuttering with joy at who stood on the other side when she cracked it open.

"Raph!" Sage flung the door wide and launched herself at her friend, nearly knocking him on his backside before he could hug her back.

"Oh—I've missed you, darling." Raph's voice sounded cheerful, with the slightest edge of exhaustion and sorrow. Sage stepped back, peering up at Raphael to assess.

"I've missed you, too." Though he smiled, his eyes didn't crinkle in the same way they had a few months prior. "Come on. I've got wine."

Grabbing his hand, Sage pulled Raph into her little abode, letting the door slam shut behind her. She practically tossed him into the seat she'd been sitting in before rushing to her kitchenette, gathering two glasses, a bottle of sweet red wine, and a basket that held haphazardly wrapped pastries and citrus fruits. It wasn't the feast her friend deserved, but it would have to do.

Setting everything on the side table that sat between the two wingback chairs, she poured them each a hefty glass. "Tell me everything," she said as she handed him his.

"I'm not sure you want to hear everything," Raphael said with a half-hearted smile. "The situation on the border is pretty..." he paused, chewing over the words he chose. "It's bad, Sage."

His voice had fallen. Her heart broke for this dear, dear friend who'd been through so much, shouldering the burdens of so many.

He cleared his throat, and rubbed his shoulders against the back of the chair as if he was trying to find a comfortable position. "Have you heard much of the Shadows?"

She nodded. Gavin had shared information as he received it via enchanted letters from Symon, Aryael, or Zeke. The horror of children dying where they stood still made her stomach drop.

"I've never seen anything like it," Raph continued, displacing her thoughts. "The ailments that developed were horrifying. They didn't respond to our healers' powers, which meant we had to watch helplessly as patient after patient succumbed. If I hadn't learned mortal medicine, I suspect we would have lost all of them."

"So, you're the only healer who's studied mortal medicine?" Sage asked incredulously. That didn't seem logical, not with a sprawling complex like the Rafalatriki dedicated to the healing arts.

"Of course not, don't be daft," Raph waved her question away. "But I am one of the last remaining healers who took their sabbatical in Meropoli. I have a much more intimate understanding of healing without using my powers. It used to be quite common, but, since the last conflict with the Dark Born...well, not many of us have had the time to venture abroad."

She nodded, understanding. For those born with magic or power, surviving without its use felt unnatural. Even in all those years in her childhood, forcing herself to suppress her elemental magic had always grated. She could imagine how a healer would feel if they were faced with a problem that resisted any and every attempt of their power.

Raph cut into her thoughts again. "I'm afraid of where this path might lead us." He stared into his glass of wine, and she wasn't sure he'd meant to say that last bit aloud.

She reached out to squeeze his knee. "We will figure it out, Raph. Don't worry. If I have anything to say about it, those Dark Born bastards will get what's coming to them."

He smiled, a genuine smile that actually reached his eyes. "Oh, well, that certainly makes me feel better."

Sage laughed. "I mean it! Just you wait. We'll figure out some way to stop them in their tracks. Then we'll put them down for good." Raphael nodded, and she lifted her glass in a cheers before taking a deep drink. The wine was just sweet enough to thaw the chill that Raph's awful news had brought.

"Let's change the topic. Tell me all about your time at the Rafalatriki."

"Well, we found what we were looking for, as far as getting Micah settled and everything." Sage felt her face fall. The realization that now she needed to focus on leaving Panchia, on getting back to her own world kept walloping her. Her heart didn't feel ready, but the soul contracts had begun tugging at her in the last few days, reminding her that time was ticking and bargains needed fulfilling.

"What is that face for?" Raphael asked, leaning forward in his seat.

Sage ran both hands down her face. "Ugh..." she began, squeezing her eyes tightly, "I guess now that I'm here, it's time for me to figure out how to get home."

"And how is that going?" Raphael asked wryly.

"Awful. First, Shiphrah confirmed what I suspected. I need the insignia to leap. And as they are lost to heavens only know, that leaves me in a bind. The second problem—I'd need to get to the temple of Maracadia." She took a deep sip of her wine, then flopped against her seat. "It's hopeless."

A pensive look passed over Raphael's face, giving Sage a shivering hint that something wasn't as it seemed. "What are you doing here anyway?" She'd assumed he was here to gather more healers.

"Actually," he began carefully, "I'm almost afraid to say this, but I might be on a journey that will help you in your first problem."

"The insignia?" Sage's heart simultaneously clenched and jumped. If he had knowledge of where the insignia were, she could finally fulfill her task. But then...if Raphael found the insignia...she would have to go.

"I don't know for sure, but my gut is telling me it might be," he continued. "About a week ago, I received this." He reached into the deep pockets of his cerulean tunic and produced a weathered letter. "It's from a distant acquaintance in Meropoli."

"Acquaintance?" Sage asked. "But you haven't been to Meropoli in ages. That'd make this person ancient for a human."

"Well, that's why I said distant. He's the progeny of someone I was close with during my time there." As he finished explaining, he handed the letter to her. "It's dated nearly a month after you first fell to us."

Gingerly, Sage opened the letter. Looping handwriting spanned the paper, spots from water damage blurring the script in places.

"I only just received it because trade between the continents has remained tense since we first established the agreements. It's likely this letter sat on a boat for months as we've tried to figure out what to do with ourselves." Raphael mimicked Sage's earlier plopping, and slumped into his chair. "I'll tell you, Sage, sometimes I wonder what we've done to deserve such challenge."

Sage reached over and squeezed his leg once more. She'd be lying if she said she didn't understand. That was a question she'd been asking herself since she became a fugitive at fifteen. She gave him a tight lip smile, gesturing that she understood, then leaned into her own chair to unfold the letter and began to read.

For the attention of Raphael, Offc. Healer to the Royal Court of Veritasailles.
From the desk of Malakai of Heronias

Raphael~
I'll begin this letter by acknowledging that I'm not confident that it will be received warmly. While my grandfather always spoke of you with the highest regards, I'd be deceitful if I didn't concede that the citizens of Heronias, and abroad, remain wary of fae and your affinity for accumulating power. I think we can all agree that the history between mortals and the fae have not always been equitable.

Nevertheless, I trust my intuition, and I trust the judgment of my grandfather even more. I believe it is in both our interests, and the interests of our respective peoples, that I inform you of some strange happenings along our continent.

*I cannot provide extensive details within the confines of this letter, but I urge you to send a representative from your court as quickly as possible. Visitors from **other** courts have already made their own offers for what I suspect might be valuable to all those in the fae lands. I also suspect that it would not benefit Meropoli, or its inhabitants, should we pursue the offers that have been made.*

This letter should provide the necessary leverage for a speedy welcome within our continental borders. Consider this an official summons.

I hope we will have the chance to meet someday. But more than that, my dearest hope lies in you heeding the call that I have sent.

Warmest regards,

Malakai

"Well, that sounds...vague," Sage said, handing the letter back to Raphael.

"I agree, but politics on Meropoli have always been more contentious. I suspect Malakai was sending this letter in opposition to other political leaders, which will undoubtedly put him in a precarious position."

"You say that as if this Malakai has some sort of sway with his people." Something about the letter had disturbed Sage, but she couldn't quite figure out what. The feeling stirred a protectiveness within her for Raphael's sake. If he was venturing into Meropoli, she wanted to be sure he'd be safe.

"From what I can glean, Malakai was elected the Governor of Heronias several years ago. He's maintained the position for a few consecutive terms, which is saying something if politics remain as polarized as they did when I took my sabbatical."

"So..." Sage began, tapping her fingers on the armchair, "do you trust him?"

"I trust that Ephraim's grandson is likely one of the most morally upstanding people to walk the land—if Ephraim had anything to do with his upbringing, I have no doubt that Malakai is acting on what he believes is best for his people." Raphael leaned forward, placing his glass on the table between their chairs. "But I'll tell you what really has me worried. I'm afraid that Speridisia has already made a move to gain a foothold on the Meropoli continent. Many mortals haven't entirely forgotten the mistreatment of their ancestors millennia ago. Yet I'm afraid that others might be fooled into thinking the Dark Born would honor any agreements made between the nations."

"Okay, then," Sage said, perking up. "Then it sounds like you have a good idea of what you need to do." She leaned forward, scooping up the notebook that had been slid beneath the table. "Can I help with anything?" she asked, flipping open to a blank page.

Raphael smiled sweetly at her. "As of right now, I don't think so. But do you think you'd be willing to keep me posted on what's going on here while I'm away?"

"Obviously!" Sage said, pushing her friend's shoulder. Raph responded by grabbing her hand and giving it a gentle squeeze. "Since we have a little time to spare, let's go down to the main hall and eat."

"My word," Raph said, grinning. "I think you might be one of the most food obsessed individuals I've ever met."

"Hush," she said back, pulling Raph to his feet. "Blame it on the trauma."

"I don't think that joke works here. If you haven't noticed, we are all dealing with our fair share," he said as she pushed him out the door so they could make their way to the hall where Sage knew the dinner buffet was already being served.

As they walked down the stairs, she refused to be distracted from her friend no matter how much her mind raced, no matter how her chest clenched with the thought that she was about to be faced with her fate.

Instead, she was going to focus on her friend while she still had the chance.

Chapter 22

❧ ✳ ☙

Sage huffed a stray piece of hair from her eyes. Since arriving in Felysia, her hair had grown longer, the ends now brushing her shoulders. She hadn't decided whether she liked the length or not, but was determined to grow out the bangs that now seemed to perpetually fall into her eyes. She wiped her palm against her soft leggings. Summer was making its final plow across the land, and even in the depths of the Rafalatriki Sage found herself sweating. If the mutterings of passing fae were to be believed, relief would soon come in the form of late summer storms. Sighing, she turned her focus back to her endeavor, a stack of books that needed to be skimmed for relevancy.

It'd been a few hours since she'd said a tearful good-bye to Raphael. Gavin still hadn't returned from the title ceremony. She knew Gavin planned on spending some time strategizing with Micah before returning, and she wondered how long that would take. Perhaps he'd be back before the evening donned.

Her hopes aside, she also realized they were busy trying to establish procedures for dealing with the topaz and orichtium extracted from the Borean valleys. Sage supposed that using fae powers were especially useful for lifting minerals and precious metals from the earth with ease, but she still found it fascinating that they'd already been able to collect enough to process in the few weeks the rogues had moved to the territory. Already, shipments had been delivered to the smitheys in Veritasailles, thanks to Micah's ability to shadow jump.

Not finding much of use from the book open on the table she snapped it shut and tossed it onto the discard pile. Daveed would be back around to scoop up the pile before the afternoon was gone, and she wanted to have her selection narrowed down to the three permitted before he returned.

She wasn't sure how long she'd been staring at the next book without really reading it when a bowl of cherries was set on top of the open pages. Startled, she whirled to find Gavin behind her.

"You're back!" she jumped up, wrapping her arms around his neck. He'd only been gone for two nights, helping the others in Veritasailles sort through the new shipment of weapons and Micah's report on some new rich seams of Orichtium he intended to extract. But she'd missed him. She was sometimes shocked by how quickly she'd gotten used to his presence as she drifted off to sleep.

Grinning, Gavin responded by wrapping his arms around her waist, "And you haven't eaten, have you?" His tone was teasing, so she let it slide as he leaned in to kiss her sweetly.

"I've grazed," she said as she turned back to the table. "And no, I wanted to get through this pile."

Gavin stepped to her side, peering at the book open on the table. "Anything new?" His voice was casual, but she could sense the slightest strain as he asked for progress on her realm leaping research.

"Nope," she replied, just as casually.

She, too, felt a sad tug at the topic. The unknowns of what came next had hounded them both over the last weeks. Shiphrah had shown Sage the underground temple of the Realm Leapers a few days prior, and the urge to return home had hit her stronger than it ever had since she first fell into Gavin's world.

The hurt she'd seen on his face when she'd explained this to him later that night had been so raw, so obvious, she'd had to excuse herself to the en suite bathroom for an hour after, spending the time "bathing". But really, she'd been sobbing over the impending departure.

The reality was, she didn't want to leave this place that had come to feel so much like home. Felysia—Mystaira more specifically—felt more like home than Thuledain ever had. Here, she didn't have to hide who she was. Here, her magic was awed and accepted. Some of the fae may have been wary of her magic initially, but by and by, she found they were willing to give her a chance.

Thuledain had never been so inviting to her. And yet...she had to go back. Not only that, but she had to figure out how to get to TupaGuara, and what exactly her Gods expected her to do there.

The weight of everything suddenly bore down on her, exacerbated by the fact that she was spiraling with worry for Raphael. He would be fine, she kept telling herself. But from everything he'd told her, she was afraid he was walking into deadly territory. Territory ruled by vengeful, untrustworthy mortals who may or may not have good reasons to fear Raphael because of what he was.

Gavin poked her arm hard. "Ow!" Sage said, peering at him sharply as she rubbed the spot. "What was that for?"

"Well, first," he began, "you were thinking too loud again. I could feel your thoughts whirring around you like gnats. And it wasn't even about what's in that book." He pushed the book out of her focus, moving the bowl of cherries back in front of her. "Second, I have something for you—another thing besides the cherries."

Sage peered at him with a sideways glare. "What is it?"

His grin had her wondering if his surprise might be a clever attempt to distract her from her research. He'd been none too happy when she declared it was time for her to figure out her next move. Then there'd been the bickering over whether or not he'd be leaping with her. At this point, she wasn't fully convinced she would manage to get herself safely out of the world. The idea of leaping with him along for the ride? It seemed improbable, at best.

Gavin rolled his eyes playfully. "Stop looking at me like that." He reached into a bag she hadn't noticed and pulled out a wrapped, rectangular package. "Here," he said softly, his breath slipping over her neck as he leaned close to watch her unwrap his gift.

Carefully, she untied the twine holding the coarse homespun around a smart leather box. As she lifted the lid, a gasp shot from her chest. Inside lay an identical pair of daggers, which shone spritely in the flickering fae light of the archives. One half of each blade was a startling white, while the other half absorbed all light into its depthless black.

"Meliza told me how good you've gotten with daggers, so I thought it was time for you to have a pair of your own."

Touched, she couldn't even whisper her gratitude. Instead, she gently pulled the daggers out from their box, testing their weight in her palms. The leather grip that spiraled around the hilt was a beautiful shade of charcoal that highlighted the wicked looking guards, which slashed out from the blades in pointy ovals. The pommels each held a polished crystal: one of aventurine, and the other smoky quartz.

"Those," Gavin pointed, "reminded me of the color of your eyes. And they add to the balance of the blades."

"Thank you," Sage finally managed to say. Stepping back from Gavin, she gripped her new daggers in her palms, then gave them each a spin in her hands, testing their feel. Quietly, she ran through a few poses and sequences Meliza had taught her for her own practice. Then stopping abruptly she turned to face him, her heart brimming. "Thank you, thank you so much Gavin. They're... perfect. When did you have the time to have these made?" She turned her attention back to the blades, unable to stop herself turning them this way and that, loving how their contrasting blades caught and played with the light. The answer rushed to her before he could answer. "Micah?"

Gavin nodded. "I gave him the idea the first time I brought him to Borea. Those were the first weapons he had made. I wanted Meliza to inspect them before I gave them to you."

"Thank you," Sage said again, grinning. "So, these blades...the black sides are orichtium? That means—"

"You should be able to use your elemental magic with them," Gavin finished for her.

Sage twirled the hilt of one dagger in her hand again. Without looking she felt Gavin step towards her. His body heat invaded her space in the way that had become so normal between them. Over the last month, they'd shared a bed every night, except for nights when Gavin was pulled away to deal with Micah and his shipments. And over the past couple of days, she'd found herself both utterly content with his proximity to her heart and frustratingly torn. How couldn't she when she'd have to say goodbye so soon?

Gavin reached a hand up to tuck a strand of hair behind her ear. "I imagine these will come in handy when we leap."

There it was, thought Sage. Quietly, she placed the beautiful daggers back in their box before turning back to him. "Gavin—we've talked about this." She took his hands in hers, looking up at him, imploring him to understand. "We have no idea if I'm strong enough to bring you with me. As far as we know, it's never been done before. And look what happened the last time I leapt. I didn't really stick the landing. "

"And, like *I* said," Gavin said, smiling back at her in that infuriatingly reasonable and calm way, "I've never even tried before. But if you think I won't try everything in my power to follow you, you're wrong. I'll follow—any world, any time, any galaxy. The stars, the Goddess, your gods themselves couldn't stop me from getting to you."

Sage's heart beat faster as he stepped even closer, his body now flush with hers. Then, slowly, he pushed her so she was leaning against the archive table.

"You cannot promise that," she whispered as he brushed his lips across her jaw.

"Yes, I can," he said, lips moving back up to her sensitive ear. "Because I mean it. You cannot escape me, Sage. Not anymore."

A short, hot laugh escaped her chest, even as his hands began skirting up her waist, wrapping around her ribs in a possessive grip. She'd be lying if she said she didn't love it when he grabbed her like that.

Suddenly, however, she remembered where they were.

The archives.

Daveed would likely be back any moment to collect the books.

"Gavin," Sage panted, "someone will see us." She felt his smile as he kissed her lips, stepping so that his legs were now situated firmly between hers.

"Good," he said, pulling away. Before she could respond, he reached around her onto the table, pulling another satchel toward them that she hadn't bothered to pay attention to. With one hand on her hip, the other hand pulling free the contraption in the bag, Gavin remained rooted between her legs, his weight leaning into her thighs.

As he finally freed the tangled mess within the satchel, he dropped to his knees and grabbed one of her feet. "Gavin!" cried Sage, not sure what he was up to.

"What?" he asked impishly. "It's a holster, for your daggers." His smile made it crystal clear he knew what he'd been doing.

Her heart still raced, her pulse throbbing in her neck. That wasn't the *only* place she felt throbbing as his hands raced up both sides of her thigh, sliding the leather holster up her leg. Having him kneeling between her legs, his hands running up her thighs then roughly adjusting the buckles so that they fit securely against the leggings she wore, made her shiver with anticipation. Finally, he stood and quickly wrapped the belt part of the holster around her waist. After pinning the buckle in place, he snatched the daggers from their box, and settled them into their respective holsters.

Gavin stepped back, and the dark gleam in his eye stole the breath from Sage. Trying to keep her voice playful, she teased, "Don't tell me you're thinking of what it'd look like if I wore these to bed."

Darkly, Gavin replied, "That's exactly what I'm thinking."

A ruffling of robes sliced through the tension roiling between them, and they both looked up to see Shiphrah turn the corner, chuckling.

"I could sense a disturbance in the area. I should have guessed it was you two."

Sage blushed fiercely. She didn't think she'd ever get used to the fae's ability to smell emotional reactions in others, especially arousal. The fact that she found herself in that state every time she stepped near Gavin made it worse. Or maybe it wasn't? She wasn't sure.

"Gavin was just helping me with these," Sage answered innocently, pulling free a dagger from its new home.

"Oh, some new hardware?" Shiphrah said as she walked towards them. As she reached their sides, Sage handed the freed dagger to her so she could admire them appropriately. "Stunning." She said, turning the blade in her hand. "They're made of orichtium," Shiphrah noted. "I suppose you plan to use them as a replacement for your wand?"

Startled, Sage's body jerked. "That hadn't even crossed my mind. I could do that?"

"Oh, well, I just assumed, with your knowledge of the substance and whatnot, that this was the kind of material wands were made of. The Realm Leapers didn't come with them when I was young."

Now that Sage thought about it, wands did sometimes use orichtium as their core element. Other materials were more commonly used, such as various quartzites that were magical conduits. Cheaper alternatives included synthesized alloys that had become widely available in the past fifty years, advancing the access to wands so that everyone could afford them. Whereas wands had been family heirlooms, passed down for generations, these days a student could purchase their own. The advantage being they were more easily replaced when they inevitably damaged them.

"I suppose it would work," continued Sage, worrying her bottom lip as she thought out loud. "I'd need to find a safe place to test out the theory, but you might be onto something."

"You could try the temples," Shiphrah offered. "They aren't visited often, we have just a few apprentices who use them from time to time." Shiphrah stepped sideways, gesturing down the hall. "Would you like to try it out now?"

"We'd both like to see her try," Gavin interjected. "But, before we do that, could you settle a little debate we've been having?" Shiphrah stopped, raising her eyebrows in response. "Sage seems to think it's impossible for me to go with her when she leaves here."

"Ah," Shiphrah said, as Sage huffed in annoyance. "Well, it would be unprecedented, that's for sure."

Turning away from the pair, she began walking towards the archives' exit. Sage and Gavin followed her, heading towards the temples that ran beneath. Centuries ago, when the Realm Leapers still jumped between worlds, Allyra and her fellow gods built a temple beneath the ground of what later became the Rafalatriki. It wasn't an expansive, sprawling temple like those on her home world, but Sage had found their presence comforting. More than once, she and Meliza had used the space as a private arena for training, something she intended to do more often now that she had a pair of striking daggers hanging from her waist.

Shiphrah's robes whispered as they swept the ground, and she trailed her fingers along the stone walls that lined the stairs which led to the temple.

"Amare and Eron were the most prominent couple to come from the Realm Leapers. There were a handful of others, but Eron was the only one to choose to stay here. As far as I'm aware, no fae had been able to leap."

As she spoke, the trio breached the stairwell leading to the lobby that allowed them to skirt past the main common spaces on the first floor. Just past the large opening that fed into the food court, Shiphrah turned right, taking the smooth steps down to the temples that only a few of the apprentices and healers ever ventured to.

"So, you're saying it's not likely," Sage suggested, cutting her eyes to Gavin. He immediately stiffened, a muscle in his jaw jerking as he visibly ground his back teeth.

"Hm, not precisely. More that I don't know if it was ever attempted," corrected Shiphrah.

Sage frowned as she caught the look from Gavin as he seemed to say, "See? It'll be fine."

After plodding down what must have been flights of stairs, they finally broke away from the stairwell, stepping out into a wide, high vaulted chamber. The floor was a smooth limestone. The walls seeming to glow with their own pale light somehow. It was a place of power and awesome majesty, and Sage couldn't understand any student or scholar of the Rafalatriki not wanting to spend as much time down here as possible.

Her breath always caught at the sight of the beautiful carvings that decorated the ceiling, so skillfully made, they almost appeared to be alive. Her eyes were always drawn to Allyra's likeness in particular, her expression caught so perfectly by the artisan crafts-fae: equally playful and triumphant. Just as she appeared in real life. The goddess was a jumbled up combination of challenge, nurture, and mischief.

Seeing her face carved into the stone above squeezed at Sage's heart ever so slightly. Was it yet another pang of homesickness? Or were the bargains becoming impatient to be fulfilled?

Either way, Sage knew her time with the fae was coming to an end.

Shiphrah turned sharply into Cerridos's corner of the temple. Sage was thankful they'd avoided Brighid's; with the oppressive heat of late summer, it was pleasant to step into Cerridos's room where a charmed breeze danced through the space, jostling the wind chimes hanging in each corner. Against the center of the back wall stood an impressive statue of Cerridos. Strangely, Sage thought, she'd not had many encounters with the God of Wind. But she'd recognize the muscled build and curling white beard anywhere. That, and his matching spears, standing at attention in each of his hands.

The three of them settled in the center of the room, Shiphrah breaking the silence. "Well, let's test out this theory, shall we?"

Sage scanned the room. She needed to try something that didn't have any elemental ties. Trying to think of a spell that didn't resemble her elemental magic was kind of difficult. But then, a pile of ribbons caught her attention. She wasn't sure what kind of practice required ribbons, but sudden inspiration left her little time to ask questions.

Extending one dagger, Sage drew a swift half circle in the air, pointing at the ribbons. At the same time, she recited the spell, "Cruth Atharraich Aderyn!"

A fluttering commotion overtook the corner of the room. The transmogrification spell spiraling the ribbons in a flurry of whirling, snapping, bending, and reshaping. Pieces of ribbon fell from the pile, then rejoined the mess until a beady-eyed bird peered strangely at the trio. The red, blue, green, and gold ribbon shaped the bird, its form resembling a crow. Shrewdly, the little bird cocked its head, assessing Sage and her companions before offering a sharp "Skwak!"

"It's a bird." Gavin looked at the bird, seemingly struck dumb by what he witnessed.

"It is," said Sage. "Honestly, I've never been able to do that spell before. I hadn't expected it to...talk?"

The bird chimed in with another loud, "SKWAK!" hopping over to the center of the room, fluffing his wings out as he approached.

"Is he hungry?" asked Shiphrah. "Will he eat?"

Sage laughed, both profoundly uncomfortable at the powerful magic she'd just performed, and immensely proud of herself. The spell was advanced, and her execution was impressive. Her mother would have been so proud of her, and the thought brought that familiar mixture of homesickness and dread of leaving. Tears pricked her eyes as she watched the crow hop around the room, then extend his arms and fly away.

"That might disturb some," Shiphrah said, and Sage wasn't sure if it was to herself or the three of them.

Gavin's arm reached around her shoulder, and he pressed a sweet kiss to her forehead. "That was...impressive."

"It was," said Sage, wiping away a stray tear.

"Well," declared Shiphrah, clapping her hands, "that solves that. Those daggers can replace your wand. Now, we just have to figure out how to use your magic with Gavin's powers."

Sage laughed again, too excited by being able to access her magic fully to argue. Instead, she turned to face Gavin, eying the satchel he clutched in his hand.

"Don't even think about it," he murmured, catching her gaze.

With a swish of her dagger, she repeated the spell. A squalling cat formed from the bag, twisting as Gavin held onto its tail. He yelped, releasing the hissing cat as it reached back to nip him, Sage cackling with laughter as Shiphrah leapt away from the creature.

"What have I done?" whispered Gavin as he stepped away from the muslin cat.

"Oh—you two are no fun," said Sage, scooping the cat into her arms. She could still hear the two whispering with each other about whether it was a good idea for Sage to be let loose with her new magic, but Sage was already making her way back up to their apartment. She had never felt so whole, so in tune with her magic as she did in that moment.

Chapter 23

❧❀❧

The next day found Sage back in the temple. Begrudg-
ingly, she'd been persuaded to turn the cat back into a
satchel, but only after Gavin had promised he'd find her
a proper pet at some point in their future, something he
seemed especially pained about. The crow made of ribbons,
however, was still flying free somewhere; neither she nor
Gavin caught sight of the colorful bird after it flew out of
the temple, although she'd sworn she'd heard its distinctive
SKWAK early that morning.

Now, Shiphrah was suggesting that Sage learn to cast
along with Gavin without touching him.

Sage stared dumbly at the older fae. "How exactly am I
supposed to use his power to cast? I'm not fae—our powers,
my magic, are completely foreign to each other. "

"Sure," Shiphrah responded coolly, "but, Amare and Eron
were able to influence each other's skills after they bonded.
Which suggests that fae and mortal powers, magic as you
call it, are not incompatible."

"So Eron learned to cast?" Sage was more than a little
skeptical. But since finding out that Eron had also been a
Realm Leaper, a part of her had latched onto the idea that
it might be possible for her to make things work with Gavin.

Still, the idea of making the leap with him in tow seemed incredibly dangerous.

"No—" answered Shiphrah, interrupting Sage's swirling thoughts. "Honestly, I met Amare and Eron when we were building the Rafalatriki. I don't really think either of them explored their bond all that much. They were just so content to be with each other." Shiphrah walked to a corner of the room and fiddled with a set of windchimes. "They were kind of awful to be around, *so* touchy-feely with each other. Actually," she said, turning to face Sage, "a bit like you and Gavin." She winked at Sage, just as Gavin entered the Wind God's temple room.

"What'd I miss?" he asked. His hair was tousled in the way it always was after he flew in his fae form, and Sage felt the familiar drop of her stomach at the sight. The male got more beautiful by the day. How was it possible for him to be so fucking gorgeous all the time?

Shiphrah cleared her throat roughly and Gavin gave Sage a knowing smile. Rolling her eyes, Sage turned to face the statue of Cerridos, even as she felt her cheeks burn slightly. It was kind of unfair, she thought, that fae could detect another person's mood so astutely. It was almost invasive and was taking a lot of getting used to. She'd never realized before, in Thuledain, how often she might feel attraction for someone else. Having her thoughts echoed back to her with knowing looks and smiles every time Gavin was even in the same room as her...it was incredibly distracting.

Heat bloomed across Sage's back as Gavin stepped close, giving her a quick kiss to her temple. "I don't think I'll ever get tired of that," he whispered in her ear.

"Alright," said Sage, turning to face Gavin and giving a playful shove, "get over yourself, Flyboy." Once Gavin had stepped back just far enough for her to feel in control of herself, Sage clapped her hands before explaining, "Right, well, Shiphrah believes that in order to leap with me, I first need to figure out how to cast alongside you."

The question was obvious on Gavin's face before he said it, but he stated it anyway. "You already do cast alongside me. So we've solved the problem already?"

"Sage needs to be able to reach out with her power, and cast with you *without* touching you."

Shiphrah came back to the middle of the room where Sage and Gavin stood. Fae lights twinkled against the swaying wind chimes, adding an ethereal quality to the room. The topic of their conversation, the setting, the thoughts rapid-firing through her head made Sage feel like she was in a dreamstate for a moment. Gavin looked between Shiphrah and Sage; back, and forth. Finally, he exhaled deeply, nodding to himself.

"Okay. Let's figure this out."

"'Let's figure this out.' That's all you have to say?" Sage raked both hands through her hair. "Gavin, our powers are different. They are from completely different worlds. How are they supposed to work together like that?"

Gavin shrugged. "I don't know. I also don't know why the Goddess would intend for the other half of my soul to have been born on a completely different world, but just look at you. You're here now."

Sage's head tilted in concession. How could she be irritated when he said stuff like that? "Ugh...fine. *Let's figure this out.*"

"Great," beamed Shiphrah, "let's get started."

Gavin and Sage had positioned themselves across from each other, both sitting with their legs criss-crossed beneath them. After what had felt like ages of answering Shiphrah's questions, she had instructed the two to get comfortable on the floor.

"Sage," Shiphrah began, "can you tell me a little about what it feels like when you access your elemental magic?"

Sage paused before replying, thinking back to the days where Raphael had helped her rediscover her power, focusing on how she'd had to drop into the depths of herself to find it.

"Well, it depends on which element I'm accessing." Sage wiggled on her butt to find a more comfortable position. "For example, when I'm using water, it's like my senses reach out, searching for where the water lives. Sometimes it's in the air, sometimes it's in a river or a puddle." She shuddered briefly, a hard memory of her friend Hyacinth crossing her mind. The way the shy fae had drained their two captors of the water in their bodies. Briefly, she let herself float along the wave of grief that always accompanied her thoughts of Hyacinth.

"Continue," urged Shiphrah softly, though not unkindly. The look in her eyes said she understood.

Sage looked to Gavin, thinking about his own power and how it was so similar, yet so different from her own. "With air, it's a little different. I still have to find it, still have to try and sense where it's most concentrated. But rather than pulling at it, I have to coax it. It's like..." Sage scrunched her face, looking for the best way to describe the feeling of working with air versus water. "It's almost like water is always eager to play. Air, on the other hand, needs to be convinced." She shrugged. "I have no idea if that makes any sense at all."

"I seem to remember a certain, powerful fae teaching you how to work with the wind," Gavin interjected, winking at Sage.

"Oh, right. Gavin, the all-mighty and amazing Lord of Mystaira, was my tutor for when I was learning how to work with air. How could I have forgotten to mention that?"

Shiphrah laughed, and Gavin muttered to himself about the statement being true, even as he grinned playfully. "And what about the other two? Earth and fire?" Shiphrah's voice was bright with her laughter, but the question brought them all back into focus.

"Fire is strange. It's not really even fire, actually. It's more like the energy that is inside everything, like the smallest particles and their potential to rub against each other and combust. It feels like a vibration, like the buzzing of bees. If I focus on it, I can access that energy and create fire. I can use the energy in the air, in certain rocks, even. I think, if I got strong enough, I could create steam with water. Although, that's just a theory.

"Earth is similar. I just have to find the energy within the ground and summon it. It feels like using a pulley system—like if I pull hard enough, what I'm trying to create just kind of comes up."

"Interesting," murmured Shiphrah. "And you, Gavin? What does it feel like when you access your wind powers?"

Gavin shrugged. "It's similar to what Sage said. I just reach out for it and ask, then it does what I need."

"And what about casting? Sage? Can you describe what it feels like for you to cast? I imagine it feels quite a bit different for a mortal."

"Well, I'll tell you one thing—I much prefer casting with Gavin than with others."

"How so?" Shiphrah leaned in, having taken a seat near Gavin and Sage.

"When I cast with Raphael, it feels like I'm being squeezed through a press, or a roller of some kind. It's like being shoved through a vat of molasses, all the air gets squeezed out of me, and for a moment it feels like my head is going to get squished."

"Really? It can't be *that* bad," Gavin said, screwing his face up at her description.

Sage squinted at Gavin, "You, hush. It is that bad, thank you very much." Sage brushed a lock of hair from her face, refocusing on Shiphrah. "It's different with Gavin. There's no squeezing and pushing. It's more like turning into mist. Like evaporating and then quickly becoming whole again."

Shiphrah's eyebrows pinched and she looked between the pair. Her freckles seemed to dance as Sage watched the fae sift through all that Sage had told her. "It's been an age since I've casted, myself. I don't have a need to leave the Rafalatriki, but I can't say I've ever found the sensation pleasant either." Shiphrah patted her knees, clearly deciding to move onto another subject. "You've both heard the other explain what it's like when you use your powers. Now, let's see if you can sense each other's power. Sage, do you think you could conjure us a set of blindfolds?"

Sage slow-blinked at Shiphrah. "Blindfolds?"

"How else are you supposed to sense each other?"

"Okay," muttered Sage. "Let's give this a try." Standing, Sage unclipped one of her new, magical daggers, picturing a set of clean cloths sitting atop the counter of her little kitchenette. They'd been intended to be used as napkins, but she supposed they'd work just as well as blindfolds. With an upward slashing motion that connected to a triangle pattern in the air, she finished the spell movement by slashing sideways through the invisible shape she'd drawn, whispering the incantation. "Galwad i mi, fy angen."

Gavin's eyes widened. "So, that's a thing?" he asked, recognizing the napkins that had been sitting in their room only seconds before. "You can just...summon anything? Do people just summon whatever they want where you're from?"

"Obviously every house, pretty much every building is bespelled to keep your belongings where they belong. Most products are, too. It's really simple, actually. Basically, when items are manufactured, they're warded so that whoever pays for it sets the intentions for its use. There are other counterwards which keep some products from being used in ways they aren't meant to be used, and others which are put in place to keep products from being harmful. Then—"

"Okay, okay," Shiphrah interrupted, standing and holding out her hands for Sage to stop. "Gavin, you'll just have to trust that a world with powerful magic, such as Sage's, has figured out how to exist with it. Just as our world has figured out how to safely exist with fae power. Even the mortals on our world have that figured out."

Gavin stood, rolling his eyes. "Fine. I just—that seems dangerous," he said, pointing to the napkins in Sage's hands.

Sage shrugged again. "Maybe it is." She held up the napkins for Shiphrah to take. "Now what?"

"Let's separate you both. Sage, go find another part of the temple to sit. Take one of the blindfolds with you."

Shiphrah tossed the other cloth to Gavin where he snatched it from the air.

Sage walked out of the temple room for Cerridos, deciding to sit by the pool at the end of the hallway. A statue of Allyra stood in the center of the pool, a gentle waterfall trickling from the wall behind. "How did all of this withstand the conflict with Rankor?" Sage asked, turning to face Shiphrah who stood outside of Cerridos's room, angling herself so she could focus on Gavin and Sage at the same time.

"I may have commissioned a few upgrades," Shiphrah said, followed by a playful wink. "Both of you get comfortable. Tie up your blindfolds. Once you're settled, use your powers."

Sage sat with her back against the raised lip of the pool, leaning so that her shoulders rested comfortably against the smooth limestone. She shook out the linen napkin, folding it into a triangle before securing it over her eyes and quickly tying the ends together. Allowing herself a few moments to become acquainted with the sudden darkness, the pressure against her eyes, she waited for her body's awareness to become heightened.

"If you haven't begun already," Shiphrah's voice lightly floated to Sage, "start with some nice, deep breathing. Inhale through your nose, and slowly exhale through your mouth."

"Oh, no. You're one of those?" groaned Sage. Raphael had always been so focused on breathing, she shouldn't have been surprised he learned it from Shiphrah.

Gavin's sharp laugh came racing to her, and Sage snorted with him. "Very funny," said Shiphrah. "But it works," she sang.

"Fine. I guess you're not wrong. Here we go...breathing." Sage heard Gavin snort again, then clear his throat. Finally, she began to feel settled again, focusing on her breath.

Inhale....exhale....

The sound of rippling water behind her bounced through the air with a coltish melody. Sage decided to lean into that part of her magic, feeling herself reach out to the water that surrounded her. Quietly, Sage allowed the essence of her body to extend itself, beyond the confines of her fleshy borders, and into the space surrounding her. She felt the encapsulating weight of the pool, all the water sitting heavily on top of itself. In the air, small particles of water drifted lazily, collecting more densely as each body in the temple exhaled, puffs of condensation hovering before gliding onward.

Slowly, Sage probed with ethereal limbs. Parts of her no one else could see reached into the pool, lifting water into the air. As if she were blowing a dandelion, she pushed, sending the water to meander through the air. As she pushed, her senses unfurled further, like a window opening so that she could see the effect her magic had on the room. A misty fog rolled along the floor of the hallway, curling away from the opening of Brighid's temple room, and bumping along the ground toward Shiphrah. Sage heard the sharp inhale as the fog wrapped itself around the healer's legs, gently floating around her and beyond.

Now fully enraptured in her own magic, Sage pushed further reaching out for Gavin's power. She could feel it: a rhapsodic hum of force whirring within Cerridos's temple room. The wind chimes had silenced, and Sage could feel Gavin funneling the power within the room into himself, pulling the wind inward.

So, too, did Sage's mist; the water vapor raced toward Gavin until it collided with the wind, both wrapping around Gavin. Sage felt her magical body stand at attention outside the room.

"There you are." Gavin's voice extended around her, and Sage's magical body turned, finding Gavin's own astral body standing, looking at her.

Sage reached out, feeling Gavin's arm as if he were real, and not some projection of his power. Her hands met his form, not quite feeling like flesh, but still feeling like *him*. Somehow, this form of Gavin was both incredibly strange and new, yet familiar. It felt like she'd been introduced to the purest form of him.

"Here I am," Sage whispered. "What do we do now?"

"Keep your breath steady," came Shiphrah's voice, as if echoing from far away.

A pained exhale came from down the hall, wet and ragged. Gavin's attention shot back to Sage's mortal body, her own gaze following. Sage watched as her body slumped over, her head dropping suddenly.

"Go back," Gavin urged.

Panic dredged up in Sage's magical body. How? How did she go back?

"Go. Back," Gavin urged again, his astral hands wrapping around her arms. Quickly, she felt him kiss her forehead. Then, turning in one step, he threw her down the hall.

Sage yelped as she felt her magical body fly through the air, the mist racing alongside her. Then her selves collided with a hammering explosion behind her eyes.

Gasping, Sage wrenched the blindfold from her face, slumping onto all fours. Footsteps rushed down the hallway towards her, but she threw up an arm, warning them to stay back. Bile surged upwards, forcing itself up and out of her throat. She retched, the sound splattering around the stone space.

"Oh, gods," Sage panted, slumping back against the pool. "That was awful." Eyes closed, Sage felt for her dagger, pulling it free and waving it with an incantation to send the mess she'd made away. She peeked through half open lids, only to find her spell hadn't worked. She reached for her water magic, pulling from the pool to wash it away.

Nothing.

Her magic lay curled deep within her, comatose to her whims.

Before she could protest, strong arms wrapped themselves beneath her legs and shoulders, scooping her into warmth and comfort. Her ear rested against Gavin's chest, the sound of his heart soothing her. "Come on," he whispered. "You'll need rest." Without the energy to dredge up a protest, Sage allowed him to carry her to their room, leaving without a word to Shiphrah.

The steady beat of his heart, the matching thud of his steps, pulled her into a sleep so deep she forgot where she'd been or how she had become so tired.

Days passed, blurring together like waves on the shoreline, endings and beginnings becoming muddled.

Sage, Gavin, and Shiphrah would meet in the temple beneath the Rafalatriki. Sage and Gavin taking their places in separate rooms to practice melding their power and magic.

And every day, Sage would be forcibly thrown back into her corporeal body, slamming back into reality with such force it rocked her senses. She'd begun bringing a bucket so that she could keep it next to her, as she inevitably got sick after every attempt.

After every challenge, Sage would find her magic weakened, dormant and stiff. Gavin would carry her back into their room, gingerly setting her on the bed before hovering over her like a mother hen. Sage naturally grew tiresome of the coddling, and found herself snapping at him. He, in turn, would huff an exasperated sigh, tell her to get some rest, then leave.

And when they weren't practicing in the temple, on days when Sage's magic refused to answer her call from burnout, Sage researched. And again, Sage found herself hopelessly out of her depth. Of all the stories and records pertaining to the Realm Leapers, very few of them seemed reliable. Instead, she found shrouds of lore tied up around the Realm Leapers.

In all, there had been six others besides the deities. Only Eron stayed behind, even though myths of Realm Leapers siring royal lineages seemed to cling to Felysian historical accounts. Sage wasn't sure how much she trusted those accounts, a sentiment only furthered by Daveed's similar contemplations.

On their tenth attempt to merge their power, a bubble of rage began to expand within Sage's chest. At least this time she hadn't passed out. But it was scant comfort. *Why* weren't they making more progress? Her head thumped against Gavin's chest as he climbed the final few stairs leading to the landing which preceded their doorway. Sage crossed her arms, her brows in a permanent furrow as she fumed.

Gavin easily opened the door, sticking out the hand supporting beneath her legs to twist the knob. Unable to take it any longer, Sage pushed out of Gavin's hold.

"Let me down."

Gently, Gavin placed her on her feet. She staggered forward, grabbing onto the wingback chair for support. Gavin reached for her, undoubtedly attempting to help before Sage cut him off.

"Stop that. I'm fine."

"You don't look fine. You still look pale." The door stood open behind him, and she glared as he crossed his arms, his weight shifting to one hip as he inspected her.

"Yeah, well, we can't all be perfect specimens, all Goddess-blessed and whatnot." Skirting the chair, Sage plopped herself into it, allowing a quiet exhale of release she hoped Gavin hadn't noticed. Her daggers rattled against her hips in the waist holster she'd purchased from a local artisan. Daveed had done her the favor of picking it up when he went to visit the market a few days prior. Restlessly, she unfastened the harness and dropped it to the floor.

Gavin circled the chair, dragging one of the chairs sitting by the table with him so he could sit directly in front of Sage. Softly, he leaned forward, elbows on his knees, resting his hands on hers. "We just have to keep trying. You're getting stronger. You made it way longer today than you have before, and look," he continued, gesturing at her, "you're still awake."

Sage scowled. "Fuck that, Gavin! Stop being so fucking *reasonable*." She sat back in the chair, eyeing him. "What if we keep trying? What if we try for a year? Two years? How long is it going to take for you to accept that this part of my journey has to be done *solo*?"

"Never." Gavin's face was calm, unbothered even, but she could feel the turmoil her words caused. The subtle flex of his fingers against her knees belied the frustration he worked so hard to keep hidden. "I do not accept the idea that you and I being separated is okay. It's not okay," he added with a one-shoulder shrug. "I will die trying before I let you go, Sage."

"Or I'll die trying to figure out how to merge our powers," Sage said, pushing herself out of her slumped position.

"No, you won't," he said, squeezing her knees. "You're strong enough to do this, I know you are."

Sage scoffed. "Hah. Gavin, you don't know. You're just hoping enough to make it true. But this," she said, gesturing between them, "this might not be what you think it is."

"Or it could be. What if we haven't been able to make our powers work together because you've been blocking it?"

"*Excuse* me?" Sage's shock rocked through her, her head pulling back with force. "So you see me pushing my magic to burnout, to the point that I pass out, and you think I might not be *trying* enough?"

"That's not what I said, and you know it. I just meant—"

"No," said Sage, pushing Gavin's hands off her knees. "No...I can't do this right now, Gavin." Squirming so that her legs were free from his, she pushed to stand and walk away. "I think I need some time alone."

"Time alone? So you can push yourself away from me?" Gavin was standing, his chair scraping against the stone floor as he straightened. "Do you think it's possible that you're actually *trying* to prevent me from coming with you? As a way to keep me from getting too close?"

"Too close? It's a little too late for that, don't you think?!" Sage's voice rose, her temper fueled by her exhaustion. "I think if I was worried about that, I wouldn't have let you fuck me."

Gavin huffed. "Is that all we did?" His glare bore into her. "Is that all you think about what we've done? *Fuck*?"

Her eyes rolled of their own volition. "You know what I mean."

"Exactly," said Gavin. "You and I both know there's more to this. But maybe that idea scares you. Maybe that's why you're trying to push me away now, because you know that if I come with you, then there's no turning back." Sage crossed her arms, looking away from Gavin as tears pricked the corners of her eyes. "Afterall, you have a habit of running away when you've gotten close." Sage's eyes snapped back to Gavin. That crossed a line, and he knew it. Immediately, he sighed, "I'm sorry, that wasn't the right—"

"Get out." Her voice was quiet, barely a breeze.

"Sage, I shouldn't have said that. What I—"

"Get. The fuck. Out."

"Just, listen. Let me—"

"Get out!" Her eyes burned. How dare he bring up Ian? As if she'd wanted to leave then. As if she *wanted* to leave now. As if she had ever wanted any of this fucking life.

"Get the fuck out, Gavin." Her voice had dropped again, a deadly thrum lingering below it. She might not have her magic right now, but she knew how to make a man hurt. Her palms itched to strike at him.

Gavin straightened, taking stock of her rage. He shook his head, his own anger still simmering beneath the surface.

"Fine." Turning, he strode back through the open doorway, slamming it shut behind him.

Chapter 24

She was walking down the stairwell of the Rafalatriki, fae lights replaced with torches, burning harshly against the darkness of night. She'd fallen asleep hours ago, sick from crying, head throbbing from her anger and sadness. How she'd ended up in the stairwell, she didn't know.

Sage ran a hand down the cold stone wall. The cold bit at her fingers, sharp in contrast to the heat that had blanketed the land for so long. Perhaps summer was finally fleeing and they'd be blessed with cooler days.

As she walked, Sage's senses prickled. The building was so quiet, so still. She'd never felt it so barren. Even on the night she'd been led to find the orichtium in the archives, the soft murmurs and rustling of robes in the distance had accompanied her. Now, the halls were still, the complex empty of sound.

She moved like a wraith, her footsteps ushering no noise as she crept downward. Something beckoned her down until she found herself crossing the threshold of the stairs into the colossal foyer. Torches burned, fastened to the walls of the foyer. Strange she thought, she'd never noticed the torches before. She assumed the entire building was equipped with fae lights, those strange lanterns that seemed to glow with some power unknown to her.

Looking down, Sage could see she was dressed in a sea foam green chiton, blue, wooden pins fastening the straps on her shoulders. It was the same dress she'd worn in the Obelisk during her first days in captivity all those months ago. Another oddity. She'd never had any of her borrowed clothes from the Obelisk sent to her. When did this arrive?

In the distance one of the towering double doors creaked open. The torches extinguished themselves one by one down the line until she was in darkness.

"Hello?" she said, her voice echoing oddly in the empty space.

Darkness permeated the air, almost like a solid thing pressing down on her, making it hard to breathe.

Crisp clacking of footsteps prowled toward her, making her heart thump in her throat.

"Hello, my darling." The slippery voice, its familiarity raising goosebumps on her arms, wrapped itself around Sage. Then the torches flared back to life. She was standing in the middle of the foyer, mere feet away from President Ranquer.

Fear was a funny thing. The way her body reacted as magic flared beneath her skin had her mind racing to catch up. How the hell had he gotten here?

Quickly, she reached for her daggers.

"Ah-ah-ahhh," Ranquer tsked, shaking his finger at her. "We'll have none of that."

Sage's hands brushed her skirts, no daggers to be found. "How are you here?"

"Oh, well, I'm surprised you haven't figured that out," he mused, stepping to the side so that he could circle her.

"This is all make-believe. Just a dream, I'm afraid." It didn't feel like a dream, especially as he leaned in close, having stepped behind her. His face brushed her hair, and her flesh erupted in goosebumps again as he whispered, "How much I *wish* this was real. That I could get my hands around that little throat and punish you for running away from *me*."

"I'll fucking kill you."

"Oh!" Ranquer laughed, stepping back around her other side, "I know you'll try."

Sage's magic writhed beneath her skin, begging to be released. "What do you want?"

"Same thing I've always wanted," Ranquer said, his voice taking on that familiar slippery tone. His smile was that of a snake's, and she yearned for nothing more than to forcibly remove it. "I want power. Dominion. I want my rightful place at the top of the hierarchy. And for that, I need you."

"Oh, is that all?" Sage said sweetly. "Guess I should wrap myself up and ship myself back to Techeduin, huh?"

"If you could do that, it'd be great," the President grinned. "But I know you won't, which is why I've come up with a backup plan. Now, don't get confused. I *will* still hunt you down, whether I need your magic or not. And I *will* find you and punish you." He stopped, letting his words linger while slipping his hands into his pockets. His pencil thin mustache was emphasized as he pursed his lips, as if he were contemplating something. "The question is, how much damage will you cause before this is all over? Shall I destroy this complex? Shall I find your little fae companion, strap him to an operating table and let my alchemists have their way with him? Or maybe...oh yes, I think this might be fun...maybe I will track down your *sister*–"

"You leave her the fuck alone you fucking, shit eating—"

"That's enough." Fingers of flame wrapped around her throat, causing her eyes to burn. Ranquer's face was centimeters from her own, blue heat roiling within his pupils. He squeezed, making her gasp for air.

This is a dream, just a dream, just a dream..."Now," he began again, still holding onto her. "You can stop all of this by turning yourself over. Cross the border, into Nysa, and I will personally guarantee the safety of those you love."

It was a lie, she knew it was a lie. But could she afford to chance it? Perhaps she could save just a few lives by sacrificing her own?

Bullshit.

She knew it was bullshit. And she knew this was a dream. There was no way for him to actually hurt her.

Her magic suddenly flared, reminding her of her own power. She'd escaped this prick before. He wasn't better than her. He was nothing.

"Get your hand off of me," she growled.

The blue flame in Ranquer's eyes grew, taking over his entire gaze. Sage called to her magic, pulling every ounce forward.

Water.

Earth.

Air.

Fire.

Punching out with both hands, Sage rocketed Ranquer back, her magic propelling him so far, so fast, that he hit the closed doors with a thunderous *crack*.

Sage whipped her arms through the air. Fire flew, water streamed from the walls, crystals and vines erupted from the ground, and air plummeted toward the President now pinned against the door.

His feet slowly turned to stone as spittle frothed in the corners of his mouth. "You'll pay for this. You'll all pay for this," he seethed, even as the stone crept higher and higher up his legs.

"Not before you will." With a final heave, Sage yanked on her magic. The stone leapt up his body as she ran forward. With a yell, she let her fist collide with the President-turned-statue and reveled as it shattered into dust.

Sage shot upright from her bed.

Her sheets were soaked, ner nightgown matted to her body. There was a stench to her sweat that made her sick to her stomach.

It hadn't been real.

It hadn't been real.

Still, the feeling of Ranquer's fingers around her neck pulsed, and the realization that he'd somehow gained access to her mind, dreamwalking with her, left her shaking, violated. The experience was so jarring compared to the dreamwalking she'd done with Raphael. She reached for Gavin, needing someone to reassure her that everything was okay.

But he wasn't there.

Recollections of their fight sifted back to her, and she leaned forward, folding in half as she scrubbed her face with her hands.

A bath. She'd bathe and feel much better.

Quickly, Sage untangled herself from her sheets, and went into the bathing chamber. Stripping quickly, she let the cool night chilled with the first hints of Autumn air dry the sweat that coated her skin as she pulled the lever that would pump water into the porcelain tub. The chill had her clasping her hands, checking her fingers for signs of that stinging cold she'd felt in her dream. The moon had moved just enough so it sat perfectly centered in the lone window of the bathing chamber. Sage guessed it was only midnight, if that. That meant she'd only been asleep a couple of hours before she'd dreamwalked.

She reached out with her fire magic to warm the water as it reached the right level, then carefully stepped into the water. Rather than feeling relaxed, being confined to the water made Sage feel more restless, more paranoid. She grabbed the soap sitting on the counter and rushed through the process of washing, skipping her hair.

She yanked on the chain, pulling up the stopper at the bottom of the tub, and rushed to step out. She stared at the moon as she hurriedly dried, watching as it crept forward by miniscule increments. She wished Raphael were here. He would know what to say.

Deep down, she also wished for Gavin. His warm arms had a talent for chasing away her fears and doubts. But she wasn't ready to face him, not yet. Wasn't ready to hear him apologize. Or admit there might have been a sliver of truth to what he'd accused her of.

Sage stomped into her room, needing the extra noise to chase away the feeling of being watched. The quiet emptiness of her room felt like a tangible creature now, and she knew there'd be no chance in hell of her falling back asleep. She pulled a dress over her head, quickly fastening the deep blue straps with pins. She made her way to the door, doubling back to grab her daggers, still fastened in the holster. As she left her room, walking down the same stairwell as her dream, she took stock of everything.

The fae lights burning in their lanterns.

The feel of the cool, but not cold, stonewalls.

In the distance, a conversation behind a closed door.

She continued down the stairs, searching for a safe place to go.

The archives?

She walked towards the hallway that would take her to the archives, but as she came closer, the sight of the towering shelves and low light twisted her gut in knots. Shadows stretched from the shelves like long fingers, flickering from the soft lights.

Not the archives.

She doubled back, not entirely sure where she was going. In the food court sat a small group of healers, drinking tea and talking quietly. Maybe she could join them?

But she didn't recognize them, and didn't feel up for making small talk, especially without the comfort of people she knew. Even after months of staying at the Rafalatriki, she had actually gotten to know only a few other fae. Instead of staying in the food court, Sage turned, taking in the opening that would lead her down to the temples.

If there was any place that felt safe at that moment, the temples seemed like the best choice. Sage rushed toward the stairs that led down, probably making a spectacle of herself to the fae sitting in the corner, but she couldn't care less.

Sage stepped quick and light, chasing a feeling of security. The smooth limestone beckoned to her as she plunged down the stairs. She was practically running by the time her bare feet met the landing, and she hurried to the pool.

She was panting, tears surging again. Her eyes were already stinging, tired from her fight with Gavin, so she forced them down.

Taking large, gulping breaths, Sage allowed her mind to still, focusing on the rippling pool, the water gently cascading from the wall. A sense of safety found her finally. She dipped a hand into the pool, letting the cool water recenter her as she focused on her breathing, letting her eyes fall closed.

Inhale....exhale.

Then, the hairs of her neck stood at attention. Heat blossomed against her back.

"What are you doing here?" a soft voice whispered, caressing her skin.

Sage whirled, and her heart raced again.

☙ ✳ ❧

Sage had kicked him out.

And honestly, he deserved it. He'd been a dick. He'd been a fucking piece of shit, and he knew it.

Equally, he knew the lecture he would have got if he went to Shiphrah and tried to explain what had happened in order to ask for a spare bedroom. Especially since he'd so eagerly announced they "wouldn't be needing" a second room when they first got to the Rafalatriki.

So, instead, he'd gone back down to the temple, determined to sleep on the floor rather than look a fool. The stiff back would be a meager penance for the shit he pulled back in their room.

What the *fuck* had he been thinking? Not only had his words been cruel, they'd been wrong.

He knew Sage didn't really want to leave. He knew she didn't have a choice. The fact that it was looking like he might have to let her go infuriated him, though, and he'd lost all sense of himself. Once again, he found himself plotting on how he could make it up to her.

It reminded him of the night he'd spent before the attack on Veritasaille back in the Spring. She'd been so hurt when she found out Symon had kept that book from her. The fact he had been spying on her for the King had filled him with shame. He wasn't sure he'd actually slept that night, instead, he had tossed and turned, berating himself for being so dense.

Tonight wasn't shaping up to be much better. It wasn't as if he hadn't slept on the floor before. In fact, his first years were spent sleeping on a floor. But that'd been dirt, and at least a tiny bit forgiving. The stone beneath him was proving to be a worthy adversary against sleep.

No matter. His mind was so full of jumbled up thoughts, he probably wouldn't have slept in a bed either.

Gavin rolled onto his side. The constant ringing of the windchimes might have been annoying to some, but he found some comfort in them. The room still flickered with fae lights, just like the rest of the Rafalatriki. The complex was rarely entirely quiet, not with all the different bodies coming and going at all hours of the day.

His shoulder hurt. The stone dug into his side, and he rolled onto the other. He'd snuck into a storage closet he'd found by chance, and managed to snag a couple of blankets. One was rolled up as a pillow beneath his head. The other was wrapped around one leg, a result of his restlessness.

Why was it that he was so horrible at expressing his true feelings with Sage? It seemed he could very eloquently tell everyone else just how much she meant to him. And yet, when it came time to talk to her, it came out wrong.

Gavin flopped onto his back, both shoulders now sufficiently sore. He sighed loudly. Maybe he should have gone back to his estate for the night, spent some time with his family. Delphia would know what to do. She'd always been so matter of fact, so action oriented, she rarely let the peculiarities of emotions get in the way of doing, or saying, what needed to be done. Nevertheless, she always managed to do so with a loving grace that was beyond him.

That was it, he decided. He'd pay Delphia a visit in the morning.

A rustling bounded down the stairwell, ricochetting softly through the temple. Dark blue skirts rushed by the opening that led into Cerridos's temple room, and Gavin detected Sage's scent: a blend of sage, citrus, and honey. Beneath her scent he also detected a sense of panic.

Quietly, he rose from the spot where he'd lain, going to the archway that led into the temple hall. At the end, Sage leaned over the pool, breathing hard and fast.

Something had happened, something to frighten her.

His first instinct was to race through the Rafalatriki and find the creature responsible for her fear. But for once he mastered his emotions, remembering the last time he let his instincts get the best of him in this regard. Instead, he watched. He stood a silent vigil as he watched her slow her breathing, gathering herself. He wanted to rush over to her, but he didn't trust himself not to startle her.

Carefully, he walked toward her, his heart pulling at him, pulsing with a need to be close, to hold, to protect.

"What are you doing here?"

He wanted to groan. What in Eternity was that?! *That* was the best thing he could ask?

Sage whirled to face him, her eyes big and bright, a mixture of fear and surprise on her face before breaking into relief. Then, she seemed to remember their fight, her shoulders went rigid and she turned back to the pool. "Sorry. I didn't know you were down here. I'll go somewhere else." She cleared her throat and pulled herself to her fullest height, which still wasn't much.

"That's not what I meant..."Gavin started, running a hand through his hair. "Just...something happened to you. I can see it all around you. What was it?"

Sage, still facing the pool, wiped her eyes. "It's nothing. I'm fine."

"Bullshit," said Gavin. He didn't want to piss her off, but he fucking hated being lied to. Even if it was her protecting herself. They needed to learn to communicate with each other. And he could take the first step at making that happen. "Come on, Sage. Tell me what's going on. Please."

She huffed a deep breath. "He found me. Again." Her voice was low, ragged.

"What? Who?" Despite himself, Gavin's power surged, begging to be let loose and find the creature that had frightened her.

"Ranquer."

"He's here?" Gavin's power, his heartbeat, his mind, all became thunderous, charging through him like a cyclone. They needed to go. They needed to warn Shiphrah. Could Symon get here fast enough—

"I was dreamwalking, and he found me," Sage continued, wiping her eyes again. She still faced the pool, but he could see her shoulders shudder. "He found me in a dream. And he hurt me. He threatened my family. He threatened you."

She sobbed then, folding forward to cradle her face in her hands.

Gavin's heart nearly broke in half. He rushed forward to gather her in his arms. "It's okay," he soothed, rubbing his face against hair. "It's okay. You're safe."

Her face whipped upward, nearly cracking him in the nose. "For how long? How long, Gavin?! We know he's here. We know the Dark Born can bypass enchantments—"

"Not ours," Gavin countered.

"Eventually, they will." Sage shoved out of his arms, and his heart fractured a bit more. She stalked down the hallway, forcefully brushing her hair from her face. She got halfway down the hall before she whipped back around to glare at him. Her face was pulled into a fierce scowl, ready to launch herself at him as if he were the enemy.

"You were right, you know." The words were flung at him, and he couldn't help but take a step back. "I am fucking *terrified* of this," she said, gesturing between them.

She took a step towards him again, pointing at him with vengeance blazing in her eyes. "What if this is something? What if this is *everything*?" She threw her hands down, turning to stomp back towards the stairs. Gavin made to follow, but she whirled again.

"And what if we *do* figure out how to leap together? Huh? And then I can't come back? What then? What will happen to your family, to Mystaira?"

Gavin took a breath, ready to console her, but she forged on. "What if I *can't* take you with me, and I finish these Gods-damned bargains, and I can't get back?" Her voice broke, and he felt his heart shatter alongside it. "What then, Gavin? What will I do?"

She sank to the floor, her head in her hands, sobs racking her body. Carefully, he approached her, sinking to his knees. He swallowed thickly, the words lodging themselves painfully in his throat before he could quietly admit, "I don't know."

Gavin gathered Sage by her shoulders, pulling just enough so she faced him. "All I know is that it doesn't matter if you go back to your world, or TupaGuara—wherever that is—if you end up in worlds yet discovered," his hands moved to her face, his thumbs brushing away the tears streaming down her face. "You could find yourself in the depths of Darkness itself, and I would find you. There is no place in creation where I won't go to find you, Sage." A hard inhale racked through her body as he continued holding her. "I would happily give my life, over and over again, even if this is all we have. But I will never stop trying to get to you, Sage. Because you're worth it." He gently swiped the tears from her eyes as she closed them, squeezing them tightly against his words.

Unexpectedly, she surged forward, crushing her mouth to his. His heart roared inside his chest. On her lips he found her familiar taste, mixed up with her fear and his. The truth was, he wasn't sure how he'd get to her. But that mattered little. He meant what he said, and had since he'd first cradled her in his arms, broken and battered.

Sage's hands slipped through his hair and he let his own hands hold her tight, keeping her wrapped up in him, never wanting the embrace to end. As she nipped his lip, he groaned into her mouth and his hands slipped down her body, gripping her waist hard against him. They were kneeling on the hard stone floor, out in the open for anyone to see. But his world was wrapped up inside a dark blue dress, who was currently raking her nails against his scalp. He didn't give a damn what else might be happening around them. There was only her.

Gavin's arm snaked around her waist, the other arm reaching to the floor as he pulled her down to the ground. As she settled beneath him, he tore his mouth from hers, brushing his lips along the column of her throat. Her breath shuddered, and her arousal filled the air around him. He'd gone hard the second her mouth reached his, but his cock now ached with his need for her.

He balanced himself over her, both letting his weight fall on her and supporting himself. She writhed beneath him, wrapping one leg around his and arching her back. The friction against his pants seam nearly drove him out of his skin, and he bit her shoulder. Her moaning gasp electrified him, making his muscles tense as she grasped his biceps. "Gavin," she panted.

Her leg lifted as he ran a hand down the length of it, hiking the skirt of her dress up until he found her bare skin. "Please," she begged, her voice little more than breath.

As his finger aimed true, spearing for the center of her, he nuzzled aside the front of her dress until her breast was exposed. She cried out as his mouth found her nipple, and his cock throbbed painfully again as he pushed aside her undergarments to find her slick and ready for him. Her hands skated across his body, and his entire body expanded as her palm gripped him hard, squeezing just enough to set him on fire.

His mouth crushed hers, stealing what he most desperately wanted from her even as she unfastened his pants, her hand diving below and gripping him fiercely.

"Fuck, yes," he growled into her mouth, biting her lip hard enough to make her cry out gently. She responded with a firm squeeze, and *fuck* if that didn't set him off.

Gavin ripped himself away from her, unfastening himself fully as she shimmied out of her undergarments. The smell of her drove him wild, and he felt himself already begin to unravel just at the sight of her. Her eyes shone, not glazed with desire, but burning with need. Burning with possession as he lowered himself, her skirts lifted to her waist.

With a quick thrust, Gavin seated himself inside her, her warmth consuming him. He didn't wait for her to adjust, and he knew she didn't need it even if he'd offered. Her body was ready, waiting for him to give her what it wanted. He withdrew, slamming home and his body contracted with the force of it, the *rightness* of it.

How was it possible for her body to feel like...*home*?

He thrust, over and over, his whole existence devoured by her as she clenched around him, her breath, her voice, her mouth and teeth and nails all marking him as hers.

"Say it," he growled into her neck. "Tell me the truth, Sage."

Her breath caught, hitched as he rocked into her again and again.

"Say it," he said, his voice pleading even as his body hardened even more.

"You're mine," she said, her head tilting up and back on the stone floor. Her body arched as he slammed home again, both breasts now exposed for him.

He licked the center of her chest, and she cried out again. "Say it again, Sage."

"You're. Mine," she growled.

"And what does that mean?" he asked into her ear, her breath hitting his neck fast and hot, rocketing down across his neck.

"I'm coming back."

Her proclamation shot through him. He felt his body pull away, leaving himself even as he plunged further into her. "I fucking love you, Sage."

As he came home, her body clenching and shuddering around him, he knew they were both close. Around him, threads of power expanded and lengthened from them both, radiating from their entwined bodies. Sage's power was the color of jade, lilac, and gold. They spiraled out from her, her legs pulling him into her even harder than before.

His power was silver, and white, threads of blue branching away from his back. As he felt his body tense, ready to release into hers, the threads of power wrapped around them both, tying themselves up.

He was entirely wrapped in her as he exploded, his entire being emptying into her with a final thrust. She cried out, her body shuddering and quaking as her own release wrecked him.

Their power hovered, wrapped around them like a cocoon. Slowly, Sage's eyes fluttered open, finding his own. She gave him a slow kiss, and he lingered, letting himself revel in her. He stayed inside her, not ready to leave, not sure he'd ever be ready to leave her.

She pulled away, letting her head fall softly back to the floor. Her eyes shifted, focusing on something behind Gavin. He felt her hand drift across his back, and damn if his cock didn't twitch again from the contact.

"What's this?" she asked quietly, plucking at one of the threads that still wrapped them tightly.

"I don't know, and I don't think I care," he said, nuzzling her neck.

He felt her smile even as he nuzzled her again. "Gavin," she said breathlessly.

He pulled back, searching for her gaze. Her eyes were soft, warm, and everything he ever wanted. "Take me to bed," she said quietly.

Not needing more prompting, he cast them back into their room, landing softly on the bed. Maybe, he thought as Sage rocked her hips upward again—reigniting his need just like that—they could stay there forever and forget everything else.

Maybe, he thought again, letting himself drown in his own wishes, this was what eternity felt like.

Gavin kissed Sage slowly, letting himself come apart inside her again. He wished the Goddess would just let him stay in this moment. He silently prayed to the Goddess, asking her to grant him sanctuary. He rocked back into Sage, hoping against everything that his wishes would be granted.

Chapter 25

Sunshine grazed the tiny apartment with a warm caress. The sun was crawling towards its height, running its fingers across the fields below when Sage and Gavin finally pulled themselves from their bed, having slept in well past breakfast. Sage had never felt more loved, more worshipped, than as they lazily bathed. As Gavin lovingly washed her hair, his hands massaging her scalp, she felt her body's final guards break down. By the time they were done, Sage thought there couldn't possibly be anything left between her and Gavin.

Her proclamation from the night before replayed through her mind.

You're mine, she'd said.

And she'd said it again, and again throughout the night. Strange that she had so readily laid claim to him. Yet, he never once made the same claim. Probably because he knew how she would have reacted to such a possessive statement.

He knew her so well, it seemed. And he was content with her claiming him, knowing that if he was hers, then she was his.

Their hands were entwined as they finally made their way down the stairwell, descending down the complex to meet Shiphrah for yet another training session.

They'd reached the food court and stopped just outside the stairwell that would bring them down to the temple when Gavin turned to Sage.

"We don't have to do this again," he said, his voice low. "If you decide right now that you can't do this anymore, I will do everything I possibly can to get you to Maracadia. Then I'll wait." He brushed her hair back, tucking a piece behind her ear.

Her heart thundered in anticipation. She couldn't lie to him and say that she wasn't afraid of trying again. The way it wrecked her body every time they practiced filled her with apprehension. But they both knew that now, after last night, they came as a packaged deal. "Let's just try again. We give it one more week."

Gavin gave her a quick, sweet kiss to her forehead. Her tight smile belied her anxiety, but it wasn't like she hadn't lived through suffering before. Hell—it wasn't even as if this would be the first time she'd caused herself pain deliberately. There had been times as a teenaged fugitive, holed up in a condemned building or abandoned barn, when the truth of her plight had been more than she could bear. There'd been times when she had been close, *so close*, to ending it all. Her own fear had been the only thing to stop her. For so long, fear had been all she had.

As they descended, Sage gripped her fear, a feeling that had once been so familiar, and held it like a hot brand, letting it burn her apprehension away. She held onto the feeling until all that was left was determination, a predator staring down a larger predator.

A wolf and a fox.

Her fear was the fox, a wiley animal with cunning, able to squirm itself into tiny spaces. It lay in wait, looking for weaknesses in the fortress of her mind, and would strike when she was unprepared.

But what was a fox compared to a wolf?

Her determination snapped the fear in half, severing the vulpine animal's head from its body.

By the time they reached the temple, Sage wondered if flames flickered in her eyes.

She could do this.

She *would* do this.

Gavin squeezed her hand hard once, and she looked up at him. The same burning determination simmered in his own gaze.

Mine, her body sang. A new thrill of resolve shivered through her as they both greeted Shiphrah, who knelt at the pool down the hallway of the temple.

Shiphrah's body snapped to attention, her head whipping to them both, an odd expression on her face.

"What?" Gavin asked.

"You've the bond," Shiphrah said. Not a question. It was said with certainty.

Sage turned to look at Gavin, who looked back at her. Their hands were still clasped and she could feel the steady pulse of his heart in the wrist that rested against hers. Memories of the ribbons that spiraled out of her and Gavin, wrapping them up, replayed in Sage's mind. Perhaps that had been The Bond settling into place?

The news—The Bond—danced around them, a pixie showering them with the reality that they'd not only committed themselves with their words, but their souls were now tied.

A bubble of laughter escaped Sage. "It seems I can't stop myself from giving away pieces of my heart, huh?"

Gavin grinned widely. His face was sunshine as he pulled her close, his hand wrapping around the back of her neck as he leaned in to kiss her.

As he pulled back away, he whispered, "But this will be the last."

"This will be the last." Sage's voice was quiet and firm.

As they turned back to Shiphrah, the healer was wiping tears away from the corners of her eyes. "This is wonderful news," she said, sniffing loudly even as she beamed a bright smile.

"Thank you," said Sage. "So...does this change anything with our training?"

"Well, for one thing," Shiphrah began, looking at Gavin then back at Sage, "it will make both of your powers stronger. Sage, you should be able use some of Gavin's strength to support your own power. And Gavin," she continued, stepping closer to him. "How does the Signum Dominari feel? Is it still trying to be set free?"

Sage's head snapped to Gavin, her face a mask of questions. Gavin merely shrugged his shoulders at her, then looked to Shiphrah and gave her a short shake of his head. "No, The Seal isn't trying to work itself out of my body."

"I thought not." Shiphrah turned to walk back to the pool. When she gracefully sat on the ledge, she addressed them again as they walked closer to join her. "It's one of the reasons we used to require those with The Seal to find a partner to bond with. The combination of two souls sharing the burden of such a great power makes it more stable. And your power," Shiphrah looked fully at Sage, "is more power-ful than most fae could dream. You wield all four elements. Of course Gavin feels more stable."

Sage looked at Shiphrah, nodding as her explanations made sense. She sensed Gavin rubbing his chest a little, as if he were admiring the feel of it, and she wondered for the first time just how much weight he'd been holding on to keep his power leashed.

"Let's try something new, today." Shiphrah motioned to the floor. "Have a seat, facing each other."

Sage and Gavin settled themselves on the floor. Sage gave one last, long exhale, blowing out any apprehension that tried to linger. She was going to master her magic mixing with Gavin's power today. There would be no other outcome.

"We've tried combining your powers with you sitting in different rooms, which might have been too difficult to start with. That's my fault," Shiphrah admitted. "I wonder if starting off like this might work a bit better."

Sage turned her gaze from Shiphrah to Gavin. They each gave each other a silent nod, then Sage watched as Gavin shifted his body weight, rolling his shoulders until he was free of the tension he usually held there. "See you on the other side," he said with a wink, then he closed his eyes. Sage huffed a half-laugh, then followed Gavin into her own focus.

She closed her eyes, beginning with the ever-familiar breathing patterns.

Deep inhale.

Emptying exhale.

She let herself be poured out of her breaths, gathering awareness and clarity with every inhale. Slowly, the sound of the trickling pool, breath racing in and out of Gavin, even the slight tremor far above as something heavy was rolled across some stone floor became a heavy blanket wrapping itself around her.

Sage's magical body began to peel away from her physical form. Her eyesight sharpened, and she could see both her physical and her magical forms sitting side-by-side. Her hair had become long, reaching to her shoulders now. Sage admired her straight posture, a remnant of her dancer's training from girlhood.

Sage's magical form turned its focus from her physical body until it stared straight ahead. Flickering into view, Gavin's astral body took shape.

"Hey, there, Fly Boy," Sage said, quirking a smile.

"Hello, yafah."

"What does that mean?"

Gavin's astral eyes warmed. "Beautiful."

Sage hummed. Of course that's what it meant. Still, her chest bloomed with warmth, even in her detached magical form.

In the distance, Shiphrah's voice broke through the barrier of their meditation. "See if either of you can move some of your power from yourself and into the other."

Sage and Gavin looked at each other, Gavin nodding slightly. "We can stop at any point."

"I know," Sage said in a whisper. Still, she'd decided today was the day she succeeded. Sage kept her gaze on Gavin, slowly reaching into her magical form to find the source of her power. Deep, deep within herself, she found it. Her magic pranced around her. She could feel its claws clacking against the surface of her essence, tail wagging with contentment.

Gently, Sage urged her magic up and out. *Come on out. Your other half is waiting.*

Ears perked up. Sage beckoned again. *Just a little bit. Let's introduce you.*

Her gaze still intent on Gavin, Sage gasped as threads of lilac power tentatively stretched out from her chest. She could feel spools of potential hovering beneath the outer shell of herself, waiting to see what happened next.

From Gavin, threads of white and silver reached out, racing towards her. Her own lilac thread responded, and matched Gavin's power for speed. At once, Gavin's threads merged with Sage's chest as her own power wove into his.

His power was cool, like the breeze racing down from a mountain top, playfully bounding through limbs and tall grass. Gavin's astral eyes shut, and Sage was overwhelmed with sensations...

Contentment.

Thrill.

Excitement.

A little bit of arousal. No surprise there.

Sage felt these same feelings, but doubled over. Some of those sensations were not her own, and as Gavin's gaze returned to her, she knew he was experiencing the same.

"It's warm," he said. "And sweet."

Sage laughed. "I'm not sure anyone has ever called me that before."

"Oh, I'm not talking about you, just your magic." He smiled roguishly at her.

Reality seemed to grow more distant, and something alerted Sage that she was nearing the time when she needed to go back to her body. "It's time," she said, tilting her head toward her physical form so Gavin understood what she meant.

He nodded once, then said, "I have an idea."

"Okay."

"Here," Gavin held out the hand of his astral body, and she grabbed it. "Now, just think about the pool, right behind Shiphrah."

A mischievous grin overtook her face, and she couldn't help herself from giving him a devilish, "Oh—yes..."

Sage grabbed Gavin's hand. She closed her magical form's eyes, and thought of the pool, just behind Shiphrah.

With a quick tug, Sage felt herself meet her physical form once again. Then, she was on her feet, knee deep in the pool behind Shiphrah.

"What?!" cried the healer, rising to her feet.

Sage and Gavin grinned at each other once, then both scooped handfuls of water and doused Shiphrah.

"Ahhh!" Shiphrah leapt forward, whirling with her fists raised. Her robes were splattered with water, but Sage was laughing so hard, she could barely register the mixed emotions warring on Shiphrah's face.

"You casted?" she sputtered.

Sage doubled over, gripping her stomach as Gavin laughed as well. "Gods, Shiphrah, I'm sorry..." she sucked in a deep lungful of air. "Your face—"

A fresh bout of laughter overtook Sage as she leaned against Gavin.

"Who would have thought the mighty Shiphrah screams like a child?" Gavin taunted, laughing just as hard as Sage.

"It was pretty funny," said Shiphrah, brushing water droplets from her robes. "And I did scream quite loud." A slow smile crept across her face. "I will tell you, I think I nearly swallowed my tongue when you both disappeared." Then she was laughing.

Carefully, Sage and Gavin stepped out of the pool, Gavin holding her hand as she lifted the hem of her soaked dress. Sage wringed her dress out over the lip of the pool as Shiphrah continued to wipe water from her head and face with the dry parts of her robes. Occasionally, a giggle escaped one of the trio until they had each recomposed themselves.

"I'm excited to know you can access Gavin's powers, Sage. If you can strengthen that ability, I really don't see you two being unable to leap together." Shiphrah's eyes held a gleam of enthusiasm. "Have you spoken about your plans with the King and Queen?"

Gavin nodded. "There's a plan for managing Mystaira while I'm away."

"Then all is set," declared Shiphrah with a clap of her hands. "We'll continue our practice in the coming weeks. Meanwhile, Sage, I'll see if any of my contacts in Jordynia have heard of the insignia."

"Thank you." Sage grinned as she thanked Shiphrah, but a cold shiver of dread slunk just beneath her happiness.

Raphael. Several times a day she wondered about her friend and his safety. That he assumed the insignia were on the mortal continent seemed more than coincidental. As per usual, it would appear as though the pieces were tumbling together like boulders down a mountain, and she just hoped this time she would be able to keep the ones she loved safe.

Chapter 26

❧ ✳ ☙

Raphael gripped the railing until his knuckles were white.

Waves were battering the sides of the ship, sending up a stinging spray. Wind tore over the planks and rain slashed at his exposed skin. The sight and sound of lightning tearing the air around him as the storm continued to pound the ship and crew left Raphael breathless.

For two days they'd been waiting at bay for a representative to emerge out of Meropoli to conduct their inspection. Two long days after a two week voyage and now this. Raphael was a stoic male, but sailing stormy seas got his very last nerve.

Raphael had forgotten how much he despised sea travel. Despite his talent as a healer, he'd been unable to stop the seasickness, thus, he was compelled to remain on the deck throughout the ongoing storm. Any time spent within the cabin brought forth the insatiable nausea, and Acantha had already warned him of the consequences should he vomit in her presence again.

The ship rolled heavily to one side as a wave tossed them, and Raphael held on for dear life. "Oh, Goddess," he whispered. "Save me from this curse." Raph's stomach gave a resounding shiver, and he exhaled heavily, trying to abate the inevitable sickness to come.

Above him, a loud "Ship, ho!" cried out, the ship's quartermaster warning of the incoming Meropolian customs vessel.

They were distant enough from the coastline that the sharp cliffs were barely outlined along the horizon. Now, with the ongoing tempest harassing them, the cliffs were shrouded in rain so that he could barely make out the barest hint of their existence. But thankfully, emerging from the almost vertical rain was indeed an official looking vessel.

"Thank the Goddess," Raph muttered, peering through squinted eyes. If all went well, he would find himself on solid land soon. He had no inkling of what time of day it was, as the storm had broken while they all slept and continued with vengeance. That didn't matter, thought Raphael, he would insist they be escorted inland immediately.

The vessel was now pulling close to their own, and Raphael gripped the railing with all his might as the ship rolled once more. Even still, the mortal sailors easily cast grappling lines from their ship, using crossbows that shot hooks and rope to the fae ship. The storm prevented the ships from attaching any sort of plank, so instead, the sailors swung through the air, their militant leather armor flapping from their waists. Within seconds, ten mortal soldiers were standing on the deck, the leader stepping forward to speak with the ship's captain. Raphael paid little attention as he fought against another pang of nausea, his cheeks full of air as he forced himself to remain composed.

"You, there!"

Raph heard the shout of the mortal captain behind him, then rapid footsteps. Next thing he knew, the mortal captain stood before him.

Raph turned to discover an angry face topped by a bronze helmet. Raph swallowed hard to keep his nausea under control; it wouldn't do to throw up on the man. By the looks of things, the mortals didn't seem all too friendly.

"You have papers for your visit?" the captain demanded, his hand jutting out toward Raphael.

"Yes, let me—here," Raph fumbled as he found the letter sent to him by Malakai. The captain quickly opened the letter, then looked over its contents. The rain battered against the parchment, and Raph hoped it would withstand the torrent.

Without warning, the captain shoved the letter back into Raph's hand. "Once we make port, be ready to disembark. We will have someone waiting to escort you to the Governor."

"Ad navem!" cried the mortal soldier abruptly. With admirable swiftness, the mortal soldiers shot their grappling ropes, swinging back across the sky to their own ship. Raphael watched in wonder, questioning how long he'd been trying to keep himself from getting sick and simultaneously admiring the strength of mortal men.

Clanking metal signaled the rising anchor, and he nearly lost his balance as the ship lurched forward. Fae shipmates rowed below deck, fighting against the tumultuous waves that continued to beat against the ship, that groaned and whined against the force of the water. Raphael found his arm looped around the railing, gripping the sleek wood like a leech.

"Is it that bad, now?" called Acantha, her footsteps splashing along the deck.

"How on earth are you remaining upright in these conditions?" Raph asked, glaring at the tattooed female.

Acantha shrugged. "It's not that bad. Keep your knees bent a little. It'll help."

Raphael scowled at Acantha as Epyllo followed her on deck, then shrugged his dark cloak tight around his body. While Acantha stood with her shaved head bare to the sky, Epyllo clutched the hood that draped over his head, peering out from beneath.

"It's fucking pissing down out here." Epyllo squinted beneath his hood, then offered a hand to Raphael. "Let's get you up."

Raphael had never felt less graceful than trying to pry himself off the deck floor, a wave breaching the side of the ship and dousing him thoroughly. "Why must it rain where it's already wet?" he muttered to himself.

The ship groaned as another large wave walloped them, and Raphael clung to Epyllo as they all staggered to remain upright. As they regained their balance, a deepening shadow overtook the sea, and Raph looked up through the slashing rain to watch as white cliffs came into focus.

The mountains that spiraled up from the cliffs looked like the bottom jaws of a sea monster in the lightning flashing beyond them, and Raphael couldn't shake the sense of foreboding that crept along his soaked skin.

As the ship continued its tossing through the waves, the trio watched as a gaping hole in the cliffside revealed itself through the darkness. The mortal ship, far in the distance ahead of their own, carefully maneuvered itself so it passed into the hole. Raphael shuddered, the dampness of his clothes and skin intensifying the feeling of being sucked into a leviathan's waiting mouth as their own ship finally entered the cave.

The silent darkness that blanketed the ship was absolute, Raph's ears almost popping with the change in pressure and total absence of the noisy, raging sea. Then, with a suddenness that startled him, light blazed as the ship continued its descent into the cave, torches lighting the way through a fortified tunnel. Mortal soldiers stood at attention with weapons drawn on catwalks that spanned the entirety of the passageway. The rhythmic sound of oars splashing echoed through the tunnel, mimicking the thundering of Raph's own heart.

What if this was a huge mistake? Raph's palms began to sweat as he wondered if Malakai's letter would be sufficient enough for what would come next. The mortals of Meropoli had good reason to mistrust the fae.

For centuries, tribes of fae had enslaved mortal men and women, abusing their Goddess-given powers to laud themselves supreme over the mortals. It wasn't until the rise of the Dark Born, when true and pure evil entered their world that some of the tribes began standing up for the mistreatment of mortals. It seemed their ancestors had needed the wake-up call before putting an end to the suffering of mortal man. Shortly thereafter, Meropoli had welcomed the mortals that fled Panchia, looking for sanctuary among their own kind.

So it didn't surprise Raphael that the catwalk remained heavily staffed with soldiers, wielding elm weapons they knew were fatal to fae-kind.

"Epyllo," Raph whispered. "Come below deck with me. Just for a moment." Raphael was overwhelmed with an uneasy feeling. The plan had always been for the three of them to disembark from the ship together. Raph wondered now if the mortals would allow all three fae to step onto dry land.

Acantha nodded at them, picking up on something in Raph's eyes. She gripped the railing, keeping her gaze on the passing tunnel wall as the ship continued being rowed toward the docks safely tucked away at the end of the tunnel. Whether the spy knew what Raphael had planned, he wasn't sure, but he wouldn't run the risk of speaking it out loud.

Epyllo barely made it to the hallway that led to the hammocks they were given to sleep in when Raphael turned and whispered, "Shift."

"What?" Epyllo asked. "Now?"

"Yes, now!" Raphael urged, shoving Epyllo deeper down the hallway. "Into something small, something that could hide on my body without being found." Epyllo's greatest strength as a spy was his ability to shift into any animal form he had previously come in contact with. That was incredibly useful for someone who needed to get into tight places quietly.

Epyllo looked at Raphael questioningly, but then shrugged out of his cloak before handing it to him. "Here, might as well take this."

Raph tugged on the coat as Epyllo shifted forms, shimmering slightly before shrinking into a light green cricket.

"Perfect!" exclaimed Raphael, clapping his hands once. "Now, where to hide you," he said, scooping Epyllo up gently into his palm. The cricket gave one loud chirp as if to say, "I don't know!"

Raphael scrambled, aiming for a pocket of the coat. "No, not there," he muttered, remembering how thoroughly the mortals had patted him down on his last trip to Meropoli. "Alright," he whispered, lifting the cricket up toward his shoulder. "Crawl into my hair, they won't check that, I'm sure."

Raphael could feel Epyllo carefully crawl into the tangled mess of wet curls that hung down below his shoulders, their weight intensified by the rainwater now soaking his locks. Tiny legs scratched his neck as the cricket crawled closer to his scalp, pinching tiny baby hairs at his nape.

"Let's hope this works," he whispered to himself, to Epyllo, and to the Goddess herself as he climbed the stairs back onto the deck.

"All good?" asked Acantha, perceptive as always.

Raphael gave a quick nod. "Listen very carefully," he whispered, leaning hard against her shoulder to mimic one overtaken by seasickness—not a hard feat. "If they don't allow you onshore, I need you to figure out a way to keep the ship nearby. Do you understand?"

"Of course."

Just then, a thunderous thud shook the deck as the ship butted against the docks at the end of the tunnel. Shouting erupted from all sides as ropes were tossed aboard and secured around posts. Sailors rolled down a large plank, creating a ramp onto the wooden dock below, which fed into stone. The stark whiteness of the cliff outside was mirrored inside the tunnel, though it glowed orange in the light cast from the myriad torches.

Raphael began to shiver from the dousing he'd experienced out in the storm.

The mortal captain from before reboarding their ship, looking again over their cargo manifesto. Both the fae captain and mortal captain discussed back and forth what items were to be unloaded: fae wine, wool harvested from Mystairan farms, gold smithied from Veritasailles artisans, and other goods commonly traded between the continents. In return, Meropolian steel and medicine would be crated onto the fae ship for delivery to Felysia.

Sharply, the mortal captain called out, "The one with the letter, come here."

Raphael turned, digging through his pocket once more for the now damp letter from Malakai.

"Yes, that's me." Raphael's knees wobbled as the ship gave a final roll on the water, cargo being lifted away byway of giant pulleys fastened to the ceiling.

"I know that," said the captain, grumbling something under his breath. "So you're to see the Governor?"

"Yes. As you can see, Malakai has requested my presence—"

"You will refer to him as the Governor while you are on Meropoli soil, is that clear?" The mortal captain barked at Raphael, startling him slightly. Why was it that soldiers always felt the need to *bark* everything?

"My apologies," Raphael stammered. "The Governor invited me, yes."

"Very well," the captain said, turning sharply. "Follow me."

"And what about my companion?" Raphael asked, causing the captain to stop short. The feathers along his helmet rippled with the force of his about face.

"I see an invitation for only one fae on that letter."

"Yes, I understand, but my friend here has traveled such a long way to see the marvels of Meropoli. I'm sure the Governor—"

"Enough!" the captain barked again. Raphael shuttered at the venom in the man's voice. "It's bad enough the Governor invited *you*."

Raphael did his best not to shrink at the harsh words. "I see. Well, then, lead the way." Raphael glanced at Acantha one last time. The spy gave him a faint nod in reassurance; she wouldn't be too far away.

The mortal captain led Raphael down the wooden plank, the beams bouncing alarmingly with the force of the man's steps. Raphael hiccuped once, fighting the last of his seasickness. As they reached the wooden dock, Raphael found himself nearly running to keep pace with the captain who stopped just as the dock met the stone floor of the tunnel. With another barking yell, the captain called over another soldier who had just finished securing a crate atop a wagon. The soldier ran over to them, stopping to salute the captain.

"Take this male to the Governor's house. Do not deviate from the path or tarry, do you understand?"

"Yes, Captain!" The soldier removed his hand from its salute, then turned to Raphael. "Have you any bags that need to be carried?"

"Oh!" exclaimed Raphael, stunned that he had forgotten his own bag. "Y-yes, hold on just a second, I believe they were—"

"Incoming!" Acantha's voice echoed off the side of the ship, and Raphael's bag flew down to the docks.

"Oh, there it is." A chirp echoed behind Raphael's ear and he stiffened, hoping the mortal soldiers didn't hear Epyllo's short outburst.

The soldier assigned to Raphael quickly collected the bag.

"Follow me," the soldier said to Raphael. His words were short, but at least his tone of voice didn't have the same vehemence to it as the captain's had.

Raph followed closely behind the soldier, dodging others carrying crates either up or down the winding path that would lead out of the tunnel. As they ascended, tiny rivers trickled down the walls and the seams of the floor. He tugged Epyllo's cloak tightly around him, fastening the buckles at the neck so it would remain secure without clutching at it, glad of the extra layer of warmth. As the tunnel darkened, Raphael braced himself to reenter the tumultuous rainstorm. The soldier barely shifted his posture as they breached the outside world, stepping into the slashing waterfall that cascaded from the lip of the cavern, returning to the wretched wetness and cacophonous storm.

Their path stretched on, feeding into a road down the ways. In the distance, Raphael could barely make out a row of wagons attached to mules. Some of the animals loosed unhappy wails at being forced to stand in the open rain.

"We will ride through the night," called the soldier. "If we avoid making any stops, we should arrive in Heronias Square by morning." He wiped at his face, which did nothing besides give him a short reprieve from the rain coating his skin. The soldier's short hair glistened from the brief illumination of lightning.

"I don't suppose you have any covered wagons?" Raphael asked.

The soldier harrumphed. Raphael supposed that was all he needed in answer. Finally, they made it to a wagon, its trunk already sloshing with collected rainwater. The soldier tossed the bag into the front and Raph followed while his new companion untied the mules. With heavy steps, the soldier pushed the mules back, their ears pinned to their heads in annoyance, until the cart was free from the row. Once the animals were pointing in the right direction down the road, the soldier climbed in next to Raphael.

"The name's August," he shouted, voice becoming muffled slightly by a rattling peel of thunder.

"Raphael." Raph extended his hand, reaching to shake the soldier's.

"Pleased to meet you. Now, let's get this show on the road."

Chapter 27

❧ ✳ ☙

Raphael jolted awake, a fresh stream of rain punishing him and his companions. A pointed *Chirp!* snapped his attention back to the road, now bumpy with cobblestones.

"Did you sleep alright?"

August's voice was raised, competing against the pattering of fat raindrops. Raphael adjusted himself. "I guess so," he said loudly, leaning into August's side. "I hadn't realized I dozed off."

"Well, it's a good thing you're awake. We're nearly there."

The wagon now bounced over the knobby street, buildings lining the sides. Awnings stretched out from shops, yet to open for a new day of business. Raphael squinted, pulling his hood close to his face. He couldn't make out much through the rainy dark, but he felt like he could just barely sense the shroud of darkness lifting from the world around them.

As the mules continued their descent into the city, a town square began to take shape. The rain slowed, still steady, but not the bedeviling pace it had been just before. Raph could make out a shape looming in the center of the square, which sat sprawling in a circular shape. As they withdrew from the tight, building-lined road, Raphael noticed other roads shooting away from the city center like the spokes of a wheel. Beyond the square, large governmental buildings loomed on a hill, reaching up over the winding roads of Heronias.

As they made their way towards a road just beyond the center-most point of the town center, Raphael shook August's arm. "Stop!"

August pulled hard on the mules' reigns. "What is it?"

Raphael stood from the bench he sat on, his gaze fixed on the statue that denoted the centermost position of the city. Tall and refined stood a statue of one of Raph's oldest friends. "Is that man's name Ephraim?" he asked the soldier.

"It is. Governor Ephraim had quite a following here in Heronias. His grandson isn't doing half-bad either." August's words were chipper. "Some might say his *other* grandchildren were doing alright, as well."

"Oh?" Raphael asked, only half listening. His gaze remained fixed on the man who'd once held so much of his time and attention. Ephraim's face had been carved into a grin, laughter close to the surface. And yet, somehow, the artist had also been able to capture the seriousness that always simmered beneath the man's gaze. Ephraim had always been a keen observer. Nothing ever got past him, so much so, Raphael used to tease that he must have been half-fae.

Looking at the statue brought a soreness to his heart, and Raphael barely noticed as his hand drifted to the spot, trying to rub the soreness away. "Do you know many of his grandchildren?" Raphael's eyes remained on the statue, even as he sat back on the wagon bench, August snapping the reins to move the mules once more.

"I am one," August said, a hint of laughter in his voice.

Raphael's head snapped to the young soldier. "You are?!"

August smiled. "One of many."

Raphael hummed to himself. If he was honest, he still found it shocking that Ephraim had bonded with a woman. He'd always assumed the man preferred other men, but it was possible he could have been attracted to both. Plenty of fae had the same preferences. Why should it be different for mortals?

"Was he happy?" Raphael asked, his voice dropping slightly.

Raph looked ahead toward the road, but could make out the slight nod of August's head. "He and my Nonno were very happy. Nonno was always joking that Pater Ephraim was too serious for children, but he–my Nonno– always had a way of bringing out the joking side of him."

"You're Nonno?"

"My other grandfather. You see," August explained, be-tween the snapping of reigns as the wagon began its ascent toward the great hill, "our parents were all adopted. All twelve of them. Adopted, obviously, because men can't bear children, at least mortal men can't...I'm not sure how it works with fae, but in mortals it requires—"

"Yes, yes, I know all of that," Raphael interrupted. "I am a healer, you know."

"Oh, are you?" August asked. "Tell me, how does that work? Fae healing? I've always wondered why the fae must import the medicine of mortals."

"Well, I can heal most things. Infections, however, are much easier to battle with medicine. And your healers are really exceptional. Did you know, August, that most of the books we have in our healing schools were written by mortals?"

"Really! That's impressive," said August. "I'd no idea our studies had such an impact on Panchia."

Abruptly, the sound of hoofbeats bounced off the buildings once again lining the streets. Ahead, the road curved tightly so they could barely make out what bounded toward them. The white horse was on them in moments, the soldier astride the horse pulling fiercely on the reins, mimicking August's heaving to stop the mules before the beasts all collided together.

"Raphael?" called the soldier.

"Yes, that's me." Raph responded, looking from August to the soldier.

"You're to come with me."

"And who are you?" Based on the curtness of the newcomer's tone, Raphael rather preferred to be escorted by August.

August huffed. "That, is Felix. Another grandchild."

"Oh, I see," Raphael replied, deflated.

Felix dismounted, then approached the wagon. "Is there a second horse for me?" Raphael asked.

"You'll ride that one," Felix responded, reaching the wagon. Felix was broad, much more broad than August. His eyes were pinched, closer together than what Raphael would consider handsome. His bushy eyebrows furrowed together beneath his helmet, and Raph wondered at how such a brash, burly man had been raised by the gentle Ephraim.

"So, I will ride that," Raph asked, "and you will..."

"I'll ride the rest of the way up with August. Part of the road collapsed up ahead; a flash flood washed away the foundation. We'll secure the wagon, then follow on foot to deliver your bag."

"I see." Raphael was wary of riding on the beast, steam bellowing from its nostrils as Raphael finally approached. "Nice, horsey," Raphael offered.

"Just stick your foot in that stirrup there," Felix offered. "He knows where to go and will get you there safely."

Raphael heaved his leg into the stirrup, then with a mighty effort, threw himself over the saddle. He nearly missed the seat and pitched forward toward the neck of the stallion. Without warning, the beast took off, galloping back the way it came. Raphael bounced ungraciously on the top of the horse, clinging to its mane.

"Goddess, help me," Raphael cried.

The stallion leapt over rubble, edges of the desecrated road just visible through the tears streaking from his face. Ahead, beige walls began to take shape, a gate punctuating two pillars topped with bowls of fire. The rain had ceased, and the flames cast shadows in large swaths.

As they approached, Raph's fingers tightly woven through the horse's hair, the gates swung open. They bounded through the entryway, and Raphael could just make out the figures of two armed guards holding open the wrought iron partitions.

A large structure made of marble sprang up in the middle of a vast courtyard, stables just visible in the distance. A lone figure stood on the expansive steps running the width of the building. Torches burned merrily along the beige stone walls enclosing the estate.

Raph was just getting his seat adjusted when the stallion stopped abruptly, throwing Raph back against its neck. He let out a scream as he nearly toppled over, and Epyllo, still safely tucked into Raphael's hair, chirped loudly in fright.

The man standing on the stairs sprinted down as the two guards hurried toward the horse, now prancing in place.

"Here, let me help you," said a clear voice. If Raphael had known better, he would have thought it was Ephraim himself speaking.

Raph threw his hair out of his eyes, lifting his head to take in the man reaching a hand up towards him. "Malakai?" he rasped.

"Yes, Governor Malakai. Pleased to meet you." Raphael waved away Malakai's hand, and gingerly let his leg slide across the top of the saddle. With trembling arms, he lowered himself from the stallion, who was held securely by a guard gripping the reins.

Once Raph's feet were firmly on solid ground once more, he turned to Malakai. Shakily, Raph held out his own hand. "Raphael. The pleasure is mine."

Malakai shook Raph's hand firmly, then tossed his arm around Raph's shoulders. "Come, it's been a long journey for you."

Raphael replied as they walked. "You have no idea."

"We can show you to your rooms so you can rest."

The idea of sleeping in a bed, instead of a never stilling hammock, was like a symphony to Raphael. "That would be wonderful."

A woman in a white chiton, her hair pinned into a demure bun, led the way through the halls. Portraits lined the walls, and Raphael admired the tasteful decor of the building as he and Malakai talked about his journey. Malakai found Raphael's seasickness amusing, and Raph decided not to hold it against the man as a favor to Ephraim.

Malakai was tall, strong, and broad in body, but not built like a man who'd spent all his time in an arena, training. He had the physique of a man who was naturally blessed with vitality and good health. His bronze skin was unmarred, except, Raphael had noticed, his hands which bore the calluses of one who has worked with their hands. His white robes swept the floors, and they somehow emphasized the strength of the man. In the torchlight, Raphael could make out sandy-brown hair flecked with streaks of blonde. All in all, Malakai was a striking figure. It was unsurprising he was a leader in the city.

As they neared the door that Raphael assumed would be his room, Malakai gently grabbed his elbow, slowing him. "Livie—I've got it from here." The woman in white turned, quietly curtsying before walking back the way they came. "Your rooms are there," Malakai indicated, gesturing to the door adjacent to them.

"Oh, thank you. I'll just—"

"Before you go..." Malakai's voice dropped, his words careful and rushed. "Be careful who you associate with while you're here. There are others who would be reticent to accept your help with the problem we are facing."

"Which is?" Raphael asked.

"I'll explain tomorrow. I'll fetch you for lunch and we can talk in my private quarters." Malakai explained his plan, looking furtively around the hallway. "In the meantime, get some rest, and try to stay out of sight."

"I'll do my best."

Malakai gave Raphael a curt nod before turning, his robes swishing around his feet. "I'll have Felix set your bags outside your door once they've arrived," he called over his shoulder.

Without waiting another moment, Raphael turned the handle to his room, quickly making his escape inside. After closing the door, Raph leaned heavily against it, exhaling heavily and taking in what appeared to be a common room of sorts. A table sat at the center of the room, along with a lounge in the corner piled high with plush pillows.

A sharp *Chirp!* broke him from his moment of respite, sending him toward the table.

Raphael slung the soaked cloak from his back, lying it over the back of a chair. Then, he carefully reached into the spiraling mess of his hair. "Just a moment Epyllo," he whispered, trying to disentangle the poor male. Scratchy legs met Raphael's fingers, and the two worked together to free the cricket from the clutches of Raphael's strands.

"I'm dreadfully sorry," whispered Raph, gently placing Epyllo on the table. "You can shift now."

The cricket chirped several times, crawling from side to side. "You *can* shift, can't you?" Raphael whispered, bringing his face close to the insect.

Epyllo gave several more persistent, loud chirps, hopping toward Raph's face. "I don't know what you are trying to tell me," cried Raphael, exasperated. He dropped his arms, hands slapping against his thighs.

Epyllo jumped twice. Raphael glared at the tiny, green insect, and was nearly startled when the bug stuck out a thin leg as if to say, *Go over there.* A darkened room was opened in the corner, and Raphael walked to it warily. Once he was there, he was able to light a candle secured in a candle lamp, using a burning torch fixed to the wall. Raphael walked into the room, candle held high.

As the light cascaded, Raphael saw that it was a bedroom, sparse but comfortable. Raphael walked quickly back to the table in the other room, only to find the cricket pointing at another darkened room. So, Raphael walked into that room. A washroom, containing a sink of sorts and a chamber pot customary in Meropoli. Nothing out of the ordinary.

"Epyllo, what is going on—"

Epyllo shifted, his fae body re-forming atop the table. "Good Goddess. It's a good thing Aryael never relied on you for spying." The male sat cross-legged on the table, glaring at Raphael. "And that's the last time I ride in your hair. Do you know you nearly squashed me when you fell asleep in that wagon?"

"I'm sorry," Raphael muttered, completely abashed at how out of his depths he was. "Oh," he began, rubbing his face with both hands. "I'm so exhausted."

"Agreed," said Epyllo, "but before we go to bed, we need to go over a few things."

"Alright." Raphael walked to the table and took a seat. Epyllo mimicked the move, and scooted off the table before grabbing a chair of his own.

"Malakai was right in warning you to be wary," Epyllo began. "Acantha and I had done some recon on the ship, but you were so ill I didn't have a chance to share it." Raphael gave a nod, indicating he understood. "Meropoli is on unstable footing, it seems. There's been a few men conducting power grabs in the last couple decades, a couple of them serious attempts. Politics are more inflammatory than ever according to several of the crew. It would seem that some political leaders have tried inciting Meropoli to war with the fae, as retribution for the past harm our kind had done to their ancestors. Some are even suggesting we pay reparations."

"There'd been some prejudice while I visited before, but it had never been that bad." Raphael wondered at how things could have become so strained.

"There's more," Epyllo whispered. "There's rumors of some men having an alliance, or some sort of association, with the Dark Born. They're on the eastern border."

Raphael let the information wash over him, all the various problems and issues swirling around while he simultaneously wondered what Malakai had called him to the continent for. In his gut, Raphael thought it had to do with the Dark Born, and Felysia's last hopes of defeating them. "Thank you," said Raph. "I'll be careful."

Raphael pushed on the table to stand, then began making his way to the bedroom before stopping. "Oh...there's only one bed." It dawned on Raph that Epyllo should stay in the singular bedroom, giving them both an opportunity for the spy to hide away should anyone come in unexpectedly.

"No worries," said Epyllo. "I'll be more useful in other forms."

Without warning, the spy shifted, shimmering and then shrinking into a tiny songbird. Epyllo gave Raphael a few merry twitters before hopping toward the double doors at the back of the common room. Raph pushed the doors open and the bird leaned forward, peering into the darkness. After a few more punctuated *twirps*, Epyllo flew into the bushes lining the walls of the private courtyard.

Deciding to leave the doors open in case the spy wanted to come back indoors, Raph muttered, "Goodnight, then," before dragging his body to the bedroom. He barely noticed the flickering candlelight as he fell face first into the stationary bed and drifted off to sleep.

Chapter 28

Light peeked through wooden slats of shutters snuggly closed against the window of Raphael's bedroom. He rolled over, shuffling across the bedding now crumpled beneath him. A chilled breeze slunk through the shutters, rattling them gently.

Raphael stretched long in his bed, then sat up quickly.

Goddess, he hoped he hadn't slept past lunch. He hadn't even known what time it was when he made it to Malakai's estate, so he hadn't the faintest idea how long he'd slept. The past twenty-four hours felt like a fever dream, rushed and flitting with different faces and places.

Raphael made his way out of the bed, entering the common room to find it empty. He supposed Epyllo was off doing birdlike things, gathering intel under the guise of fauna.

Remembering Malakai's words, Raphael stuck his head out of the main door of his quarters, finding his bag presumably delivered by Felix. He hastily grabbed it and shuffled back into the common room. He haphazardly tossed the bag onto the table, then rummaged through the contents. Inside, he found a pair of breaches and a tunic he had not touched during his voyage on the trip. They smelled of sea salt, but were otherwise clean and presentable. Raph took his time cleansing himself in the washroom, taking special care to rinse and detangle his hair.

"Oh, that's better," Raphael mused once he'd bathed and changed into fresh clothes. He was rubbing scented oils into his scalp and hair as he thought through everything he'd learned since arriving in Meropoli. To think, already he had met *three* of Ephraim's grandchildren. Raph wondered how many there could possibly be wandering the streets of Heronias.

Raphael replaced the cork in the bottle that held his hair oil, his hair now feeling alive again after being so punished by the sea. He was just unpacking the rest of his clothing, et al, when a sharp knock came from the main door.

Raphael slipped on a pair of sandals, similar to those worn in Meropoli, and quickly answered the door. "Ah—August!" exclaimed Raphael.

"Good to see you, healer. How was your rest?" August's deep brown eyes shone genuinely.

"Beautifully," said Raphael. "Would you like to come in?"

"Actually, I've come to escort you to Malakai. He's expecting you for lunch."

"Excellent," said Raph. As he closed the door, he couldn't miss the birdsong fluttering in from his quarter's courtyard. Hopefully, that was Epyllo signaling that he wouldn't be too far behind.

Raphael followed close behind August, who hummed merrily to himself. The man was a picture of contentment, clearly comfortable and unbothered. It had an incredibly calming effect on Raphael, he realized, as they turned a corner heading down another hallway.

"So this is Malakai's estate?" asked Raph.

August shrugged. "It belongs to whoever is Governor. But that means we all grew up here."

"Because Ephraim was Governor?" Raphael was trying to piece together the events that had taken place since he'd last spent time in Meropoli. Over a hundred years of history had elapsed.

"Yeah. And then Felix's father. And then our cousin Remmi. And now Malakai. You could say it's a family business." August shrugged a shoulder, then continued his humming.

"When I was last here, the people of Heronias would have considered that nepotism."

"Oh, trust me, that's been brought up before." August's steps slowed, allowing Raphael to walk beside him. He grinned at Raph, his youthfulness a reminder of how aloof and carefree Gavin had been at one point. "But...Pater Ephraim is kind of a hero around these parts. Other families sort of just...stopped running for the position after he took it. We nearly didn't have a Governor after Felix's father retired. Remmi had to be dragged onto the House floor to be nominated."

"I see."

Raphael actually didn't see. Ephraim had been quiet and serious, but he'd had the most entertaining mischievous side that Raph had always found enchanting. And the man had never been one for politics, much more concerned with studying the world around him than associating with the upper echelons of Heronias. Instead, you'd sooner find Ephraim nose-deep in a book or playing a prank on a fellow scholar. A feeling like homesickness struck Raph, and he suddenly remembered why he'd left Ephraim all those years before.

August slowed again, nearly stopping. "See, Pater Ephraim is the reason Heronias, and possibly the rest of Meropoli, is a free state. He led the charge against Brutus."

"Brutus." Raphael spat the name, remembering the lumbering oaf of a man who had loved tormenting any of those he deemed unworthy. He was especially prejudiced against fae, and even more so against those who dared break the social norms of gender in Meropoli culture. Obviously, he and Brutus had *not* gotten along.

"Yes, Brutus," August repeated. "You see, there'd been a famine, and there didn't seem to be much our people could do about it. He convinced a small circle of followers to assassinate the Governor of the time, then tried to secede from the nation."

"And, I'm sure, he also tried to make *himself* King."

"Bullseye," August replied, snapping his fingers at Raphael.

They began walking at a normal pace again. "It was Ephraim who stood against Brutus. A bunch of citizens of Heronias fought back, but Ephraim was the one to get support from Cynia and a few cities in the Pyhhria Desert. Without his leadership, Heronias would be a dictatorship, not a republic."

"A hero indeed," mused Raphael. A tiny flutter of pride grew in his chest. He would have loved to see Ephraim as a leader.

"Here we are," August said, interrupting Raph's thoughts.

He nodded his thanks to August, then pushed aside the curtains that separated the room from the hall. Inside was a lavish common room. There was a section of the floor sunken into itself, lined with luxurious pillows. A long table ran along one side of the room, flanked with dark mahogany chairs with rigid backs. Doors spanning the width of the room stood open to the elements, allowing the rain-cleansed air to breeze in, supplying a steady stream of coolness.

Malakai sat at a desk in the far corner, his chair facing out toward the common room. His brows were pinched, stylus held firmly in his grip as he focused on a piece of parchment sitting in front of him.

Raphael waited quietly near the entrance for Malakai to take notice of his arrival. The Governor scratched several lines quickly, before stuffing the parchment into a folder and looking up.

"Oh, you're here," he grinned.

"I'm here." Raphael clapped his hands together to emphasize his arrival.

"Let's eat," said Malakai, gesturing to the table as he vacated his desk.

Arranged along the table was an assortment of fruits, chilled meats, and cheeses. What appeared to be wine sat between two chairs at the far end of the table, and Goddess, Raphael truly hoped it was wine. Both males took their seats, and Raphael followed Malakai's lead, serving himself a variety of food before taking a few bites.

It was...divine. Weeks of sustaining on hardtack and cured fish, which he hardly kept down, led to a more ravenous feeling than he was used to. It dawned on Raphael that he hadn't been so hungry since being freed from Rankor's work-camps.

"August," called Malakai.

The young soldier peeked into the common room, pushing aside the purple curtains. "Cousin."

"Secure the room for me, will you? We mustn't be disturbed."

August gave a playful salute. "Felix is in the courtyard. I'll keep the hallway cleared."

"Thank you." Malakai's eyes bore the same gravity, the same intensity as Ephraim's once had. To think, the men hadn't a drop of blood to share, but Malakai clearly took after his grandfather's demeanor.

Malakai took a deep breath, dropping a piece of bread he'd been eating onto his plate. Raphael waited, sensing that Malakai was readying himself for whatever news Raphael had traveled so far to hear. Malakai took a sip of wine, rolling his lips in before finally looking up at Raphael.

"I'm trying to figure out the best way to go about this. I have this grave feeling that one way or the other could have dire consequences for my people, but I haven't quite figured out which way is best."

"I get the sense that you have some questions for me," said Raphael, wiping his fingers on his linen napkin. "I'm happy to supply you with answers."

Malakai penetrated Raphael with a searching stare. "How did you know my grandfather?"

Well—that wasn't the question Raphael expected. He cleared his throat, his sip of wine suddenly tickling as it got stuck. "May I ask what you know of me, first?"

"Hmmm...no. I'd rather hear the truth from you." Malakai was still. Good, Goddess...the man was so much like Ephraim. Malakai possessed the same intensity as Ephraim, and could easily have passed as fae on Panchia. All he needed were the tipped ears.

"You are so much like him," Raphael heard himself say. He shook his head slightly, trying to rattle sense back into his mind. Raphael exhaled deeply, leaning back into his chair to try and determine the best place to begin. "As you know, it was not uncommon years ago for fae healers to take a sabbatical to Meropoli. I gather that relations between the states were more stable at the time."

"That's an understatement." Malakai sipped at his wine, his eyes still pinned on Raphael above the glass.

"Right. Well, I took mine when I was in my sixties—"

"Relatively young for a fae," Malakai said, grinning.

Raphael smiled back. "Yes, and I felt it. I met your grandfather, Ephraim, at the academy here in Heronias. I'd already visited Cynia, had spent a year there."

"What were you in Heronias for?" Malakai's eyes once again held the same intensity as before, and Raphael felt the weight of it.

"I'd heard of some research being conducted on antiseptics. It fascinated me because, as a fae healer, I have the ability to fix plenty of ailments using my gifts. But battling infection is something our powers cannot master. It's theorized that killing infection would mean killing something living, thus counteracting the purpose of the gift. As such, any other resource that could defeat such an obstacle was something of an obsession of mine. I desperately wanted to know what made something powerful enough to kill infection."

"I'm happy to say that research is still being carried on today." Malakai asked before popping an olive into his mouth. His gaze still hung on Raphael, making the healer squirm internally.

Raphael shook the curls from his face, his mind racing with thoughts and questions. "Anyway, that's where I met

Ephraim. We did some research together and became very close...friends."

"Is that all?"

Raphael fought the urge to squirm under such intense scrutiny. "If I'm honest, we were a bit more than friends." Raphael's heart raced. He wondered if Malakai would hold it against him that he and Ephraim had once been lovers.

"I'd say so if you two lived together for nearly four years."

"You knew about that?" Raphael asked in exasperation. Raphael gaped, shocked that Malakai had led Raphael down a field of memories when he was clearly familiar with Raph and Ephraim's history.

"Of course I did. We all grew up hearing the stories of the fae who nearly stole Ephraim away. Our Nonni seldom let Pater Ephraim forget."

"Who exactly was *Nonni*?" asked Raphael. It must have been someone who had known of their relationship.

"Niko." Malakai's grin grew wide, joy bubbling beneath the surface.

"Niko? Of course it was!" Raphael laughed. "I'd always teased Ephraim that Niko had his eye fixed on him."

"You'd be right," said Malakai. "Nonni adored Pater Ephraim."

"I'm glad," said Raphael. And he was. He was thrilled to hear that Ephraim had lived a life full of love. What's more, it seemed that the man had created an impressive legacy for himself.

"I wanted to hear the story from you so I could get a sense of what details to tell you." Malakai pushed away his plate and leaned back in his chair before scratching his chin. "I wanted to see if you were as honest and brave a male as Pater Ephraim considered you to be."

Raphael blanched. He'd never considered himself especially honest or brave. Spying on Sage for Symon ran through his mind, and he was suddenly very glad mortals didn't possess any sort of mind reading powers.

"I'm assuming I've passed?"

"You did." Malakai's gaze turned intense again, like a fire that had been rekindled, suddenly blazing to life. "Several months ago, the Western front was bombarded by a celestial shower. It came out of nowhere and sent our astronomers into a panic, causing them to spread prophecies of imminent doom for our world. As it turned out, the falling stars were only medallions. There were four of them."

As August would have said...*bullseye*, thought Raphael. Just as he'd suspected, the insignia had found their way to Meropoli.

"What about these medallions?" asked Raphael, trying to play cool.

"I think you already know, but since you'd like to play coy," Malakai smiled. "The letter I received included drawings. It appears they belong to the Realm Leapers."

Raphael cleared his throat, unable to conceal his anticipation.

"You are a terrible liar," said Malakai.

"Yes, well...incredibly honest and brave, remember?"

Malakai laughed at that. "I remember." He leaned forward and Raphael could scent change in the man's mood. Something akin to excitement lingered in the air, mixed with anticipation and fear. "There's been a special hearing called in Heronias to debate what to do with the medallions. There's two arguments being made: keep the medallions for ourselves, in hopes of finding some sort of power to use in our defense. Or, turn them over to the fae, probably Maracadia."

"You can't do that!" said Raphael, scooting forward on his chair.

Malakai nodded. "I expected you to react that way. But I need a good reason."

Raphael squinted his eyes, trying to decide which route was best in this instance. Pure honesty? Selective truth?

"There's been another Realm Leaper. She's not a goddess, but she's very powerful. And she needs the insignia to get back to her own world."

"And?"

"And if she doesn't, then the homicidal maniac who followed her into *our* world is likely to burn it—and us along with it— in the wake of his wrath."

Malakai leaned forward, patting Raphael's hand. "That was what I feared. I've had word from one of my diplomats that they believe one of our Representatives has made an alliance with the Dark Born—"

"You cannot be serious!" Raphael snatched his hand away, standing up abruptly.

"Oh, I'm deadly serious," Malakai explained. The tone of his words matched the deadly calm in his eyes. Ephraim had never stared at Raph like that before, but he could recognize it. It was the same gaze Symon took when faced with the cumbersome weight of leadership. "There are those on Meropoli who still wish to overthrow our government and rule as our monarch. Those men are generally very greedy and would do more harm than they ever could do good."

Raphael reached for his seat, his hands shaking. How had the Dark Born already discovered where the insignia were? If they got their hands on them, Sage would be stranded on Panchia. What kind of death would she face with three unresolved bargains tied to her soul?

"If the Dark Born manage to find the insignia we are doomed," Raphael said, his voice low and raspy.

"Don't worry," assured Malakai. "Now that I know, I can convince the others to give the insignia to Felysia. It's possible we can have them on board with the next shipment of goods by next week."

"And you truly believe you can convince the others?" asked Raphael. Malakai held the type of aura that simmered with influence.

"I do," he said, and Raphael could tell the man believed in his abilities to persuade. "I'll begin working with my colleagues this afternoon, drafting a letter arguing that the insignia should be turned over to you. That you were so close with Ephraim should be a strong enough bargaining chip."

"And in the meantime?" asked Raphael.

"In the meantime, would you like August to take you to the academy? I hear there's been new research surrounding something called an antibiotic. We are getting powerful results, I'm told. "

"That would be delightful." A huge weight lifted off Raphael's chest. This was just the kind of boon they needed. Finally, it seemed as though things were taking a positive turn for Raphael and his loved ones. By next week, he could be back on a ship, bringing Sage the insignia so she could finally rid herself of those awful bargains.

As he walked back to his rooms, Raphael couldn't help but hum along with August. He'd opted for an evening alone, still feeling like he could use the rest. But he was more relieved than he'd felt since the Dark Born had attacked them in the Spring. Maybe, just maybe, everything would finally be settled.

Maybe, they would finally rid the world of Ranquer and they could focus on ridding the world of the Dark Born, once and for all.

He was just thanking August for the escort as he closed the door. As he turned, Epyllo was shifting from bird form.

"I think you should write to Symon in that fancy book of yours."

"I think you're right," beamed Raphael. And how nice it would be to include some positive news.

Chapter 29

✧✦✧

To Queen Aryael~

First, I want to send my regards to you and King Symon. I hope you are both well, considering. My heart breaks with the news that we still do not know about the well-being of your brother. He has always been such a good fae, and I will continue to pray to the Goddess that she will protect his spirit.

I am writing to update you on Gavin's progress. As I've said before, I don't think you need to worry about him, so. He has done an excellent job of combating the side effects of the Signum Dominari. Additionally, I think his relationship with Sage may prove useful for us in the long run.

On that note, I should let you know that the bond has begun to set for them both. Already, their scents have begun to merge, and Sage has learned how to use her own magic to cast alongside Gavin without them touching. I've sensed Gavin's power stabilize as well. They've been working to try and make sense of their differing power and how to use the bond to enhance it, and while that's been somewhat effective, I'm perplexed that the bond hasn't completely settled in place yet.

Sage continues to try and find a way to realm leap without using the insignia. So far, we've had very little luck. I suspect we will never find out if she can manage the journey without them unless she goes to Maracadia and tries. She's mentioned an idea of trying to craft new insignia using orichtium.

I know this is a lot of information to contain in a letter. I've tried to encourage Gavin to come talk to you on his behalf, but he's insisted on staying with Sage for the time being.

I will continue to guide the two as best I can, and will forward any relevant information as it develops.

Give Symon my best.

~Shiphrah

Aryael placed the letter on the table. It had been delivered by a raven shifter early in the morning, but the Queen was only just getting a chance to read it. The day had flown by in meetings with merchants of Biznia who had been evacuated out of the province. Many of the families had been irate at the disruption of their business. Aryael always wondered at how some could value wealth over the safety of their own families. Had they learned nothing from the past hundred years?

Her body ached. Months of stress had her muscles locked in place. Her head constantly hurt. And on top of everything else, now she carried around the weight of guilt from her fight with Gavin.

She'd pushed him. She knew she'd always been pushing him, but she really thought it was for his own good. She still believed it was for his own good. Had he not been given the title of Lord of Mystaira when The Seal made its appearance, the effects could have been drastic.

Nevertheless, she felt shitty and like a bad friend. She should have mentored him more, *been* there for him more.

Now, she was stuck getting updates from Shiphrah. Gavin wasn't responding to her letters, and despite what Symon said, she worried their friendship was damaged.

Symon stalked into their room, the door banging the wall. She'd been sitting in an oversized chair, but jumped to her feet in surprise, the sound startling her from her wandering thoughts.

Symon stomped into the bathing room, a hand held over his face.

"What in the Goddess?" Aryael asked, following him in.

Symon stood at the sink, rummaging with one hand. "I need a cloth," was all he said, still clutching his face.

Aryael snatched one from the armoire pushed against the opposite wall and rushed to his side. Quickly, she ran the cloth under the cold running water and handed it to him. As he removed the hand from his face, Aryael took in the long, angry welt that spanned one side of his face, over his eye. "What happened?"

Symon cleared his throat, turning to rest his backside against the countertop. He swallowed, and Aryael could feel a war of emotions through their bond. The silence grew, and she reached out to stroke his arm, unsure of what caused such a discord of thoughts and feelings within him.

"I went to visit Petra."

"And it didn't go well."

"I think that's self-evident." Symon removed the cloth, turning to run it under the water again. "She's worse than I've ever seen her. She blames us all for Hyacinth's death, for the attack on the city. She thinks it will happen again, and accuses us all of being naive."

Aryael rolled her eyes. "I know she's hurting. But does she really think that's an excuse for hurting her bonded?"

"I don't think it matters to her. I think she'd burn the whole world down for what's been taken from her." Symon dropped the cloth onto the counter. The welt had calmed slightly, but it still looked menacing, like he'd been whipped with a belt.

Part of Aryael wanted to cast into the Obelisk and teach the bitch a thing or two about hurting her love. But the other half of her knew it would only hurt him more. That, and a small grain of guilt agreed with Petra. They'd all been blind to the threats of the Dark Born.

Symon gathered Aryael to him, settling her body between his legs and resting his forehead to hers. A sweeping sadness rushed down the bond, and Aryael fought the tears that accompanied it. Oh, how he hurt for his sister. For Zeke. For the world.

"Tell me something good," he whispered.

It was a game they used to play when they first met. Over a decade ago, when they were both dressed in rags, whipped and degraded by their captors, he and Aryael would play this game. In spite of all the bad, all the evil they experienced, they'd look for something good. Just one thing. One thing that could feed the dying embers of hope deep in their souls.

"Gavin and Sage have bonded." Aryael hoped the whispered words were enough, would suffice.

Symon pulled back, his hands moving up to Aryael's upper arms. He smiled, "I knew it!"

"You knew it?" Aryael laughed. "How'd you 'know it'?"

"Just a feeling. He looks at her like I look at you."

Her heart fluttered. This male was her everything, and she just wished she could fix it all. Make all the bad go away so that the joy that sparkled in his eyes now could stay there forever.

"Shiphrah wrote with the details. I got the letter today."

"Has the bond been completed?" Symon asked, wrapping his arms around her once more and pulling her close.

"Not yet. And it may take longer than with fae. She's mortal, after all." Aryael wondered if the bond would complete at all. As far as she knew, it had never been done before.

"Have they tried dreamwalking?" Symon asked, his jaw working as it rested atop her head.

In the early days of their own bond, Aryael and Symon had dreamwalked together. It had happened by accident at first, but soon became something they did regularly, and still did to that day. With Symon's mind powers, they assumed it was a subconscious reaction on his own part, his body looking for ways to create a more tangible bridge between their souls and minds.

"That's an excellent idea. She's already able to cast without touch. Perhaps the dream world will unlock the rest." Aryael inhaled deep, relishing the smell of Symon so close. "I'll go write to Shiphrah."

"Later," said Symon. A finger slipped under her chin and she let him tilt her mouth up. "First, let me take you to bed." He kissed her deep, his soft lips moving intently over her own.

Fire erupted within her, and suddenly she burned with the need to have her King. "Gladly."

Symon reached down, grabbing her backside and lifting her up against him. Their mouths moved feverishly against each other and Aryael let herself be consumed. As he laid her on the bed, pushing up against her and hitting her exactly the way her body craved, she marveled at the beauty of him.

Then, she reached down between their bodies, grabbing hold of him and commanded, "Now."

Symon gave her a wicked laugh, a rumble against her chest that she felt all the way to her toes. "As you wish, my Queen."

Goddess, thought Aryael...*this* is something good. And what came next was even better.

Chapter 30

⸎❈⸎

"Good afternoon," hummed Shiphrah, breezing into Sage and Gavin's apartment. They'd just sat down to enjoy some dark brown ale when her knock had interrupted them. Sage hid her disappointment behind a friendly smile. She'd been excited to share the beverage with Gavin.

Back home, beer had been a regular commodity, and while she liked the wine produced in the Mystairan province, she'd been homesick for a hearty beer. The cooler weather, brought on by the changing season, had emphasized her homesickness. When she and Daveed had taken the morning to visit the nearby market, she'd been thrilled to find a vendor selling bottled and chilled ales.

"Shiphrah," said Sage in greeting. "And how are you today? Would you care for an ale?"

Sage walked to the counter where a bowl of ice and water sat, sealed bottles submerged to stay cold.

"Did you get that from Vesta's stand?" asked Shiphrah. Sage nodded in answer, grabbing a bottle. "Then yes! I didn't realize Vesta had made it back to market already."

Sage sat next to Gavin, who already sipped his ale. The table was empty except for a bowl of olives and pickled vegetables Sage had also grabbed while shopping with

Daveed. Shiphrah sat at the table, lifting her own bottle in a salute before taking a sip. She hummed, and Sage had to agree. The beer was fantastic. Nutty. Rich. Smooth. The combination of flavor and carbonation soothed a raw ache that had been present in the past weeks, and she let herself savor the momentary respite.

"So," began Gavin, "I assume you didn't come all the way up here just for ale." Shiphrah placed her bottle on the table, tilting her head in admission. "What is it?" Gavin's gaze was probing, his shoulders immediately rolling in the all too familiar way. He could sense something was amiss, thought Sage.

"I came to check on you," said Shiphrah, her eyes drifting to Sage. "Daveed said you had another attack."

Sage rolled her eyes. "Oh, he's just a worrywort."

"Maybe," Shiphrah admitted, "but you can't deny that they are becoming more frequent."

In the past week, since the bond between her and Gavin had begun forming, Sage had started having what they referred to as "attacks." As far as Sage could tell, it was the bargains urging her to make good on the promises she'd made. Today, in the market, she'd had a particularly bad one, scaring the wits out of Daveed. One moment she'd been fine, walking and laughing with Daveed, admiring the handmade wares in the marketplace. Then, she'd gotten lightheaded, and had rushed to find a place to sit.

Her heart had raced, beating as if it were trying to escape her chest. Then, it would feel like her heart clenched tightly, the beating becoming only a tremor. Dark spots had invaded her vision and she'd nearly passed out; Daveed had been forced to use his weak healing powers to keep her conscious.

She'd had several other episodes just like it in the preceding days, and they were coming more often, and with greater strength.

"Well, there's not much can be done for it." Sage said, popping an olive into her mouth and shrugging. "Until we've found the insignia, or made new ones out of orichtium, it's a lost cause."

"So, then what?" asked Gavin. "What's your plan, Sage?'

She shrugged. "Don't know."

"Goddess, Sage. You sound as if you've just accepted your fate. What happens if you don't fulfill the bargains?" Gavin asked. She could feel the heated sting of irritation travel down the threads of their bond.

"She dies." Shiphrah held her bottle between her palms, looking at the table.

Sage shrugged again. She knew the answer. She would die. And maybe that would be okay. Maybe, she'd have helped Felysia just enough that they could actually defeat the Dark Born *and* Ranquer. She didn't see it as giving up. She would continue looking for some sort of answer. But she also refused to be afraid anymore.

"Daveed and I have read every single text referring to the Realm Leapers that we could get our hands on. The answer may lie in Maracadia, but we will have to get there first."

"Which means," Shiphrah interjected, "that we need to strengthen the bond between you two." Gavin huffed, his shoulders rolling again. It had caused him no small amount of vexation that the bond had not fully settled. He hadn't asked Sage whether it was because she was holding back, but she knew he wondered.

She'd interrogated herself over the past several days. Was she holding back? The answer was a resounding no. But, try as she might, their powers just seemed to miss *something* in order for them to form a fully intact bond. They were at a stalemate.

"That's the other reason I came up here." Shiphrah took another sip of her ale, her eyes lifting in anticipation.

"And that is?" Gavin asked when the healer refused to elaborate.

"Have you tried dreamwalking together?"

Sage's head pulled back in confusion, her brows pinching together. "Dreamwalking? Isn't that basically the same thing we've been doing?"

"Not really," said Shiphrah. "Dreamwalking won't take your powers, your magic, out of your bodies. The dream world is in an entirely different place."

"And what will that accomplish?" Gavin asked. His gaze was pensive, apprehensive even.

"I'm not sure. But it was a suggestion sent by the King and Queen."

Gavin stiffened. "You've heard from them?"

"We've kept up our correspondence," Shiphrah said, waving away the question. "Based off their recommendation, I think dreamwalking could help unlock any subconscious barriers still in your way."

"Let's do it," said Sage, her beer bottle clinking loudly as she set it on the table. "It's not like we have much to lose. Besides, I already know how to do it." Gavin shifted in his seat, his gaze dropping to the table. "We should do it tonight."

Gavin nodded, but his gaze didn't meet theirs, and Sage wondered what was making him hesitant. He was the one so adamant on the bond settling.

She wasn't against it, but it also didn't matter to her whether the bond completed itself or not. Gavin was hers, and that was all that mattered to her. She'd do everything she could to complete the bargains so they could live their lives together. And if things didn't work out, then at least she'd been here for a little while. At least she had experienced this feeling of completeness.

Finally, Gavin agreed. "Tonight."

"Then let us toast. Hopefully, after tonight we will see you two happily bonded." Shiphrah lifted her bottle, and they clinked them together.

Maybe, thought Sage, by the end of the night, she'd be one step closer to taking Gavin to her home world. And they could pay back the bargains. And then they could come back, and start their lives in Mystaira.

Maybe... she could make this all work.

The moon had risen to its zenith. Its glow illuminated the halls of the Rafalatriki as Sage and Gavin made their way to the temples below. Shiphrah had insisted on them conducting the dreamwalking from there, stating simply that she would be better able to monitor them as they slept. It could be dangerous wading into the dreamworld, and she wanted to be on her guard in case either of them ended up in trouble.

Sage felt the slightest bit of unease. Partly from imagining what kind of trouble they might find in the dreamworld, and partly from her experience with Ranquer violating her dream space not so long ago. She decided against worrying about it. If she thought about it too much, she might lose her nerve.

They'd just entered the stairwell that led to the temples, when Sage reached out, grabbing Gavin by the elbow. He turned to face her as she pulled them to a stop, a question written on his face.

"Gavin, before we do this," she began, her voice a soft rasp, "I need you to know...whatever happens, I have no regrets. Whatever we find out, I need you to know that I'd do it all again. I'd choose to do it all again just to find you."

Gavin pulled her close, a hand wrapping around the back of her neck. She had to lift her chin high to look into his eyes. "I'd do it all, a million times over," he said as he pulled her into a soft kiss. "I still mean what I said. I'll follow you anywhere, Sage. Even into eternity."

She nodded, then quickly kissed him once more before saying, "We'd better get this over with."

Gavin held her hand as they descended. A disquieted nerve had begun shivering somewhere deep within her, but she couldn't think of why she would be so on edge. She'd dreamwalked before. Granted...there was that one time she'd become trapped within her dream, unable to find Raphael or her way out.

She shook her head, trying to dislodge that thought. It would be fine. There wasn't a reason she'd get separated from Gavin this time. She remembered everything. They were just looking for a barrier, something that was blocking the bond from completing itself.

As they entered the temple, Shiphrah was finishing up the final preparations. She'd somehow gotten two cots down into the main temple, situated just under the carved mural of Allyra.

"There you two are," she said, clapping her hands together as Sage and Gavin approached. "All ready?"

"As ever," said Gavin. He still bore that same look of unease. Perhaps her own nervousness was bleeding into him. Sage tunneled into the thread of the bond, investigating. Once she was there, she could sense her own anxiety twining around his own.

So they were both nervous, then.

"Go ahead and get comfortable," said Shiphrah, placing a pillow on one of the cots. Sage and Gavin each eased themselves onto a cot, Shiphrah taking a seat on a short stool just behind them. "I will help ease you into sleep, but I won't accompany you on this journey. This is for the two of you to experience without me. I'll just be here in case you need to be pulled out quickly."

"Got it," said Gavin.

Sage inhaled deeply, allowing her exhale to whoosh out of her body. Some of her tension eased as she did so, and she got a sudden bolster of bravery when Gavin reached out and took her hand.

Together.

They'd do this together. To whatever end.

Shiphrah placed a palm on Sage's forehead. "Begin with breathing," she said quietly.

Sage snorted, causing Gavin to chuckle as well, easing the tension. It was an on-going joke for them any time Shiphrah had them practice breathwork after Sage's jokes about Raphael doing the same.

"Hush," Shiphrah reprimanded, but there was laughter in her voice as well. "It is how we must begin. Breathing connects us to the deepest parts of ourselves, which is exactly where you both need to go."

"Okay, okay," whispered Sage, wiggling on her cot to settle herself. Gavin squeezed her hand three times. *I love you.*

He always did that. She adored it, and a warmth blossomed in her chest as she squeezed back. Four times. *I love you more.*

Gavin responded. One long squeeze.

Sage matched her breathing to Gavin. A large, long inhale through her nose. A deep, full exhale through the mouth.

For countless moments they breathed, muscles relaxing, a falling sensation, surroundings fading into darkness. Her mind drifted. Her body lost its weighted feeling.

Then she stood in a dark void. Gavin's hand was no longer in hers. All around was an eternal void of empty blackness. A tiny part of Sage's brain pondered how she could see her hand stretched out in front of her with no source of light.

Smoky images blurred into focus. A stone wall, gray and purple, rose up from the surrounding blackness. Her mind always landed here, in front of the wall.

Bypassing that thought, Sage gave a slight tug at the thread she'd come to covet. She could see it now: a silver and lilac thread that stretched out from her chest, disappearing through the wall. The thread tugged back.

One by one, she watched as the bricks dissolved into nothing. Standing on the other side was Gavin.

She felt her smile, as broad and warm as it had ever been. He was beautiful. He stood tall, *shirtless*, and winged. It'd been so long since she had seen his wings. White with black tips, and she marveled at their beauty as he approached her. Warmth flooded her body as he wrapped his arms around her and kissed her fiercely. A sudden urge to touch his wings materialized, and before she knew it, she was running her fingers along the edges of one. Soft, silky feathers played between her fingers, and Gavin stiffened against her.

He groaned, "Remind me to have you do that again later."

Sage grinned up at him. "You like that? I was kind of worried I'd offend you."

Gavin responded by nipping at her lip, his hands spanning her backside and pulling her into him.

"Oh," she whispered. *He did like it.*

Gavin kissed her again, and her head swam with want. "I wonder what it would be like to take you here," he said, his voice growling against her neck.

Sage was ready to let him do it, the Goddess knew she'd had him in her dreams often enough.

Just then, a loud chime echoed through the darkness. Sage pulled away from Gavin, her head turning toward the sound.

Through the black, the chime echoed again. A ringing, like a bright bell being struck on its side. Sage pushed out of Gavin's arms reluctantly, but her body sensed she was meant to follow the sound.

"What is it?" Gavin asked.

"You don't hear it?" Again, the bell chimed, rippling towards her as a bright light took shape in the distance.

"No," said Gavin. "Where are you going?"

"Come on. Let's go see what it is." The light grew brighter, its white circle enlarging as Sage walked toward the ringing bell.

"Sage, where are you going?" Gavin's voice was distant.

"Just follow me!" This was it. This light was where they'd find answers.

"Sage! Where'd you go?" Gavin's voice was pitched, alarmed.

Sage turned, spanning through the darkness and finding nothing. That wasn't right. She'd only taken a few steps, and Gavin had been right behind her.

Again, the bell chimed, and she looked at it. Far in the distance, she could hear Gavin yell for her. His calls becoming frantic.

"Gavin?" Sage cried. "Where'd you go?!"

The chiming surrounded her now, enveloping her, thrumming through her body. Then the light exploded, the world condensed. The darkness was ripped away leaving a harsh light stinging her eyes so she had to shield herself.

When she could lower her hands, when the light no longer penetrated through every sense and feeling, Sage blinked rapidly, trying to adjust to what she saw.

A beige stone room illuminated by torches. In the center stood a rotating statue of the Tri-Goddess. Haestas held aloft a pair of scales, which rocked back and forth. Anthephone cradled a basket of flowers, strands of wheat piled at her feet. Dianis clutched a bow, a quiver of arrows visible over her shoulder.

The statue stopped at Dianis, and Sage spun, looking behind her for a way out. No exit was visible in the room. Just walls and torches and the statue.

An echoing voice filled the space. "Do not fret, child of Allyra."

"Who said that?" asked Sage, whirling again where she stood. As she stopped, facing the statue once more, Sage stumbled back landing on her bottom. The statue dissolved, leaving the form of a woman in its place.

Dianis stood tall, her jawline sharp as a razor's edge. Her form blurred and stiffened. "Do not be afraid." Dianis took a step down, her strong legs rippling with muscles beneath her cropped chiton. Bracers strapped to her wrists and shins glinted in the torchlight, and the Goddess shimmered like moonlight. "Stand, child of Allyra."

Sage pushed herself to her feet. "Where's Gavin?"

Dianis shifted, taking the form of Haestas now. She wore a gold chiton, its sleeves billowing from her arms, her scales rocking from her fingertips. "Again, I say, do not fret. Gavin is where he needs to be."

"And that's where I need to be," said Sage. "Please, send me back to him."

"You cannot be with him right now," said Haestas. The circlet on her head wobbled as her form vibrated. "He is on a path that must be traveled alone."

"What does that mean?!" Sage cried. "Please, you have to send me back to him."

"I cannot." Haestas' voice was powerful, rumbling through the room. "He must take the journey alone. But do not be afraid. All will be set right on the other side of the path."

"What does that mean?" whispered Sage.

Haestas shifted. Now, Anthephone, Goddess of love and fertility stood before Sage. Her soft, curling hair flowing down past her shoulders. Petals floated through the room, and the sweet smell of wisteria permeated the air. "There is something Gavin must uncover for himself. In the meantime, sweet child, how would you like to hear a story?"

"A story?" croaked Sage.

"Think of it as a bedtime tale." Anthephone smiled sweetly. Her motherly powers wrapped themselves around Sage, the energy soothing and relaxing the tension from her shoulders.

She desperately wanted to go to Gavin, to save him from whatever he faced. But who was she to argue against the Goddess?

"Are you sure I can't go? I can't help?"

Anthephone smiled sweetly again, shaking her head. Haestas appeared again. She waved her hand, and a cushion appeared. "Have a seat, young Sage."

Not knowing what else she could do, Sage followed the orders of the Goddess. With a flourish of her hand, her scales no longer present, Haestas transformed the room. Space spiraled into itself until Sage found herself surrounded by the void. She recognized the void. She had fallen through it once before.

"This is the story of beginnings. The story of life and death." Haestas waved her hand again. "Millenia ago, I found myself. I do not know where I was before, or what was before. But I grew from an ember that floated through eternity. I was not only me, but three sides of the same entity."

A light flashed in the darkness, and Sage watched as it pulsed. "Eventually, I learned what existence was. I learned about creation. And I desperately yearned for more than myself."

Another flash, and a world began to take shape within the void. Stars blinked into existence. A sun, a moon, celestial bodies swirling into position. Anthephone, her body swollen with child came into focus. "With creation, came life. I bore life to many races, namely fae and mortals. And they lived happily together in the world I'd created."

Space blurred, and now Sage watched as images of fae and people cohabitating flitted around her. "The fae provided for the mortals, cared for them. And there existed a great and wonderful harmony."

Sage watched as a group of fae brought offerings of food to the mortals, who traded their wares with the fae.

"At some point, however, I grew lonely. Watching my loves grow and prosper was fulfilling, but I yearned for someone to share it with."

Again, Sage was thrown into space, surrounded by stars. Anthephone was joined by another creature. Burly and horned, he had a charming smile and penetrating eyes. "Balor," said Anthephone.

"Balor was meant to be my companion. One I could share the burden of creation with."

Anthephone changed, growing into Dianis. "I made the mistake of sending him to Panchia, giving him the power to walk amongst the fae and mortals. I thought, if he was able to witness them on their level, we could provide them with more prosperity than ever before." Dianis squeezed her bow, and her skin shimmered. "But I was wrong. Balor was jealous of my power, and worked to turn my creations against me."

Space streaked by. Now Sage watched as fae whispered to each other. Soon, mortals were in chains, and there were fae who laughed and jeered at their new captives.

"Balor conspired against us, planting greed and malice in the hearts of fae, which spread to the mortals as they were abused and mistreated. I knew I couldn't leave Balor there, so I removed him from Panchia."

Now they were back in the temple room. Haestas took the place of Dianis. "I love all that I create. And I feared that if left in this world, Balor would corrupt all I had created. So, I banished him, and made him his own world to rule. I'd hoped he would take the opportunity to care for those lesser than him."

Green mountains came into focus. A forest spotted with large lakes, and mortals hunting amidst the woods played through the room.

"That's Thuledain," said Sage.

"That's right," Haestas beamed. "Such a beautiful world." She spoke softly watching as the mortals of Thuledain discovered magic, both elemental and more. "But Balor was still envious. He begrudged my power, and begrudged being banished. Instead of caring for his people, he began sacrificing them, stripping them of their power."

Now, Sage watched in disgust as the horned god drank the blood of mortals, her people. Anthephone came into focus. "He had discovered that by consuming the elemental magic of the people in Thuledain, he could build a spiritual bridge between the two worlds. And so, again, he corrupted the mortals. They sacrificed their own, not knowing they were serving a dark god."

"Why didn't you stop him?" Sage cried. She felt the tears slowly collect in her eyes, a tightness growing in her chest as more and more people were consumed by the god.

Dianis now. "Don't you think I wanted to?" she seethed. "But there are bounds for even gods."

Haestas. "Balance."

Anthephone. "Patterns." The Goddess rippled, all three forms moving in and out of each other. "While we couldn't destroy Balor ourselves, many warriors tried. That is where your gods came from. They led the final war against Balor, and trapped him deep beyond the Otherlands."

Sage was whipped out of Thuledain, through the Otherlands where spectres of people meandered, some sleeping, some walking through fields of golden wheat. As she was pulled further and further, she gasped when everything finally stopped.

The space was purple with a greenish hue. The ground soft and mucky. Pits of bubbling green acid dotted the landscape, accompanied by a rotten stench of decay and despair. As she turned, Sage watched as a great battle took place, down below the precipice of a plateau she hadn't realized she stood atop. Mortals wielded magic against the horned god and demons alike. Brighid cried out, her war-cry unmistakable, burning demons that emerged from the pits of acid. The battle waged on, warriors both falling and triumphing.

Then, the four gods, currently mortals, surrounded Balor. Together, they wielded the element they were each strong-est with even as the horned-one raged against them. Slowly, with the battle spiraling behind them, Balor was turned to stone.

Demons disintegrated. Allyra, Cerridos, Brighid, and Th-erysid collapsed. Then, Sage stood in the temple room once again.

"Your gods, once mortal, spent the next few centuries ascending. When Balor's power found a way back into Panchia, the gods answered my call and became the first Realm Leapers." Haestas was back, her form clearer than before. "It was the Realm Leapers who helped the fae re-member their goodness."

"So why can't they help now?" asked Sage. "Shouldn't they be the ones to leap? Couldn't they have stopped Ranquer?"

The Goddess rippled again, all three forms standing tall in front of Sage. "Your gods have fully ascended. They can-not interfere anymore than they already have."

"And what does all of this have to do with me?"

"King Rankor and President Ranquer are of the same ilk. When Balor somehow managed to find his power, although still trapped, he began sending out his demons. They've been working all this time to find a way to free his true form."

"How long has a demon been leading my people?" asked Sage, the pieces all beginning to fit together.

"How long have your people elected Presidents?" Dianis asked.

Hundreds of years. For hundreds of years, Thuledain had been led by a demon.

"Now that Balor has captured Therisyd through his demons, he is closer than ever from escaping. And if he does, your world and Gavin's will not survive."

Sage's body was yanked against itself. Shiphrah's voice echoed around the room, calling her name. Time was running out.

"TupaGuara?" asked Sage. "Why TupaGuara?"

Anthephone spoke, her tone urgent. "When I first realized Balor was able to use his powers once more, even from his stone prison, I created one final world. In that world, I've hidden a weapon. It will destroy Balor, once and for all. But be warned Sage—"

Haestas interjected. "With every action comes a reaction. All creation has a balance. You must be sure you accept that before you venture there. You, or any of your comrades."

"What does that mean?" asked Sage.

She was yanked, hard. The world blurred as Sage's body was catapulted into the sky, into the void. She thudded as she came back into consciousness.

She gasped loudly, sitting up and turning to seek Gavin, but all her grasping hands found was empty space where he'd lain.

"Where is he?" Panic gripped her heart.

Shiphrah, normally bright and shining, was pale. Her eyes darted all around. "I don't know."

"You don't know?"

"I-I-I...I don't know. His eyes snapped open, then he was gone. He cast away."

"Where?!"

"I don't know." That was all Shiphrah could say.

Gavin was gone. He'd left her. Something had happened and he'd left.

Sage tried yanking on the thread. She could feel its presence, but it was distant. He was so far away, and she could do nothing.

Sage pushed off the cot, and ran to her room.

What the fuck?

What. the. Fuck?!

Ranquer was a demon? Balor, an evil god of some underworld realm, made real by the Tri-Goddess? Everything her world believed in was a lie?

Her heart raced and her mind whirled as she paced her room, waiting for Gavin to return.

Night turned to day, and he didn't come back.

Sage wondered if he ever would. Or could.

She wondered if maybe she should have died in that van when she was fifteen.

She wondered if they were doomed. If this was it.

She wondered how a girl like her could possibly defeat a demon, or if she was capable of the balance the Goddess had warned her about.

She wondered if she'd ever see peace at all.

She wondered it all as a feeling of despair echoed her own down the tremoring thread that connected her to Gavin, and she curled up on the bed and let herself succumb.

Chapter 31

꙳✳꙳

Gavin stood in the darkness, alone.

One second, Sage had been right in front of him.

Then, she'd taken two steps, following a sound only she could hear, and disappeared.

Gavin whirled, spinning around, desperate to find her. He couldn't see her, couldn't feel her, couldn't smell her. The tug of their shared thread, gone.

She'd been ripped away from him.

His heart thundered in his chest and he fought against the darkness, trying to scrape himself through the sludge and back into reality.

He had to find her.

In the distance, a soft voice began murmuring. "Sage?" he called out.

His insides turned to icy liquid at the thought of her panicking, struggling to find her way back to him. Urged toward the sound his body nudged him to go, to follow. The voice continued, a sing-song canter to it, and he squinted as the faintest slice of light began to form, curving around the horizon.

As he walked through the empty void the voices became clearer. Memories welled up, and Sage slipped out of the grasp of his mind as he realized who the voices belonged to.

Delphia. His mother. That chuckle, there...that was Papa. And beneath it all, the bubbling laugh of a toddler.

He screwed his eyes shut as the light swelled to a head splitting brightness before fading. Blinking, he found himself back in the hovel where he'd been born.

The work-camp.

In the corner, on a crudely constructed stool, sat his mother, Lydia. She was clapping, and singing a song about a shepherd herding his goats into a corral, only for them to jump the fence, causing him to start the task all over again. Delphia, no older than seven years of age, twirled and sang along. And in the center of it all, sat a young, cherubic Gavin.

Baby Gavin clapped along, rarely on beat, but laughing and babbling with the innocence of childhood. The room was sparse. Gavin's Papa sat on the floor, cross-legged, so that his love could have the only seat available. A small fire crackled in the pitiful excuse of a fireplace, and Gavin choked at the sight of the thin pallets laid out on the floor.

As a family, they'd been afforded one of the few private rooms, no larger than his bathroom in the Obelisk. Most prisoners slept in gargantuan barracks, lined up side by side in lumpy cots. Not all families had private quarters, some were forced to stay in the barracks. But Gavin's family had been respected. His mother's insistence on continuing to teach the younglings in secret had earned them the respect of the community of prisoners.

It had also been the cause of her injuries, given to her by Dark Born guards who discovered her private lessons before Gavin was born.

Yet, it never stopped her. She continued educating the younglings despite the peril it put her and her family in.

Gavin's mother stopped singing, her voice cutting off abruptly. Delphia, slow to notice, continued twirling until the unmistakable *whoosh* of wind caught her attention.

In the center of the room, baby Gavin bounced his arms up and down. Blankets fluttered, the fire spit and hiss.

"Hushhh, now baby..." cooed Lydia. "Shhh...." she said, making her way to Gavin.

Before she could reach him, Delphia reached over and scooped him up. "Gavin! Let's play peek-a-boo!"

The wind picked up, rattling the few tools that Jethro, Gavin's father, was allowed to keep in the room. Lydia continued, "Husshh, now baby...Shhh..."

"Peeeekkk," Delphia said, holding Gavin on her hip and shielding her face with the apron she wore, "a-boo!"

The wind picked up, then died down suddenly when Delphia dropped her apron. Baby Gavin squealed in delight.

"Peekkk," Delphia said again, "a-boo!" Once again, Gavin squealed.

The scene dissolved, sifting like sand around Gavin. He reached out for his mother one more time before everything returned to the void it had once been.

The world lurched, the darkness clearing again to return Gavin to the same room. Now, the fire had been put out, only a lone candle burned. Delphia and baby Gavin lay curled up on a pallet of blankets, his parents on the opposite side of the room.

Hushed voices came from the corner, and Gavin strained his ears to hear.

"What are we going to do?" Lydia's soft voice came.

"I don't know." Jethro's admission was barely more than a breath. Pain laced the admission, and Gavin's heart broke for his parents.

"It's getting worse," said Lydia. "He's already wearing the iron. We've even added a band, Jethro. And he's still able to reach his powers." The silence stretched, then, "If he gets caught, they'll take him from us."

A soft noise whooshed out of his mother, and Gavin realized she was crying, sobbing into his father's shoulder.

Again—the world shifted.

Now, Gavin was older. Maybe six or seven. Levi was with him. They were playing in one of the long halls that had been dug out of the hills the work-camp was nestled into. Torches lined the walls. In the distance, the sounds and calls of people working echoed down the corridor.

It wasn't often that younglings found themselves alone with time to play, occurring only rarely. Yet Gavin had no memory of this event.

Levi bolted past young-Gavin. "Oh, no you don't!" he cried, running after the rambunctious toddler.

Levi was fast for a youngling his age, and easily slipped out of Gavin's grip. The toddler sidestepped, then ran squealing toward a pile of crates stacked against the wall. Before young-Gavin could reach him, Levi was already clamoring over the piles of rubbish, reaching for a precariously balanced box.

A whoosh of wind, and young-Gavin disappeared, landing just behind Levi and peeling him away from the dangerous obstacle.

"What in Eternity are you doing?" Delphia cried, running towards the boys. Her head was wrapped with a rag to keep her wild hair from her eyes. Her brown clothes were splotched with stains, the hem torn and frayed in places. and torn at the hem. She bore the confidence and maturity of a much older fae, a tribute to her hard childhood.

Delphia yanked Gavin to her, snatching his wrist so he yelped. "What in the Goddess do you think you're doing? What if you had been caught?" she hissed.

"What should I have done?" said young-Gavin, glaring up at her. "Let him climb up that and get squashed?"

Delphia huffed, rolling her eyes. "Enough. Come on you two. Let's get you indoors where you can't get into any trouble."

The world tilted again, spinning Gavin around before coming to a stop.

Now, Gavin stood on the sandy dirt that covered the work-camp. Outside, the light was pale, gray and muddy. The air held a bite to it that told Gavin it was winter.

Again, the surroundings felt familiar, but the events were like witnessing somebody else's life.

Young Gavin, now roughly eight years old, walked alongside Levi. The youngling, probably four now, teetered under the weight of a laundry basket, overflowing with the clothes and linens of guards. Gavin carried an overly large bag bursting with more clothes thrown over his shoulder and a smaller one in his hand, filled with tack, the tasteless, dry as leather bread that passed for extra food rations in this hell pit.

Gavin watched, keeping pace with the younger version of himself, waiting to see what would come next. He could hear the cries of someone in the distance, likely catching a beating from a guard. The sounds of hammering rang out from the work yard, where able-bodied males and females were forced to carve huge bricks from stone hewn from the mountainside. It was demeaning work, especially for those whose earth powers were continuously ripped from them.

"Ugh—" groaned young-Gavin. "These Dark Born pricks stink."

Levi giggled. "What does that mean? *Prick*?"

"Don't worry about it," said young-Gavin in a rush. "And don't you *dare* repeat it around Papa. He'll beat my backside red if he finds out."

Levi giggled again, whispering to himself, "Prick."

"I mean it," said young-Gavin, pausing to hoist the bag back onto his shoulder. "Don't tell anyone you heard that word from me. Or I'll—"

Young-Gavin stuttered to a halt as three teenage boys stepped in front of them. . One of the boys smiled wickedly, a missing tooth belying his habit of starting fights in the halls of the work-camp. The others took up stations on either side of their leader, both shaved bald, smacking their palms with wooden clubs. Old-Gavin would've laughed at their textbook attempts at bullying kids half their age if it weren't for the fear that came off little Levi in waves.

"Alright lil' whelps. Time to pay-up." The teen with the missing tooth stepped toward Levi, who dropped his basket. Young-Gavin dropped his bag, too.

Gavin's heart raced. What was happening? Why didn't he remember this?

Before he could figure it out, Levi began crying, the tiny four year old whimpering pityingly, tugging still further at Gavin's heart, prodding The Seal deep inside him. Young-

Gavin tugged on his stained tunic, rolled his shoulders and then stood as tall as he could.

"No." Old-Gavin admired the boy's courage.

"Oh, stop it now. Just give us your tack, and we'll be on our way."

"That tack is ours," young-Gavin said, clenching his fists and edging in front of Levi. "We took the extra shift hauling their filthy clothes, so we earned it."

Tack was used as a tool for bribing the prisoners to do extra work, Gavin recalled, compensation that was happily accepted when rations were meager, and used as currency by the inhabitants of the work-camp.

Levi shrunk back, edging his way further behind young-Gavin. Before the youngling could reach his brother, the teens pounced, launching themselves at the boys. The older teen grabbed hold of Levi, and then—

The scene exploded.

YoungGavin disappeared. The wind roared.

First, he appeared behind one of the club-holding teens, wielding a hammer grabbed from somewhere. Young Gavin slammed the teen's knee in with the tool, leaving him howling on the floor.

Then, young-Gavin disappeared again, reappearing beside the one holding Levi, taking a swing at him before he had a chance to organize his limbs and respond. Young-Gavin cast over and over, until all three teens were bloody and bruised.

Levi crouched trembling as the wind ripped through the work-camp. Doors rattled on their hinges. Shingles on the outlying buildings hummed as they were pried up, flapping hard against their roofs.

Finally, with the three teens writhing in agony, young-Gavin grabbed Levi, and they ran.

The scene changed again, tipping Gavin heavily back into his family's hovel room.

Now, young Gavin lay sleeping on his pallet, Levi curled around him. The younglings snored softly, their faces the picture of innocent repose only a child could muster in the depths of safe sleep.

Delphia stood in front of her parents, speaking animatedly in hurried, hushed tones, her hands alternately flapping and wringing anxiously, determination etched across her face.

"If we don't do something, he's going to get himself *killed*, or worse."

"But what else can we do?" Lydia whispered. "Delphia, we've tried everything. The iron, the herbs..." Gavin's mother leaned forward, rocking in her seat the way she did when she couldn't find a comfortable resting position. "I don't know what else we can do." She was close to tears.

"I do." Delphia's voice was strong. Gavin had always admired how confident she was. She always had a plan, always saw the world in the biggest picture, details intact. "Papa, take this off my wrist." Delphia held out her wrist, pointing to the iron band soldered to it.

"Why?"

"Because then I can use my powers to make it so he can't access his powers. " Delphia tilted her chin in the way that meant she had a plan that was foolproof, and nobody should dare to argue against her.

"How?" Lydia asked. "You know they poison our food so we can't use our powers, girl. Don't be foolish." Lydia rarely raised her voice to her children, but there was something foreign in her eyes now. Gavin realized, it wasn't just fear, it was the kind of terror that went right through to her marrow.

"The guards let you take home those pliers still, right?" Delphia continued as if her mother hadn't spoken.

Jethro nodded, mute.

"Good. Then go get them and take this thing off. It only takes us three days without that poison to regain our strength."

"Three days?" asked Jethro. "Three days without food *or* water?"

"I can do it, Papa. Please." Delphia held her father's hands, they seemed to be communicating on another level. Jethro started to rise resignedly.

"No!" Lydia pushed to stand, shoving Delphia's hands away, tears pouring down her cheeks. "No! I cannot allow it. It's bad enough one of my babes is at risk. I can't risk another."

The break in his mother's voice nearly unmanned Gavin as he watched, transfixed.

"I'm not asking for your permission." Delphia growled at her mother, who sat back down abruptly. "Besides, if he draws attention to himself, the Dark Born will start looking at the rest of us, too. We are all at risk if we do nothing." The command this girl wielded at just thirteen was astounding.

Nobody moved. The silence thundered through the tiny space. Delphia looked from her mother to her father, but neither could meet her eyes.

Then her father looked up. "I think we should try it." Jethro's voice was weak, nearly broken to Gavin's ears.

No...it couldn't. This meant—

Lydia painfully lifted herself from her chair, hobbling toward the fire. She looked like a bent and broken old fae in that moment, centuries older than her actual years. " If you do this," Lydia began quietly, gazing into the faintly glowing embers, "He won't have any memory of what he can do?"

"None. But... it means I will have to...rearrange some of what he remembers as well."

A choked sob came from Lydia, she leaned against the wall, the other hand held tight across her mouth. Eternity seemed to pass while she mastered herself. Then she sniffled, straightening before turning. "All right. Get the pliers, Jethro."

The world dissolved, falling back into darkness.

She'd...

Delphia had changed his memories. Had erased them...

His access to his powers had been blocked to him.

She'd taken a part of him away, and never told him about it.

"Do not blame her, Gavin." A crisp, staccato voice echoed from behind him. Gavin turned, and Dianis stood tall, her bow and arrow notched and ready, but lowered.

"She took them from me," whispered Gavin.

"She only did what she must. And it worked." Dianis looked away from him, peering through the darkness. "There is something else you must know," the Goddess continued. "Your powers...you are not only a Wind Wielder."

Gavin shook his head, turning away from the Goddess.

Too much. It was all too much.

"Your sister *had* to hide you away because you would have never escaped otherwise. None of you. And without you...let us say that the fate of the worlds is entwined with your own.

"You see," the Goddess paused. "You do not wield the wind. You *are* the wind."

Everything melted.

Gavin was pulled back into reality.

He was the *wind*?

What did that mean?

He slammed back into his body, his eyes snapping open. Shiphrah jumped, words tumbling from her mouth, but Gavin could barely hear them. With a thought he threw himself outward, tumbling through the sky.

The next moment, his feet hit the wooden floors of his family's home.

"Delphia."

Chapter 32

꧁ ✳ ꧂

Delphia shot up from her bed, clinging the sheet to her chest. A second form quickly sprang from the other side of the bed, a blade whipping from out of nowhere.

Meliza, wearing nothing but her sleeping tunic, glared at Gavin. When she recognized him, her stance softened, lowering her blade.

"Oh, Gavin," Meliza breathed. "What is it? What happened?" Meliza was already grabbing her pants from the floor, stepping into them.

But Gavin didn't care about her. His stare was pinned to Delphia, who returned his look with a hint of trepidation, the first time he'd seen any uncertainty on her face that he could ever remember. But then, he thought wryly to himself, he couldn't truly remember the early years thanks to his sister. It was hardly surprising.

"Meliza, get out." Gavin's voice was pure animal, the growl of a jungle cat before it pounced.

Meliza straightened. "No." Her gaze darted between him and Delphia, lifting the blade again. "I don't think I'll be doing that."

A rumble left his throat then. He'd blame it on the Signum Dominari if he knew better. But it wasn't The Seal driving him. His family had lied to him, had manipulated him. They'd ripped a part of himself out, as if it were an infected canker. Denying him the depths of his power, his truest self. The betrayal was deep, biting, and he would stop at nothing to get the answers he was owed.

Delphia swung her legs out of the bed, still clinging the sheet to her chest. "It's alright, Meliza. I've got it from here."

"Dee—listen to me," Meliza's voice buzzed, "come over here and I can cast us away."

"A fair thought," said Delphia, grabbing a robe and slipping it over her shoulders before turning and securing it, dropping the sheet in the process. "But as I said, I've got it. Gavin's here for answers by the looks of it."

His sister had to feel his gaze, hot like daggers, piercing into her. Even so, the female stood tall, unwavering, any earlier uncertainty gone. And, damn it, that pissed Gavin the fuck off. How dare she not show even a little remorse? She clearly understood why he was there.

Meliza stalked toward Gavin. When she reached his side, she pointed the tip of her blade at his chin. "If you hurt so much as one hair on her head, I swear to the Goddess I'll make you pay for it."

Gavin still didn't look at Meliza, her blade be damned.

"Go on, Meliza. He won't be hurting anyone tonight." Delphia had turned back to face Gavin, her face as relaxed and neutral as ever.

The door slammed as Meliza exited. Gavin and Delphia stood, rooted to the floor, glaring at each other for countless breaths. His chest felt hot, boiling over with rage. Despite it all, there weren't any thoughts running through his mind. Only empty hurt and betrayal.

"I take it you found out about the memorywalking," said Delphia, as if it weren't a complete violation. As if she hadn't erased parts of his life.

"You stole my power from me," Gavin ground out, his teeth clenched so tightly the sinews in his scalp went painfully taught.

"I saved your life." Her words were tossed back at him. No remorse. No sorrow.

"You *stole* from me, Delphia. I should have had a choice in it."

"And what if you'd declined? Hmmm?" Delphia's head cocked in the way that indicated she was ready to wage war. Another fae may have been intimidated. "What if you'd decided not to let me change your memories, change your understanding of your power? I should have let you die? At the hands of those fucking *monsters*? And had our parents brutally tortured to get the truth out of them?"

"You should have helped me."

"I did! How else could I have done it?" Her voice pitched up. She leaned forward now, her hands gripped tight. "We already had the smithey add iron bands to you. You ate extra doses of that poisoned food that kept the rest of us stifled from our powers. And what? They still rose. You had no control over it, Gavin."

Gavin exhaled heavily, his breath hot against his face. "You lied to me."

"I did what I had to do. I did what no one else could bring themselves to do." Delphia turned, walking toward her window, then turned sharply back to face him. "Have you even considered what I had to give up to save you?"

Gavin paused, looking more intently at his sister.

"I starved myself—for days," Delphia spoke slowly, deliberately. "Not even letting a single drop of water pass my lips. *Just* so I could access my powers again. I was *twelve*." Her chest heaved, her breathing heavy and exaggerated. "I was on the brink of death when I walked for you, Gavin. And I'd do it again in a heartbeat." Her hand raised, her finger outstretched, pointing at him. "So don't you dare accuse me of *stealing* from you. I *gave* you your life."

"You at least should have told me." His anger still prodded him. But now, it was caught up in feelings of revenge, a desire to burn Speridisia to its core for what it had done to his family, to him.

"When would I have done that?" she asked, her voice bouncing off the walls. Her arms outstretched, then she dropped them loudly to her sides. "You were never here."

Gavin looked away. The statement was a slap of bitter truth. He had neglected his family for years.

His feelings warred against each other, a torrential cyclone within him of anger, regret and shame.

Gavin stepped, heading for the door, then turned to say something else.

"Don't bother," cut in Delphia. "You know the truth now, so you can be gone." The unspoken 'again' hung in the air between them. And *fuck*, the calm neutrality in her face hurt worse than the truth.

Unable to bear it he turned to the door, snatching it open and stepping outside. The house rattled as he slammed it shut, and his boots shook the pine plank floors as he made his way to leave.

"Going so soon?" His mothers voice caught him like a hand reaching around the wall.

Slowly, he made his way back to the living room, embers still crackling in the stove's grate.

Lydia sat in her favorite chair. It was plush, yet supportive. A haven of sorts when her injuries plagued her. Not that Gavin had much firsthand experience of the pain his mother still suffered he admitted to himself, as Delphia's words of his absence grated on his soul.

The click-clacking of needles was a gentle rhythm in the dim light as Lydia looped yarn, the beginning of a scarf or blanket taking shape. The room suddenly felt oppressive, and Gavin had the distinct childlike recollection of being reprimanded by his mother.

"Sit." Lydia continued looping yarn; over, under, over, under. Her eyes were fixed on her hands. Still, Gavin swallowed thickly at her command. No doubt she'd been listening to his argument with Delphia. Did his mother harbor the same hurt from his absence all these years?

With a sigh, Lydia placed her yarn and needles in her lap. "You know, all the texts in the world cannot prepare you for raising young. It doesn't matter how prepared you might feel." She reached toward the side table, lifting a mug to her mouth.

She still didn't look at him. Her gaze rested on the candle lantern that lit the space. The flame bounced around inside the box, casting shadows in the room. Gavin felt like the flame, his insides pinging off his ribcage with the turmoil of his emotions.

"We tried for years to start a family, then King Rankor took over and we thanked the Goddess we hadn't been able to. It had been such a blessing in those early years. So many were lost..." Her voice trailed off, the meaning clear and evident. The tragedies had been far more brutal in the first years of the occupation.

"When I first realized I was carrying your sister, I was terrified. I didn't know if I'd be allowed to carry her to term. I was so afraid that we'd succumb to disease. I'd already been punished once for teaching the younglings in the camp." Lydia paused, sipping from her mug once more. "And by some miracle, there she was. The most beautiful little baby you've ever seen. And then I had to watch as that light, the spark in her eyes, became clouded. When you came along, she turned even more serious. She vowed to protect you at all costs."

Lydia looked at Gavin, her eyes soft. "I should have protected her more. At the time, I was thankful for her protectiveness, especially as your powers grew. But now, I look at her and wonder what could have been if we'd protected her innocence a little longer. Sometimes, I wonder if we even could have protected her in the work-camp."

"Mama, you can't think like that."

"Of course I can. It's a mother's job to worry about her young." Lydia placed the mug on the table. "I know you feel like we betrayed you. I've been waiting for you to realize what had been done, and I've been pondering how best to make it up to you." Lydia picked up her yarn and needles, reorganizing them. "Then I came to the realization it wasn't you who deserved the apology."

Gavin sat straighter, surprised at her words. He'd expected—no, felt he *deserved*—some sort of apology from his mother, from someone.

"You see, it wasn't *you* who lost anything. You're gaining your powers back. You got to live the last few years as if you weren't the leader you were meant to be." Needles began moving again, working their way through the yarn. Lydia's focus fully returned to her project.

Gavin tensed, sensing something more was to come from his mother. The click-clacking nearly drove him mad as he waited.

Then, "If you truly want to feel better about what's happened, then *you* need to make things right with your sister."

"*Me*?" Gavin was ten years old again. He was coming around to understanding what Delphia had done, and why. But surely Gavin wasn't in the wrong for any of this.

"Yes, you," said Lydia, placing the yarn in her lap to look at him. "She gave her life for you, has been doing so since she was five years old. If you want to make things right, then you need to figure out how to find your own happiness. And let her find hers."

"It's not like I've been stopping her."

"Haven't you?" Lydia raised an eyebrow, making Gavin squirm at her insinuation. "You may not have intentionally, but what sacrifice have you made while she made hers for you, over and over again? She will continue to worry for you until you've settled." She picked up her yarn again. "Once she believes that you are well and good, I think she might let herself finally find her own peace. I think she may already be on her way." Lydia smiled slightly, an ember of knowing written on her face.

Gavin's brows pinched, confused at what his mother was referring to. Meliza. Of course. In his anger at his sister he'd not fully taken onboard the importance of finding Meliza in his sister's bed. Or realized that he'd actually never known his sister having a partner in her life. Someone to share the burden of ruling in his stead through his long absence, running the farm, caring for their parents, raising Levi.

Goddess, he'd been such an ass. Delphia had put *everything* on hold for him. He really did owe her more than his life.

"How do I make things right with her, Mama?"

Lydia's eyes cut to him before returning to her knitting, a satisfied peace settling across her features. "You start by showing up for the ones you care about. Then: you love. You love hard. Show her that you are capable enough to handle your own burdens, and strong enough to ask for help when you need it."

"I'm already doing that, aren't I?"

"Give it time, son." Lydia placed her needles down again, looking at Gavin with so much love, so much pride it made his heart ache. "I love you, boy. Now, get out of here and go back to where you need to be. We'll see you once you've finished what you've been called to do."

Gavin cleared his throat. "What if I fail?" The anger had subsided, but now he was overwhelmed with worry and remorse.

"Did I raise you to fear failure?" Lydia's eyebrow lifted.

He laughed under his breath. "No, you didn't."

Gavin pushed down on his knees, standing to his full height before walking to his mother. He bent down, kissing her on the cheek. "Love you, Mama."

"I love you, too. Now, get out of here."

Gavin grinned, and walked down the hall.

"By the way," his mother called out to him. "Congratulations on the bond. I expect to see you and Sage soon so we can celebrate."

Gavin smiled. "Will do."

Then, he cast back to the Rafalatriki, into his and Sage's room.

She was curled up on the bed. A loud sniffle indicating she had been, or still was, crying.

"Sage?" he asked, quietly.

She sprang up from the bed, her eyes splotchy and swollen, and ran to him. "Thank the gods," she cried, throwing herself at him.

Gavin crushed her to him, squeezing as hard as he dared.

"I'm sorry," he whispered into her hair.

Sage pushed him hard, hitting him in the chest. "Don't you ever fucking do that to me again."

"I'm sorry," he repeated.

Sage sniffed loudly once, then wrapped him in her arms again. "I'm so glad you're okay. What happened?"

"Can we lay down?" he asked.

He was suddenly weary to his bones. So much had happened, and already the sun was making its appearance for a new day. They'd not slept at all. Dreamwalking wasn't restful and he was ragged from all that he'd experienced and learned in a few short hours.

Sage grabbed his hand, and he let her guide him to the bed then wrap him up in the blankets before nestling in beside him. She pulled him close so that his head rested on her chest and he could listen to the steady beat of her heart. She pressed a soft kiss to his head, and he exhaled hard, finally letting the last of those heavy emotions go.

"Tell me what happened," she said, her lips moving against his hair.

So Gavin did. He told her about the dreams, his memories, his sister's sacrifice.

He told her about the Goddess. Apparently he was the wind? He didn't know what that meant, but he was content to find out another day.

For now, all he wanted was to sleep in the arms of his soul-tied. He'd make everything right, he told himself. It would all be okay.

A burgeoning feeling of hope began to sprout somewhere within him. He could see his path stretching out before him. He could imagine his homeland finally free of the evil that'd plagued it for so long. He could see himself and Sage building a life for themselves. And in it all, there was his family. Safe. Happy. He'd make it happen.

His eyes closed, and he let himself fall into sleep. He knew where he was going, and he'd be damned if anything got in his way.

Chapter 33

❧ ✳ ❧

Sage and Gavin stood in the middle of a field. It'd been a whole day since their dreamwalking episode. In that time, they'd both shared their experiences multiple times over. Now, they stood next to each other preparing for what came next.

In theory, now that Gavin knew the truth of his powers and his past, there should be no barriers to the bond completing. Already, Sage could feel the thread that bound them pulsing. It had been her idea to spend the day outdoors, testing the limits of the bond, to see how well they could access the thread. Sage was curious just how far away Gavin could go for her to be able to cast to him.

She and Gavin had slept most of the day away, then spent the evening sharing with Shiphrah all that they could about their dreamwalking. The healer had been palpably relieved to see them walk through the doors of her study.

Details about Ranquer, Rankor, and Balor were still muddy, at best. Sage couldn't quite piece together what the Goddess had meant when she said the President was part of Balor. How could a demon, trapped in an eternal stone prison, send his demons into the world? Wasn't that the point of the prison, to keep him powerless?

Still, parts of the story were adding up. How could her world worship elemental gods, and simultaneously be so prejudiced against magic wielders of the same ilk? That was a detail that had bothered Sage for years growing up, even more so once she was on the run. Ian himself had pondered the hypocrisy of it late into the night after one of the high holy days.

Now, Sage stood in a field, staring at Gavin who stood roughly ten feet from her. She took a deep breath, steadying herself and her magic. Her daggers pressed into her legs, reassuring her and calming her nerves. The thread of the bond hummed down its line, and she gave it a little tug.

With another deep breath, she exhaled and focused on the sensation of casting with Gavin. She disappeared, breezing across the field on an invisible wind. She landed right in front of Gavin, giving him a kiss on his cheek and then cast back again. This time, she shot back further, landing with a heavy *thump* on the ground.

"Not bad," said Gavin. "You got further than last time."

Now, she stood probably fifteen feet from him. She wanted to push further. "Again?"

He nodded once, and she cast again, landing behind him and flicking his ear. This time, she shot to the side, gliding across the land. "Hey!" called Gavin. "Keep it up, and I'll come after you."

"Ohhhh—don't tempt me with a good time," laughed Sage.

Again. She cast again, landing next to his side. She pinched his bottom, and he yelped. Her laugh lingered even as she cast away.

"Hah! That's got to be over thirty feet."

"Yeah, and you're in for it." Gavin's gaze held a promise of pay back, and gods damn it, Sage liked the kind of pay back he was thinking of. She could feel it pulsing down the thread of the bond, and she'd be lying if it didn't have a profound effect on her. She rubbed her thighs together, trying to quell the sparking need.

"Again," whispered Sage.

She cast. Before she landed, Gavin grabbed her by the waist, somewhere in the astral-plane. Their bodies twined, and when they landed, their lips were locked.

Sage panted against Gavin. Oh, gods, this male made her melt like nothing she'd ever experienced before. How was it possible that his hands in her hair, his hands running down her back to grip her hard made her body come alive like this.

This was more than lust. It was her soul catching fire.

Gavin's tongue slipped in and out of her mouth, rolling across her lips. She answered with a soft bite to his lower lip, and a rumble vibrated through his chest.

"Gods," moaned Sage. Gavin's hand was reaching behind her, running across her ass and reaching up. He was guiding his hand between her legs from behind, and Goddess, fuck it all...she let out a cry.

His hardness was rocking against her, and she was so fucking close already as his tongue ran down her throat.

She was loosening the fastenings on his breaches when a throat cleared behind them.

"This better be *really* fucking important," muttered Gavin. Both arms were gripping Sage so she couldn't twist to see who interrupted them.

"We have to go to Veritasailles."

Sage turned. Meliza stood, white as parchment, her spear in hand.

"What happened?" asked Sage. The fire crackling inside her was ice cold now, the look on Meliza's face enough warning that something terrible had happened.

"Suda's back."

⚐ ❋ ⚑

Their footsteps bounced off the polished marble walls of the palace, matching the cadence of Gavin's thoughts.

Fuck. Fuck. Fuck. Fuck. Fuck.

If Suda was back, then that meant he was either dead, or something worse was happening. Meliza hadn't had anything more to say. She'd casted to the Rafalatriki as soon as Symon had sent her the letter. She wouldn't say how long it took her to find them. Shit, she would hardly say anything.

Sage had quickly run to grab Meliza's hand, convinced that their combined powers could cast them all. She'd been right. Perhaps Sage understood his powers better than he did.

Aryael's ranting greeted them as her war room came into view.

"I'll kill them! I'll burn the whole fucking country to ash!"

Gavin and crew walked into the war room, Zeke and Symon braced against the round table where the image of Speridisia smoked.

"Where's Suda?" asked Sage.

Aryael panted, "In my room." Her eyes seemed to sizzle as she looked around, a lioness rabid with hunger. "I'll fucking kill them all," she said, her voice deadly quiet now.

Symon looked up at Gavin, "They've declared war."

"Declared?" said Gavin. "That's hardly their style."

Aryael chucked a letter at Gavin's feet then growled at the table once more. A lone Dark Born figurine flared, charring the map beneath it.

"Goddess, she's going to burn the whole castle down," muttered Zeke. His gaze was fixed on the table, but Gavin could still see the dark circles beneath his eyes.

"Can we see him? Can we see Suda?" Sage's voice was soft. Symon gave her a pleading look and shook his head.

It's bad.

Symon's voice cut through Gavin's mind, and he could tell it had done the same for Sage and Meliza.

Raphael isn't here, but even so...he might not last long.

An image floated through Gavin's head. Suda, bleeding from lashes across his body. And his limbs....He was missing his leg, arm, and eye on one side of his body. His face sagged with a ragged wound on his face. The once handsome fae lay sprawled across the front steps of the Veritasailles. The bastards had *nailed* the note to Suda's chest.

Sage cleared her throat, and Gavin glanced at her quickly, noting the tears gathering in the corners of her eyes.

Aryael's nails scratched against the table as she gripped her hands to it.

Meliza snatched the letter from Gavin's hand, striding to stand next to the Queen as she read over it. "Looks like you'll have your chance, Queen. They'll walk right into your clutches. And we'll help you."

Gavin stepped next to Meliza, taking the letter for himself to see just what the Dark Born had said.

After reading it, he agreed. It looked like the demonic twins would play right into their darkest fantasies. Finally, Gavin would get the revenge he'd quietly been smothering.

At last.

Dearest King Symon and Queen Aryael,

While it has been our utmost pleasure hosting your brother, we are no longer beholden to his services. We have savored our time together, but alas, all good things must come to an end.

You've stolen something of ours, something that rightfully belongs to us. And so, take this gift as our last act of goodwill. It is only fair that we give you this final week with your dear brother, if he makes it that long. Besides, the fae of Felysia will cease to exist once we are done with you.

I am giving you a week's warning. In that time, make amends for your failures. Pray to your stupid Goddess. And rest assured, when we march on your city, Darkness comes with us.

I look forward to your screams as we slaughter your people.

~Abbadon

Chapter 34

✴

A jaunty wind rolled down the streets of Heronias, tumbling leaves into gutters and doorways.

Raphael had spent the last several hours at the bustling Academy. He was astonished with the advancements mortal medicine had made. Antibiotics, it seemed, could *kill* bacteria. And not just kill it, but eradicate it from the mortals' bodies. Raph was curious to find out if the same medicine would work in fae.

Sunlight bounced over the pitched roofs lining the roads of Heronias as Raphael trudged up the steep road that led to the Governor's House. He'd secured his hair in a plait so that his pointed ears remained pinned beneath, effectively disguising him as another mortal. Men and women hurried through the streets, some tugging on children's hands as they walked, others bartering with the various vendors nestled between residential homes.

Within the next few days, Malakai would be meeting with the other leaders of Meropoli. As far as Raphael could tell, all the leaders would be in attendance, fifty in all. He supposed he was lucky to have arrived when he did. Hopefully, with Malakai's help, Raph would soon be back aboard a ship heading to Felysia. A flutter of excitement beat against his chest.

A cheery, "Hello there!" greeted Raphael as the tall walls surrounding the Governor's House came into view. August stood in front of the walls. He wore the common soldier garb: tan, homespun tunic that hung to just above the knees. Leather armor studded with bronze rivets was strapped to his chest, accenting the bracers on his legs and forearms. August, Raphael noticed early on, did not make a habit of wearing the helmet that usually sat atop soldiers' heads. Instead, the man chose to keep his head bare, exposing his close cut hair. The look accentuated his sharp jawline and mischievous eyes.

In spite of himself, Raphael found himself very fond of August. Not in a romantic way of course; even if that were possible, the idea of being attracted to one of Ephraim's grandchildren felt...off-putting.

Raphael waved at the young soldier, adjusting the canvas bag that sat heavily on his shoulder. One of the scholars had been kind enough to share several texts on antibiotics with Raphael. He'd promised to make sure the books made it back to the academy, and hoped either August or Malakai would make sure it happened.

Raphael was about to turn around and ask August while the subject was on his mind when he nearly collided with another man.

They simultaneously pulled up short, Raphael stumbling backwards just briefly, nearly knocking into the gated wall.

"Watch where you're going," exclaimed the man.

"Oh—I'm so sorry," said Raphael, regaining his balance.

The man standing opposite of him was slightly shorter than himself. From his vantage, the man's hair, oiled flat so that it sat in meticulous curls across his forehead, Raph could see the hairdo disguised a balding pate. Despite his shorter stature, the man's sneer had a weight of its own. According to the purple cape attached to the man's shoulder, he was a political leader of some sort.

"You—" said the man, his voice pinched. "Who are you?"

"I'm a friend of the Governor. Raphael, nice to meet you," said Raph, offering the man his hand in greeting.

The man looked down his nose at Raphael's outstretched hand. Raphael waited a couple of beats before realizing the gesture wouldn't be reciprocated.

Raphael withdrew his hand, wiping it on his thigh. When had it become sweaty?

"A friend of the Governor?" The question seemed rhetorical. If Raphael wasn't a friend of the Governor, why else would he be walking into the estate?

"Yes. Just visiting on sabbatical. I've been working with the Academy on some new research." Raph adjusted the bag once more. A cool breeze ruffled his hair, and Raphael cleared his throat once more. "And you are?"

"Sahl. Of Balam."

"Ah—nice to meet you, Sahl." Raphael stepped to the side, ready to get to his rooms and set down his bag. "I hope you enjoy your stay in the city."

He was just making his way past Sahl when the man called out. "I look forward to talking to you. Perhaps you will attend the Governor's feast tonight?"

An unsettling feeling wriggled beneath Raphael's diaphragm. Why would a healer have dinner with other political leaders? "I'm afraid I've yet to receive an invitation. Have a nice night." Once again, he turned to leave.

"I'll send word to Governor Malakai. Expect an invitation within the hour." Without another word, Sahl pivoted, causing his cape to billow behind him. A rollicking sound came from the road. A chariot pulled up beside the gate and Sahl climbed in, muttering to the driver. With a snap of the reins, horse hooves rattled as the chariot was pulled down the road.

Raphael hurried through the halls of the great house, hustling to get somewhere safe. Something was not quite right with that man.

He'd just gotten into his room, closing the door with a sharp *snick* when a squirrel bound into the room. With a shiver, the rodent transformed into Epyllo.

"I don't trust that man," said the spy.

"No, neither do I."

"He seemed rather interested in you. Do you think he knows?"

"That I'm fae? Or the reason I'm here?" Raphael tossed his bag of books onto the table. "I'm afraid I can't tell. But I get the distinct feeling that his arrival is a wicked omen."

Epyllo sat on one of the table's chairs, resting his elbows on it. "I think I know where they are keeping the insignia."

Raphael took a seat next to Epyllo. "And?"

"And, we could avoid whatever theatrics come with the House meeting. I can get into the vault, get the insignia, and we could be on the ship with Acantha by tomorrow morning."

Raphael sighed. "Then what? Pray tell, Epyllo, what is your plan then? If we steal the insignia, we effectively create enemies out of Meropoli. What's stopping them from allying with the Dark Born altogether?"

An alliance between Meropoli and the Dark Born would be disastrous. Sure, the mortals of Meropoli didn't possess powers like the fae. But their weapons were catastrophic. If the Dark Born were supplied with a steady stream of explosives and elm weapons...Raphael shuddered to think at how Speridisia would wield that advantage.

Epyllo shrugged. "It was just a suggestion."

"Leave it to Malakai. I have full confidence he will convince the mortal leaders to join our cause, even with the outlier. Surely, they won't out themselves by admitting they've made a deal with Speridisia."

A sharp knock startled Raphael, and Epyllo quickly disappeared. A mouse scurried across the floor, crawling beneath the chaise tucked away in a corner. Before Raphael could open the door, a letter slipped beneath the door, skidding against marble tile. He stooped to pick it up, cracking open the wax seal. Inside was the neat handwriting of Malakai.

Raphael~

I see you met Sahl. He's suggested I invite you to tonight's feast. I'll oblige.

Please wear something suitable. I will send August with a selection of robes for you to choose from.

Gathering begins as the sun sets.

~Malakai

Raphael folded the letter. Oh, bother. He was already dreading the evening. But perhaps it would give him the opportunity to locate the Dark Born allies. That could be useful information for their cause.

"Very well, then," said Raphael, to himself, Epyllo, and the air around them. "Tonight is a night for espionage."

The mouse beneath the chaise gave a loud squeak. "Oh, hush," chided Raphael. "This will be fine. It will all. Be. *Fine*."

As Raphael walked into the washroom to clean and re-plait his hair, he wondered whether he was reassuring Epyllo or himself.

Chapter 35

The evening passed in a blur. August had arrived with an arrangement of tunics and togas. Raphael had attempted to convince the man to fetch a pala for him to drape around the robes, but the young soldier had been reluctant to consent. It seemed, as the palas was usually reserved for married women, that it would be off-putting to some in attendance of the feast. Raphael huffed, discouraged that the mortals had made so little progress in the matter of evolving gender norms.

By the end of it all, Raphael stood with his hair down adorned with a wreath of olive leaves supplied by August. Raphael made sure to secure the wreath and his curls so that his ears would remain hidden throughout the night. Having finished dressing, Raphael took one last glance in the mirror. His robes were the common white of Meropoli, embellished with a deep blue silk cape pinned to both shoulders, fastened with wooden pins. He opted to wrap the end of the cape around one arm to add some additional flair. He hoped the robes would help him blend in, glad now he'd been denied the pala.

Raphael exited his bedroom, taking note of the mouse laying on the chaise lounge. "I'll see you on the other side."

Epyllo gave a squeak in response, and Raphael told himself it was a vote of confidence from the spy.

Raphael stepped out of his room, surprised to find someone waiting for him. "I've been told to escort you, healer."

Felix's gruff voice reassured Raphael, and he nodded in thanks. "Thank you, Felix." The soldier was dressed in his typical military garb with the addition of an ornate sword affixed to his belt.

The echoing noise of chatter shuffled down the hall as they headed towards what Raphael assumed was a formal dining room. As they entered, he took in the openaired space, lined with marble columns. Bronze braziers alight with fire dotted the perimeter of the room, casting the space with warm ambiance. The sun was setting, the visible sky painted in lilacs and pinks. The effect was lovely, creating an incredibly inviting atmosphere.

Raphael thanked Felix once again, and headed toward a buffet that held silver chalices filled with wine. He delicately lifted one, then took a spot against one of the columns, sipping his wine in silence as he observed the people gathered there.

The room was filled with leaders from across Meropoli and their partners. Governors and other politicians were dressed in togas, their wives in stolas and palas. Women wore their hair braided and pinned in buns, curls framing their faces. Many of the men had oiled their hair close to their scalps, their curls in symmetrical patterns.

Then there were the men and women from the Pyrhhia Desert. The men wore white double kilts, fastened with ornate golden broaches. Silk capes draped over their shoulders, fastened by jeweled pins. The women wore silk dresses with capped sleeves, belted at their waists to emphasize their trim figures. Some of the men and women wore their dark, straight hair down to the shoulders. Others wore braids, embellished with gold beads and clasps. All of the Pyrhhia representatives wore kohl around their eyes. A few even sported piercings in their noses.

Raphael was still admiring the fashion of the desert people when a pinched voice came from behind him. "You came."

From another individual, Raphael might have taken the statement as an invitation for flirtation. However, this voice whined with such self-righteousness he wondered if the man had ever said a kind word to another creature.

Raphael turned to greet Sahl, planting as pleasant a smile on his face as he could muster. "I did. Thank you for seeing that I was invited. It was very kind of you."

"Yes, well, I was intrigued by you." Sahl kept his chin tilted, his gaze sloping down his own nose. Raph was curious whether the male ever got a crick in his neck.

"I must warn you," Raph said with a light-hearted grin, "there isn't much that is intriguing about me." That was a lie, thought Raphael. He was the most interesting person he knew, besides Sage. But something about this man made Raph's skin crawl. He wanted to be out of his presence as soon as he could.

"You will sit with me at supper. I have many questions for the healer invited to visit the Governor of Heronias himself."

Well, damn. Raphael had hoped to observe Sahl from a distance. But, he supposed he could glean some information from the source itself during dinner. "It would be an honor, Sahl of Balam."

"It's Governor Sahl, by the way." The nasally drawl of the *Governor's* voice grated against Raph's skin.

"Of course." Raph wasn't sure what else to say.

"Come," said Sahl, looping his arm through Raphael's. "Let us mingle."

"Oh—" exclaimed Raph. Sahl was pulling him through the crowd, aiming for a group of Pyrhhians. Sahl's grip was firm, a tad bit possessive, and Raphael squirmed, trying to free himself.

Sahl cut his gaze sharply at Raphael. "I'm sorry," said Raph. "I mustn't."

"Are you entangled with someone else? Perhaps Malakai?" Sahl had stopped walking, and Raphael took the opportunity to turn to face him, successfully pulling his arm free.

"Oh, no...not Malakai," blurted Raphael. Thinking quickly, he lied, "But I am currently betrothed."

"I see," said Sahl, "where was it you said you were from?"

Raphael swallowed thickly. "I-I don't think we ever happened on the topic," he stammered. *Shit*...he thought. Something warned Raphael not to admit he was fae. A dangerous hint writhed in his diaphragm, telling him it was time to go. Spying would have to wait for another day.

Just then, Malakai's voice broke through the crowd. He was striking. He wore a deep red cape pinned to one shoulder of his white toga. A wreath of fresh olive leaves sat atop his head. August stood in the background, red feathered helm hiding his eyes. He stood relaxed, but even a mortal could sense that the soldier was alert and ready.

"Friends. Colleagues. I thank you all for making the journey. For some of you, it has taken weeks of travel. I am humbly indebted to you all for your diligent commitment to our great state." He lifted his chalice into the air. "May we toast the Goddess in thanks for her continued blessings to Meropoli."

"Here, here," echoed the crowd, men and women alike lifting their own chalices.

"Let us feast. And tomorrow, we will continue the tradition of republic and brotherhood." Malakai gestured to the table, which had been set by servants as he toasted.

The crowd made their way to the table, and Raphael speared toward the direction of Malakai. He hoped Malakai would see him and offer him a seat next to him, thereby offering Raphael the opportunity to escape Sahl and his pesky questioning. And the man's advances. That had been unexpected.

"Ah—Raph," said Malakai, a warm smile gracing his face, but if fell slightly as he looked over Raphael's shoulder "I see you have met Governor Sahl."

Raph turned slightly, acknowledging the Governor who it appeared it was becoming impossible to shake off, then turned back to Malakai. "Yes. I just wanted to thank you for the invitation."

"Of course. I'd be honored to have you, both of you, sit with me this evening."

Goddess above! For once on this intrepid journey, thought Raphael, could one thing go his way?

The three of them took their seats, Malakai sitting at the head of the table. Plates of pickled vegetables and soft cheese were placed at intervals, loaves of bread were being passed around. A group of women, wives of politicians, laughed loudly at something, and Raphael noticed a few of the men glare in their direction. Sahl was one of them.

"We should enforce the formality of such events. These dinners are not suitable environments for those of the weaker sex," said Sahl, his lip curling on one side.

"Oh, I disagree," said Malakai lightly, ripping off a piece of brown bread and handing the loaf to Raphael. "I think a diverse crowd makes for excellent conversation. Besides, at least half of our constituents are female." Malakai tilted his head, eyebrows lifted, daring Sahl to argue with his logic.

"Do you not agree that women exist for man's ability to repopulate? That hardly makes them suitable guests for political functions."

Malakai dropped his hunk of bread, his eyes taking on their serious quality. "Now, Sahl. I considered you to be a more educated man than that. If we mistreat the women, who's to say they will even agree to continue bothering with us?"

Sahl's lip curled even higher, nearly touching his nostril. "I forgot, Malakai. You are one of those permissive politicians."

"I think you mean progressive," replied Malakai, not missing a beat. "And yes, I am. I can't imagine how anyone would forget."

Sahl, seemingly tired of the topic, turned back to Raphael. "You were just about to tell me where you are from when we were...interrupted." Sahl punctuated the last word by glaring once more at Malakai, who was now focused on his food.

Raphael's heart thundered in his chest, and he grappled, searching for *anything* that he could use to get himself out of such a pickle.

"He's from a small town in the southern half of the continent," said Malakai, not even bothering to look up from his plate as he scooped cheese and pickled onions onto a hunk of bread.

"Interesting," said Sahl, pausing to sip his wine. "What's it called? I'm surprised to find a healer worthy of the Academy's attention from a village."

"Pletoria," said Malakai. "I'm sure you've never heard of it. The only reason I ever did was from one of my diplomatic voyages. I'm sure you remember that I'm assigned to that area." Malakai took a deep drink from his wine, his eyes cutting to Raphael.

"Oh—" said Raphael, "yes...that's how I met Malakai. He was..." Raphael's mind whirled. why would a Governor have any business meeting up with a small town healer? "...he was suffering from a case of dysentery. I was the closest healer available."

"Right," smacked Malakai. His eyes carried a hint of disbelief in them, and Raphael hoped Sahl wouldn't notice. "Dysentery. Raphael was an excellent caregiver. In thanks, I invited him to join us in Heronias for further learning."

"So you're a commoner?" Sahl said the words like they were poison.

"Aren't we all?" Raphael laughed.

"I'll toast to that," said Malakai, raising his glass.

Plates were swept away by servants, chalices refilled with wine. Before Raphael could be served, Sahl covered his chalice. "Please, I insist." The Governor of Balam gestured over a servant standing in the distance. He wore a pale purple tunic, reflecting Sahl's deep purple cape. Raphael realized other servants wearing the same color were dotted around the room. "This wine is from my province. It is the prize of all Meropoli." The servant poured a generous measure into Raphael and Sahl's chalices. When the servant turned to

Malakai, Sahl sent the servant shuffling back where he came from. The insult was clear, but Malakai grinned despite it.

Plates of roast venison, carrots, celery, chickpeas, and pasta were placed in front of the guests. Platters of steamed oysters and mussels were laid in the center of tables, and the room filled with the excited chatter of the diners. Wine flowed, and Raphael's chalice was refilled by Sahl's servant more than once.

It was as the plates of venison were removed that Raphael began to notice the effect of the wine taking place. If he wasn't mistaken, his speech had begun to slur slightly, and he'd found himself surprised by a fit of giggles more than once. Raph hadn't expected mortal wine to have such a profound effect on him. Fae wine was customarily much more potent.

Dessert was placed in front of the guests. A layered pudding of brown bread sweetened with cream, honey, and spices. The smell was overwhelming, and Raphael felt his head begin to spin.

"I'm so sorry, Malakai," began Raphael. "I'm afraid I've overexerted myself today. I will kindly excuse myself for the night."

"Should I have August escort you?" asked Malakai, his brows pinching.

"Oh, no. I'll be just fine," said Raph, patting Malakai on the forearm. My, thought Raphael, the man had quite the muscular forearm. Raphael stunned himself, hiccupping loudly. He felt his cheeks redden. "I'll see myself out."

Raphael had just made it to the hallway that would lead him back toward the residential part of the estate when his mind grew fuzzy. The world tilted, Raphael staggering hard against the wall, using it for balance as he sluggishly took one step after the other toward his room.

"I'm impressed," came the nasal voice, close behind Raphael.

"Oh, please. Don't worry. I'll be just fine." He said, trying to brush Sahl off as he made an attempt to hurry toward his room.

No luck. Sahl was in front of him, arms braced on either side of his body. His breath reeked of roasted meat and vinegar, a sweet aroma lingering around his body. "Most would have succumbed to my wine within the first glass. You took three."

His nose was close to Raphael's face, and he squirmed, screwing his eyes closed.

"You...drugged me?" It was all becoming clear now. That was why Malakai hadn't been offered the drink. "But you—"

"I drank the wine, too...yes. I make a habit of dosing myself. You can build a tolerance to almost anything." Sahl leaned in, running his nose down Raphael's jaw.

"I told you before, I'm already with someone. Betrothed—"

"That has no bearing on what I have planned for us," said Sahl, licking Raphael's cheek.

Raphael made to push the man away from him. "I decline your offer," he said, fighting against him as Sahl pushed up harder.

Sahl's shoulder jabbed into Raphael's chest, and he cried out softly at the hurt. Then, Sahl's hands were rifling through his robes, hiking them up along his leg. "I said, no." Raphael shoved again. No use, the man was strong despite his shorter stature. Raphael's body, despite his disgust, felt fuzzy, ungrounded, like he wasn't connected to his limbs.

"Shhh..." said Sahl, his lips pressed to the fleshy part of Raph's earlobe. "You'll be begging for me by the time I'm through with you."

Raphael tried pushing again, and his ribs throbbed from the pressure of Sahl's shoulder. Then, a hand was on him, cupping his balls and squeezing. Raphael was mortified to feel his body respond, cursing its betrayal. Once again, he stammered. "Stop. I don't want this." The hand stayed, gripping him harder. "You're hurting me," said Raphael.

"You like it," said Sahl, his teeth clenched.

"Stop it," repeated Raphael.

Then mercifully, his mind cleared. The effects of the drug finally metabolized thanks to his fae blood. He felt himself come back into its power. He mustered everything he could.

With a mighty yell, Raphael jerked himself away, throwing a knee up into Sahl's groin.

The man grunted, but he moved quickly, a blade in his hand.

"How'd you—" he started, a hand squeezing Raphael's throat, the blade aimed for his artery. "You're a fucking fae," said Sahl, his lips curled back in a feral snarl.

Time slowed. Sahl's blade drew back, and Raphael heard himself scream as it began plunging toward him. This was it.

Then Sahl shuddered. And froze. He looked down at where his robes began to bloom. Bright crimson flowed outward from where the tip of a blade just barely showed through. The blade yanked out, and Sahl slumped to the floor.

Epyllo stood there, blade in hand.

As Sahl hit the floor, his mouth moving in silent gasps, blood bubbling from his lips, Epyllo spit on the dying man.

Thundering feet pounded toward them, and Epyllo grabbed Raphael's hand. Before they could move, Raph heard a familiar voice.

"Ah...fuck!" August had his hands on his head. Malakai stood next to him.

"This complicates things." Malakai didn't seem terribly surprised, and Raphael wanted to throw a punch at the man, if he knew how to do such a thing.

"You think?" asked Epyllo.

"I assume you're with him?" asked Malakai, gesturing to Raphael.

Epyllo nodded once, then pulled Raphael so that he stepped over the now dead Sahl.

Raph's body began to tremble. That man, that *dead* man, had tried to hurt him, had tried to take him against his will. In all his years, even in his time in the work-camp, he had never been violated in that way. He had never expected to be harmed that way.

He should have been more careful. He should have been more aware. Maybe, if he'd just never gone to that feast, he could have avoided this whole thing. And now...now everything was in jeopardy. He'd ruined everything...

"Stop that," whispered Epyllo. "Look at me Raph. What he did is none of your doing, you understand? Nod and let me know you understand."

Raph's gaze was stuck on the bleeding form of Sahl. He nodded.

"I need more vigor than that. Look at me," Epyllo's voice was soft. "Monsters answer to no one but themselves. That means, they get to blame no one but themselves when they get what's coming to them."

"And that, there," interjected August, "was a monster I'm jealous I didn't get to kill."

"Nevertheless," said Malakai, "this does complicate things."

"What will we do?" asked Raphael. His eyes, round like saucers, felt like he couldn't close them. His hands shook furiously, and his desperate attempts to get his body under control were—for the moment—failing him.

"Sahl had many alliances. His death will cause an uproar. We'll have no chance of swaying the House now," said Malakai softly.

"Could we just...relieve the state of the medallions?" asked Epyllo.

"I'm assuming you know where they are?" Malakai looked sharply at Epyllo, who shrugged.

"Comes with the job."

"Good." Malakai walked to Raphael. Heavy hands landed on his shoulders, forcing Raphael to look into the man's eyes. "You have to get those insignia and get out of here. August and I will hold the House off for as long as possible."

Raphael nodded, his tongue thick and uncooperative.

"Can you get him safely aboard a ship?" Malakai asked.

"We've got one anchored just south of the nearest port." Epyllo had a rag in his hand. He was cleaning his blade. Raphael's stomach rolled. He might be sick.

"I don't recommend going to port. Can you..."Malakai waved his hand in the air, searching for the words. "Can you do that thing? The one where you disappear?"

Epyllo nodded.

"Good. Now, make haste. You haven't got much time."

"You heard the man," said Epyllo, grabbing Raphael's hand once more. With a tug, Raph felt himself pulled through reality as Epyllo cast them. They landed outside in the street, now darkened besides the sparse lantern light. Epyllo peered around the corner of a building, pulling his head back quickly.

"I need you to go up to those men down that alley. Occupy them." Epyllo's voice was a hurried whisper.

"Occupy them? How?" Raphael swallowed hard, his stomach protesting at doing anything beyond melting into the cobblestone ground.

"Act drunk, or something, I don't know. I need less than a minute to get by them."

"Fine," Raphael hissed. He stumbled down the alley, finding a bush. He leaned into it, finally letting loose the contents of the feast. He vomited into the bushes, letting the sick splatter against the rose petals.

"Hey—what's this?" asked one of the guards. He hurried over, his feathered helmet bouncing atop his head.

"He looks like one of them that's at the Governor's place," whispered another.

"Oh, yes," stammered Raphael, taking a handkerchief from his pocket to wipe his mouth. "I beg your pardon. I was at the feast and suddenly felt terribly unwell. I'm afraid I may have come down with something."

Both soldiers suddenly stepped back. "Alright, well, keep it moving then. And keep your vomit to the waste pots, will you. This is private property."

"I will. Thank you," said Raphael, stepping back out of the alleyway. "Terribly sorry." He gestured with his head again, nodding his apologies.

He saw the mail flap of one of the alley doors quickly and quietly slip open then closed. The elm doors prevented powers from being used within, which also meant Epyllo hadn't been able to cast out of them. A snake paused at the bottom of the door, a bag grasped in its tail. It waited, staring at Raphael, and the soldiers began to turn toward it. Realizing Epyllo needed another distraction, he gagged, sounding as though he might be sick again.

The soldiers hurried over to him. "No, no, no...not here you don't." One of them pointed down the street. "You can handle your business down the street near the tavern, just like everyone else."

Epyllo's snake form shimmered, casting away. "Terribly sorry," muttered Raphael again. He shuffled quickly down the street, hurrying away from the Governor's house and whatever business Epyllo had just breached.

Raph made it two blocks, constantly looking over his shoulder when a hand jumped out of an alleyway.

"Ahh—" screeched Raphael.

Epyllo's hand smacked over his mouth. "Shhh..." he hissed. "I've got them. Are you ready?"

Raphael nodded. They stepped out from the alley, then Epyllo cursed, pulling Raphael back into the darkness. "Fuck," he cursed.

"What?" Raphael hadn't seen anything.

"Shhh..."

"Stop shushing me," said Raphael in a sharp whisper.

"Two Dark Born soldiers. Just down the block." Epyllo leaned his head out, peering the other way down the road. "And two more heading toward the Governor's house. We've got to get out of here."

"Can we cast to the ship from here?" asked Raphael.

"I doubt it."

The distance to the port was further than Raphael had ever cast.

The sound of short, clipped hooves rang down the street. Raphael and Epyllo stood transfixed, this was it. There was no escaping now. The two fae looked at each other, Epyllo handing the bag with the insignia to Raph with a clink as he loosened his blade in its scabbard.

"If you have to, use them as a weapon. Otherwise, stay behind me."

With his heart in his mouth it was all Raph could do to nod back. He wanted to howl in frustration at this entire trip, it had been nothing but hardship. And the irony of having found the very things they'd been looking for, and right at the last rung of the ladder, having their escape fail...

Moments later, Felix appeared out of the shadows navigating a horse drawn wagon straight toward them. He guided the horses into the alley, pulling them to a halt.

"Need some help?" he asked. His arrival couldn't have been better. His scrunched face was possibly the most beautiful thing Raphael had ever seen.

"Thank the Goddess," Raph breathed.

"How'd you find us?" asked Epyllo in bewilderment.

"I'm an excellent tracker, and an even better spy." Felix winked at Epyllo. "I've been watching you ever since you both got her."

"So you knew?" Felix winked again. "Mortals truly don't get the credit they deserve," said Epyllo, clapping a hand on Felix's shoulder as he hauled himself into the wagon bed before turning to drag an almost limp Raphael up behind him.

"Now come on. We're about to have company." Felix hurried into the wagon after them, kicking the bottom of it so that a door to the side slid open. Raphael and Epyllo carefully squeezed into the false floor, holding onto the top and bottom to secure themselves. Felix struck the wagon again, and the floor snapped closed.

Raph heard a muffled curse, followed by a tugging at the edge of his robes. There was a sound of ripping fabric, hurried footsteps and then a lurch as they moved off.

The two fae settled into the bottom of the space, Raph's delicate stomach still complaining from the drugs he'd ingested. "What is that smell?" gasped Raphael, his stomach positively heaving.

"Garbage," said Epyllo thickly. "He's using it to mask our scent."

A few more nauseating maneuvers later, and it appeared they were finally heading out of Heronias.

Any relief Raph felt around his queasiness was quickly snuffed out. A muffled shout of challenge was followed by rapid discussion between Felix and whoever was between them and freedom. Questions and answers were tossed back and forth. Raphael could make out Felix's question about what the Dark Born were doing here. They claimed to be guests of the Governor.

Felix was masterful. He feigned naivety, pretending to buy the story that the Dark Born were any sort of companions of Heronias's leader. The challengers seemed content to buy the feints Felix parried, and with a jovial farewell, Felix snapped the reins, and the wagon rumbled down the road.

The sensation of rocking combined with the overwhelming smell of garbage plagued Raphael. The only way he could find comfort was in dissociation, using his fae powers to take his mind to another plane of existence. It also helped quell the shame at the violation he'd suffered that evening. Whatever Epyllo had said, Raphael still blamed himself for the horrible turn of events.

Finally, after what felt like an age, they halted. Felix's footsteps were quick. A strike to the bottom of the wagon caused the false door to open, sending Raphael landing hard on the ground. Epyllo, having braced himself, gracefully dropped one foot, then the other.

After they had each extricated themselves, Felix hustled them toward what appeared by the smell of it to be a dump.

"This is as far as I can take you. I must get back to Malakai," he said, apologetically.

"Thank you, Felix," said Raphael, squeezing the man's shoulder.

"Be safe," said Epyllo. Felix gave him a salute in return, then unbridled the horse. He rode the steed bareback, dust kicking up behind him.

"I can cast us to a spot I've marked. I'll need you to get us onto the ship. You've always been more precise with your casting," said Epyllo, gripping Raphael's shoulders and turning him. "I need you to listen. No matter what happens next, you get these onboard that ship. You hear me?" Epyllo clasped his hand over Raphael's that held the insignia to his chest.

Raph nodded, swallowing his feelings, absorbing strength from his companion. "Here we go, then."

Once again, Raphael was pulled out of reality. Time and space squeezed at him, and he focused on traveling with

Epyllo. He focused on the male's breathing, the feel of his skin against his palm.

There was a pop inside his ears, and they thudded to the ground. Epyllo was panting with exertion. They'd cast a vast space, and the male was clearly spent.

Yells of alarm sprang up. They were on the peak of one of the mountains at the border of Meropoli. Below the peak, waves broke against the bone white cliffs. A shack built on an outcropping of stone just below them burst open. Soldiers with spears and crossbows all began yelling at each other. Raphael looked at his feet. They'd landed on something.

He registered the warning bells then. They'd landed right on top of a trap. The bells warned soldiers of invading fae. Epyllo pushed himself to his feet. "Shit." He looked down, then quickly jumped back, dragging Raph with him behind a boulder. Elm arrows flew over the peak of the mountain.

"They're shooting at us!" cried Raph.

"No shit. Look out at the sea. Do you see the ship?" asked Epyllo, peering through the darkness.

Waves crashing. Soldiers yelling. Bells ringing. Epyllo cursing. Arrows whizzing. Spears thudding.

It all clouded his senses.

Finally—

"There!" cried Raphael. In the distance floated a ship, its sails standing out against the dark sea. Raphael reached behind, grabbing Epyllo's hand.

He looked back at the ship and willed them both to jump. Raphael felt a hard thump, then they were casting, landing solidly onboard.

"Epyllo!" screamed Acantha.

Raph looked at the spy, who gaped. An arrow speared through him, the fletchings just visible above his shoulder. Epyllo hissed as his knees buckled.

Horns blared from the mountain. The ship's captain began calling orders to the crew. Fae below deck heaved mightily on their oars. Wind wielders cast their powers to the sky. The sails snapped open, and the ship took off.

Raphael dropped next to Epyllo.

"That hurt," hissed the spy.

"Don't you dare fucking die on me you asshole." Acantha had a knife out, sawing at the arrow shaft, just behind the sharp head.

Raphael helped her push the shaft through Epyllo's body. Already, angry black streaks were working through his shoulder. "Don't worry, Epyllo. We can fix this." He held firm to the wound, applying pressure. "Go get my medicine bag from below deck."

Acantha took off, running toward the bag that Raphael was now grateful he'd left behind.

He tried pouring his power into the wound, but the sorcery of the elm tree fought back. Acantha was back with the bag. Together they worked to stop the bleeding, applying medicines to staunch the wound.

Once they'd patched him up, a couple of crew members helped them carry Epyllo down to their quarters. The spy was breathing hard, his skin already flushed red with fever, a sweat breaking out on his brow.

They'd done everything they could. The ship raced against the tides, the wind being controlled by fae powers.

If they could just keep Epyllo alive for the journey. Once they returned to the Rafalatriki, Raphael would be able to combine efforts with the other healers. They just might be able to save Epyllo.

Raphael prayed to the Goddess. He prayed over Epyllo with all his might that they would make it.

They just had to make it Felysia.

And then, he could make everything alright.

Chapter 36

✧◆✧

Gavin stood on a wide open field, the rolling hills of Mystaira reaching up in the distance. The place felt unfamiliar, and he was barely aware enough to realize he was dreaming.

The past weeks had been harrowing. Somehow, he and Eshmael had been able to deliver several additional shipments of orichtium and topaz weapons. Smitheys, earth wielders, and enchanters had all worked around the clock to prepare Felysian soldiers for the Dark Born's impending attack.

And now, he found himself on the eve of battle in a strange dreamland. He and Sage had spent the night relishing each other's warmth, and he'd collapsed into sleep. In all honesty, he was surprised to be dreaming at all, considering how exhausted he had been.

A foreign breeze rippled across the grass. The sky held a peculiar green tone, and Gavin watched as the land grew rocky and sparse. It melted from the lush pasture land of Mystaira, into a wasteland of cesspools and dust.

"The Wind Walker himself. My, my...what a treat."

The snake-like voice shivered through the air behind Gavin, and he turned slowly. Standing several yards away was a tall man, wearing a pin-striped suit and pencil mustache. President Ranquer.

"Can't say anyone's ever called me a treat before," said Gavin, shoving his hands into his pocket. While his spirit boiled over in rage that this demon had the audacity to seek him out in the dreamworld, Gavin wasn't afraid of what would happen. He wanted to make sure Ranquer knew it, so he refused to look even half as incensed as he felt.

Ranquer hummed, taking a few steps toward him. "I have to say, I expected a little...more from the famed Wind Walker. Tell me, what was it the Tri-Goddess saw in *you*?"

"Does this meeting have a point?" asked Gavin, rolling his eyes. "I have an appointment with your minions tomorrow. I'd hate to miss it."

"I've come with a proposition." Ranquer replied smoothly, ignoring Gavin's jab. The demon strolled forward, advancing on Gavin. "I had initially planned on taking Sage for myself. That task has proved...more cumbersome than I anticipated."

Gavin snorted, and he took no small delight in witnessing Ranquer's moment of frustration from it. The President's lips tightened briefly, but sidestepped the moment by beginning to circle around Gavin. Gavin let him, not bothering to track the man's movements.

"Instead, I've developed a new plan. All I need are two things from you," Ranquer stopped, standing directly in front of Gavin. "Give me with Fire Queen and Truth Teller, and I'll leave this world alone. You'll never hear from me again."

Gavin sighed in boredom. "And why would I do that?"

"It's obvious, my boy. To save Sage. You love her, don't you?" The President's words were pragmatic, but Gavin could sense the barest hint of frustration beneath the words.

"Ah, you see...but that's where you have it wrong. Sage doesn't need saving."

"She does from me," said Ranquer. He balled his fists, a glare beginning to simmer behind his eyes.

"Your past history with her says otherwise," shrugged Gavin. "Besides, I'm looking forward to watching her kill you." Gavin grinned wickedly.

Ranquer shot forward, grabbing Gavin's shirt. "You dare insult me?!" he hissed hotly into Gavin's face.

Gavin winked. "Couldn't help it. It's just too easy." He let his wings unfurl from behind him, Ranquer still gripping tightly to his shirt. Before the demon could react, Gavin flapped his mighty wings hard in his face, a pummeling wind barreling into Ranquer and sending him flying backward.

Gavin stood tall on the spot, his wings still flexed and ready. "Next time you want to bribe someone, it might help if they're actually afraid of you." Gavin slammed his wings down, shooting into the sky before erupting back into his body.

His heart beat fast, and he took a moment to reorient himself. Sage lay sprawled against his chest. Gavin took several minutes to take stock of his surroundings.

His dresser stood where it was meant to. His armor ready for the morning was situated on a chair. His sword was leaning against the dresser, his crossbow in a case nearby. Everything was as it should be.

He steadied his heart, taking comfort in his love sleeping in his arms. In the morning, they'd go their separate ways. But by the Goddess, he was determined to watch her get revenge if Ranquer had the balls to show up. He couldn't think of anything that would make him more happy, and he nearly laughed at the idea as he let himself drift back off to sleep.

Chapter 37

✧✦✧

Sage stood in front of the castle, looking out through the gates that led into the city of Veritasailles. Reality seemed superimposed after the whirlwind week, the city busy preparing for the Dark Born's march.

It had been decided that they would allow the Speridisian Army to march on the city. With the wards preventing the King and Queen from leaving the city at the same time, and neither willing to miss the battle, it had been the only viable outcome. The added benefit was that the city had already been laden with protective wards that would hopefully stall the opposing army long enough to sway the battle in Felysia's favor. Not to mention, Suda had barely survived the mistreatment from the previous months. All through the week, healers had poured their efforts into the male, trying desperately to save him. Somehow, the male persisted, but he was still too weak to be moved. His injuries were permanent, and Sage shuddered to think of what had been done to him. It made her magic writhe within her, begging to be let loose on the monsters who had been so cruel.

Also in the past week, Raphael had arrived with Acantha, Shiphrah, and a badly wounded Epyllo. Somehow, they'd managed to heal the male, but it had been a close call. The elm-arrow wound had festered something awful. Raphael had wept when Symon told him that a note had appeared in the journal they used for communicating. Raphael had left it in Meropoli on their flight out, and Malakai had found the book. Taking a chance that it was enchanted, he'd sent a note to say that they were all safe...for now. Dark Born soldiers had taken over the city of Heronias. His last remarks were "not to worry; mortal men do not take kindly to captivity." Sage hoped the mortal lands would be able to fend off their attackers.

Back in Veritasailles, they'd evacuated all the citizens they could, starting with Bithnia. All merchants, civilians, and soldiers had been moved out of the providence in preparation for the Speridisian march. Symon and Aryael worked tirelessly to find lodging for everyone in Mystaira and Jordynia. Some civilians had opted to stay and fight.

Which meant that the other feat they'd tackled over the week was training. Training soldiers on how to use the orichtium amulets that Micah and his court had rushed to complete. Training civilians on how to fight. Gavin spent a lot of time training Sage on battle strategy.

Now, Sage stood waiting for what would inevitably come. Her breath just barely fogged the darkened morning air, and she shivered slightly as her neck hairs stood at the end of goosebumps.

She'd already said her goodbyes to Gavin, who now stood atop the Obelisk with Zeke, lookouts for when the Dark Born finally made their appearance. She'd said her farewells to Raphael, who remained huddled deep within the castle complex, guarding the few citizens who'd been unable to evacuate at such short notice.

Petra manned the entrance of the fortified keep. She would be the last line of defense should everything go wrong. Sage was amazed they'd been able to get the female to leave the Obelisk based on everything she'd heard. But, she couldn't say she felt sorry should any Speridisian soldiers find their way to the female. A hard shudder made its way down her spine as she remembered the males who clawed themselves to pieces after killing Hyacinth. They'd gotten what they deserved. Still, Petra's powers were unsettling, to say the least.

At present, Symon's spies came strolling out of the castle, each wearing scraps of armor. Acantha, her head freshly shaved, wore leather bindings across her breasts, a leather kilt, and bracers. Daggers were strapped everywhere, and Sage was stunned to see the female walk so fluidly in spite of them. Epyllo wore leather armor on each shoulder, and a leather kilt similar to Acantha's. Short swords were crossed on his back. He'd painted his upper body black with ash.

"Don't you think you'd best put on a little bit more armor?" asked Sage as they walked past.

"Nah," said Epyllo. "We're much faster this way."

"Besides, once we get started, you'll see. I bet you'll sweat your tits off in that thing." Acantha flicked Sage in the chest, poking fun at the leather armor she'd had commissioned. It was black, thick and corded around her body. It'd been carefully designed to bend at her joints while still offering protection against anything sharp. In all honesty, she felt incredibly badass wearing it. Especially when Gavin had belted her dagger holster to her waist, securing the bottoms of it around each thigh. She'd finished this morning by tying her shoulder length hair in a tight bun, using oils to slick her hair to her scalp so no strands would whip her in the face.

Sage scrunched her nose up at them. "Can't help that I'd rather not get stabbed."

"'Specially not in the tits," laughed Epyllo. "I bet Gavin is fond of them."

Acantha guffawed as Sage's eyes grew round and she blushed.

"Come on, Epyllo. Let's get ready." Acantha's laugh could still be heard as they left the gravel drive that led to the castle.

Sage took one more glance up at the Obelisk, then she walked through the gates of the palace. It took her fifteen minutes to walk up the steep road that opened into a wide city center. There, Queen Aryael stood proudly with her all-female unit of soldiers. They wore white armor embellished with gold piping, a red or orange feathered helmet, and deep orange capes. Short swords and long swords hung at their sides.

"Ho-ly-shit..." whispered Sage. Each female stood so tall, so strong. Sage had never seen anything quite so impressive.

Meliza stepped out of line, gesturing to Sage. "Welcome to the Fire Unit, Realm Leaper. Are you ready to kick some ass?"

Sage laughed. "I'm starting to wonder if I'm in over my head."

Meliza shrugged. "Maybe. But you've got to start somewhere."

Spread across the city, other units were dispersed. The Shadow Unit was tucked into alleyways and buildings, waiting for opportunities to ambush marching soldiers. The

Water Unit held the line on the beachy shore of Veritasailles. The Wind Unit was also scattered, positioned so that
flyers could spring into the air quickly and suddenly. Those
without wings or flying abilities were armed with crossbows, catapults, and various sling weapons. Earth Unit held
the line along other borders of the city. The units weren't
named to indicate fae power abilities, but was a device the
King and Queen used to strategize.

Stepping into line with the rest of the Fire Unit, Sage
took everything in, marveling at them. Their hair was down
or braided. Some wore red face paint beneath their bronze
helms. *Fucking badass*, thought Sage.

Whoops and hollers rolled through the city, and Sage
tensed, not sure what to expect. She looked to Queen
Aryael who had just been speaking in low tones to one of
the Lieutenants standing next to her. A broad smile broke
across the Queen's face as she turned toward the sound.

On the road, warriors walked, beating spears against
shields made of woven wood. Lions, cheetahs, rhinoceros,
apes, leopards, and even...an elephant led the procession,
each letting loose their own thunderous calls. The warriors
whooped and shrieked, someone carried a drum and called
out in time with the marching.

"The Sekiri have made it to the party!" cheered Aryael as
the animals arrived, the warriors close behind.

A shimmer, and then each animal shifted into fae form.

At the front of the line now stood three warriors. A tall,
lithe female with tight braids skating across her skull stood
from her cheetah form. Another female, her hair curling outward from her head like a halo, stood in the center where a
lioness was once positioned. And the elephant shifted into
a large man, his huge pectorals bare to the crisp morning

air. Sage nearly choked at the size of him. From where she stood, she guessed that the size of his palms were equal to dinner plates. His skin was dark, nearly ebony, and glinted in the rising sunlight as if he were carved from stone.

And yet, he exuded warmth as he greeted the Fire Unit, wearing the brightest, most genuine smile Sage had ever witnessed. She supposed one could be so happy if they were literally the largest creature anyone had ever met, in animal and in fae form.

The elephant shifter laughed. It was staccato and booming. He stretched out his arms and greeted, "Queen Aryael. We meet again!"

Aryael met him halfway in an embrace. "Prince Aghbalu! It's been too long." The two embraced in the way that two long-lost friends might, squeezing tight and rocking side to side.

Aryael and Aghbalu stepped away from each other, and the Queen turned to the lioness shifter. Aryael put her fist to her heart and gave the female a short bow. The lioness shifter returned the gesture. "Queen Dihya."

"Queen Aryael," the female said back. Then they hugged.

Finally, Aryale embraced the cheetah shifter's forearm and they each smiled at each other. "Now you are a Queen? Last time I saw you, you were running around with scraped knees."

"It's good to see you, Amastan."

"Now...when do we get to fight?" said Amastan, her grin wicked. Sage thought she saw the glint of pointed teeth and wondered whether she could partially shift similarly to winged fae.

"Whenever those bastards decide to show up," said Aryael.

Meliza approached. "Sekiri, it is an honor to fight beside you." Meliza placed a fist to her heart and bowed.

"And ours to finally see the famed Truth Teller in all her glory." Aghbalu cracked his knuckles, his fur cape shifting as he rolled his shoulders.

Dihya interjected, "Do we stand a chance against the Death Shadows?"

Meliza lifted her bracers, each embellished with Orichtium amulets. "With these we do." She flexed and the amulet hummed with energy.

"I can't wait to watch them burn," said Amastan.

"Here, here," sang the chorus of several Fire Unit soldiers who had gathered round. They all broke apart as Meliza and Aryael began to shout orders, getting their soldiers ready for battle. The sun was just cresting the ocean, glinting off of domed rooftops.

Another disturbance rumbled towards them. Hooves beat stone and Sage turned in time to see what looked like a cyclone of sand and dirt spinning toward them. In the distance, Sage could hear the cheers of Felysia warriors as the cyclone passed tightly down the road, never reaching the buildings, only kicking up dirt and dust.

"What's happening?" whispered Sage.

"It's the Kalipha tribe," said Aryael, her face pinched.

"They're from the desert of northern Nysa," said Meliza when Aryael didn't provide more. "They usually keep to themselves."

"And why are they cheering?" asked Sage. Obviously, some from Nysa had survived and now came to their aid. That was a good thing. She was confused as to why the Queen wasn't as excited as she was about the Sekiri Tribe.

"They are excellent earth shapers. Masterful even." Meliza stood tall, her arms crossed.

"Okay..."

"But not everyone likes them. They find the Kalipha hard to trust."

"Okaaay..." said Sage again, drawing out the word to imply she'd like to hurry up and find out what was going on.

"They're venomous," supplied Aryael.

"Venomous? Like...as in...they bite?"

Aryael nodded. "If they should get their fangs in you...well, let's just say it's unpleasant."

"Have you ever been bitten by one?" asked Sage.

Aryael looked at her, an almost pitying expression on her face. "I'm alive, aren't I?"

Sage swallowed thickly. Noted, she thought. Do not let the Kalipha bite.

Finally, the cyclone stopped, the dust hovering in its wake before falling with a whisper. Seven riders sat atop horses. They wore black robes and veils, their faces covered with black silk except for their eyes. Small scimitar swords were tattooed beneath their eyes, and Sage guessed at least three of them were female. They all had dark tan skin, and eyes so brown they were nearly black. The overall effect was striking.

The horses glistened. Their manes were black, flowing like oil. Their tales stood tall behind them. Sage especially liked the one that was the color of gray smoke, white dappling covering its body. She wanted to stroke her hand down its coat, but remembered what Aryael had said of the riders.

The rider in the front called out with a stilted accent, "Representatives from the Kalipha tribe have come to fight alongside the Realm Leaper."

"Setarrah," said Dihya sharply. "It's nice to finally see the Kalipha outside their desert."

"The Kalipha do not respond to lies," responded Setarrah.

"Sounds like you just did." Amastan chuckled behind Dihya, and caught a swift elbow to her ribs when Setarrah's eyes cut to the female.

"Setarrah, we are honored to have the help of the Kalipha. You are welcome to fight in Fire Unit if you prefer." Queen Aryael held her head high, her posture ramrod straight.

"The Kalipha fight where they are needed," said another rider, his voice deep and melodic.

"Excellent," said Aryael under her voice. "Of course."

Setarrah gave Aryael a nod, touching her forehead with two fingers. Then, the riders gently kicked their steeds. The horses walked calmly down the wall of soldiers, who now stood at attention. Some drew their swords, others kept their eyes fixed on the horizon. Some leaned close to another, whispering low.

The sun rose, higher into the sky, and they waited. Sage's palms began to grow sweaty as they waited, and waited. Acantha was right. She hadn't even begun to fight, and her tits *were* in fact sweating. Someone passed her a water jug, and she took several deep gulps.

The air was no longer crisp and cool. The sun had chased away the autumn air, intent to have one last day of glory. Maybe that was an omen, thought Sage. Aryael was basically the personification of sunshine. Maybe this was the Goddess's way of saying they were favored.

Time ticked by. Occasionally, a soldier cast into their unit, carrying a message for Aryael or Meliza. Sage, growing weary of waiting, bounced on her toes, letting her limbs bounce as well, willing her muscles to loosen.

"This is your first battle?" Aryael asked.

"I fought off the Dark Born's possessed," said Sage, referring to the last time the city had been attacked.

"That was different. That was an ambush. *This* is your first battle." Aryael's gaze was fixed on the horizon, but Sage could feel her attention.

She cleared her throat. "Yeah, I guess."

"Are you nervous?" asked the Queen. Sage didn't answer. "Let me help you. You'd be a fool not to be nervous."

"Then yes. I'm very nervous."

"Good." The Queen nodded. "Are you going to vomit?" she asked quietly, so quietly Sage was hopeful no one else could hear.

Now that she thought about it...Yes, yes she was going to vomit. Sage nodded.

"I suggest you do it over there, in the bushes. Go ahead and get it over with before the fight begins."

Not waiting, Sage hurried toward a building at the edge of the city square. She stepped into the alley and grabbed hold of the bushes, letting her meager breakfast of oats loose from her stomach. She groaned, wiping her mouth with the back of her hand.

Now that it was over with, she felt much better. She breathed deep. Letting the air flow through her body. She stilled her mind, allowing herself to focus. They could do this. She breathed, telling herself again. *They* could do this.

Sage rejoined the unit. Meliza was waiting.

"Remember what I told you. There's no honor in battle. The only way to win is to survive."

"Got it," said Sage.

"You make them hurt. Make them pay," said Meliza. Her voice was tight and sharp. Violence radiated from the female's body, and Sage let it fuel her own anger.

Make them pay...

Yeah, she'd make them pay.

They'd pay for Hyacinth. They'd pay for Ian. They'd pay for hurting Raphael. They'd pay for Suda, who now lay in the care of Shiphrah, half the male he used to be.

A persistent thud came from far away in the distance. It rattled the ground, windows and doors rattled.

"Here we go," said Meliza, a wicked glee edging her voice.

The thread of the bond pulsed, tugging at her chest three times. *I love you.*

Sage tugged back. *I love you more. Don't die.*

The shimmering echo of a soft laugh rippled through her, and Sage let it bolster her.

The Fire Unit began banging their swords against their shields. Some held spears, slamming the butts to the ground. Some of the soldiers began to yell in rhythm to the bangs. Sage found herself joining in, grabbing her daggers and clanging them together.

The Sekiri Tribe whooped, a baboon shifter returning to animal form, springing forward and banging its chest as it screamed to the sky.

The Kalipha Tribe yelled, high pitched and sharp, rolling their tongues. The effect made goosebumps erupt across her entire body.

Sage stepped forward, a scream of defiance ripping from her until her voice was raw. She was panting, letting the yells, battle cries, clanging of swords and spears feed into her until she was at a fever pitch, ready to smite any poor soul who might step into her path.

Then, the world fell silent.

They'd arrived.

Chapter 38

✧✦✧

From their position, they could see the approaching army just at the peak of the horizon. Swaths of black lined the hills that bordered the city. Some Speridisian soldiers flapped in the air, black smudges against the sky. Two figures flew higher than all the others, their wings expansive and rippling with smoke-like shadows.

Sage's heart beat fiercely.

"All ready then?" came a familiar drawl.

"Micah?" asked Sage, turning to see the Shadow Master.

"Yes, yes. I made it after all." He took a swig of something from a waterskin, then burped. The syrupy sweet scent of wine followed.

"Are you drinking?" asked Meliza in shock.

"Well, I might die," said Micah, as if it were perfectly clear. "Might as well die drunk." He took a long swig, drops of red trickling from the corners of his lips.

"He has a point," muttered Aryael, grabbing the waterskin and taking a swig of her own before handing it back.

"I expect a huge funeral if I die, by the way." Micah capped the waterskin, then threw it into the air. With a wave of his hands, it disappeared into shadow. "Elaborate.

I will require at least three wailers to mourn for me as I'm carried through the streets like the hero I am."

"So help me," Sage barged in, "if you don't shut up, I will cut your tongue out."

"Go ahead and try. It might be fun to tussle with you." The rogue turned Lord waggled his eyebrows, and Sage rolled her eyes.

Shouts interrupted their tête-à-tête. In the distance, the sounds of whirring and buzzing could just be heard. Something about the noise made Sage's stomach drop. She racked her brain trying to place the sound and came up short. But something about it put her body immediately into defense mode. Her muscles tensed beneath her armor. She readied her stance.

Then, silver orbs lifted into the sky. The whirring intensified as they spread out away from them.

"Shit," said Sage. She shouted over to Aryael. "They've got drones!"

The machines began pummeling the city with fire, shooting at the city limits. Light flared, the city's enchantments sparking to life against the threat. The drones continued, firing in rapid succession until the enchantments finally glowed a hot yellow. A ringing sound reverberated throughout the city as the enchantments failed.

Magic only lasted so long, thought Sage. They'd come with the drones knowing that their magic used a higher frequency of energy, just to knock out the enchantments.

"Fuck," whispered Micah.

"Got anymore of that wine?" asked Sage. Suddenly, being drunk seemed like a good idea.

"Nope." Micah stood with wide eyes, staring as the drones flew into the city.

Wind Unit jumped into action. Winged fae flew through the air, aiming directly at the drones. The drones fired at the fae, who dodged and dipped. Some fae went down. Some drones were knocked out by catapults on the ground.

A horn blared from the Obelisk. More airborne fae sprung up, spearing toward the border, toward the Speridisian forces where flying fae trickled over the city line.

Swords, spears, arrows, projectiles all clashed in the air. Shouting rang through the streets.

The fighting remained confined to the sky and ground at the edges of the city. Now it was Aryael bouncing on her feet. "Hold!" she yelled to her unit, as much to them as it was to herself.

Fire Unit soldiers tensed, preparing themselves to sprint toward the fight. Sekiri warriors whooped again, lions roaring loudly through the streets.

There, in the sky, Sage saw Gavin. He dove from high above, hitting a drone with his sword before they both fell to the ground. Sage's throat clenched. Then, he was airborne again, his wings beating strong as he took on a Dark Born soldier with big, leathery wings.

The whirring intensified.

Sage looked toward the horizon. A trio of drones speared toward the Fire Unit.

Aryael called yelled, "Ready!"

The drones drew closer.

Aryael yelled again, "Fire!"

Earth shapers, wind wielders, fire wielders, and water workers all let loose, their amulets glowing as power coursed through them. Sage's daggers hummed with intensity as she let loose a series of stones and water.

One drone went down, crashing into a building with a fiery finale.

Two drones continued on, dodging the missiles shot at them.

Aryael yelled again, "Give it everything!"

Another drone crashed, spinning wildly before it imploded on itself.

One drone left. A Sekiri baboon shifter screamed wildly. Then, he leapt into the air, smashing the drone with his fist. The drone flipped end over end, out of control. In half a moment, the drone righted itself and took aim even as it sparked.

Tiny barbs shot out of the drone, striking the baboon.

The drone exploded. The baboon thudded to the ground.

A Sekiri soldier ran to the animal, now shifting back into fae form. He shuddered, blood bubbled from his mouth.

"Fuck," growled Meliza.

"They have elm!" yelled Amastan who was trying to revive the fallen warrior.

Aryael turned to Sage and Micah. "I need you two on the drones. Take them out with everything you have." Her teeth were grit, her fists clenched.

"We will go with you," yelled the leader of the Kalipha tribe.

Next thing Sage knew, she was being tossed onto the back of a horse, a rumbling voice calling "Hold on, Realm Leaper."

"Fuck me running," Micah said beneath his voice as a large, silk wrapped arm grabbed him and hauled him onto the back of a horse.

Setarrah let out a series of shrill yips, and they were off. Shadow engulfed them; dust flowed over them stretching out through the street. Anyone caught in their fray would become hopelessly lost.

The horses galloped hard and fast beneath them as they followed the sound of the drones overhead, the noise vibrating through the streets. The clanging of weapons rang out around them, but they paid no mind. Overhead, a drone shot a laser through the dust cloud, scanning for bodies.

Even as the horses galloped, Sage yelled, "Micah! Up!"

The Shadow Master reached out with his power, shadows wrapping around her. Then, she was in the air, Micah by her side. They were falling, probably fifteen feet above the drone. Sage's daggers, gripped tight in her hands, hummed as she shot fire and stone. Each shot struck true, and the drone exploded.

Micah's shadows wrapped around her again, shielding her from the blast. Another pull of power, and now Sage was back on solid ground.

The Kalipha Tribe were on their feet now, scimitars drawn and ready.

"Where are the horses?" Sage cried.

"Gone for now. We go on foot." Setarrah took the lead, running forward.

Dust swirled, wreaking havoc on the eyesight of enemy soldiers galloping toward them.

Sage allowed herself one breath to take it in. The Dark Born soldiers were gargantuan. Many of them bore tusk-like piercings in their lips and noses. Their pointed ears sagged at the bottom, and some of them were covered in what Sage took to be scar tissue. They were hideous.

One behemoth of a male charged right at Sage. He flung out a hand, sending a stream of smoky shadows at her. She swung a dagger, whisking it away. Then she stomped her foot and the earth crumbled beneath him. He stumbled, then sprang forward, free of her trap. He reached her, slashing down with his broadsword. She dodged the slash, swiping up with a dagger and catching him in his under arm.

She whirled, catching an elbow to her shoulder as her enemy slammed it into her. She let the momentum of his weight carry her, leaning into and falling away, her other dagger catching him across his quad.

Her shoulder throbbed, but she hardly noticed as she stepped back, missing another strike of the sword. She stumbled, the sword was heading back to her. She threw up her daggers, braced for impact as it came right for her.

Rippling shadows, pure and free from the smoky malice of the Dark Born, formed in front of her. Micah appeared, and blood sprayed.

The Dark Born soldier fell to his knees, Micah stepping aside for him to thud onto the ground.

"You're welcome," said Micah, wiping his blade on his pants.

"That one was mine," said Sage, through clenched teeth.

"Too bad, too slow." Micah stuck his tongue out, then ran toward another fight.

Before he got far, Sage yelled again. "Micah! UP!"

Just above them, two drones whirred, their laser beams scanning the area. Micah flung out his cloak, shadows wrapping around her again.

They were above the drones, falling again.

But this time the machines spun, sights locked on Sage and Micah.

She flung everything she had. Earth. Fire. Water. Wind.

It all pummeled the drones at the same time. She gave them everything she had, just hoping it was enough to keep the drones from firing.

Boom!

The drones went down. Imploding on themselves in a fiery spectacle.

Sage was dropping like a stone, plummeting to the earth until Micah grabbed her with his power. They thudded to the ground.

Sage gasped greedily for air. Her head throbbed. It had been so much power. More than she had ever wielded before. She swiped at her nose. It was bleeding, and something deep inside her was pulsating with a painful rhythm.

Sage looked up in time to see Setarrah rip free her veil. Scales lined the female's face, and sharp fangs protruded. The female leapt forward, sinking her fangs into the Dark Born soldier who screamed and writhed as she held on.

The soldier struck back with his dagger, sinking it deep into the Kalipha leader's side. It spurted bright red blood. She let go, and gasped for air. The Dark Born soldier whimpered, then crumpled in on himself. A few seconds later, he was quiet.

"Micah," Sage whispered. When he looked at her, his eyes went wide. "Get her to Raph." Sage pointed at Setarrah.

"You're bleeding." Micah grabbed her by the elbow.

"No, shit. I'm fine, but she's dying." Sage pointed at Setarrah, even as one of her fellow warriors scooped her up. "Get her to Raph, now." Sage growled at Micah, urging him to go.

"Be safe, sorceress. If you die, Gavin will never forgive me."

"Just go."

Fire Unit was rampaging toward them, taking out Dark Born that had wrapped around the dust storm the Kalipha had struck up. The Sekiri Tribe fought savagely, ripping through Dark Born soldiers as if they were ribbons.

Aryael struck down enemies with her blade alight, a white hot flame engulfing those she struck. They screamed as they were consumed with the fire.

Meliza was by her side, fighting with sword *and* spear at the same time. Sage wiped her nose one more time, thinking she'd love to just watch the Commander fight at her full strength.

A mighty yell took Sage out of her reverie, and Sage turned to see another Dark Born heading right for her. Sage whipped her daggers out, whirling them in a circle. Water collected around the enemy soldier until he was fully encased. Sage ran forward, causing the ball of water to move backward until it was against the wall. She burst the water bubble, then tossed her dagger. It struck the soldier in his neck before he could collect himself. With her wind power, she ripped the dagger free so it flew through the air into her waiting hand.

The whirring was gone. Either she'd destroyed the last of the drones, or they'd been pulled back. Fire Unit was finishing off the last of the Dark Born in the area as far as Sage could see. Aryael yelled something, pointing her sword down toward the city lines.

Everyone ran. Lions. Cheetahs. A warthog led the charge.

The road leveled out, into what Sage recognized as the marketplace she had once perused with Gavin, chaos had broken loose. Gavin battled against three hulking Dark Born at once, one of which was impossibly fast. A strong wind pummeled two of the Dark Born back.

Then, Gavin was gone. He cast behind one Dark Born, running his sword through him, before casting to the other. Over and over, Gavin cast and struck. Three Dark Born soldiers now lay on the ground, bleeding out.

Overhead, Sage heard a mighty bellow.

"Shit," Gavin yelled.

Meliza looked up, "Shit."

Zeke tumbled through the sky, plummeting through the air toward them. Gavin cast. Meliza cast. The two met Zeke, each grabbing for him in their winged forms.

Gavin grabbed an arm, Meliza a leg. Together they were able to slow the fall. A wind howled, and Gavin cast them all to the ground.

An arrow protruded through Zeke's black and gray wings. The feathers drooped, many already falling free.

Sage had a second to see Meliza scoop Zeke onto his feet, his arm draped around her shoulder, and they both began a limping run out of the battle zone.

A yell vibrated behind her. Sage whirled, her daggers up just in time to stop a sword from striking her. She pushed back, sending flames down her daggers. The flames caught on her attacker's sleeves and he staggered back. Shadows seeped from his body, spearing towards Sage. She dropped her arms, spinning to miss the sword once again, his sleeves no longer alight. Sage slashed down with her dagger then drew a line across it. "Reo Corff!"

The spell took hold. Frost covered the soldier's body. A blue sheen coated his skin, his eyes glazing.

She withdrew her dominant dagger arm, then struck the air, commanding, "Chwyth!" The frozen body broke apart, shattering into a thousand tiny pieces.

Symon's Unit, the Shadow Unit, was now a part of the fray. They were edging toward the city lines. The enemy was being pushed back.

Aryael let loose, a whole horde of Dark Born incinerating on site, Gavin feeding the flames with air. Arrows whizzed from rooftops, striking down the enemy.

Despite their advantages, despite their numbers, despite their grotesque size and brutality, Felysia was winning.

Speridisia soldiers were going down, one after the other. They were almost there.

Deafening wingbeats boomed overhead. Two males, with smoky shadows twining around their bodies hovered above the fray.

Abbadon and Apyllon. They watched, occasionally sending down a shadow or two of their own.

Sage fought the shadows, sending bursts of her elemental magic up toward them. It worked. Each blast of all four elementals shredded apart the shadows.

But Sage paid for each hit.

Aryael saw what she was doing. "Sage! Is it working?"

Sage looked at the Queen, nodding quickly before wiping her bleeding nose.

"Gavin, with me!" screamed the Queen. Just then, Meliza was back. "Sage, you cover water. Gavin, Meliza, hit them with your power, use your amulets."

Gavin and Meliza squared up next to Sage and Aryael, surrounded by members of their own army. Together, they sent rhythmic blasts of power at the twins. Each combined hit tore apart the shadows, bit by bit. Apyllon screeched, diving down at them once before being called back by his brother.

The twins flew upward, increasing their elevation. Sage grit her teeth, forcing everything she could through her water magic. The blasts still hit the twins, but it was becoming weaker.

One shot hit Apyllon square in the chest. He stuttered in the air, then caught himself. Then, with a wild glare in his eye, he shot to the earth.

His wings dragged against the stone ground, talons forming from his fingertips. His arms were outstretched, and he aimed for Sage. She sent out a wild gust of wind, followed by Gavin's own blast. It threw the twin off course, sending him tumbling backward.

"Fucking cowards!" screamed Apyllon as he slammed into a wall. He seemed to shudder for a moment, then villainously sharp fangs erupted from his gums as he began to grow into something unworldly. His skin grew paler, his eyes glowed red. "I'll enjoy drinking your blood once I've ripped you apart."

Apyllon's wings disappeared. He sprang forward, aiming for Sage, again. She steadied herself, planting her feet, not willing to back down. His talons were long, black, and glinted with their sharpness. Before he reached her, she slashed up with her daggers. Vines exploded from the ground, grabbing hold of Apyllon. He tore at the vines, ripping free of them. But by then, Sage and Gavin had cast to the other side of the road that had become a battlefield.

Abbadon had landed, engaging Symon and Aryael. Sage supposed she and Gavin were left to deal with the wild twin.

Apyllon huffed, spittle foaming at the corners of his mouth. In his hand, shadows formed a longsword the color of obsidian. "I'll capture you. And make you watch as I torture you both, each in turn," he seethed, panting as he walked forward erratically like a drunk.

Apyllon lunged forward, Sage and Gavin stepping away from each other, out of his reach. Sage dropped to the ground, swiping out with a foot. Apyllon saw it and stomped on her leg, hard. She screamed, and punched upward with a ball of flame before he could strike.

Gavin met the twin with his short sword, striking upward. But Apyllon caught the sword, striking against Gavin even as his shirt flamed. It was like the male couldn't feel anything, for all that he acknowledged his singed flesh.

Gavin and Apyllon struck at each other over and over. Gavin cast out of the way of a blow, landing behind the twin. Apyllon reached back, blocking Gavin's strike before spinning around and countering the blow.

Sage drew a circle with her dagger, "Slaodach!"

Apyllon slowed, her spell striking true. Gavin used the opportunity to slash the Dark Born through the center. But the sword passed through smoke. The sword hit nothing.

Apyllon laughed wildly. "Oh—that was a bawdy trick by your little President, there." Apyllon spun in a circle, his arms outstretched. "I cannot be killed! Not by you!"

An arrow zipped by, passing straight through Apyllon with a wisp of smoke. Nothing.

"Fuck," whispered Sage.

Now what?

Now. What?

Apyllon struck out, hitting Gavin with his longsword, Gavin parrying every blow. Over and over they parried. The battle raged on around them.

Gavin cast out of the way, moving out of reach from Apyllon.

Then a thought struck Sage. She knew how to kill the Dark Born. She could do it herself.

Sage reached into herself, grabbing hold of the thread that tied her and Gavin together. With a mighty heave, she yanked her and Gavin down the road.

They landed heavily, Apyllon left in the distant heaving, looking for Gavin.

"Trust me," whispered Sage.

"Always," said Gavin.

Sage tugged again. Now, Sage landed behind Apyllon, Gavin right in front. Sage leapt on the twins back before he could react and stabbed both daggers into his neck. She poured every ounce of magic she possessed into the twin. Earth. Water. Wind. Fire.

All of it. Her daggers sparked. Her body trembled with the force.

The Dark Born beneath her howled, his talons jabbing into her wrists. She screamed, but never relented. Gavin sliced with his blade, and it hit flesh. Dark Born blood spilled out.

Finally, he was down, falling to his knees.

Apyllon's skin grew ashen. Talons withdrew. Black blood pooled beneath the lifeless body.

A mighty roar bellowed across the battlefield. "NOO!" Abbadon's scream pummeled the world around them, knocking over several Felysian soldiers.

Before anyone could react, Abbadon pulled out a vial and threw it into Aryael's chest. It smashed into her, splattering her with a sticky purple liquid. She froze, her arms dropping to her side, her eyes rolling back into her head.

Symon ran forward, her name on his lips.

Abbadon scooped her up, then shot into the sky.

"You fucking fools! You'll pay for what you've done this day! " he screamed down to them, Aryael limp in his arms.

Then, he disappeared.

The Speridisian soldiers still fighting faded into nothing, leaving the streets free.

"ARYAEL!" thundered Symon.

He cast, light erupting hundreds of feet above the city. Sage watched in horror as the King fell from the sky. Then, he disappeared, casting again.

Again, the sky exploded, yellow light sparking from the King.

He fell.

Again, cast.

Again, light erupting.

Symon's wings were out, and he screamed to the sky. Calling out for Aryael. Over and over again.

When he finally came back to the ground his eyes were red with burst blood vessels. His breath heaved.

He sunk onto all fours. "Get me an enchanter," he yelled. "Get me a FUCKING enchanter, right now!"

"Symon," said Meliza quietly, commanding the King, her brother, to look at her. "We have to play this smart."

Symon grabbed her by the throat, his eyes wild with rage. "Get me a fucking enchanter right now or I'll tear this whole city apart."

"If you really wanted to do that, you'd already be mind controlling me, brother," said Meliza. Her voice was soft, empathetic. "We both know you'll make the right choice."

Symon roughly pushed her away. He walked back toward where his sword lay on the ground. He faced an ally, raking his hands through his hair, then yelled, a heartbreaking, torrential sound that went on and on. When his voice was breaking, losing its ability, he turned.

Tears ran down the King's face. "Meet me in her war room. Five minutes."

Everything around them came alive.

Sage turned to Gavin, her eyes wide and savage. The battle was over. They were both alive, and unhurt...well, mostly unhurt. Her knee gave out suddenly, and it throbbed with an angry pang.

Gavin rushed forward, grabbing her. "Thank the Goddess," he said, his face buried in her hair.

"Let's get to Raph, then see how we can help."

Gavin nodded. "First," he said softly, then crushed his lips to hers. Then, "You're bleeding," he pulled back, running a tender finger across the blood that coated her upper lip and nose.

"I'll explain later," she said. "Right now, Raph."

Without another word, they cast into the castle foyer, where Raph was already busy with other injured soldiers.

His face shone with sweat when they walked toward him. "Oh, thank the Goddess," he exclaimed.

"You need to heal Sage, then go to Aryael's war room." Gavin's tone was curt.

"What does she need?" asked Raphael.

"She's gone," said Sage. Raph jumped, covering his mouth with his hand. "We need to hurry," explained Sage.

"Of course," muttered the healer, then stooped to his knees to investigate the leg with the limp.

As Raphael's magic flowed, Sage let her thoughts roll over her like waves. All magic had a price. Everything required balance.

In order to save Aryael, Sage would need everything she had. But Sage was wondering now if she still had enough to give.

And if she didn't, then who did?

Chapter 39

✧✦✧

Gavin and Sage finally made it to Aryael's war room, Raphael hot on their heels. They'd passed more wounded scattered throughout the palace and the sentry's barracks, but Shiphrah had swiftly stepped in to take the lead. Healers bustled around at breakneck speed, heeding the calls of the injured.

Symon leaned heavily on the round table that sat at the center of the room. The same table Gavin had seen Aryael lean upon so often. It felt wrong. She should be there.

To think that she was in the clutches of Abbadon. It made his stomach turn, especially now that they had Suda back. The evidence of their malicious cruelty had turned his stomach. The Queen's once handsome brother now lay in a darkened room, refusing to take visitors apart from Raph and one of his trusted assistants, who cared for him around the clock.

Had anyone told him? That his sister had been taken? Gavin would suggest that Raphael go once they'd determined some sort of plan.

At the table stood Epyllo and Acantha, one on either side of the King. Acantha sported a busted lip, which only served to make her more fierce looking. Micah leaned against the wall, tucked away in the corner. He was covered in blood. Gavin looked twice to confirm it wasn't his own. Petra was nowhere to be seen. Gavin assumed she'd skulked back to the Obelisk, although, they could do with her specific type of shadow skill in this situation.

Meliza and Zeke were busy pointing at the map, arguing.

"You are a fool if you think you're in any shape to go to Speridisia," said Meliza, her tone sharp.

"And you're a fool if you think I'll stand by and let those monsters torture our Queen!" Zeke was positively rabid. A vein bulged from his forehead, and his skin was an angry, mottled red.

"What do you expect to do, hmm? Your powers have all but dried up. You can't even shift out of your winged form."

Meliza was on a roll, she'd have Zeke cowed within the next few moments, thought Gavin.

It was true, however. Zeke was in no shape to fight against the Dark Born on their own turf. His injured wing drooped heavily, its tip lolling on the floor. And, Gavin knew Zeke was further weakened by Petra's continuous attempts to break their bond. Gavin's fists balled, and he stepped involuntarily toward Sage, his own bonded. Now that he'd experienced the bond, the idea of breaking it made his blood boil. In his mind, Petra was an insufferable brat. He empathized with her trauma, but was her trauma all that mattered?

"You'll not be going," Symon said, his voice low and deadly. The King stood, pushing off the table. "And neither will you, Meliza." She nodded once. "I need you both with me."

"Then who will go?" asked Zeke, defiantly pushing past Meliza and staring down Symon, his hands shaking. "Are we just going to let her rot there while you wait for an enchanter? What are you thinking?"

Symon looked at Zeke then, his eyes colder than the frozen glaciers in Borea. "I cannot sacrifice myself, or my two most powerful warriors for a rescue mission. It isn't what she would want." Symon's gaze turned slowly back to the table before he leaned onto it once more.

Just then, the rustling sound of skirts perforated the growing silence.

"Zeke!"

Petra rushed across the room, running to Zeke. She threw her arms around his neck. Zeke stood immobile, his arms hovering out in the air as Petra clung to him, sobbing into his neck. Slowly, the warrior let his arms fall around Petra's back, and he buried his face in her hair.

The room fell silent. Everyone watched as the two held on tight. Zeke's hands fisted her dress, clinging to her like she'd evaporate into thin air if he ever let go.

For an eternity the two of them held onto each other, while frozen in time their closest companions looked on. Something eased in Gavin's chest, a knot he hadn't even known was there. The beauty of that moment had tears burning his eyes. He looked to Sage, a knowing look passing between them as their hands joined.

"Zeke..." Symon said softly. "Go. Sit this one out."

Zeke and Petra pulled away from each other enough so they could look deep and long into each other's eyes. A silent message seemed to pass between them, a promise that never again would they lose hold of the other.

Petra looked thin, dark shadows of mourning marring her eyes, still.

Zeke nodded and let Petra walk him out from the room.

Everything seemed to still once the couple had finally left, a crackling energy at once deafening in its silence and electrifying in its potency thundering through each of them. Gavin thought the dust motes even froze as they all let what had happened sink in.

She'd finally come back. She'd come back and saved Zeke.

Symon's head hung low between his shoulders. Gavin couldn't help but notice a tear fall onto the table beneath the King, mirroring his own stifled emotions. The hands that seemed to be pushing against the table to keep himself upright shook slightly.

Finally, with a loud sniff, Symon lifted his head. "Alright, who do we send?"

Meliza cut in first. "We need someone who can get as close as possible to the Speridisian borders. Their enchantments will prevent any of us from casting into their territory."

"We've done it before." Acantha licked her busted lip, hands propped on her hips as she spoke. "Epyllo and I are probably your best chance of crossing the border undetected."

"Won't that be pitting the Queen against time, though?" asked Micah. "I mean, how long do you reckon they'll keep her...intact?"

Symon punched the table, sending a shivering crack down the center of it. "They won't harm her. I will not allow it!"

"Then we need a way to get to their keep, and do it quickly." Meliza crossed her arms, her brows furrowing.

Sage rocked from hip to hip. Gavin side-eyed her, noticing a strange feeling humming along their bond. He thought this might be the feeling she got whenever an idea had struck her, and her mind began moving a million miles a second. She chewed on her bottom lip, one arm hugging her torso, the other hand propped against her cheek.

Micah offered, "I reckon I could get us pretty close to the keep if I used shadows. It wouldn't be precise. And..." he paused, pushing off the wall and walking toward the table. "I'm not sure how the shadows would respond in Speridisia."

There'd always been rumors that shadows behaved differently in the Dark Born lands. Legends of revenants being sent to serve the punishment of unspeakable crimes, locked in a land of pure evil, had been passed down for generations. The thought made Gavin shiver.

"No—" Sage cut in, "it can't be you." She was shaking her head. Then, she stopped, becoming completely still. And she looked at Gavin. "Gavin can do it."

Symon looked at him, his face stern. "How close can you get?"

Sage answered for him. "He can get us all the way there."

"Sage, the wards protecting the Spearsan Pass are different than you've experienced before. They're *incredibly* powerful. There's no telling how much more powerful the enchantments are once you get closer to the keep, especially if they've been using blood sorcery all this time." Meliza spoke patiently, clearly not convinced. Gavin wasn't sure he felt differently.

"Can wards keep out the wind?" asked Sage. She looked at Gavin again, the whisper of a smile reaching her eyes in spite of the situation.

"No..." began Meliza.

"Then they can't stop Gavin."

"I'm sorry. Can one of you love birds explain to the rest of us what you are talking about?" asked Micah.

Gavin locked eyes with Sage for a moment. He hadn't shared this particular revelation with anyone other than her and Shiphrah. He turned to Symon. "When we dreamwalked, Dianis visited me. She told me I wasn't just a wind wielder. I *am* the wind, a *true* wind walker." Gavin turned his gaze on Sage again. He was so fucking proud of her. She'd once again solved the riddle.

"You see, when Gavin casts...it's different from all of you," began Sage. "When I've cast with Raphael, it was like I was being squeezed through giant rollers until I popped out on the other side. When Gavin does it...it's just different. It's like walking through fog, almost."

"He becomes the wind," finished Meliza.

"Which means he's fucking unstoppable when it comes to wards." Epyllo nodded his appreciation. His paint was streaked down his body from the exertion of battle, so Gavin could see his expression a little more clearly. "So its me, Acantha, and Gavin."

"And me." Sage leaned forward, placing her palms on the table firmly. "Where he goes, I go. I can disable Ranquer's fucking machines. And I want to see the look on his face when we destroy his dreams."

Symon pierced them both with her glare, his teeth clenched tightly. "Bring her back. I don't care if you must destroy the whole fucking country. Bring her back to me."

Gavin stood straight, gripping Sage's hand in his. "We'll bring her back. Or we'll die trying."

The King gave one final nod, then he shimmered into nothing.

Gavin turned to Sage. Her gaze echoed his own. They'd bring back the Queen. And they'd rain punishment on anyone and everyone who had hurt the people they loved.

He'd make sure of it.

Chapter 40

✧✦✧

Sage looked up at the darkened mountains before her, holding tightly to Gavin's hand. He'd opted to take them as far as the Spearsan Gap, a test to see how accurately he could land while not knowing exactly where he was going and hauling three other bodies with him.

Not surprisingly, at least to Sage, he'd landed in the exact place he'd pictured from looking at the map. Epyllo, Acantha, and Gavin now all looked at a map rolled out on the ground before them, discussing the location of the Dark Born keep before casting again.

"They've got several rows of smithies lined up in this area. The last time I was able to cross this border, the smithies were serving the alternate purpose of being armories and an extra layer of defense. Their smiths are also their soldiers." Acantha toyed with a blade strapped against her bare stomach as she spoke, staring at the map intently.

"So I should take us straight inside the walls of the fortress, then?" asked Gavin.

Epyllo, crouching low to the ground, countered. "I'm not sure about that. It might be best to land over here," he pointed at a spot on the map, a little east of the fortress. "There's a hill over here where we might get a better look at

470

what kind of defenses they have within the walls. We don't have a clear picture of their numbers, but this vantage point could give us some insight."

Gavin nodded. "Agreed. Then we'll cast there," he jabbed the spot on the map with his finger, "and make a decision."

"Then let's get going," said Sage.

Epyllo stood, rolling the map with nimble fingers. The four of them looked up at the mighty, gray mountains before clasping hands. Sage grabbed hands with Acantha, closing their small circle. With an exhale, Sage felt her body dissolve into air and get swept through the valley that created the Spearsan Pass.

Seconds? Minutes? Passed as their bodies drifted and glided, the ground becoming craggy and jagged beneath them. Blurs of reality streamed by as they cast far beyond the borders of Nysa and Speridisia. The earth was gray, full of volcanic rock and geysers that steamed.

Every now and then, a small forest stood resiliently, as if it were daring the Dark Born to try and wipe the land clean of vegetation. It seemed, thought Sage, that even in the darkest of places, small pockets of hope and defiance could be found.

Sage felt Gavin's hand against her, squeezing tightly as they were pulled onto a different course, whirling past and around heavy artillery lined up in rows. The wind drifted through the machines with ease until they'd passed the blockade, not a single one whirring to life in alarm.

Sage breathed a sigh of relief. If only the rest of their mission could be so simple.

A moment later, they were standing on a hill made of huge boulders piled on top of each other, stacking upward until a miniature mountain had been created. They landed on unsteady footing, tiny rocks cascading from their feet. Sage leaned heavily against a boulder, fighting for purchase as the rock she stood on wobbled. A strong hand grabbed her shoulder, pulling her back. She fell heavily against Acantha, who held on tight as the boulder she'd just been standing on toppled to the ground.

"Shit," whispered Acantha. "Did we mention this hill was precarious?"

"Not at all," said Gavin.

"Hopefully they're making too much racket to have noticed," said Sage, finally reaching Gavin and leaning into him.

They stood, nestled in between several overlarge rocks, many of them jutting out at strange angles. It provided decent cover from the fortress in the distance.

Down below, ringing up to the sky against the hill, smithies worked overtime, hammering, clanging, and stoking roaring fires. The noise was so great, Sage could feel the vibrations of the synchronized hammers in her ear drums.

"What are they building?" asked Epyllo.

Sage squinted, looking down at the fortress. If she focused, she could just barely make out the shapes of several orb-like structures.

"Here," whispered Gavin, in her ear. "Use the bond."

She nodded, leaning into his power. Her eyesight sharpened, no doubt a boon from his hawk form. "Drones," she said. By the looks of it, there were fifty or more drones lined up in a field near the fortress.

She focused harder, pushing her heightened eyesight to its maximum potential. Large cylinders—human-sized glass tubes—were arranged in tiny rows. "What the hell are those?" she whispered to herself.

"You've never seen them before?" asked Acantha.

Sage shook her head. She couldn't fathom what they would be used for, but something in her gut screamed that they all needed to be destroyed.

"We have to destroy them." She spoke, the words leaving her before she realized she was speaking. "We have to destroy them all."

"We lose the element of surprise if we hit them first," said Gavin.

"And we might also lose the chance to destroy those machines before they're let loose on Veritasailles. If all of those drones make it to the city…"

"It'd be a massacre," finished Epyllo. "I'm with Sage on this."

Gavin huffed. "Okay. Ideas?"

"Do you trust me?" asked Sage. Gavin nodded. Acantha shrugged. "I think I have a plan."

◆◆◆◆

Aryael lay strapped to a padded board tilted slightly so her feet were lower than her head. The walls were streaked with what she could only imagine was blood. Chains and hooks hung from the wall. Something shiny stood against the far corner. Occasionally, a small green light blinked, and the object would let out a beep.

She wished her heart would beat in time with the thunderous rhythm of panic that she felt, but instead it kept a sluggish, uneven staccato. She tried flexing against the bindings that kept her strapped to the board, but it was no use.

She could feel her limbs, but no matter how hard she tried, she couldn't consciously control her body. She couldn't even swallow, could barely move her eyes. Drool leaked down the side of her chin, her head drooped toward her shoulder.

Bits of glass still stuck to her. The sticky, purple poison that Abbadon had smashed onto her clung to her skin like a sickly, sweet syrup. She didn't recognize the substance, though she was no poison master. Abbadon had thrown her against the board, and stripped her leather armor from her body. Now, she only wore the muslin bindings across her chest, and cotton leggings.

The moments dragged on in the room, no one coming to see her, torture her, kill her. She almost wished they would come. The waiting was becoming unbearable.

Her eyelids drifted closed. Maybe she'd fall asleep and wake up to find this was just a nightmare. Maybe when she reopened her eyes, she would roll next to Symon, who would comfort her and tell her everything was all alright.

A rattling from the corner startled her awake. Near the beeping machine she could make out a squat male hunched over a cart of glass vials and bottles. He muttered to himself, his voice gratingly squeaky from what Aryael could decipher. His white jacket shifted slightly as he stepped around the cart, his gaze never lifting to Aryael's.

Then a dark, hateful voice crawled from the archway that led to only the Goddess knew.

"There's my prize."

Abbadon stood in the archway, his form cloaked in rippling darkness that seemed to ooze from his skin. His eyes pierced her, and if she'd had the ability to, she'd return the gesture. How her insides boiled to see the male stand there. Her spirit writhed inside her, desperate to fight. But the cord to her body had been severed when that glass bottle shattered against her chest. All she could muster was the whisper of a growl, which sounded more like a whimper.

"Do you have her prepped?" Abbadon asked, stepping into the room and striding towards her.

"Nearly," was all the squeaky male said.

"Hurry, Cian. I can hardly wait to see what horrors we design." Abbadon walked to her, a strange gleam to his eye. Then he straddled her, both hands braced against her face. "When this is over, you will be a marvel. You'll be unrecognizable. And you'll *hate* it."

His breath smelled of strong liquor with a rancid undertone, and she would have gagged if she'd had the ability to.

A hand was on her face, squeezing her cheeks as he moved her head so she faced him. "Should I scar you? So that when Symon finally sees your dead body, he'll think of me, and all the fun I've had with you?"

Aryael's insides clenched. This wouldn't be the first time a male had forced himself upon her. If anything, the work camps had taught her how to go numb in order to survive the ordeal of being female. In fact, the feeling she had right now was eerily familiar, and that felt like more of a violation than being poisoned.

How was it that she was once again beneath a Dark Born male? And this time, the son of the King that had slaughtered her parents.

She prayed to the Goddess, begging her to release her from the poison so she could burn the fucker from the inside out.

She'd blow up the whole damn fortress by the time she was done with this.

The cart rattled close, bottles clanking against each other. Abbadon pushed away from her, letting Cian near.

"I have the elixirs ready. Which was it you'd like to try first?" asked the spectacled male.

"The last one." Abbadon's mouth broke into a sick smile, and for the first time since being captured, Aryael felt truly afraid. No one had come to rescue her, and how could they? It would be a day, at least, before anyone could make it to the fortress. And how long would it take them to make it into the keep?

Cian grabbed a syringe, dipping it into a vial. It made an abhorrent slurping sound as a dark liquid was pulled into it.

Aryael's eyes darted from the syringe to Abbadon and back again.

"Ah—yes. This, is going into *you*." Abbadon stepped back to give Cian more access to her. "This is a concoction Cian made with the last sacrifice your *dear* brother made for us." He clapped his hands once to emphasize her brother. "You see, we started with his forearm. Oh, you should have heard him. He would wake up, take one look at what we had done, then scream. He has the most beautiful voice." Abbadon began pacing a little bit. "That was how Apyllon got his power. He was the first to taste the sweetness that is Suda. I'll admit, I was a bit jealous at first." Abbadon's grin was pure madness now.

Cian moved forward, rubbing something wet and cold against a vein bulging from her forearm. Abbadon continued.

"But, I didn't want to be the test rat, afterall. So once we knew your brother's powers—enhanced strength and speed —could be used to enhance our shadow powers? Well, it was only fitting that I was graced with the next gift. So I had Cian take his upper arm. So he will always think of me when he uses the other." Abbadon had stopped pacing, staring at Aryael like he were a fox about to kill a cornered rabbit.

"Then, Apyllon took his eye. It was a bit...uncouth, the way he went about it, I'll admit that. But jussst before we sent him back to you, I had Cian take one. last. piece."

The needle stung as it stabbed her skin, penetrating the vein. A stabbing of electricity ran through her as Cian pushed the plunger to the bottom. Something wild coursed through her, her heart kicking from feeble flutterings into hammering overdrive. She could suddenly feel *everything*. And it was too much. Too fast.

Her body jerked forward, her head thrashing as the power coursed through her veins. She gasped hard, her throat aching as the air rushed into her.

"That right there, is the contents of your brother's left leg, concentrated into one, tiny bottle. You've been injected with double the dose we've tested as being effective. Or safe. So now, Cian and I will wait and watch to see just how long you can withstand the inevitable end, when your powers burn you alive."

Aryael's body jerked against the board.

She was hot. So fucking hot.

Her forehead was sweating. Her whole body was sweating.

There was a ringing in her ears.

Someone was screaming.

It was her voice. She was screaming. Something in her ear popped as a pressure began building within her. She felt as if the entirety of her insides were expanding, while her outer shell contracted, crusting and shrinking painfully, stretched over her power-bloated body. She would explode before too long. The pressure was too much.

Her head jerked to the side, and she saw that she was glowing. An incandescent glow, the color of sun rays. They were shooting out from cracks forming in her skin.

She was screaming again.

This was it. She was about to die. They'd used her own brother's blood against her, the one thing she had fought so hard to protect, and now it was killing her. Now, it was tearing her apart from the inside out.

Something hissed loudly, but she was hardly able to focus on it as a mighty force began pulsing deep within her. The power wanted out. It desperately wanted out. She wasn't strong enough to contain it.

With a mighty yell, everything went bright white.

Moments passed, Aryael wasn't sure how long.

Perhaps she'd made it to Eternity. Perhaps the Goddess had finally granted her rest.

She was on the ground. It was littered with glass and debris. Choking, acid smoke filled the room. In the corner, something smoldered.

She was naked.

She pushed herself up to standing, faltering as she cut her foot on a sharp piece of broken bottle.

There, an archway. Something told her to go through that.

As she headed toward the archway, she passed a body. Deformed. Crumpled.

A pair of spectacles lay nearby, the lenses blackened with smoke. The smell of burnt hair and flesh stung her nose.

She scanned the room, looking for evidence she had killed her other captor. In the corner, a roiling ball of shadows twisted and twined on top and around itself. It churned like the contents of a bubbling cauldron filled with an elixir of pure evil.

Aryael turned and ran through the archway, limping as she made her way out. She tried reaching for her powers, tried to cast away from this hell she'd woken up in.

But there was nothing. Not even an ember of her powers sparked within her.

A sob escaped her as she ran, not knowing where she was going, only knowing she had to get out.

Something rocked the building. A huge noise rumbling from the outside. Shouts tumbled through the stone hallways, heading in her direction. She stepped into the first room she found and quietly closed the door behind her.

It was sparse. Containing only a bed, a set of drawers, and a wash table. She rushed to the drawers. A cotton tunic was stuffed inside. She threw it over her head, yanking her arms through the holes. Next, she found a pair of pants. They were faded black, and likely four sizes too large. She stepped into them, rolling the waistline down so they would stay up while she ran.

She scanned around the room. No shoes, although with the condition of her feet, she wasn't sure she'd be able to tolerate them anyway.

Slowly, Aryael peeked her head out of the doorway. The shouts were going in the opposite direction, away from her current location. Down the other way, she could hear the crackle of something smoldering. Why hadn't anyone come to check on the Dark Born twin?

She left the room, taking pains to walk as carefully and quietly as possible. She left bloody footprints on the floor as we walked, but she saw no other way to make her escape. She couldn't cast. Her powers had shriveled up inside her.

Whatever Abbadon had done to her had caused her power to burn out. A quiet panic bounced around deep within her soul, a question as to whether she would ever get her powers back.

She broke into a limping half-run, heading toward what she thought might be an exit. The hallway broadened. In the distance, she could hear the murmurs of voices. They were stern, but not the same panicked tone as the shouts from outside. She stopped, realizing she was heading straight for them, and tried to gain her bearings. There was no indication, marker, or hint of familiarity about her surroundings that told her what part of the fortress she might be in. She was hopelessly lost and vulnerable.

Another rumble rocked the fortress. The ground shuddered and shook, the walls rattled.

A mighty roar broke through her deliberation. Abbadon.

He was raging, his voice barreling down the hallway toward her.

"You cannot escape, you fire-wheezing shrew!"

He was nearly on her, she could feel his power rippling toward her, down the hallway. Heedless of any further danger she ran toward the closest room to her.

She made it safely inside. Mercifully, it was empty. The voices had disappeared, probably heading toward the chaos happening outside. She closed the door, turning to find someplace to hide. In one corner stood a tall glass tube, large enough to fit several people inside. Shiny boxes with buttons and lights beeped and hummed. A table was scattered with maps and figures, stacks of parchment, and a box that seemed to glow. Small letters scrolled across the front of the box.

But there was no place to hide. Everything was sparse, open, transparent. She was ready to give up, ready to turn and fight with what remained of her strength.

A hand appeared from a crack in reality, gripping her by the throat.

Lightning hot power shot through her neck, deep into her veins. Her body writhed beneath her.

Two bodies slowly began taking form.

Rankor.

No...not Rankor. This form was similar, but his close cropped hair highlighted rounded ears. A pencil thin mustache twitched with amusement as she gasped in his grip, her body alight with fire and pain. An eyepatch covered ragged scars running from above his eyebrow to his nose. This was the President from Sage's world, and he had Aryael under his control.

Aryael's body went limp, her energy finally expired from the devastation of his power. She crumpled to the floor, and a booted foot rolled her to her back.

A woman with slicked back hair and long lean legs wrapped in fitted black pants crouched down to Aryael. She tilted the Queen's face up so she had to look into her eyes. "Look what we have here."

"Dullahan—I do believe this solves our little problem, don't you agree?" asked Ranquer.

Dullahan, her voice ice cold, "A fire wielder. It's almost as if the Goddess is *trying* to help us win the war."

President Ranquer laughed. The sound sent shivers down Aryael's paralyzed spine. She wanted, more than anything, to jump up and fight her way out. But her body was once again incapacitated. Useless.

The door blew open, blasting off its hinges.

Abbadon stood in the doorway, panting. "Back away from that." He glared at Aryael.

"I don't think so, my dear boy," replied Ranquer. He smiled, it looked sinister on the man.

"She's mine. I'm going to rip her to shreds." Abbadon took four large steps towards her, his hair sticking up in wild angles. Black smudges covered his face.

Dullahan stepped in front of Aryael. "I wouldn't do that if I were you."

"Or what?" growled Abbadon, lunging around Dullahan, aiming for Aryael.

The temperature in the room dropped, the lights flickering. Ranquer's form swelled, rippling as if something were trying to rip free from his mortal body. His shadow distorted, horns framing his head. An unearthly, primeval power erupted. Aryael's head felt as if it were being squeezed in a vice, she squinted her eyes against the blue lightning racing toward Abbadon. Before the Dark Born could react, the lightning latched onto him, writhing through his body. Abbadon screamed, his shadows hurling out from his body, trying to tackle the lightning.

But it was no use. Aryael watched in horror as Ranquer stepped up to Abbadon, opening his mouth as he pulled the Dark Born toward him by his throat. A squelching sound made her stomach turn as the President pierced Abbadon's throat, drinking the blood that rushed out of the male's neck.

Lightning cocooned the two, and Aryael tried shrinking away, but she still couldn't move her body. Dullahan grinned, watching as Abbadon kicked out.

The Dark Born's face grew gray and gaunt. His skin shriveled. His body shrank to the size of a doll.

The lightning and charred smoke cleared revealing Ranquer clutching a sickly green heart, still softly beating. He let it fall to the floor with a thud.

Ranquer flexed his shoulders. Shadows swirled around him, his gift from his ally turned prey. And he laughed. "Oh, these will be delightful. And extremely useful." His gaze turned to Aryael, still immobile and exposed on the floor, completely at this monster's mercy.

He flicked his fingers, and the shadows raced to Aryael, scooping her from the floor, stretching her arms out to either side of her. She hovered above the floor, hanging from her wrists. More shadows wrapped around her ankles, binding her so there was no hope of her regaining her autonomy.

Ranquer stooped, grabbing the heart from the floor. He tossed it to Dullahan. "Be a dear and put this back to incubate. Perhaps his next form will be less...willful."

She nodded, heading toward the glass tube, green heart in hand. "And—" said Ranquer as he punched a button on one of the big silver boxes, "tell the others to prepare for a new power cell. Once I have the wind wielder and Sage in hand, we'll be ready."

Dullahan gave a salute, a gleeful look on her face. The top of the glass tube whirred and beeped incessantly. The tube glowed bright. Then, the woman was gone. She'd disappeared.

Ranquer stepped away from the silver box. He gripped Aryael's chin, pulling her head forward. "I'll admit, I won't miss Abbadon. He was a pest." He chucked her under the chin as one might a child, then pushed her head back painfully to the side, making her see lights popping behind her eyelids. "But...I will say he did me a great favor, bringing you *and* your friends to me. He didn't realize it, but he saved me the trouble of capturing you myself."

He laughed. The sound snaked around her body, making her skin erupt in goosebumps.

Something bright white flashed. A dagger flew, end over end, then stuck itself in Ranquer's side.

A pregnant pause hung in the room.

Then, all chaos erupted.

Chapter 41

✧✦✧

The group cast into the middle of the field where the battery of drones stood at attention. Crouched low to the ground, they hid beneath the machines, Sage noting the bristling array of elm projectiles and what looked like biological weapons. Her instinct that these drones would destroy Veritasailles had been spot on, these things were lethal and much larger than the ones they'd already fought, or she'd seen in her home world. They were easily the size of an automobile, if not larger.

"Looks like they planned on gassing the city," Sage whispered to Gavin, jutting her chin towards the torpedoes that would contain the poison. "With those. Most likely, the gas would immobilize the victims, making them easy targets. It'd be a massacre." Her stomach shuddered at the thought.

Gavin followed her gaze, his face blanching as he took in row after row of the deadly weapons. "It'd be genocide," he whispered back. "Our people would have no chance."

There were ten guards manning the perimeter of the field. Another ten stalked the rows, up and down.

In the distance, Sage could hear the telltale clanking and drilling sound of more weapons, possibly more machines, being built and assembled. How many would the Dark Born army bring to Felysia?

Sage sank cross-legged to the floor, grounding herself. Her part of the plan was to create a sound barrier, to add to the element of surprise. She gripped her daggers in her hands. She began chanting the spells she'd learned in school, adding to them spells she'd learned from Ian. She combined every spell she knew to strengthen the barrier, to make it unbreakable.

Her brow beaded with sweat as she poured her magic into the spells.

Then, she felt her surroundings shift. A pressure formed, creating the barrier.

Gavin, Epyllo, and Acantha cast at once. Moving through the rows, taking out the guards. Sage focused on her spell, not letting the sounds of fighting, grunting as soldiers hit the ground, distract her from holding the spell in place.

Someone yelling was heading straight towards her. "They've breached the defenses! Sound the alert!"

Hard footsteps stomped down the row where she sat.

Shit, she'd have to fight him.

Then, Gavin landed in front of her, hiding her from the soldier. She felt his wind power whip from him. The soldier who was yelling stopped, a gurgling sound coming as Gavin ripped the air from his body.

Sage felt her spells waiver. She was running out of time. She could only hold it for a short while longer, fighting against the enchantments the Dark Born had placed on the weapons. She grit her teeth, pushing her magic further.

We need to hurry, she thought, pushing the feeling down the bond.

"We're done." Gavin's feet were in front of her. He crouched to the ground, helping her crawl out from under the spherical drone.

Her ears popped as the spell vanished, the sounds from before filtering back to them. "Part two," said Sage.

Gavin grabbed her hand, and they cast to the front of the artillery line, between the rows of drones and glass tubes. Epyllo and Acantha were already there.

Acantha stooped, squatting to the ground. She placed her hands firmly on the rocky terrain, scrunching her brow. With a flex of her fingers, viney plants erupted from the craggy earth. The vines sprang forward, punching through the glass tubes. Lights blared from the devices, alarms ringing loudly. Shouts bound up from the fortress.

Sage followed Acantha's suit, using her magic to decimate the drones while Acantha continued using her plant powers to destroy the glass tubes. Sage brought her hands clenched around her daggers together, pointing the blades down toward the ground. She pushed down, as if she were driving the blades into the earth itself. When her hands reached her pelvis, she opened her arms to the side, arcing them up over her head in a circular movement. She was gathering earth power, letting it build within her. She felt the buzz of excitement as the earth began responding.

Her blades pointed up to the sky. She pulled her hands down to her chest. She was ready.

Soldiers began running out of the fortress, crossbows locked on the four intruders. Sage didn't wait. She stomped into the ground with her right foot, slashing the air with her blade. The world crumbled beneath the drones. She repeated the movement with her left. Again, the earth rumbled.

Boulders and rocks bubbled to the surface, the running soldiers losing their footing on the teetering earth. Then, Sage stepped back on her right foot in a reverse lunge, one blade by her ear, the other stretched out in front of her. She pulled back, then lifted up on her front toes, both arms whipping up over her head. With a mighty cry, she drove the daggers into the earth.

The world seemed to explode. Earth separated from earth. Soldiers cried out as they were swallowed into a large crater, the drones swiftly following them.

Dirt, dust, debris flew around them. The ground tilted, and Sage lurched back to stop herself sliding into the cavernous canyon she'd created.

Gavin grabbed her, and they cast to the front of the fortress.

The jig was up. Now everyone knew they were there. Arrows whizzed through the air, Gavin easily whipping them away with his wind power. Epyllo cast to a turret, a guard falling from the top moments later. Acantha ran forward towards another guard wielding a giant ax above his head. One moment, Acantha was in the guard's sights, the next a black viper sprang up in her place. The serpent wrapped its body around the guard's neck, long fangs sinking deep into the guard's throat. Then, Acantha's snake form cast back to Gavin and Sage.

The double wooden doors to the fortress ponderously opened, hoards of Speridisian soldiers pouring out to line up with spears, axes, and bows. Sage tunneled into her powers again. There was a water line deep beneath them. She yanked on the thread, pulling it up to her. The earth rumbled, ominously.

Sage reached out with both arms, calling forth a towering column of water to erupt from the ground behind her. She reached up to the sky, drawing the tower forward to cast a shadow down in front of her.

The soldiers faltered, looking up as the mighty stream of water took the form of a water dragon: half horse, half serpentine. The water crashed down in front of Sage, barreling into the fortress and burying the soldiers beneath its wake.

The courtyard of the fortress flooded.

Screaming perforated the space around them.

Gavin, Sage, Epyllo, and Acantha joined hands once again. Sage felt Gavin withdraw slightly, reaching out with his wind power to cast them.

Then, they were gone, shimmering into nothing. Their bodies dissolved, floating through the chaos, into the fortress's sprawling complex half buried into the hill behind it.

They whipped through hallways, bounding through space.

Then, they were in a room. A glass tube in the corner, light leaking from inside of it.

Before anyone could say anything, Sage had her target.

Fucking Ranquer. He stood gloating in front of a limp Aryael, who floated above the ground, her arms stretched out to the sides, wrapping her in choking, greasy shadows.

Sage let her dagger fly, end over end. It struck Ranquer, punching deep in between his ribs with a meaty thud.

"YOU!!" he screamed, turning in shock to see Sage, her hand still outstretched. Then he looked at the dagger sticking out of his side. Bright, purple liquid oozed from the wound.

The room changed temperature, plummeting into icy coldness. Lightning began crackling from Ranquer's fingertips. Acantha and Epyllo cast, meeting two guards who had run into the room. The spies engaged the newcomers, metal clanging against metal as they fought with swords and daggers.

Ranquer whipped his lightning at Sage, but too slow. She and Gavin cast out of the way. Then, Sage was casting a spell at Ranquer, trying to immobilize his lightning.

With a wave of his hand, he waved the spell away, casting another round of lightning at her. She shielded herself with a spell, her arms crossed in an X.

Gavin swung down with his short sword, aiming for Ranquer's neck. Out of nowhere, a sword the same color as his blood materialized in Ranquer's hand. The demon blocked Gavin's blow, and Sage rushed forward.

She blasted him with a spell to stun. Ranquer blocked it with his sword, then met Gavin's next swing. He was impossibly fast. He shouldn't be so fast, thought Sage.

Purple blood dripped from her blade still sticking from his side. Keeping her distance, she reached with her magic for the blade.

Lightning sparked from Ranquer's sword, striking Gavin and blasting him back against the tube. Ranquer aimed at Sage now, and she shielded just in time.

His moves had been a trap for moving closer to her, he reached out for her just as she lowered her forearms from the blocking spell. He'd aimed for her throat, lightning sparking from his fingertips, but she ducked, stepping behind him. She grabbed the dagger, and pushed her magic through it.

Earth. Water. Wind. Fire.

Everything she had leapt out of her body and into the President.

His one good eye grew round. Sage redoubled her efforts, pushing herself harder. Staring into that eye, every bit of her pain, anger and fear from the past ten years driving her need to destroy him, she watched the color leaching from it before becoming a black hole to the void.

His back arched as he bellowed.

She felt the trickle of blood roll from her nose.

One more push of power. It was all she had.

Ranquer's elbow crashed down into her temple, her legs crumbling beneath her. Her dagger ripped free, blood bursting from the wound.

Gavin was on his feet, casting back to Sage in a moment.

Her vision blurred. Her tongue thick and sluggish. She wanted Gavin to go after him. To get Ranquer and put him down, but no words came.

Instead, Gavin gathered her to him.

Ranquer slapped a bloody hand against a button on one of the machines, then staggered to the glass tube. He crawled inside, closing the door behind him.

"This isn't over Sage! You belong to me! I'll have you and your power before this is done. You—" his words were drowned out by a deafening hum as a tremendous light broke through the glass tube.

Then he was gone.

Aryael fell to the floor, the shadows that had held her evaporating to nothing. "You have to destroy it," she moaned, gasping.

Sage didn't know if she had any magic left to spare. Then Gavin squeezed her hand, and she felt his power entwine with hers, bolstering her energy.

Acantha and Epyllo ran back to them. "Time to go!" they yelled.

The earth rumbled beneath them. The ground quaked. Something was wrong.

"Abbadon is dead," whispered Aryael, as Acantha lifted her to her feet.

Everyone stood in a tight circle, staring at the machine, fighting to stay upright as the earth tried to shake them to their knees.

"You have to destroy it," Aryael said again. "We have to be sure he can't come back."

There was blood on the Queen's face. Her normally dark brown skin, ashen.

Another wave of power rippled down the bond.

"Do it," said Gavin.

Something in the building rumbled hard, a crashing noise raced toward them.

Sage grabbed hold of Gavin's power, then threw her magic at the tube and its machines. Earth erupted inside, water sprang out from the ground, flooding the machines. Electricity sparked from them. Then, she let her wind and fire magic meld. She pushed all she had. They incinerated, glowing bright red, the glass of the tube melting.

"They're going to explode! Time to go, now!" Epyllo yelled.

They all grabbed hands. Sage held onto Aryael, her hand clammy and trembling. Just before they cast, Aryael's head lolled, her eyes rolling back into her head. The Queen's knees hit the ground, and she fell.

Sage cursed, just as they evaporated into nothing. She fought to hold onto Aryael, deadweight now as their bodies were thrown through space.

Moments. Minutes. Hours. Days. Time lost all meaning.

Then they were standing in the courtyard of the palace in Veritasailles, on the gravel drive that led to the expansive, white doors.

Aryael fell forward, landing heavily on her front.

Sage's head grew dizzy. The spies rushed to the Queen. Someone was shouting from the doors.

Gavin was speaking to her, but she couldn't decipher anything through the ringing in her ears. She staggered. Something warm and wet ran profusely from her nose.

Gavin had her by the shoulders trying to hold her steady.

Her knees softened. They hit the gravel beneath her.

Shadows were dancing as she felt herself being lifted into Gavin's arms.

Everything grew quieter and quieter, even as she recognized Gavin's steps had broken into a run.

She was so tired. All she wanted to do was sleep.

Gavin laid her on a bed, yelling frantically in her ear, something she couldn't hear. He held her shoulders, tears pouring down his face.

She turned her head. In the corner of the room she now lay in, stood Allyra, the Water Goddess. Next to her was Nehelannia, half-wolf, half-woman. They both held battle axes. Allyra nodded once to her, then they were gone.

The Darkness was closing in around her.

She was done. She'd done something, something she was supposed to do. Her heart stuttered, the bargains protesting. She hadn't completed everything, but she was done. She'd given it everything and now she was ready to go.

Sage used the last of her strength to reach up to Gavin's face, cupping it softly.

He looked at her, his eyes wide with panic.

She gave him a soft, half smile.

He grabbed her hand, holding it against his cheek, then kissing her palm. She thought back to the first time she'd seen him. She thought he had been an angel, and now she thought maybe he was. He'd saved her, not her body, but her soul. It'd been lost and wandering, and he'd helped her find the strength to bring it back home. He'd shown her how to love with confidence. He'd given her a home.

And she was so thankful. Because now, she could look toward eternity knowing she'd once had a home. She looked at him one last time, taking in that beautiful strong face. She wanted to tell him not to give up. That she'd wait for him on the other side. That she gave everything so that they could all have a life full of love. She only wished she could've stayed a little while longer.

Her body heaved a heavy, wet exhale.

She was done.

Darkness wrapped itself around her completely and she fell into it.

✧✦✧

Meliza's heart stuttered.

They'd returned from their task, but what had it cost them? She'd immediately moved to help the Queen, but Raphael was already there, gently pressing Symon to the side so he could ministrate to her. Petra and Zeke looked on. Plus the spies, Epyllo and Acantha.

It was like something from a nightmare.

Gavin on the other hand was racing into the palace, screaming for a healer, Sage gathered in his arms. Meliza took off after him. He'd made it to a sitting room close to the foyer. He was yelling at Sage, yelling for a healer.

"Fuck," Gavin grunted. "Come on, Sage, fight it. Stay with me, stay with me!"

He turned, his eyes wild. "Get someone! She's done too much." Meliza turned to run and find a healer, when Shiphrah flew into the room. Gavin continued muttering, "She's done too much, she's done too much." He was crying.

Meliza was by his side, now, trying to pull him away even as Shiphrah walked to Sage's head and laid her hands there. Sage's skin was ashen. She'd never seen the girl so pale, not even after she'd fallen from the sky.

Blood poured from her nose, too fast to clot. A bubbling sound rumbled in her chest as she gasped for breath. And Meliza could feel it, could feel the beating of Sage's heart stutter and slow.

"Fuck!" screamed Gavin.

Sage's hand shook as she reached up and placed it on Gavin's face. One side of her mouth crooked into what might have been a smile. Gavin stilled, grabbing her hand. He kissed it sweetly.

Then Sage's eyes closed, her head slipping from the pillow it was propped on. Gavin rocked back on his heels, and a sound she'd never heard from Gavin racked through him. His shoulders shuddered. "No...no, no, no," he said softly, still clutching her hand to his chest.

Shiphrah still stood at Sage's head, muttering softly to herself. Something warm and light glowed beneath her fingers, but Meliza could sense it, could feel the magic leave the room.

Sage was gone.

Meliza laid her hand on Gavin's shoulder. "Gavin," she whispered.

"Leave us," he said.

"It's okay, Gavin. We're here." It was just Shiphrah and herself; she hoped it'd be enough.

"What the..." Meliza turned at the sound of Micah's voice, she couldn't have been more relieved to see Gavin's childhood friend.

Shiphrah's muttering continued, the glowing beneath her hands growing brighter. But there was nothing to do once someone had passed. Meliza had seen it time and time again on the battlefield and in the work-camps.

Eshamel laid his hand on Gavin's other shoulder. He remained silent, and they held on as Gavin sobbed, his body rocking as he clutched Sage's hand to his heart.

Shiphrah's muttering stopped, her eyes remained closed.

"Gavin," Shiphrah's voice echoed strangely, and Meliza looked to the healer. Her body was framed in celestial light. Power rippled through and around the healer, skating out from her cream robes. "Are you prepared for what comes next? Will you follow Sage into the next phase?"

Gavin stopped his rocking, still holding tightly to Sage's hand. "Yes," he said. His voice was steady.

Meliza's heart thundered. He couldn't be serious! They needed him. The battle was won, but the war had only just begun!

"Then so be it," said Shiphrah. Her voice galloped around the room, swirling into a frenzy. It wrapped around Gavin, kicking up locks of his hair.

Shiphrah's body levitated, and she glowed brighter, the power expanding and filling the entire space around them.

Micah let go of Gavin and he yanked Meliza away. They staggered back as Shiphrah's power slammed into Sage and Gavin. The light broke into thousands of fractal rays.

A loud gasp pierced the air. The light was too bright, Meliza had to shield her eyes. Gavin yelled something. She had no idea what was happening, and that scared her.

Then everything fell still. The room seemed dark after the brightness of the light.

Meliza looked up. Shiphrah was gone.

Gavin's forehead rested on Sage's chest, his body completely still. Sage's body shifted, her eyes fluttering open.

Meliza ran forward, hoping she wasn't right. Gavin couldn't have sacrificed himself for her. She grabbed his shoulder, yanking his body up.

He shrugged her off, lunging forward again to gather Sage into his arms. The look of pure love and relief Gavin gave pierced Meliza's heart.

"Thank the fucking Goddess," Gavin said, crushing his mouth into Sage's, blood be damned.

"What the fuck just happened?" asked Micah.

Shiphrah.

The healer was gone.

It wasn't Gavin that had sacrificed himself. It had been Shiphrah.

Sage clung to Gavin's neck, crying into his shoulder. "I'm sorry," she wept. "I'm so fucking sorry."

"It's okay," he hushed, kissing her hair.

Shouts came from the hallway. The sound of footsteps running down the corridor. Symon's voice could be heard commanding sentries and servants alike. But Meliza stood rooted to the floor.

Shiphrah was gone. But Sage and Gavin remained.

They'd gotten Aryael and Suda back.

Apyllon was dead.

Petra had crawled out of her manic depression and rescued Zeke.

Did this mean they were saved?

Meliza allowed one lonely tear to roll down her cheek before she cleared her throat. Then she leaned toward Micah, who stood with what looked like shock written on his face.

"Come on, Shadow Master. We deserve a drink," she whispered. She grabbed Micah's arm and pulled him through the door. They walked quietly down the hall, away from the chaos coming from the opposite end.

Maybe, once they had shared a glass of moonwater given to her by Delphia, they'd have the courage to find out what would happen next.

Chapter 42

✧✦✧

The weeks had passed in a blur. The Sekiri tribe had immediately left to scout the Spearsan Pass to see what they could find out about the Speridisian troops now that both Dark Born twins were dead and gone.

Aryael had explained how Ranquer had killed Abbadon, and now Meliza wondered what that meant for their world. Ranquer, presumably, could no longer reach their world with his machines destroyed.

Meliza had gathered with Symon, Aryael, Raph, Zeke and one or two others in his war room to hear the Sekiri tribe's report. It was morning, the sun barely up, the chill of winter starting to bc felt in the northerly breeze. Amastan was saying that they had traveled all over the Speridisian planes. Not a single Dark Born soldier could be found. She had mused that it was almost as if they'd dried up and evaporated from the land. The Dark Born fortress had caved in on itself.

Not an ounce of Dark Born power could be sensed.

Their world was free for good from the evil that had plagued them for millennia. Meliza had whooped out loud, throwing her fist in the air. Symon, of course, had remained more stoic. He still bore heavy, dark circles beneath his eyes.

Aryael had come back from darkness itself. The intervening weeks had seen the Queen often tortured with nightmares at night, and Raphael still had not discovered how to get her powers back. Aryael was powerless, the Dark Born experiment draining her of her fire wielding abilities. Meliza could tell that the result had been catastrophic for the Queen, who now sat in her bonded's war room with a disquieting malaise about her.

Aryael's eyes often darted around the room, as if she was looking for something. Occasionally, Meliza witnessed the Queen snapping her head to the side as if she'd seen or heard something that startled her.

Regardless, Meliza couldn't help but be thrilled with the news that the Dark Born were gone for good. And Ranquer could torture them no more.

They had the insignia, so the next step in their plan was to help Sage find a way through the Maracadian wards, and into the Realm Leaper temple.

But that would take some time. Sage was still healing from their ordeal. She'd weakened herself using so much magic at once, and Gavin had sequestered them both in the Big House in Mystaira.

Meliza shook Amastan's hand, grasping the female's forearm in her own. "Thank you, Amastan. We are forever grateful for the help of the Sekiri Tribe."

"And as are we to Felysia. May this be the beginning of a new, and improved, alliance between our people."

One final shake of hands, and the cheetah shifter walked out of the council room.

Symon said a few last words of parting, dismissing Zeke, Meliza, and the few others that had attended the meeting.

Meliza cast back to her rooms, scratching out a quick message to her lieutenants, outlining what she expected to be completed while she was away. She'd decided to spend the next days in Mystaira, away from the chaos of Verita-sailles, and in the arms of her love. Now that she had the official word that there were no more threats, she could breathe easy, and let her lieutenants do their job.

She smiled broadly as she stepped out of the palace and into the weak sunshine, letting it warm her face until she cast over the mountains, landing heavily on the dirt path that would lead her back to her heart.

She couldn't stop the smile from spreading as she walked toward the small, stuccoed house. Smoke curled from the chimney, and she broke into a run as she spied Delphia around the corner, trimming herbs that grew from bushes.

Meliza's heart swelled as Delphia turned at the sound of her footsteps, dropping the shears and trimmings and meeting Meliza with open arms. They clasped each other hard, and Delphia buried her head in Meliza's curly hair.

"I missed you so much," whispered Delphia.

Meliza laughed, "So did I."

They pulled back, and Meliza kissed Delphia, relishing in her soft lips.

They stood there for several moments, holding each other and staring. Finally, Meliza's body seemed to breathe. Finally, she'd found it. She'd found the thing she'd been missing.

And, she realized, they were free. Finally free to live. To feel joy. To grow.

And there wasn't a Dark Born bastard to stand in their way.

The path forward was filled with light. And for the first time in her life, she believed that they could be happy.

She believed *she* could be happy.

And she thanked the Goddess for it.

They walked hand in hand toward the barn in the distance, Delphia chatting about all that'd happened on the estate in the past weeks. Meliza beamed as she realized what she'd found.

It was hope. And it was real. And it was good.

Chapter 43

❈

She'd been walking for four bloody weeks. Through Jordynia. And now through some place called Mystaira.

When she'd first landed in Maracadia, she'd been shocked to find people who seemed so different from those she was familiar with. But their powers were strangely similar.

It'd taken her six months to convince a small band of Maracadian sailors to help her escape the tiny island nation. The leaders there had wanted to keep her under protection, or so they said. She wasn't so sure she believed them.

Besides, her mission all this time had been to find the Realm Leaper. She'd found significant favor in Maracadia being one herself. If she was honest, her aching legs and feet were beginning to miss the temple acolytes. They'd been incredibly generous with their food and shelter.

But, while she'd been more comfortable at the temple, she'd felt herself grow further and further away from her goal. *Finding the Realm Leaper.*

Now, she cringed as one of her feet spasmed from exhaustion. But she was close. So fucking close to finding what she'd been after.

She'd gone from one area of the nation to the other based on rumors from the local people. Then, she'd had to hole up in a hovel somewhere to brew the body disfigura-tion tonic that kept her ears pointed. While the after effects hadn't always been pleasant, she'd found it easier to travel from place to place under the guise of a fae female.

She'd nearly given up all hope a couple weeks prior, feeling like she was on a wild-goose chase. But then, one of the homes that had offered her a place to stay boasted runes etched into their window sills and door frames. She'd recognized those runes to be necessary for many of the protection spells she knew, although some of them were unfamiliar. But it had told her she was getting closer. Ac-cording to her hosts, the Realm Leaper was living nearby, only a few day's travel away on foot.

Her body ached. Her stomach growled loudly.

Her disfiguration tonic had worn off the day before, but she was close.

According to the rumors, she would make it to the estate where the Realm Leaper could be found before nightfall.

Her shoes kicked up dust beneath her as the road wound on.

Finally, she breached the shade of a pine forest, shield-ing her eyes from the setting sun ahead of her. A small, stuccoed cottage sat merrily by a creek. Livestock bleated in the distance. She smelled smoke from the chimney, and she shivered slightly against the chilling night air.

The temperature had dropped steadily as she made her journey on foot, and she pushed her body harder to find the main house that sat on the estate. She refused to spend another night in the woods, shivering as she struggled to maintain a campfire.

She clenched her dress in her fist, gritting her teeth as she walked on over the crest of a hill.

A big house came into view. It stood tall, impressive double staircases leading up to large double doors announcing the estate house. She found the thing pretentious. She bet the fae that owned the place was a snob.

She'd found herself becoming more and more resentful to the fae who'd kept the Realm Leaper safe and sheltered all this time while she had been forced to travel alone.

Step after step, mile after mile, her anger and frustration had risen.

And now she was here, and her resentment was close to bubbling over. She was on the stairs, climbing heavily up toward those ostentatious front doors. They loomed in front of her. She raised her fist, banging loudly.

A cheery voice sounded from behind, "Coming!"

Her heart leapt into her throat. This was it! That was the Realm Leaper.

The door squealed as it was opened. In the doorway, in a light green dress, stood Sage, holding a bowl of cherries.

Her eyes widened as she looked out and saw who waited for her. The bowl crashed to the floor, her hand snapping to her mouth.

Heartbeats dragged by, and they stared at each other.

Then, Sage whispered, "Aimee?"

Acknowledgements

Writing a book is just...so much.

It's not really possible without a solid village rooting you on through all the tears, doubts, and struggle. I'm so honored to have such a tough village. I'm a lucky gal, I'll tell you that.

First- I want to thank my editor, Claire. You are amazing. I'm so, so, so....eternally grateful that we found each other on that Facebook page over a year ago. Working with you is a **dream**. You are so talented, so thoughtful, and just such a blessing to this baby-author. I cannot thank you enough for all the help you've given me. I can't wait to get to work on book 3!

Second, Amanda B.: Girl! What would I do without you in my corner? Where would I be? Probably still in a corner doubting myself. Thanks for being my hype girl. Being your friend is just the best.

Last- My mom...You've always been so supportive of our dreams. Seeing you so excited for this journey I'm on has been one of the things keeping me going when it got really tough. On days where I wasn't sure if I could keep this train moving, knowing you were out there telling everyone under the sun about my book gave me the fuel I needed. Thanks for being best. I love you!

Of course, I have to throw in a quick thanks to my husband and kids. It never gets old hearing you guys talk about my work. I know it can be tiresome seeing me tinker away on my laptop, but you guys never complain. I love you guys so much. Being yours will always be my favorite.

If you've stuck around this far, I'd like to thank all the readers! I'm honored you've followed me down this path. Get ready...book 3 is going to be a doozy!

P.E. Craven has spent her whole life engrossed in the fantasies of others. As a former dance teacher and choreographer, creative storytelling has always been a source of nourishment for her body and mind. Now, as a mother and school teacher, telling stories in print is how she pours her creative soul into the world.

In her debut novel, she has answered the call to write stories about people facing down their destinies on their own terms. She continues this work with the next installments of The Realm Leaper Series, in addition to her next project: The Tree Kings Series.

In her spare time, P.E. Craven loves basking in the outdoors with her family, exploring her hometown Chattanooga, and jumping into perilous journeys written by other authors.